ALSO BY JESSE BROWNER

Conglomeros

TURNAWAY

LODI PUBLIC LIBRARY
LODI CA 95240

Fiction
Browner,
Jesse

TURNAWAY

JESSE BROWNER

VILLARD NEW YORK

Copyright © 1996 by Jesse Browner

All rights reserved under International and Pan-American
Copyright Conventions. Published in the United States
by Random House, Inc., New York, and simultaneously in
Canada by Random House of Canada Limited, Toronto.

Endpaper map courtesy of the I. N. Phelps Stokes Collection,
Miriam and Ira D. Wallach Division of Art, Prints and Photographs,
the New York Public Library,
Astor, Lenox and Tilden Foundations

Library of Congress Cataloging-in-Publication Data

Browner, Jesse.
Turnaway/by Jesse Browner
p.   cm.
ISBN 0-679-44788-1
1. Indians of North America—New York (N.Y.)—Fiction.
2. Island—New York (N.Y.)—Fiction.   I. Title.
PS3552.R774T87   1996   813′.54—dc20   95-51007

Printed in the United States of America on acid-free paper
2   4   6   8   9   7   5   3
First Edition
Book design by JoAnne Metsch

FOR JUDY

TURNAWAY

Cokoe went home last night. My nurse, Daphne, who comes from Jamaica and believes that the cool autumn breezes will help heal my injuries better than air-conditioning, must have forgotten to close one of the windows before she left. I always kept the door to Cokoe's cage open, in case he wanted to make the journey that I assume he began last night, but until to-day he was always there, perched inside with one eye to the skyline, when the pain or the garbage truck woke me just before dawn. But today, when I saw that empty cage, I didn't even bother to call for him, much less attempt to get out of bed to search the apartment. I can understand why living in Manhattan might have unpleasant connotations for him. I'm glad he's gone—I really am—though I'm afraid his jour-ney's end will be a bitter shock and disappoint-ment to him. I imagine he's reached Turnaway by now.

Owls are more inscrutable than most people understand. Even after you've lived with one for a while, as I have, it's often hard to tell what they're thinking. In all the time he lived with

me—and it wasn't long—Cokoe never once looked me in the eye. He
must have associated me with what happened, which I can appreciate; he may even have blamed me, and maybe he wasn't too far off in
that, either. But if he did, in any case, he never told me so. Why
would he? His thoughts and plans were none of my business, though
I knew what they were—of course I knew—from the first day I came
home from the hospital. Even Daphne, who's been hearing my story
in dribs and drabs, could tell he had something on his mind. As for
me, I may be no seer, but I knew that he'd be preparing for this trip
as soon as his tail feathers grew in. When my own wounds heal, I
might just follow him. He'll never survive the winter out there alone.
That's probably what he's counting on.

If I close my eyes, I can picture the entire journey he undertook
last night. I would guess that the first tentative step to the windowsill
was the hardest, that he was trying to steel himself to the sight
waiting for him on the other side. He wouldn't have flown far, probably just to the cornice of my building, enough to get his bearings
before committing himself to flight. Of course, he won't have found a
single familiar landmark, either below on West Forty-fourth Street or
anywhere to the south. It was probably even worse than he'd imagined, and even in his resilience he'd have been pretty shaken by the
view. Turning to the west, it's possible that he recognized the broad,
sluggish waters of the Hudson—his beloved Mahikanituk—and the
great gray wall of the Palisades beyond, home of the wily Hackensack. Keeping that reference point behind him, he'd have turned
again to the northeast and taken wing, sparing little time to wonder at
the treeless landscape below. He'd have to pause often for breath,
though the balmy air of New York in October tends to agree with him,
a native in every sense of the word. Maybe he stopped for a rest on
top of the RCA building, sniffing with disdain at the filthy, huddled
pigeons, wretched descendants of a once proud and tasty race. This
perch will have given him his first unhurried look at the entire island, from Kapsee all the way to Shorakapkok, and it must have been
a nasty shock, despite everything he'd seen so far. Still, the greenery
of Central Park would have been a soothing sight, and the East River
even more so, its restless waters gleaming copper in the dawn light.

With a bolder heart, and maybe a brief stopover in the park to browse among the daisies, he'd have continued making his way northeast, disappointed in his scanning of First Avenue for the least trace of Konandekonk. As he crossed the Harlem River—his Muscoota—he would have been confused by the sight of a large island jutting into Hell Gate where there were once three, before they were connected by landfill. The walls and turrets of Riker's Island, and in fact the island itself, would also have been new to him. But his confusion will have been short-lived as he recognizes with joy and relief the familiar shoreline of the Bronx, which he follows eastward, fruitlessly searching for signs of the rich fields of Quinnahung under the sewage works and the Con Ed plant on Hunts Point, or the busy longhouses of Snakapins among the beach huts of the Shore Haven Beach Club on Clason Point. He's distracted and terrified by the jets as they make their sharp turn over Throgs Neck and plunge on toward the runways of La Guardia, and he hurries onward, lured by the sparkling waters of home as they open out into Maminketesuck, the Long Island Sound. To his right now, as he veers north over Locust Point, stretches Sewanhacky, the long island, and the finger of land called Menhadenock—the land of fish, Great Neck—in whose dark woods he has often hunted under a full moon. It points him homeward, over Aqueanonk—Eastchester Bay—and what is left of the home of his youth, Lapechwahacking, in Pelham Bay Park. And now he begins his descent, with fluttering heart. Over the Chimney Sweeps, past Hunter's Island where his ancestors rest, across the Blauzes and the Nonations, and down. Down toward the last island—the very last—in New York City. He's home—home on Turnaway.

But maybe, tired as he is, he doesn't land just yet. Maybe he takes a moment or two to survey the situation. It isn't a very big island— twenty acres and some—and he hovers above it, or makes a few passing sweeps before coming down for good. From this height, not much seems to have changed. He can't spot any rabbits among the lettuce, or any lettuce for that matter. (How can he know that the rabbits ate all the lettuce and starved to death weeks ago?) And the house looks a little strange. But other than that, he can't see any obvious reason why he shouldn't land. The trees are all standing and still in full leaf; the beaches are empty, as always; the launch rocks gently in the tide and bumps with a soothing, hollow clop against the pier; the wind chime in the observatory can be heard ringing, even from up here; no intruders anywhere. Just as it should be. He swoops down, fans his wings to brake, and lands gingerly on the ridge of the roof, dislodging a cedar tile, which slides and clatters down the slope and plummets with a muffled thud into the shrubbery. All is quiet.

But something *is* wrong, after all. The quiet is too pervasive. And why is there a gaping hole in the roof? What is that lingering scent of charcoal and burnt timber? How did all the windows come to be smashed? Mustering all the courage in his owl's heart, and suppressing another shudder of apprehension, Cokoe drops through the hole to investigate the dark cavity of the attic.

The first thing he notices as he patrols the cavernous space is that the floor is covered in whitish droppings; looking up, he notes that bats have taken roost under the rafters—dozens of them hang sleeping from the collar-beams. On another occasion he might have been tempted by these easy pickings, but right now he's too distraught to entertain thoughts of food. The smell of smoke is very strong in here, but even with his excellent vision enhanced by the shadows he detects no evidence of any recent fire. A mouse brushes past him, and he stomps on it mechanically, abstractedly, pinning it to the beam between his powerful talons. A sparrow lands on the edge of the hole in the roof, cocks its head into the darkness; it sees the owl and freezes momentarily before dropping out of sight below the eaves. There is nothing more to be learned from the attic, and the trapdoor leading to the lower floors is closed. Cokoe unfolds his wings and with one beat leaps out into the open air. The mouse, having prepared itself for death, scurries off to its hidden nest.

The owl arcs down to perch on the porch railing. Several support posts have collapsed, and half of the awning hangs limp against the side of the house, like the lid of a great winking eye. The house itself is covered in a sooty film, and licks of blackened, blistered paint rise above every first-floor window. Cokoe ignores the yellow sheriff's seal on the front door as he hops onto the stoop of a shattered window and peers into the gloom. Finally, after standing there motionless for several minutes, he brushes away some loose shards of glass and squeezes himself through an empty pane.

The devastation is appalling. Every inch of wall is singed and begrimed with an oily wash of soot and water. Charred floorboards hang from the rafters; all the furniture has been overturned and smashed; paintings lie twisted and soiled on the floor; the stairway, or what's left of it, is leaning precariously into the center of the entrance hall; every light fixture has exploded. In the library, most of the books have escaped the flames, but none the hose. By contrast, the kitchen is burned beyond recognition, a mere blackened shell. A large wound in the ceiling affords a view of the ruined bathroom directly above. The living room, like the library, is a revolting, sodden mess, and Cokoe pokes desultorily through the artifacts strewn across the carpeting. He picks up a flint arrowhead with his talons and examines it. He's seen enough—or almost.

Returning to the entrance hall, he approaches a low door beneath the stairwell. It is ajar, and there is just enough room for him to squeeze through. Inside it's pitch-black, but that's no problem for an owl. Before him is a simple stairway of raw timber, and he hops down it, step by step, into the basement. It has been left unscathed by the fire upstairs and, except for rivulets of ash-laden water that have stained the plaster walls, is just as he last saw it. In the center of the room is a table—a platform, really—that is so large it leaves little room along the walls to move. From edge to edge, the platform is covered in tiny green hills and valleys, blue streams and bays, rocky beaches, grassy dunes. Cokoe jumps onto the far end and begins to inch along, careful to avoid crushing the tiny, delicate balsa-and-clay models. The miniature landscape at his feet is all too familiar. For the second time that day, he finds himself above Manhattan Island, towering like some avian monster over the southern tip of the island. But now there are no skyscrapers to perch upon, only trees and rocks, and the tallest man-made structure is dwarfed by ancient oaks and beeches. The island is thinner, too, and its ragged shores wend an uneven way northward. Here, as he rounds Kapsee and Nechtanc, there are no bridges connecting the lands of the Marechkawiek and Canarsee tribes, only canoes, a few beached right below him in the village of Rinnegachonk. He makes his way up the East River, gaz-ing down fondly upon the cornfields of the Maspeth. He pushes northward until he rejoins his route of that morning at Monatanuk—Hell Gate. And now, like before, he has a bird's-eye view of the final leg of his journey home; only this time, as he hovers above Quin-nahung, no jet plane threatens his way and no sewage flows from the Aquehung brook. Again he rounds Throgs Neck, where the Ma-tinecock still paddle in dugouts to their fishing grounds. This is the homecoming he'd hoped for. He wades into Aqueanonk, steps over the islands that bejewel its crystal waters, and stands now over his home: Manapinock—Turnaway Island. He stares down on it, then lifts his right leg and lowers it gently upon the tiny island, forming a protective cage around it with his talons. There, in the pitch dark-ness where he will die, and where nothing I can say or do will touch him, he pulls his head down deep between his shoulders and closes his eyes.

In the far southwest corner of the City of New York, there is a quiet place called Pralls Island. It lies in the narrow arm of water that separates Staten Island, in New York, from Union and Somerset Counties in New Jersey. It can take, literally, hours to reach from midtown Manhattan. You have to ride the subway, then take a ferry, then another train, a bus, then walk—and, of course, swim. You can also sail down the Hudson, across the Upper Bay, into the Kill Van Kull, through Newark Bay, under Goethals Bridge, into the Arthur Kill and past the mouth of the Rahway River.

It's worth the effort. Pralls Island is a little wilderness of marsh reeds and mallow, heron and toad, soughing breezes and gently lapping brackish waters. If you lie on your back on the deck of a little dinghy on a late summer's afternoon, as I often used to do, looking up at the passing clouds and hearing nothing but the wind and waves, you could be anywhere in America, in the world almost. Where do you choose to be? Lake Titicaca? The Danube delta? The Mekong? I chose them all, one day or another.

But sit up and it's a different story. If your prow is pointing south, you'll have Fresh Kills to your left—the world's largest garbage dump, hundreds of acres across and hundreds of feet high, visible and smellable for miles. On your right, Carteret, tank farms stretch as far as the eye can see and the air is freighted with petroleum. Garbage barges and oil tankers ply the waters around the tiny nature preserve on Pralls Island. Of all the many, many miles of waterfront in the metropolitan area, this was my favorite spot to come and paint.

It was late August. I'd been boating at this spot all summer, ever since I'd bought the *Spirit of New York* and my first set of watercolors. Now, in the hazy glow of a late-afternoon's sun, I stood back and admired the canvas I'd been working on since midday. The oil tanks and machinery were all sketched in and filled out, but I hadn't gotten to the foreground—the shimmering, oil-filmed water and marshlands. I didn't know how to paint water yet, much less reproduce anything as ephemeral as light dancing on its surface, but the tanks weren't bad. I was pleased with the effect of the white pastel I'd used for the blinding lines of reflected sunlight that flashed from every curve. I'd learned to do that only recently, from a show of drawings at the Morgan Library. Of course, the entire sketch was a failure, as I'd known it would be before I started it, but that hardly bothered me. I was never going to amount to anything as a painter, not even an amateur landscapist, but there was still something about my work that made me smile with satisfaction. I think it was precisely that clumsiness, the lack of attention to detail and coloring, that seemed to comfort me. I'm not happy in the natural world; a man-made setting is less challenging and emotional, more soothing, a sketchy reproduction even better. You can concentrate on what you know and understand, without being distracted by all the world's pointless, irritating filler. I think that was the effect, if any, that I was striving for in my painting. Yes, it really wasn't bad at all.

But I'd been thinking for a while now that it was time for a change. I'd painted just about every inch of interesting shoreline from Port Mobil to Chrome. It might be time to move on. It wasn't that I was tired of the Arthur Kill and its beautiful wastelands, but New York has hundreds of miles of waterfront and I'd barely begun to explore them since I'd bought my old dinghy in May. Even now, in this tropical humidity, you could smell the change of season coming on. After Labor Day, most of the pleasure boats would disappear, and I'd have the chance to explore stretches that I'd been avoiding till now, unable to stomach the sight of all those sleek, polished speedboats and their vapid, wholesome, All-American occupants. Try as I might, I knew perfectly well that you can't get away from other people altogether, but it's pretty easy to figure out the kind of places they shun—docklands, gasworks, poisoned inner-city creeks. Luckily for me, those were just the places I tended to seek out. As I motored slowly back to Manhattan, my head was already dancing with the magical names of waterways still unexplored—Harlem River, Gowanus Canal, Newtown Creek, Bowery Bay, the Bronx River.

By the time I pulled into the boat basin and tied up at the floating pier, it was almost seven-thirty. The sun had set but the sky was still on fire, glowing strata of carbon monoxide and particles of incinerated fuel and garbage. It had been another summer of drought, but rain had been predicted for weeks; now, the only clouds were some bedraggled strands of cirrus so high they'd continue to catch the sun even as it set over Trenton. Now they pulsed, bloodied, like the heart of a dying man. It was impressive, I guess, but I jammed my hands deep into the pockets of my Bermudas and limped through the park to the subway. On such a lovely summer's evening, with the first coolish breeze in nine weeks, the lovers and homeless were out in force, not just in Riverside Park, but citywide and up and down the eastern seaboard, I imagined. I pulled my head down between my shoulders and kept my eyes on my feet.

I don't think there's anything so beautiful in the whole world as a New York City street—and for certain I don't mean some quaint, cobbled throwback in Greenwich Village or Brooklyn Heights. I mean that long, pitiless slash receding in perfect perspective to the horizon—now that's a street, man-made to the last pothole. I'm no poet, but every time I find myself on some corner and I look up to see the canyon ahead, and turn back and see the canyon behind, with the sky above as insignificant and neutral as a neon strip, it makes something resonate deep inside of me. It's like the street is telling me the story of my life, better than I could ever do myself. I recognize it without understanding it. Whenever someone accuses me of being cruel or callous, I have to smile to myself, because if they could make me feel the way I feel alone on the sidewalks of New York, they could have anything they wanted from me. No one ever has, and who can blame them? I'm not holding my breath. There are already enough idiots in the world, clinging to their pathetic hopes. On the subway, a nice old lady tried to offer me her seat, but I snarled a little and she sat back down.

By the time I reached the Peking Garden West, at the corner of Tenth Avenue and Forty-fourth Street, my thighs and hips were throbbing. It would rain tomorrow, most likely. The humidity on the water always made it worse, but it was something I'd come to expect and I put up with it. Almost home, though, and I yearned for painkillers. You weren't supposed to take them on an empty stomach, but if I washed them down with a little scotch before dinner I could put my feet up on the coffee table before the carton of Kung Pao chicken was even half empty. Now, I had the exact change ready and my food was brought out to me in a white plastic bag, even though there were half a dozen customers ahead of me still waiting to be served.

My landlord was sitting on the stoop in his undershirt, the fabric clinging to his sweaty, drooping breasts and fat belly. A group of the old neighborhood boys was standing around. Every one of them had been a stevedore thirty years ago, when the Irish gangs ruled the waterfront. My landlord was usually a nice guy in private, but he was afraid of losing face before the boys if he was polite to the soft-skinned cripple who rented the top floor of his limestone. I couldn't blame him for it, either—I'd have done the same thing in his place. Anyway, I'd rather be spat at than pitied. The boys fell silent as I approached the stoop.

"Why don't you sweep the sidewalk once in a while? It's disgusting," I said as I squeezed past him on my way up the stairs.

"Why don't you kiss my ass, gimp?" We all laughed. I could still hear them laughing through the open windows when I reached my apartment.

There was one message on the machine. "You're an asshole," a woman had said and hung up. I didn't recognize the voice. It had been so long since anyone had bothered with these messages that I was almost inclined to think it was a wrong number, unlikely as that was. I kicked at the TV and listened to some highway patrol show as I went into the kitchen to fix my drink. The cop was making some redneck touch his nose and walk in a straight line. A baggie fell out of the guy's pocket. I knocked back my pills.

"Lookee here," the cop said, deadpan, as I limped back into the living room and stripped off all my clothes. The baggie was filled with coke, probably. I took a quick, cold shower then ate my dinner from the carton and watched the rest of the show in my undershorts. Afterward, I fetched my bottle of vitamin E oil and spent a half hour massaging my scars during *Star Trek: The Next Generation.* When that was done I poured another scotch and went to my armchair by the window in the bedroom. The fronds of an ailanthus tree, whispering and rustling just a few feet away, blocked a wider view of the city, but I could still look down the length of the next block to Eleventh Avenue. Sometimes the johns from New Jersey parked their minivans and Cherokees directly below and I had a perfect view of the action through their windshield. That was for later, though. I shifted and settled in the chair. There'd been a time, not so long ago, I might even have thrown on some clothes and hobbled down to the corner myself, see if Annie or Desirée were hanging around the Park Rite, sometime after midnight when my neighbors were asleep. I hadn't really needed it or wanted it, but I'd made myself go to them every now and again just to remind myself that I was a man. I never brought them upstairs, but still, you never could be too discreet in a neighborhood like this.

I hadn't gone down there in a long while, though, not since the accident. I don't mean to imply that I was maimed, sexually, or anything like that; only I'd gotten to the point where I couldn't even pretend anymore—not even for the five minutes it took her to get the job done—that I was with someone who might love me, in the right circumstances. It had been pretty pointless after that, even at Hell's Kitchen rates. Besides which, negotiating the stairs was painful and clumsy at the best of times these days, let alone in the dark of night with every neighbor lying in bed, listening to the poor crip slouch and slither off to his lonely, disgusting rendezvous.

It was easier to stay at home, go to bed early. Then again, I might just sit in the window for the rest of the night. Sometimes I even managed to get a little sleep that way, cradled in the arms of the city, the distant sounds of car horns, breaking glass, the occasional disembodied laugh floating in on the breeze.

Overnight, a warm front moved in, pushing wind and the threat of rain with it, as predicted. I wasn't afraid of the rain—the *Spirit of New York* leaked at every joint, and my feet were perpetually damp anyway—but wind could make open water a dicey proposition for an eleven-foot dinghy with only fifteen horsepower behind it. I couldn't risk the Upper Bay or even the lower Hudson. If I was going to take her out at all today, it would have to be in the shelter of the Harlem and East rivers. The Weather Channel had issued a small-boats advisory for the next few days, but that, too, I figured, applied more to sea-bound vessels than to mine. A quick scan through the bedroom window showed the sky still clear, and I made up my mind.

By mid-afternoon the clouds were piling up, heat lightning flashed on the horizon, and I was far from home. I'd been carried away with the excitement of discovery and had lost track of the time. But I'd seen some gems that day, perfect painting sites I'd filed away for future reference. On Newtown Creek, in the stinking shadow of the Brooklyn Union Gas grounds, I'd found a trash heap marked on my map as Mussel Island and a toxic open sewer called Whale Creek. Mussels and whales—I had to laugh. This was just what I was looking for. The Harlem River, too, was a rich apocalypse of highways, junkyards, razor wire, and weed-choked lots.

I couldn't help myself, the scenery drew me in. I knew it was time to turn back—the distant thunder was unmistakable even through the roar of the Bruckner Expressway. I promised myself that I'd swing her about once I'd reached Randalls Island, but instead I veered gleefully east into the narrow Bronx Kill, past the railyards, and into the East River. I was enchanted, in thrall: more oil tanks, subway tracks, elevated highways, and sewage works cluttered the shoreline all the way to Hunts Point.

At the Shore Haven Beach Club, the speedboat owners were busy wrapping their vessels under tarps against the approaching storm. I should have taken my cue from them and put off the final leg of my journey for more promising weather. The sky was dark with menace by now, and a growing wind was beginning to raise whitecaps on the river. Common caution should have persuaded me to make for safe mooring on Seventy-ninth Street, still a good two hours away by even the shortest route. But once the rains began they'd be unlikely to let up for days and I was too excited to give up so early, with a good four hours of daylight left. So instead of returning home like I should, I gunned my engine to its full five-knot capacity and headed for open water.

By the time I rounded Throgs Neck Point, I knew I'd made a mistake. A light, misty rain had begun to fall, precursor to the advancing showers, and visibility was dropping rapidly. Though it was barely two, a gray, viscous twilight had descended on the city, and I switched on my halogen lamp. Its beam was swallowed up by the gloom, useless. Only a hundred yards from the Coast Guard station, I dared not approach the rocky outcropping, and I had no radio. The smartest thing to do was to pull into protected water, such as Little Neck Bay to the south or Eastchester Bay to the north, and wait out the storm. But with my barely seaworthy dinghy and lack of familiarity with the dangerous local shoals, it seemed safer to look for a mooring. I could still see a good forty or fifty feet ahead of me, probably enough to avoid any oncoming traffic, and the water, though increasingly rough, was still manageable.

I looked over the map. Armed with a compass, I was sure I could make it as far as City Island Harbor before the rain came. I turned the boat to the north, but I hadn't gone two hundred yards when the clouds broke and my visibility was cut to twenty feet.

At this point, I had little choice but to continue groping blindly forward. I kept my halogen beam pointed straight ahead and strained to hear the sounds of any approaching ship above the roar of the rain and my own little engine. On the water, day was as black as night, just about, and I was beginning to feel distinctly queasy. I'd gone about halfway from Willets Point to City Island when a light appeared off my starboard bow. At first I thought it was another boat, and I let off a series of pathetic blasts on my foghorn. It took me a minute or two to realize that it was actually a buoy—the Stepping Stones light, according to my chart—which meant that I was on course. If I turned north-northeast here, maintained that heading for half a mile, then veered due north for another mile, I should find myself at the mouth of the harbor, with any luck. But as I was preparing to make my turn, the light suddenly disappeared. A moment later, a great steel hull emerged from the darkness and bore silently down upon the *Spirit of New York* from the northeast.

A spryer boat than mine could easily have revved up and crossed the path of its bow with time to spare. But I had neither the speed for that nor the braking power to reverse. Instead, I did the only thing I could, which was to veer hard, directly toward, and hopefully athwart the oncoming freighter. The ship passed ten feet to my port and its bow wave threw me to the floor of the cockpit. By the time I was on my feet with my hands on the wheel, the ship was gone and the thud of its engines, momentarily audible from astern, was swallowed in the pounding of the rain. My hand-held compass was nowhere to be seen, and the boat was swamped.

I'd hardly had a chance to catch my breath when the engine sputtered to a halt. I hit the ignition a few times, but the motor was clearly flooded. The water on deck was shin-deep. No doubt about it: the dinghy was foundering and would have to be abandoned. I slipped on my life jacket, kissed the boat goodbye, and jumped overboard, legs splayed as I'd been taught to do at summer camp. Moments later, the *Spirit of New York* went down without a sound. The last thing to disappear beneath the waves was my easel, bolted to the stern gunwale.

I bobbed motionless for a few moments, the rain lashing at my face. Thrashing, I spun myself around once or twice, looking for some familiar landmark, but it was hopeless. Between the downpour and the waves and the sting of salt water, I couldn't make out a thing. I struck out in what I hoped was a westerly direction, toward Hart

Island or Orchard Beach. I swam a leisurely breaststroke to conserve my energy and concentrated on breathing through my nose to avoid swallowing too much water. The two-foot swells were more impressive at eye level than they'd been from the helm, and it wasn't long before I realized that they could easily sap my energy before I'd be able to reach shore. I swam.

I closed my eyes and tried to visualize my chart of these waters. If my memory served, I had at least half an hour in the water before I could hope to spot land, and I tried not to allow morbid thoughts to creep into my head. I reached down, untied my waterlogged sneakers, and kicked them off. One floated up between my legs and bounced off my life jacket before leaping from the water and smacking me in the face. I watched it bob away to my right, and as my eyes followed it I suddenly became aware that I was staring directly at an island, not three hundred yards away. Between the rolling waves and my preoccupation I'd almost swum right past it. I couldn't remember seeing an island anywhere near here on the chart, but there were so many little ones in these waters it was easy to confuse them. Maybe this was Pea Island, off the Westchester coast. I'd find out soon enough, anyway.

I did what I could to pace my strokes, but with each one I felt my strength ebbing and my legs—weak at the best of times—going numb. I couldn't sink with my life jacket on, but I could easily pass out and die of hypothermia or be hit by a boat. I focussed on the island's rocky shore, overhung by great oaks and chestnuts, and tried to picture myself crawling from shallows to beach. I passed into a kind of reverie with this image, replaying it over and over and somehow confusing it with an idea about a primordial amphibean creeping onto land for the first time and seeing myself as that creature, and by the time the dream played itself out I found myself within shouting distance. There was no one to shout at—the island seemed completely deserted—but I shouted anyway. Even then, my foot touched bottom, and I waded up to a sheltered cove with a tiny crescent of pebble beach. I collapsed and rolled over onto my back. A gnarled tree bough, silhouetted against the brightening sky, loomed over me and dripped.

I opened my eyes. If this was it, this was it. Something had to be done. I'm familiar enough with accidents to know that you have to fight the weariness, the pain, and the sense of distance they bring on and force yourself back into the present moment to do what needs to be done if you want to live. I didn't think I was in any immediate danger of dying just yet, but I could get myself in trouble if I didn't take some precautions right away. Still, it was peaceful there on my back: the sun was beginning to emerge, birds were calling tentatively through the greenery, the sound of roiling waters had finally faded. I lay there a few minutes longer, absorbing energy from the light, then rolled over and pushed myself to my feet.

The first thing to do was to strip off my wet clothes. For once ignoring all my doctors' warnings about the danger of sunlight to scar tissue, I stood with my arms outstretched to let the sun dry every inch of skin. It was only after I'd been standing there for a while that I realized how silly it was to leave my underwear on: a thick wall of forest behind me, miles of open water ahead, who was the modesty for? I usually felt self-conscious and uncomfortable being naked anywhere that people might see me, but just now I didn't care. After all, I was a castaway, wasn't I?

My eyes scanned the horizon. To my left, the Sound stretched on beyond sight. Ahead was a wooded promontory, two or three miles away—Kings Point, maybe? To my right, a bay, possibly Little Neck. I had no idea where I was. I tried to recall my lost chart of these waters, but the only island I could place in this vicinity was Davids, and that was covered in ruined army barracks. One thing, at least, was certain: the far side of the island was the one facing west, toward Orchard Beach and the Bronx, and that was where help would be coming from. I grabbed my clothes and headed down the beach to a spot where the undergrowth seemed to thin out. There I found a narrow trail concealed behind a screen of bracken and forsythia. Going from the sunny, open expanse of water and beach into the dank, gloomy forest was like being in one of those television commercials where a weary traveler steps through a billboard into a whole new world. The temperature dropped suddenly. Only the hardiest shafts of sunlight managed to pierce the greenery. Water from the recent storm continued to drip from the thick canopy of leaves overhead, as if in a tropical rain forest. There was little undergrowth on the forest floor, which was covered in a thick mat of glistening mosses, humus, and islands of lily of the valley, still in bloom. A rabbit startled me as it scampered across my path; my eyes followed it into the woods, where I saw others, dozens of plump white bunnies grazing on the lichen. They seemed completely tame, or maybe they were unafraid like animals that had never seen a human before. From the corner of my eye I caught a flash of tan as a white-tailed doe and her fawn bounded away into the depths of the wood. Songbirds of many different species played and called to each other in the crowns of the towering, ancient trees.

I walked deeper into the woods, the trail twisting and turning so that I was never able to see more than a few paces ahead at any time. There were no sounds other than the dripping of water and birdsong. The light was emerald, liquid and muted, as if the whole forest was underwater. But then, gradually, after I'd been walking and shivering more and more violently for about five minutes, the trail began to rise and the light grew brighter. I supposed I was approaching the far side of the island, that I'd come out on a bluff overlooking the mainland. But I didn't. A minute later, I stepped out of the woods and into a large clearing. I was at the foot of a sloping lawn bathed in sunlight. And I was looking up at one of the strangest houses I have ever seen, perched at the top of the hill like a vulture on a carcass.

It wasn't a large house, not by any means. In many ways, later, when I came to know it very well, I found that it was actually quite modest, but seeing it there for the first time, I felt as dizzy as if I were looking at Versailles. It had a looming quality, especially from that perspective, the way a monument seems from a great distance to dominate a landscape that dwarfs it.

It was difficult to take in at the first glance. Like some cubist exercise, it had a crazy profusion of perspectives, planes, and elevations that made it seem to shift and shimmy, never allowing the eye to rest or to accept a final, definitive version. No two details were quite the same, no two façades fully perpendicular, no gable entirely orthogonal, no window perfectly aligned. And even that wasn't true, but there was just no grasping the house in its entirety. Like a butterfly, your gaze might set down briefly on some florid detail but couldn't hold still more than an instant. So, even after standing there in awe and confusion for some time, I was able to piece together only the vaguest jumble of hood moldings, sunbursts, lancet windows, finials, pendants, all awash in an ocean of dolphins, sailing ships, mermaids, anchors, and leaping swordfish. It also happened to remind me of a house in Queens where I'd spent a few unhappy years. I was overcome by a wave of exhaustion and sank to my knees at the edge of the lawn, my head in my hands.

It was all so unreal that I was almost surprised when I looked up again to find the house still there, unchanged. But now, like in a dream, there was a man standing before me. Where he'd come from, or how he'd approached me so silently, I had no idea. He was just there, as if he'd coalesced from the mist that was beginning to rise from the grass. He was in his late middle age, dressed in an old-fashioned three-piece suit of brown tweed, and he carried the sort of black leather doctor's bag you see in bad westerns. In his free hand he held a plaid blanket, neatly folded. I was kneeling, naked and wretched, and I don't remember saying a word, but he spoke to me as if in answer to a question.

"No, it is not a dream," the stranger said as he draped the blanket over my shoulders. "You are on Turnaway."

I let it go at that. He'd spoken clearly and deliberately enough, in a vaguely Eastern European accent, but I had no idea what he'd just said. I was "on turn away"? What did that mean? That I was being turned away? The way nonsense can often seem perfectly logical in dreams, the thought crossed my mind—even as I gibbered on the lawn—that he meant I'd been placed on some rotating expatriation roster, like being on stand-by. This only reinforced my conviction that I was dreaming, but I didn't have the strength to question him. Despite the blanket, the warmth of the day, and the fact that the sun was growing stronger by the minute, I was still shivering uncontrollably from head to toe. I had just enough warning to roll over on my side before vomiting profusely and painfully. By the time my eyes were clear of tears, the stranger was grasping me by the arm and helping me to my feet. I went along without protest.

"We had better get you inside, don't you think?" the stranger murmured, almost to himself. He helped me across the lawn and up the steps of the porch. In my delirium I took in very little as my guide marched me through the front door and across a wide foyer toward a broad wooden staircase—passing glimpse of a living room to my left, a library to the right, all in the semishadow of twilight— and then I was climbing the stairs, past a blur of portraits, land- scapes, and gold-flocked wallpaper, and herded into a small bedroom at the end of a darkened landing.

The stranger—now, I suppose, my host—led me to the side of the bed, on which I sat while he went rummaging in a closet. Why had I allowed myself to be led around so passively? At this point, aside from his first, enigmatic remarks, we hadn't exchanged a single word. As a New Yorker, naturally suspicious and wary, I would never nor- mally enter a stranger's home without prior introduction or a very good reason at least. Maybe it was the fever and my helpless condi-

2 2 / J e s s e   B r o w n e r

tion that made me so tractable, but there was also something about my host, despite his inscrutability, something assertive and yet gentle, a kind of take-charge sympathy. What it was: he behaved like a doctor, and that's exactly what I seemed to need. So I sat there like a docile refugee in my blanket, in a strange house in an unknown place, while a stranger turned his back and strange metallic sounds issued from the closet.

A moment later, the stranger himself emerged from the closet, wheeling a cart of brushed aluminum. On its tray was a neat arrangement of surgical instruments, as well as various phials and philters, bandages, and a stack of folded white clothing and towels. He pushed the cart to the foot of the bed and chose a gleaming pair of tongs from among its implements. He used them to pick up a large swab of cotton wool, which he dipped into a kidney dish filled with a viscous white liquid.

"Antibacterial soap," he murmured comfortingly. He then knelt at my feet and dabbed the cotton wool gently over bleeding abrasions on both my knees, which I hadn't even noticed until that moment. He removed a few embedded pebbles with a pair of tweezers, then bandaged my knees with gauze. Then he went to the sink to wash his hands. With his back to me, he said: "Please remove the blanket and lie down on the bed." Sensing that I hadn't moved, he looked over his shoulder with an ironic smile. "I am a doctor," he said, aspirating the r. I did as he asked.

Once he'd dried his hands, he wheeled the cart to the side of the bed and sat down next to me. He slid a thermometer under my tongue and took my pulse. Then he began his examination, beginning with my feet and working his way up. Was this a perfectly normal sequence of events or was it truly weird and maybe dangerous? I had no idea. I lay there in a daze, unable to focus my thoughts. When he reached my thighs, the doctor glanced up sharply and let a thin hiss of breath slowly leak from his lips.

"This is recent?" he asked, almost severely.

"Almost two years now."

"You are lucky to be walking."

"I'm a lucky kind of guy."

The doctor shook his head a few times, as if he disapproved of my accident, then continued his examination. He palpated my abdomen, auscultated my chest, prodded at my neck and shoulders, peered into my ears. He pulled the thermometer from my mouth and held it up to the light at the window, squinting. I watched placidly.

He was a thin-boned, elfin man of about sixty, with a horseshoe of wiry gray hair extending from ear to ear around a shiny and some-what knobby bald dome. But it was only the filigree of crow's feet radiating from the corners of his eyes that gave away his age. Other-wise, he had a virile, ageless face that seemed to grow backward from the tip of a muscular nose in planes of taut olive skin. He had high cheekbones, bushy eyebrows, thin gray lips, and a deep dimple in his fleshy, bulbous chin. I'd noticed during the examination that his fingernails and cuticles were immaculately groomed and oiled. Like I said, there was something kindly but austere about him, particularly in the parentheses etched around his mouth and the shifting grays of his eyes, now almost silver in the evening light and the shaded glow of the lamp overhead. He wore a simple brown knit tie tightly knotted beneath a high, stiff collar, and exuded a subtle aura of powder and lilac.

"Who are you?" I asked.

"My name is Dr. Joseph Ross," he answered without looking up from his work.

"And this is your house?"

"I have lived here for forty years."

"But where are we?"

Ignoring my question, the doctor flicked the thermometer a few times, then placed it in a dish. He picked up an old-fashioned glass hypodermic, screwed a needle onto it and filled it with a clear liquid from a small, rubber-covered bottle. "You have only a slight case of hypothermia. This is a mild sedative. You will feel better tomorrow when the fever has dissipated." He administered the injection with professional efficiency into my left arm. Then he covered me with several heavy blankets that he'd brought from the closet. He tucked them in and made hospital corners.

"You are in Turnaway House on Turnaway Island," he said in a low monotone that emphasized his accent. "But you must try to get some rest now. You have had a bad trauma. I will come to see you in the morning and answer all your questions."

I was beginning to feel groggy, and the bed kept tilting to the left, but I persisted. "My boat . . ."

"All that has been taken care of," said Dr. Ross, rising to his feet. "Just sleep now."

He padded across the room and placed his hand on the light switch by the door before turning around. "Good night," he said, smiling. "Sleep well." He switched off the light and the door clicked shut.

I lay on my back in the dark. From the woods came the distant hoot of an owl. To slow down the revolving bed and anchor it, I turned my head toward the window. Only then, for the first time, did I notice the view. I looked out over the treetops and across a stretch of inky water. Beyond hunched the black shoulder of Throgs Neck, and beyond that a distant strip of glimmering lights, like the fiery tail of a comet. It was Manhattan, already lit up for the night. A few land-marks were visible—the Citicorp building, the Chrysler, the Empire State, and further, separated by a dark gulf, the faint embers of the twin towers. They were far away now and growing fainter, receding, the entire island receding, silently gliding away over the horizon, following the sun into the west, ever farther, until they dipped behind the curve of the earth and their blaze was extinguished in the black ocean of the night.

I awoke toward dawn to the riotous chatter of starlings. I climbed from the bed and went to the window. Manhattan, Throgs Neck, and Eastchester Bay were no longer visible, shrouded so thickly in mist that I even wondered momentarily whether my vision of the city the night before hadn't been a drug-induced hallucination. Directly be-low me was the porch roof—my room seemed to be almost above the front door of the house. On the lawn and in the treetops, birds wheeled and dived on the last of the nocturnal insects. Further than that I could see nothing but a few shreds of cirrus cloud glowing pink in the first rays of the rising sun. There was a door leading out onto a narrow porch facing west, but the view was the same—mist, birds, and treetops. The city was gone.

As I stood there, gazing and wondering, I gradually became aware of things that weren't right with me: my body ached and smelled—an unpleasant combination of dirty seawater and sweat—and I had an urgent need to piss. First things first, I made for the sink in the corner, where I prepared to relieve myself until I realized that the door to my room had no lock. I grabbed one of the washcloths that hung in neat rows from a brass towel-rod by the sink and sponged myself down with warm water. After patting down with one of last night's soiled towels, I went into the closet where, among the instruments, bottles, syringes, and shiny bedpans, I found some hospital pyjamas, a doctor's white robe, and a pair of cotton slippers. I slipped into the pyjama bottoms, draped the robe over my shoulders like a boxer, and kicked my feet into the slippers.

Like any guest, I was shy about padding out into an unfamiliar house while the host, as I assumed, was still asleep. I opened the heavy, paneled door. The excitement and terror of this first step, relics of an entire childhood spent creeping around strange houses with untested masters, made me catch my breath and hesitate a moment. I hadn't been a criminal, just a foster child, and yet every time I found myself alone in a new home, however kind my new guardians, I was overcome with guilt and shame, as if merely being there was cause enough for punishment. I'd felt that way everywhere I went as a boy and every time anyone had a reason to pay attention to me; I hadn't been sorry to put my humiliation behind me as a man, but the feeling rushed back now as fresh and familiar as if I were twelve all over again. I mastered myself quickly, as I've learned to do over the years, but my palms were still moist and my throat dry when I stuck my head out and listened.

The house was silent, so I stepped into the hallway. It was long and wide, with polished oak floors reaching from a double lancet window at one end of the house to a single at the other. The dogleg stairwell was about midway between the two. Directly across the hall from my door was another, identical and firmly shut. I'd enter it only as a last resort, since in my experience closed doors are usually closed for a reason.

I tiptoed down the hall. The gold in the flocked wallpaper, which I'd noticed last night, now glowed in the morning light streaming through the windows. It was the background to a pattern of wine-brown interlocking fleur-de-lis, thoroughly dull and faded. The entire hallway was papered with it, and the overall effect was of walking through a halo of golden mist, as if the whole world had become a soft-focus photograph. Many paintings, ornately framed in gilt and cherry, hung from the crimson picture rail: naïf nineteenth-century land- and seascapes, ancestral portraits, and several romanticized scenes of American Indian life. Opposite the stairwell was a dark, narrow hallway with a stairway and a bull's-eye window at the far end. That, too, I decided to explore only if absolutely necessary.

The next door I came to, on the left, was ajar. I tapped once, again, then stepped into a small study. Rows of wooden boxes with glass casings lined the walls, housing columns of pinned butterflies, moths, and beetles identified by labels, some typed, most in long-hand. A large desk under the window was strewn with optical micro-scopes, loupes, petri dishes, and dissecting implements. Every surface, including the semiopaque windows, was covered in a layer of dust, as if the room had fallen into disuse long ago. There were cobwebs in every corner and hosts of live spiders, mosquitoes, and harvestmen going about their business. The far wall was lined with bookshelves, and between them a door stood wide open, revealing the welcome sight of claw-foot tub and toilet. After a long and explo-sive piss, I washed my hands and ran them wet through my dishev-eled hair. They came away smelling of salt water, seaweed, and something I didn't care to identify. I left by a door in the right-hand wall that led back to the hallway, made my way to the top of the stairs, and called down. Still there was no answer—the house seemed to be deserted, or else inhabited by very sound sleepers. Hanging on tightly to the handrail for fear of losing my footing on the worn and gleaming teak treads, I crept downstairs.

I paused at the bottom of the stairs, my hand resting on a polished newel cap carved in the form of an oyster shell. The foyer was papered in a once-iridescent blue strewn with golden scallop, clam, and conch shells, while pink starfish formed pallid constellations in the sky-blue ceiling. Directly ahead of me was the front door; now, with the light behind it, I noticed the intricate stained-glass profile of a fully-rigged frigate set into its window and a pearly sunrise in the fanlight above. Next to it was an elephant's foot crammed with black umbrellas and walking sticks. For some reason, it was the sight of this elephant's foot more than anything else I'd seen that brought home to me the strangeness of this empty house. Walking through it was more like being in a museum or on the set of some overproduced haunted-house movie than in someone's home. I've been through more homes than most people and a few of them have been pretty grim, but none has ever struck me as being so inappropriate a place for human habitation. I sneezed and went on with my self-guided tour.

At the bottom of the stairs, I turned left under an elliptical arch supported by two doric columns and found myself in the library. Every wall was lined with mahogany bookshelves filled with well-oiled leather-bound volumes, not a single cloth- or paperback book among them. I ran an index finger casually across the spines—Victorian and Edwardian ethnographic studies mostly, a little archeology, no fiction or poetry. A windowseat in the bay was upholstered in sea-green velvet—real, if threadbare, I noted as I brushed my hand across it—and the windows were hung in draped taffeta of a matching color. The furnishings were sparse but heavy, all of mahogany black with age: a long, low captain's desk, covered with neatly stacked papers and envelopes, squatted under the front windows behind a matching armchair; a small, round pedestal table in the bay; and a suite of chesterfields, wing chairs, and ottomans upholstered in cracked morocco before a massive fireplace in the corner. A long-nosed ancestor in a stiff collar gazed down blandly from a murky portrait, framed in mahogany, above the mantel.

I wandered across the foyer into the living room. Though larger, with an enormous bay that encompassed half the room, and maybe a little livelier in tone, it was hardly more comfortable. Several ensembles of high-backed sofas were grouped about the room in little cliques, as if awaiting a visit from the ladies of the Temperance Society. Some Persian rugs, their patterns barely discernable, were strewn about the floor; prissy brass sconces hung on the walls, with a few ancestors, one in a sea captain's uniform. As in the library, all the wooden surfaces were dusted and polished, the furniture and fixtures about as clean as their age and condition allowed. But there was one extraordinary thing about the living room that immediately distinguished it from every other space in the house: it was crammed, floor to ceiling and jamb to jamb, with American Indian artifacts. Stone-headed arrows, peace pipes, and beaded leather tobacco pouches covered every horizontal surface. Mocassins danced on the windowsills, councils of ceremonial feather headdresses conferred on the walls, rivers of stringed beads flowed below the wave molding. There were combs and needles and necklaces of weathered bone, straps and loincloths and togalike dresses of leather, hatchets and tomahawks and blades of stone. There was artwork by Indians— obscure effigial figures prancing through abstract zig-zag hills and valleys—and about Indians—soft-hued riverside idylls, hunting scenes and death throes. A moth-eaten bearskin in front of the fire-place snarled at a framed replica of the 1645 deed to Manhattan on the wall. There were more, countless unidentifiable fragments of wood and horn everywhere the eye turned, all exuding clouds of mildew that set my head spinning and clogged my lungs and throat. I staggered through a narrow door by the fireplace and found myself in the dining room. More ancestors, and the doctor. He was seated at the end of a long mahogany table, eating half a grapefruit and read-ing the *Times*. My wallet, sodden and bloated, rested by his elbow. A place was set at his right, and a cup of coffee was already steaming there. A bowl of porridge, a thin layer of cream on top, was also waiting at the empty chair. The doctor, his mouth full, gestured for me to join him.

"I trust you slept well?" he inquired as I took my place.

My tour of the house had made me distinctly edgy, and my throb-bing head only exacerbated my irritation. When I spoke, the light-hearted inquiry I'd intended came out as petty peevishness. "Dr. Ross," I said, "what's going on here?"

He paused before answering, evidently put off by my tone, but more out of surprise, to be fair, than annoyance. "The ancient Greeks," he said thoughtfully, "valued hospitality above all other virtues, in case a stranger invited into their homes should turn out to be a god in disguise." A wry smile bloomed on his face. "I don't know if the old gods ever lost their boats at sea, but you'll forgive me for taking no chances."

I sipped at the hot coffee to mask my embarrassment, and burned my tongue. "I'm sorry," I spluttered. "But you have to admit this is pretty weird, my being here like this."

Now the doctor was genuinely amazed. "What is weird? You have an accident, I am a doctor. You are wet and traumatized, I put you to bed and sedate you. You awaken, I give you coffee. Later, I will lend you clothes and call for a taxi. Then you will return to your home. Please, what is *weird* about this?"

I felt my cheeks redden with shame. "I really am sorry. It's just that . . . I suppose where you're from all this is perfectly normal."

"You are correct," he said, then turned his eyes to the newspaper so as not to appear too solicitous. "How do you feel?"

"Lousy."

"Too bad, such a promising patient." He continued to pretend to peruse the headlines while he pushed my wallet across the table to me. It left a trail of slime, like a snail. "I must tell you, on the beach this morning, I looked through it, to identify you. Just so you know, since you find the kindness of strangers so alarming."

"Thank you."

"May I ask you, what were you doing out there in such weather? The shallows around Turnaway are notorious and treacherous, if you are unfamiliar with them."

"I didn't hit anything. My boat was swamped."

"Ah, then you were lucky twice. People have died. They know to stay away."

There was a pause while I considered this information.

"I guess I should notify the Coast Guard," I said finally.

"I have already done so, last night. They will be in touch with you."

"Thank you."

Another pause. We seemed to have said all there was to be said.

"You have a very interesting house," I said.

"Thank you, but it is not my house."

"You rent?" Here was something a New Yorker could discuss.

"I serve."

"I'm sorry . . . ?"

"I am a servant. There is a master of the house."

"You're a . . . doctor?"

"I am a servant and a doctor."

"You take care of the house. The owner doesn't live here."

"The master of the house lives in the house. I take care of the house and I take care of him."

"And where is the . . . master now?"

"He is out. Hunting."

The doctor was clearly relishing my confusion. Though he never lifted his eyes from the newspaper throughout this exchange, a wicked glee had crept into his voice, and he kept rustling the paper to emphasize each remark. Was he toying with me? Who was this so-called master? Had I stumbled on to some strange cult, the kind of thing you read about in the tabloids? After my tour of this unnerving, uninhabitable mausoleum, I was ready to believe anything. In any case, whatever the truth, there was no gleaning it from the doctor's inscrutable behavior. I was beginning to think that, for once, my instinct for caution and suspicion had been well-founded.

And as if to confirm this, I was startled from my dark thoughts by the sound of the front door slamming and the unmistakable patter of naked feet running across the oak floors of the foyer. The door—not the one I'd come through but another, directly across the table from me—burst open. And there stood a skinny boy, with tousled black hair and flashing gray eyes, naked except for a tan leather loincloth and a string of purple beads around his forehead. He was panting heavily, and his long, tapering face was bissected by a dazzling smile. In either hand he held a white rabbit by the ears, both very much alive and kicking. He turned to the doctor and held his trophies above his head.

"I got two, Ross, two! Oh, you beauties!" And he lowered one rabbit to eye level and kissed it smack on the snout with evident affection. The bunny booted him on the chin with equal and opposite affection, and swung away like a pendulum. The boy, unharmed and undaunted, turned to me and unleashed another open-mouthed grin.

"Hello, Mr. Givens," he laughed. "I'd like to meet you. I'll come down for you in a moment." And he was gone. I sat there flabbergasted while the doctor pursued his grapefruit and reading unperturbed. Presently, he swallowed the last segment, dabbed at his lips with a linen napkin, and turned a page. Again without looking up, he spoke in the same tone of mischievous pleasure I'd heard him use earlier.

"That," he said, "was the master of the house."

The enigmatic doctor, the wild child, the mysterious home on a desert island—it had to be a setup, some sort of elaborate practical joke. There may have been one or two people in the world who'd go to that kind of trouble on my account, but none of them had the imagination for it. Obviously, it wasn't going to do any good to question Dr. Ross—he just sat there with that knowing smile under his little apple cheeks and brushed off all my inquiries. "Ask the master," he said. I could hear the little Apache upstairs, banging and stamping around to wake the dead. I made up my mind to try to get off the island as quickly as I could.

A few minutes later the "master" came down. He'd changed out of his costume, to be sure, but his new getup was even more outlandish than the first. Now he was dressed up like something out of *Babes in Toyland:* a three-piece suit of gray worsted, the lapels wide enough to touch the shoulders, severely tapered at the waist, a gold watch chain strung across the vest, plus fours tucked into tartan kneesocks, canvas saddle shoes, a flat cap cocked jauntily over his right eye. He was even carrying a polo seat, a walking cane with a point at one end and two little fold-down wings at the other. After pausing for effect in the doorway and registering my amazement with a triumphant smile, he strolled into the room swinging his hips and shoulders like a runway model, jammed the point of the cane into a crack between the floorboards, unfolded the seat, delicately eased himself onto it, crossed his right knee over his left, and finally came to rest with his chin balanced on his fist and his face not nine inches away from mine.

"Mr. Givens," he piped. "Welcome to my island."

I'd had him pegged from the moment I first set eyes on him. A child of wealth; arrogant, secure in his immunity, and accustomed to having every whim catered to, costumes included, but at the same time very lonely, uncertain of the social graces, having to mask his fear of being thought a fool behind gestures of opulent foolishness. A familiar type: I'd known a lot of guys like that in college—smug and not too bright for the most part, but they still made scholarship students like me feel small and ugly. It was easy for me to dislike people like him, even if he was just a boy.

I gave him a curt "thanks," but instead of starting a conversation he just sat there staring and grinning at me like I was his new-found darling. His smile was so wide, his teeth so straight and white, and his boyish face so narrow, that it would have been more accurate to say that he had a face on his smile than a smile on his face. I was deeply, deeply embarrassed. I glanced over at Dr. Ross for guidance, but he was pretending to be engrossed in the business section. Finally, having gazed at me for a full thirty seconds with an expression of outrageously languid affection, my host offered me his hand.

"My name's Hutchinson," he said. "Elias Hutchinson of the Turnaway Hutchinsons, in case you didn't guess. But my friends just call me Wulamewet."

"What if I call you Elias?" I asked through gritted teeth, trying my hardest to remain polite.

"By all means, do," he beamed. "I don't have any friends anyway."

Dr. Ross coughed discretely into his paper but carried on reading as if we weren't there. I knew I had to be patient and subtle, but I felt like I was going nuts.

"You know," I said, rising a little too quickly. "I should be getting back to town. Can you tell me where I—"

Elias Hutchinson jumped to his feet, a genuine look of alarm on his face, and clasped me by the shoulders.

"Going? But you've only just arrived," he cried, clinging to me in real earnest as if he wanted to prevent me physically from leaving. "Ross, tell him he must stay!" He seemed on the verge of tears.

I pulled away, horrified and sickened. Why did the boy think I was here? Hadn't the doctor explained to him about my accident? How could he even imagine that I might want to stay? And suddenly it dawned on me. The boy wasn't spoiled—he was an idiot, the retarded or slow-witted son of wealthy parents who'd abandoned him to the care of a personal physician and trusted family retainer. This, too, was a familiar type: the weak, sensitive boy who was always bullied and picked on. There was one in every class. But he'd have an unfailing nose for the reluctant heart among his tormentors; when he found it he'd cling to it with all his might and either bring his sympathizer down with him or force him to be doubly cruel. He'd have to break that desperate grasp just to save himself.

But the doctor beat me to it. Without looking up from his paper, he asserted his authority. "No, Elias, he must go," he said. "You see he is unwell. He needs attention without delay. You and I will escort him to Felicia when she gets here."

The boy looked sincerely crestfallen. "I get so few visitors, especially ones my own age," he whined. I couldn't help smiling: his every expression, his every gesture, was so comically exaggerated that his disappointment verged on the tragic. Despite my consideration for his condition, I had to stifle a snicker. I caught Dr. Ross darting an amused glance in my direction before turning back to his paper.

Elias wrung his hands dramatically. "Couldn't you stay just a little while longer? Please, Mr. Givens? Ben? Can I call you Ben? Please, Ben?"

"No, I really have to . . . I should be getting home. Doctor's orders." I'd said that as a joke, but it wasn't taken in the spirit in which it was meant.

"Pooh, doctor!" Elias spat out the word like a bitter cherry. "Some doctor!" Snatching up his cane, he turned on his heels and stormed out the door, slamming it behind him. Three other doors banged somewhere in the house, each more distant and muffled than the last, before it fell silent again. I could only stand and contemplate that exit in silent awe. Behind me a newspaper rustled, and I turned to find Dr. Ross staring into his coffee cup, the *Times* folded neatly on the table in front of him.

"I am sorry about that," he said. "He is not usually so . . . petulant. He gets excited to see a new face."

"He could use a little discipline, that's all." The words sounded strange in my mouth, severe and humorless, but I was more embarrassed for the doctor than for myself. I needn't have been. He raised one bushy white eyebrow thoughtfully.

"He is a little old for discipline, I think."

"No child is too old or too slow to learn basic manners."

"I agree," the doctor said quietly. "But Elias is no child. He is twenty-nine years old."

"Twenty-nine?" It seemed impossible. Elias was only two years younger than me. It wasn't only his tantrums or his costume dressing that made him appear so childish; physically, with his slim shoulders and waist, his bony chest, his hairless face and smooth skin, he was a boy—no older, I'd have guessed, than sixteen or seventeen. It occurred to me that his problem might be genetic, a missing growth hormone or something like that.

"Is he . . . completely . . . healthy?" I ventured.

"Oh yes, yes," the doctor chuckled. "I know what you are thinking, but he is in excellent physical and mental health. It is only that he is so very . . . untouched by the world, he has remained young in every way. Generally, he is a very warm and generous person. But it is only your presence that enervates him—he sees so few people, he wants to make an impression but he does not know how to act. He becomes flustered."

"Doesn't he have any friends?"

"Where would he be finding friends?" The doctor looked to his left and right to show me there were no friends in the room. "We are alone on the island, he and I."

"Why doesn't he get out more? See other people?"

"There is no need. He is very busy here, with his studies and our work. And then, I provide him with all the company he needs."

"Do you?" I said. I hadn't meant to sound skeptical or judgmental, but I guess that's how it came out. The doctor's face shut down as if someone had pulled a switch. He'd just started to warm up, too, it seemed to me, but whatever I'd said, whatever line I'd crossed, drained all the emotion from his features and cast him in stone. All his professional courtesy and what I'd come to think of as personal kindness, which had been so comforting to me the night before, dried up. All this time he hadn't once looked up from his cup; nor did he do so now.

"The mail boat arrives in the late morning," he said icily. "It will take you across to City Island. They have buses there to Manhattan, I believe, or to the subway."

"I'm sorry. I—"

"In the meantime, please feel free to walk about the island. If you have any feeling for insects or botany, you will find much to interest you. Good day."

With that, the doctor pushed his chair abruptly from the table, stood up stiffly, and exited the room via the kitchen, giving me a nod that was more of a snub than a courtesy. I was left standing by myself in the middle of the dining room, unsure what to do. In the house, there was not the least sound to indicate the presence of another human being. The floorboards clicked, a moth beat its wings dully against a windowpane, the jury of ancestors glared down from the walls with ancient contempt. I wanted to kick myself. I seemed to have a knack for making people dislike me. I was always doing this sort of thing, alienating people for no good reason. Why couldn't I just get along? Well, the damage was done now. I shoved through the swinging door and strode briskly through the musty parlor. The telephone rang before I could make it to the front door. I stood there

hesitating, waiting for someone to pick up another extension somewhere in the house, but no one did. At the fifth ring, I answered.

"Dr. Ross?"

"No, he's not here right now."

"This is Corporation Counsel. Can you tell him—"

Just then, the doctor came scurrying through the door from the
kitchen and swiped the receiver from my hand so violently that I
backed up a couple of paces, as if from an attack. He glared at me
until I continued my retreat through the front door. I took a few
seconds to recover, then turned my face into the dazzling sunlight.

Before me stretched the great lawn, sorely in need of a mowing.
Down at porch level, I could not see beyond the palisade of vibrant
green forest that enclosed the house and its grounds on all sides.
Strangely, despite the fresh air and the trees and the wild bird calls
and the sunshine, to me the whole setup seemed oppressive somehow, as if it had been designed for reclusion, like a gulag hidden
deep within a forest. But when I stepped off the porch onto a white
gravel path that encircled the house, the sound of crunching gravel,
mingled with birdsong and the rustle of leaves, brought to mind
instead the image of a Victorian mental hospital. In my white robe
and slippers, I was dressed appropriately—the only thing missing
was the genteel *pock* of croquet balls. I turned to my right, with the
hot sun at my back, and set off down the path, exaggerating my limp
and crunching the gravel under my heels so as to be sure not to
surprise anyone who might be lurking. I was feeling decidedly
cranky and, now that I'd managed to insult both my hosts—the only
two people in the world who knew where I was—a lot like a reluctant, awkward kid who's just been dropped off for his first summer at
camp. I found myself listening intently for the engine of the mail
boat.

I continued down the path. Up close, the house showed all the
signs of age and weathering that had been invisible from a distance.
It was painted in three shades of green, like the woods—a deep sea
green for the structural elements; a very pale jade for the siding; and
a brighter chartreuse for the ornament—and was faded, flaking, and
in desperate need of refinishing. The gravel was dappled with flecks

of green, like sea foam, and there was a clear case of rising damp on the baseboards of the limestone foundation wall, which rose to about hip height. Long rectangular windows set into the wall gave onto the basement; I shaded my eyes with my hands and pressed my nose to the glass but could make out nothing in the subterranean gloom, the panes having been blackened with paint or tar. Ancient, powdery grout was falling off the chimneys in fist-size lumps. Several pottery chimney pots had dropped to the lawn, and those that weren't smashed were tilted at odd angles like old headstones, completing the picture of abandonment and decay, indoors and out.

I followed the path around to the back, where the sweep of the lawn and the solid forest wall were broken only by another gravel path leading from the small kitchen porch, across the grass, and into a gap between the trees. Still, there was no one to be heard or seen. The only sounds were those of birds, cicadas, breeze, water, and the occasional roar of a jet banking over Pelham Park to land at La Guardia. Where had my hosts vanished to? Just a few minutes earlier they'd been so solicitous of my health, my comfort, my company; now they seemed to have forgotten all about me and left me—a total stranger—to roam their private estate at will. What if I were a criminal? Didn't they read the papers? Just the idea of such carelessness and naïveté was enough to rile me up all over again. Still, where were they? It was hard to imagine that they'd just abandoned me on the island.

I rounded the third corner, coming to the eastern side of the house. Here the lawn disappeared. In its place was a wide kitchen garden, stretching from the edge of the path to the verge of the woods some thirty yards away. But this was no ordinary kitchen garden. Instead of the usual tidy rows of spinach, beans, onions, and herbs, this one was all lettuce—Boston, as best I could tell. It was a good quarter-acre of tightly spaced lettuce protected by a waist-high fence of stakes and chicken wire. The garden was obviously well tended, too: the lettuce seemed healthy and plump, like little green guinea hens, and there wasn't a weed to be seen along the narrow pathways crisscrossing the patch. A big lettuce patch is more impressive than you might think, especially to a city boy, and I stood contemplating it for several minutes, not that I had anything better to do. Then I noticed a small clearing in the woods behind it, developed with what seemed to be a block of chicken coops. I strolled around the lettuce and into the clearing.

They were not chicken coops but rabbit hutches—four large huts raised off the ground on brick pilings and surrounded by fencing nailed to shoulder-height wooden stakes. The corners of the fence were anchored with tall concrete buttresses, which made the compound look like a scale model of a concentration camp. Its inmates were large white domestic rabbits of the Easter bunny variety, the kind I'd seen in the woods the day before and in Elias's hands that morning. Obviously, the lettuce was being grown for the bunnies. A very efficient little farm, apparently, clean and orderly, but it seemed weird that Elias would need to hunt rabbits when he was breeding them by the hundreds. Maybe he had a vermin problem, like the Australians in the 1950s; maybe he hunted the rabbits and imprisoned them here in the compound but couldn't bring himself to slaughter them. It didn't make much sense, but neither did anything else on Turnaway. Nailed to a post was a weathered, hand-painted sign that said RESERVATION PROPERTY.

As I absorbed it all in bemusement and disgust—I've never had much use for bunnies—the prisoners started to riot. At first it was a sort of low-intensity nervous shiver running through the crowd, but soon they began to scramble, jumble, scamper, and boil, kicking and pawing and climbing over each other in apparent desperation to escape. I thought they were reacting to me—animals don't care much for me, as a rule—but then the door to one of the hutches swung open and Elias Hutchinson emerged in a crouch onto the ramp. Once again dressed in a loincloth, and nothing else, he was carrying a dustpan piled with pellets. Unaware of my presence, he was muttering to himself, or to the bunnies, in a gibberish language full of glottals and swallowings. It wasn't until he'd pulled himself clear of the doorway and stood up that he noticed me watching him. He broke out his most unself-conscious smile.

"Aha! So we meet again, Bumppo m'lad!" he said.

"Any idea when the mail boat is due?" I asked.

Elias Hutchinson emptied the dustpan into a galvanized bucket, slapped his hands together, and stepped through the gate of the enclosure, herding a few errant bunnies back inside with his naked foot. Then he strode over to me and clasped my right hand in his right and my left forearm in his left.

"Forget about the boat. Stay here with me. The island is a beautiful place," he said earnestly, glancing nervously over my shoulder toward the house.

"I really can't." This time, I was careful to convey a tone of regret. Instead of jerking away, I eased myself gently from his embrace.

"You have a job to return to, I dare say?"

"No, not exactly."

"Well, well," he tisked thoughtfully. "I suppose you must go." But he brightened instantly. "But the boat won't be here until eleven. That gives us . . ."—he squinted up at the sun—"about half an hour. Come. I'll show you round the res." He hooked his arm through mine and led me down a trail into the woods. I didn't even consider protesting, though strolling arm-in-arm with half-naked hysterics is not necessarily my idea of a good time. Still, the day was beautiful, and as we walked in the sunlight filtering through the canopy of chestnuts, Elias Hutchinson began pointing out the native flora and fauna of the "res." Squirrels and shrubs don't do much for me either, so after a quarter hour or so on the nature trail I was glad for the chance to change the subject.

"What kind of reservation is this?" I finally managed to interrupt. He seemed genuinely surprised by my question, and stopped dead in his tracks.

"Why, an Indian reservation, of course."

"Indian?"

"Yes, certainly. Manapinock Reservation. The only Native American res in New York City."

"And do any . . . Native Americans . . . live on the reservation?"

Now he stared candidly at me as if I were crazy, his jaw dropping dramatically.

"Why, *I* do. Don't tell me you didn't know I'm an Indian?"

I didn't, of course, but now I took the opportunity to examine him more closely. It was true that his hair was dark and relatively straight, and it was very nearly black, but it could just as easily be called brown. His eyes, too, were a dark brown, and his skin copper, but tanned rather than naturally Asiatic looking, I'd have said. I squinted, trying to see him the way he saw himself, but I admit I just couldn't do it. He didn't look like an Indian to me—his nose was slim and slightly upturned, his cheekbones high but not too high, his eyes large and oval—but in all honesty, never having known any Native Americans personally, I wouldn't have known what to look for. Maybe it isn't fair to expect every Native American to look like Sitting Bull. All I can say for sure is, he looked nothing like the extras in *Drums Along the Mohawk* or *Dances with Wolves*, the only Indians I'd ever seen up close. But the tone of his question had made it clear: he had no interest in hearing any doubts I might have been entertaining. I humored him.

"I suppose so," I managed to stammer. That seemed to please him, because he smiled in a gentle, modest way.

"Not full blood, of course. Our blood was mixed with Europeans' almost from the first contact. But I *am* the very last registered member of the Siwanoy tribe."

"Sue . . . ?"

"Siwanoy. A chieftaincy of the Lenape nation, now called the Delaware. We used to own the north shore of the Sound from the Bronx clear up to New Haven. Manapinock is all that's left. And me."

The trail ended abruptly at the water, a sharp escarpment of stones and pebbles overhung to eye level by ancient oaks that leaned precariously over the current. Through their leaves I recognized the crescent of Orchard Beach, maybe two or three miles away. Elias picked up a handful of pebbles and began tossing them one by one into the water.

"How long have you lived here?" I asked tentatively.

"All my life. I was born here. My father was the last of the Siwanoy, too. He was born here. And so was his father, who built the house." He paused for a moment, deep in thought. "So will my children, when they come," he said, almost under his breath. After another pause, he absentmindedly dropped the rest of his pebbles into the water and turned back toward the house. I followed.

"What about the rabbits?" I asked. The question seemed to draw him from his reverie.

"The rabbits? New Zealand whites—they're my prey. I stalk them," he said proudly.

"But you raise them."

He saw no contradiction in this. "Sure. These fluffy white beasts, they're not native to Manapinock. I raise them then release them into the wild, like they do on pheasant farms."

"And you eat them?"

"Good god, no. I wouldn't have the heart to kill those little cuties. I do it to hone my aboriginal hunting skills."

"And what happens to the bunnies?"

"There's a home for bunnies somewhere on Long Island that Ross knows about. When it gets too crowded, he packs up a hundred or so in a crate and ships them off. And the owls always get a few. You can't prevent it, Manapinock's full of them. Here's Ross."

By now we were in view of the front of the house, having approached it from a different path, and there indeed was the doctor, walking—almost skipping, in a strange, birdlike gait—toward us. He was wearing a brown herringbone suit with a white shirt and black tie. In his hand he held a plastic shopping bag. He beckoned us to approach.

"Felicia is here. She is a little early," he called to us. "Mr. Givens, I have your shorts here, cleaned to the best of my ability. Perhaps you'd like to change before you leave? I've laid out some clothing upstairs that I believe might fit you."

I grabbed the bag and stumped upstairs to my bedroom. Draped across the bed, crisply remade with hospital corners, were a gray pinstripe suit, a white cotton dress shirt, black ankle socks, and a pair of black leather oxfords. Slightly to the side—as if to say "We know you are the casual type, but in case you wish to do things the right way . . ."—was a broad tie in blue-and-white club stripes. I dressed, without the tie, then stepped over to the mirror to gauge the effect of my new duds. Considering that I was a good deal taller than both my hosts, the clothes fit surprisingly well. I couldn't help laughing—I looked like a completely different person. I never played dress-up or any other make-believe games as a kid, but I could see its attraction for someone who was starved for company. I even felt a passing twinge of pity as I imaged little Elias, all alone day after day, trying on costumes for the mirror to laugh at. I did my feeble Cary Grant imitation for the empty room.

"My father was a bigger man than me."

I spun around to find Elias Hutchinson leaning against the door frame, smiling wryly at the fit of the suit. How long had he been standing there watching me preen? The door was reflected squarely in the mirror, but I hadn't noticed him until he'd spoken. Maybe he was an Indian after all—weren't they supposed to be good at creeping and spying? To cover my embarrassment, as well as my revulsion at having been caught admiring myself in a dead man's clothes, I turned back to my reflection.

"These belonged to your father?" I asked indifferently.

"Every stitch I own, except this," he said, indicating his loincloth. "Most of it hasn't been worn since he died, fifteen years ago."

"I'll mail them back to you."

"You can bring them next time you visit. Felicia's here."

The doctor was waiting for us at the foot of the stairs. We walked through the house, across the big, old-fashioned kitchen with its Norge and Royal Rose appliances, and down the back steps, all in silence. We followed the gravel path that led through the woods, winding gradually downhill to the waterfront, where it opened out onto a small concrete levee with a rickety wooden jetty pointing north toward Larchmont. Roped to a bollard on the jetty was a small blue launch with a U.S. MAIL sign affixed to the cockpit, and standing by the bollard was a plump young Hispanic woman in a baggy postal uniform, not unattractive in a cuddly sort of way, sorting through a pile of envelopes in her hand. She looked up and smiled sweetly as we approached; the pin over her left breast read FELICIA LOPEZ.

"Hiya, Doc. Hiya, Elias."

"*Hola, Felicia,*" said Elias in the earnest, eager tones of a student. "*¿Qué tal?*"

"Muy bien, amor."

"Felicia, mi amigo, Señor Givens."

"Mucho gusto," Felicia said, turning to me.

"Likewise," I said.

"Felicia, would you be kind enough to give Mr. Givens a lift to City Island?" the doctor said quietly, holding out an upturned hand for his mail.

"Sure, Doc. Here you go." Felicia held out a newspaper and the stack of envelopes, and since I was nearest to her I reached for them. But the doctor, with a speed that was surprising for his age, stepped between us and grabbed them from her rudely, slipping them into his inner breast pocket. I noticed, in the split second in which he looked down to lift his lapel, the glance and smile exchanged between Elias and Felicia—it was exactly the look you might expect from two teenagers conducting an illicit romance under their parents' noses. Brief as it was, Elias caught me watching and blushed like a virgin.

"Mr. Givens was shipwrecked yesterday," he said.

"No shit?" Felicia said without much interest. "Let's go," she said to me. "I'm late on my rounds already." She jumped without further ado into her launch, then turned back toward us. *"Hasta mañana, caballeros."*

Ostentatiously ignoring her familiarity, Dr. Ross took my left hand in his and spoke in the commanding tones of his profession, though he wouldn't look me in the eye. "Mr. Givens, please get some bed rest for the next few days, and take plenty of acetominophen. And please stay out of boats."

"Thanks for everything, Dr. Ross," I said, and then he did something strange. He reached up, pinched my cheek, and slapped my face. The idea, I'm sure, was that this was some sort of sign of personal affection in the old country, but the pinch was a little too insistent and the slap a little too resounding to make the gesture anything but ambiguous, at best. I turned to Elias, who was prancing by his side like a nervous show horse. He, in contrast, met my gaze boldly, as if we were lifelong friends, and his intimacy was much more unpleasant to me than the doctor's hostility.

"When will I see you again?" he pleaded.

"Well, I don't—"

"You must, you must come back to the res. We have so much to talk about." The doctor tisked sharply, rolled his eyes heavenward, and walked off toward the house. Elias threw an anxious glance at his retreating figure. When the doctor was out of earshot, he draped an arm around my neck and drew me into conspiratorial proximity. "There's a great deal you need to know about me," he said as if he were revealing a deep secret. I nodded my head sagely, and Felicia sounded two short blasts of her foghorn. I climbed awkwardly down into the boat before venturing my reply. "Well, thanks for every-thing," I called with false good cheer. "See you around some time."

I knew very well that this wasn't even close to the response Elias was fishing for, but now that I was safely off the island I was done humoring him. Whatever problems he had, however pathetic he might be, my giving him false hope and insincere sentiment wasn't going to help. It was better to be brutal and honest, as I knew from experience. I certainly had no reason to feel guilty. And yet, though my debt of gratitude could be paid off with the quickest of thank-you notes or a token gift, and though I felt as if I'd been much kinder and more indulgent toward nutty little Elias Hutchinson than most people in my situation would have been, as the launch pulled away from the jetty in a wide arc and moved off across Eastchester Bay I somehow couldn't quite bring myself to look back at his lonely little figure on the levee. The fact is that, despite myself, I *did* feel a little guilty—not responsible, never, just a little stingy maybe. I knew what it was like, standing alone on shore and watching someone gradually recede without a backward glance, though it had been many long years since. I could feel Elias's gaze of sad reproach fixed on our dwindling figures, and I knew that if I turned around now those ridiculous puppy-dog eyes of his would stay with me longer than was comfort-able. But in the end I didn't look back because I also knew that I never intended to follow through or, frankly, even give him a second thought.

It was a beautiful morning on the water and I didn't much feel like talking. At one point, Felicia asked: "You live in the city?" and I said: "Hell's Kitchen." There was a pause, and then I asked: "You know them long?" to which she replied: "Long time."

"How come you deliver the mail by boat?"

"Got to. Island has its own zip code."

"Ah." Pause. "Nice guy, Elias."

"Real nice," Felicia said, and looked away toward Westchester. The rest of the ride, no more than five minutes, passed in silence.

Felicia landed me at the Fordham Street pier. A cab had just dropped a fare at the yacht club, so I grabbed it and was back in Hell's Kitchen in forty minutes. I swallowed four Tylenol, switched on the air-conditioner, white-noise machine, answering machine and alarm clock, and fell into a light, troubled catnap. I was grateful to be home in my own bed, but I went to sleep with a curious sense of having left something undone.

When I got up an hour later my legs were aching, so I took a cab up to my doctor's on Park Avenue. He couldn't find anything wrong—at least, nothing new—but he renewed my painkiller prescription. There were three messages on the answering machine by the time I got home. The first was from a man who said: "Damn you to hell everlasting." His voice seemed vaguely familiar but I couldn't place it. As the machine played the second message the tape began to crackle, the sound of an open line, but there was no voice. Finally the line was disconnected and an electronic tone indicated the end of one message and the beginning of another. Again, the line was opened but no one spoke. This time, though, after a ten-second pause, a voice with a German accent spoke into the machine.

"Allo? . . . Allo? . . . Mr. Givens? . . . Is this? . . . Mr. Givens, this is Dr. Joseph Ross speaking to you. . . . I would like to leave a message for Mr. Benjamin Givens, please. . . . The message goes . . . please to call me. . . . Thank you . . . thank you very much. . . ." He left his number and hung up.

Assuming that I'd left something on Turnaway, or that the doctor was simply following up on his treatment, without thought or hesitation I picked up the receiver and dialed. He'd only left seven digits and I automatically dialed the 718 area code. It was only after twice

connecting to a Korean wedding shop in Jackson Heights that I
remembered that, as a Bronx exchange, Turnaway Island would be in
the 212 area code. It was funny and somehow unsettling that his
home and mine should share the same area code. Already, Turnaway
seemed like something out of a dream, and its two sad, eccentric
inhabitants the characters of some half-forgotten Christmas panto-
mime last seen in grade school, the by-products of some overwrought
Dickensian imagination brought to life as I lay traumatized on the
beach. But it was a very real Dr. Ross who answered his phone on
the second ring—on Turnaway Island, less than fifteen miles from
Hell's Kitchen.

"Mr. Givens, I'm so glad you called."

"Yes, Doctor, what can I do for you?"

"Well, I have a request of you. It is strange, you see. I will get
directly to the point. Mr. Givens, you are on your summer vacation,
are you not?"

"No, not exactly."

"But you have time to spare, if I am not mistaken?"

"Yes, a little."

"How much? A week?"

"Well . . ."

"Two weeks? Three?"

"What is it you want, Dr. Ross?"

"Mr. Givens, Elias Hutchinson would like to extend an invitation
to you to spend two weeks as his personal guest on Turnaway Island.
Will you accept?"

"Personal guest?"

"I must tell you that I myself am opposed to such an invitation.
Elias has no experience and no use for visitors and strangers. This is
not the first time he has expressed such a desire, and I have always
been compelled to disappoint him. But he has been peculiarly insistent this time, and I fear a refusal now would be more harmful than
acceding to his whim. So I ask you again: Will you accept?"

"Such a gracious offer . . ."

"Mr. Givens, I have been frank with you, please, no games now."

"Why doesn't Elias call me himself?"

"I wished to speak with you to make sure you understood everything. From Elias you might not get both sides of the story. He is a candid boy, but sometimes when he wants something . . . Now you know. Will you accept?"

"I can't—"

"I must make an honest attempt to persuade you: you will have the country air, the woods, the boating, the swimming, relaxation. And Elias can be excellent company when he wishes. As for me, if you accept I promise to do all I can to make you comfortable. Will you accept?"

"No, I don't think so."

"Very well." And the line went dead.

Now, there may be people who find it painful and difficult to make snap decisions. For them, every aspect of the question at hand becomes a moral issue and every issue is a quandary that has to be solved in its own right before the core decision can be approached. That's how decisions do not get made. I don't have that problem. Growing up, I had certain responsibilities and decisions to make that don't usually fall on people so young, and I learned how to deal with them quickly and dispassionately. I'd made my decision before the doctor had even hung up: nothing could ever induce me to spend two more minutes, let alone two weeks, on Turnaway Island. I was able to say this with conviction because I thought I knew myself. I'm not too fond of the countryside and its so-called pleasures, and even if I were, calling Turnaway the country would be like calling the Bronx Zoo Zimbabwe. I wasn't so taken with the locals either: neither the "kindly" old doctor with his old-world charm and thinly veiled tyranny or the high-strung young squire with his delusions of noble savagery. In any case, whatever opinion Elias might have formed of me on the basis of such a brief encounter, he was wrong to imagine that I was anybody's idea of a good houseguest and companion. And I certainly had better things to do with my leisure than sit around some dank old firetrap wet-nursing Peter Pan. I shuddered at the very thought and put the whole issue out of mind.

Besides which, I had some serious business to attend to. The *Spirit of New York* had been my entire life since my retirement the previous year. It hadn't been much, I know—a leaky, secondhand tub with a top speed of five knots—but still, it had been enough to fulfil a lifelong dream. Shunted from home to home as a kid, I'd had a hard time fitting in. I didn't play sports or cowboys and Indians, wasn't an easy socializer. I wasn't exactly bookish but I did read a lot, I suppose since every new bedroom was the same with a book in my hand. I was aloof and dreamy, and one thing I read and dreamed about more than anything else was boats. My own experience was so far removed from anything even resembling boats that I fixed on them as the very embodiment of freedom. I kept a scrapbook of images cut surreptitiously from magazines and library books: sailboats, yachts, cigarette boats, ocean liners, tall ships, even refugees' rafts—any scrap of wood that could bear me away was a worthy vessel for my imagination and yearning. Lots of boys dream of running away to sea, but I really meant it. I'd have done it, too, if some busybody philanthropist hadn't foisted a college scholarship on me. Anyway, one thing led to another, as it usually does in life, and suddenly I found that I was a grown-up with a job and less dramatic means of keeping the world at arm's length.

So when the opportunity presented itself, I jumped at it, so to speak. This was the jackpot: not only a boat, but infinite leisure to enjoy it. Sure I'd paid a price, but it was worth it. The settlement from my accident let me quit the civil service, where I'd worked since graduating from college; safely invested, it returned just enough every quarter to keep me off the breadline. And it bought me the *Spirit of New York*. A pretty modest luxury, I thought—and the only one I'd allowed myself—but she'd served her purpose dutifully. I'd taken her as far north as the Mohawk, all the way out to Montauk, and even to the Delaware Water Gap via Cape May and Philly.

And now she was gone, uninsured. I'd already sold off all my suits, the Italian shoes, and most of my books. There was nothing left to sell except the TV, and I was keeping that. There was no money to replace my boat without dipping into my capital, which would create a shortfall in my annuity that I'd feel for the rest of my life. The only alternative I could come up with after days of desperate brainstorming was almost as bad. Facts were facts and I'd faced far worse than this, but still I could hardly think about it without having to repress hot tears of frustration. Just eight months after I'd made a solemn promise to myself in a hospital bed that I would never work another day of my life, I was going to have to look for a job.

Once I'd resigned myself to this twist of fate—not after several days of hand wringing, sedation, and sleeplessness—I began to examine my options. I had skills and experience in management, administration, and word processing, and there seemed to be plenty of high-paying freelance work available. My Ivy League degree ought to be worth something, too. I figured that, saving every penny I'd earn except what I'd need to buy a couple of cheap suits, some dress shirts, and a new pair of shoes, I could put enough aside to replace the *Spirit of New York* in three months. If I worked for six, I could probably buy something more reliable and insure it. Five months of leisure had gone by in the blink of an eye; six of drudgery seemed to stretch out ahead of me like a bleak, endless prairie, but I was going to have to get used to it. I started combing the daily want ads.

And that was exactly what I was doing one morning, four days after I'd left Turnaway, when the phone rang. I usually monitored my calls on the answering machine before picking up, to screen out the undesirables, but for some reason I'd forgotten to switch it on. I waited seven rings, hoping the caller would give up, then answered.

"Mr. Givens, this is Dr. Ross of Turnaway calling you."

"Yes?"

"I am calling to repeat my offer to you. Won't you please come and visit with Elias for some time?"

"I'm sorry, Doctor, but I've already told you I can't. I'm looking for work right now."

"Looking for work, is it? Well, never mind, you can spare a week I'm sure, can you not?"

"No I can't. What is it with you people?"

"Ahem, Mr. Givens, it is not with me, as I have told you. It is with Elias. He has not been at all the same since he met you."

"Hasn't he? How's that?"

"He has become very agitated and I fear for his mental health."

I wanted to say: "A little late for that, isn't it?" but held back. "How do you mean, agitated?" I asked instead.

"*Ach,* I don't know. He mopes, he forsakes his books, he stares in the waters."

"He stares in the waters?"

"Yes he stares, and he doesn't eat."

"Look, Doctor, is Elias gay or anything?"

"I am telling you, he is very unhappy."

"I mean, is he homosexual? Because if he is then I—"

"No, no, no, no. You do not understand Elias. He is a sensitive boy. You have made him feel, how shall I say, the need of a . . . of a . . . peer."

There was an awkward silence.

"Please, I am worried for him," the doctor whispered. His voice was so pathetic, especially in contrast to its usual authoritarian tone, that I took pity on him and lied through my teeth.

"Look Doctor," I sighed wearily. "Tell you what—You tell Elias to call me himself and maybe I'll consider it. Maybe. How's that?"

"Thank you, that's good." He hung up. I barely had time to find my place in the help-wanted section when the phone rang again. It was Elias.

"Please, Ben, please come. It would mean so much to me," he said breathlessly.

"Elias, I already explained to Dr. Ross that it's impossible. I need to find a job."

"Why, Ben, why? Why do you need to find a job?"

"I need to buy a new boat, for one thing."

"We have a beautiful boat here, a real admiral's launch. You didn't see it. We don't use it much because of the cost, but you could use it as much as you pleased. It's a beautiful boat."

"It's not only the boat."

"What then?"

"Hang on a second. Why pick on me, Elias? You feel sorry for me because I'm a cripple, is that it?"

"I'd hardly call you a cripple, Ben, but yes, I do feel sorry for you.

You have so much pride and you are so ashamed of yourself. I can help you with that, and in return you—"

"Excuse me, did I ask for anyone's help?"

"Ben, I sense that we have something important in common, that we might learn from each other. I don't know what it is yet, but I sense it. We're both orphans and we need—"

"I'm no orphan."

"Of course you are. You needn't lie to me, Ben. I knew it from the moment I set eyes on you. We are like brothers, you and I. We complement each other."

"Listen to me, Elias. I'm sorry to say it, but as far as I'm concerned you're a sad case. We have nothing to learn from each other, nothing at all. I'm nobody's brother, I'm nobody's anything. I don't know what you think you know about me, Elias, but you're just wrong and you'd better accept that. I'm nobody to you, got it?"

"You're upset now, Ben. You wait awhile, calm down. When you do, you'll see I'm right. You'll see."

It wasn't only the invasion of privacy, although that was bad enough. It seemed to me I'd made it pretty clear that all I wanted was to be left alone. People had been leaving me alone all my life and I liked it just fine that way. I'm no fool, I can't be flattered by attention and kindness the way some of those real lonely, pathetic souls are. But Elias hadn't stopped at inviting me to visit—he'd even suggested that I stood to profit from it! Something in common? Nobody had ever spoken to me that way before. And he'd come right out with it, without the slightest hint of shame or embarrassment. Had he really dared to say that we complemented each other? Had he actually claimed that we were like brothers? Me, somebody's brother! Who did he think he was, offering me his friendship? It was like a thief walking right up to a tightly locked, heavily armed house and ringing the front door. I was so upset I was close to tears.

An hour or so later, once I'd managed to calm myself down, I began packing. In the end, it was the admiral's launch that swayed me.

Elias's singsong voice rose and fell in my ear like a distant tide:

"*Siwanoy* is a Dutch transcription of the word *Shawani,* meaning 'of the South' in any number of Algonquian dialects—like the much larger Shawnee nation, 'the Southern people,' or the Swanee River, the 'southern river.' They were called Siwanoy because they were one of the southernmost chieftaincies of the Munsee-speaking Lenapes on the east bank of the 'great tidewater'—the Mahikanituk, or Hudson River.

"The Lenape lived in New Jersey, on Manhattan and Staten Island, the western tip of Long Island, and the western bank of the Hudson all the way to the Mohawk Valley. They shared the east bank with the Mahican, but there was little antagonism between them. They spoke mutually intelligible languages of the Algonquian family, which stretched unbroken from Canada to the Carolinas and as far west as Wisconsin. They shared customs, summer fishing grounds, winter hunting grounds, fratries, and presumably families. They could afford to: in what is now the greater New York area, with a population of some seven million people, there were probably no more than two thousand people of the Lenape, Mahican, and Matouack nations.

"*Nation,* of course, is a European word. It's hard to apply it meaningfully to tribes like the Lenape and the Mahican—they had little sense of being bound to distant villages by a common cultural identity and they had no central power or ability to come together for defensive purposes. They lived in small communities, ruling themselves with elected or hereditary *sakimawak,* or sachems. Occasionally, through some random fluke, a *sakima* might end up with leadership over two or several villages, but that was the extent of his power. It didn't necessarily bind those villages forever, especially since any leadership was held strictly by the consensus of the led. Not even the name of a chieftaincy was necessarily permanent—a band of Lenape might take the name of its current *sakima,* its present place of residence (which could change and did), or a place or an event in its past. That's why, for instance, historians are divided over whether the original inhabitants of Manhattan were called the Manhattes, from the Munsee *menaten,* for 'island,' or the Reckgawawank, after their chief Reckgawak. And that doesn't even include the Wekweskik in Inwood or the Canarsee in the Wall Street area. In other words, in its time, New York was a kind of Switzerland of Algonquian culture.

"Look, here were the Canarsee, and the Merric, and our neighbors the Matinecock just across the water. We knew them all, we got along. We weren't the same tribe, not quite, but we understood each other, we got along. Our tribes called each other brother, nephew, cousin."

"Elias," I interrupted sleepily. "Why are you telling me all this?"

Elias was taken aback by my question, as if the answer was self-evident. "Why, because these are things you need to know."

"They are?"

"Isn't this why you came to Turnaway?"

"No," I snorted derisively.

"Why then?"

"I don't know. Fresh air. Scintillating conversation. Boating."

Elias took this in with a frown, absentmindedly rubbing his palm in circles over his bare chest. For a moment there I thought I'd gotten to him, but then his frown dissolved into giggles and he swatted me playfully across the top of my head.

"Silly!" he laughed. "Now where was I? Oh yes."

I sighed. Elias and I were on the lawn, he in loincloth, I in T-shirt and jeans. A large map of New York City and environs was spread out on the grass, held flat by glasses of iced sassafras tea against the gentle easterly breezes off the Sound. Lying on my back, my head cradled in the palms of my hands, I drifted into a daydream. Through half-closed eyes, I contemplated the pale cyan sky and the occasional cloud that loitered over the city before pursuing its indolent journey into the heartland. The cool breeze on my belly was lulling me to sleep. My impromptu history lesson droned on, Elias's voice gradually receding and merging with the hum of honeybees in the clover. I was exhausted. It was hard to believe I'd been on Turnaway less than twenty-four hours.

It had all started out so well. At least Elias hadn't been lying about the admiral's launch. It *was* a beautiful thing, eighteen feet of polished teak and brass, simple, elegant curves, two benches of padded white leather—the sort of boat you see being driven by madcap millionaires in thirties musicals. I whistled softly through my teeth as I approached the dock. The doctor was at the controls, dressed in his usual brown suit.

"Where's the chief?" I asked as I clambered down, throwing my duffel into the backseat.

"Elias does not ride in the launch," he said stiffly, staring forward like a chauffeur.

"Mind if I take the helm?"

"Please. But you must keep to the channel I show you, as the shallows are everywhere."

I followed the doctor's directions, taking a circuitous route across the bay that snaked between tiny islets and jutting rocks. Turnaway was the last bit of land before the wide open stretch of the Long Island Sound. Even from half a mile away, I could make out the dark figure of Elias standing on the jetty, his hands clasped before him like an idle waiter. He seemed, as usual, to be dressed weirdly, but it wasn't until we were much closer that I saw he'd worn a tuxedo to welcome me. It was ancient and ill fitting, its silk lapels frayed and elbows shiny with wear. Though it was obvious from his little skips and barely suppressed squeals that Elias was as giddy as a puppy dog, he was clearly under strict orders to be on his best behavior, and I was escorted wordlessly from the beach to the house like a visiting dignitary. The doctor insisted on carrying my bags—his pace was strong and sure despite his age—and we circled all the way round the house so as to enter ceremoniously by the front door. In the foyer, at the foot of the stairs, the doctor lowered my bags gently to the floor, nodded briskly to me, then headed for the kitchen. Like a greyhound at the starting gate, Elias then snatched up my luggage and began racing up the stairs, taking them three risers at a bound. But he'd barely reached the landing halfway up when he was stopped short by the doctor's hail through a crack in the kitchen door.

"Elias," he called out. "Don't forget to remind our guest that we dress for dinner."

Elias nodded, almost to himself, and disappeared up the stairs.

I'd been assigned the "infirmary," as I thought of it, the room where I'd spent my first night on Turnaway. By the time I reached it, moving slowly to spare my legs, my two bags were already on the bed, open side by side, with Elias perched restlessly on its corner. He pointed past me to the closed door directly across the hallway.

"That's my room," he said, almost panting in his eagerness. "At night we can leave our doors open and talk to each other in bed."

"Won't that be nice?" I said as I began to unpack. I was a little concerned about that "dressing for dinner," especially with Elias all got up for the opera. I'd packed sparingly, and I doubted that my one polo shirt and shapeless linen jacket would pass muster. Elias crossed the room, drew aside the muslin curtains, and walked out onto the consumption porch. I spread my clothes across the bed and eyed them skeptically. It wasn't a happy prospect. I sighed and began undressing. Just then, Elias sauntered back into the room. He stopped short when he saw my legs, then pretended he'd seen nothing. He turned away and began fiddling with knickknacks and framed photographs on the dresser. He was a terrible actor and I knew he couldn't keep it up for long. Sure enough, a minute or so later he tossed out his burning question like it was a piece of lint from his pocket.

"How did you hurt yourself?" he asked casually, still turned away from me.

"I fell on the subway tracks."

"You were run over by a train?"

"No. I slipped in a puddle and fell, that's all. They had to put my hips back together with screws and pins. The scars are from the operations."

"Poor, poor fellow."

"It's not so bad. My life needed changing anyhow. Plus I'm a rich boy like you, now, courtesy of the MTA. Now, do you mind if I dress in private?"

"I'll go change into something more comfortable and meet you downstairs in ten minutes." He shut the door behind him as he left.

I slipped into chinos and loafers and hoped that I wouldn't look too out of place at the dinner table. I could always borrow a tie from Elias, in a pinch. I wanted to fit in, to disrupt the household routine as little as possible, like a naturalist trying to observe a pristine habitat. That, I'd decided before leaving for Turnaway, was the most sensible approach to take if I really wanted to go through with it. The last thing I wanted was to get emotionally involved with these people, especially my brother orphan. The situation had some potential for mischief, but I'd need to stay aloof. Back at home, I'd even found myself growing excited at the prospect of dipping into this little domestic enigma, observing it from a distance, throwing in the occasional firecracker to test their reactions, and then withdrawing, as easily as changing the channel, unaffected but thoroughly entertained. If I played it right, it could be like spending two weeks in one of those theme parks that tries to emulate, say, life in the Old West, with cancan-dancing whores and six-shooters loaded with blanks; only in this case the environment wouldn't be simulated and I could leave any time I wanted. I could walk away. It was their life but my vacation. There was no risk to me—no risk whatsoever.

But now, as I finished unpacking and gave myself a last once-over in the mirror, I had to admit that I could no more hope to fit in on Turnaway than my naturalist could hope to go unnoticed in a herd of zebras. I took a deep breath and a couple of painkillers, then headed downstairs.

I found my hosts on the front porch. The doctor, mixing drinks at a sideboard, was wearing the same brown suit. Elias sat in a decrepit rattan armchair, eyes closed and face turned to the sun low over Manhattan; he wore a khaki World War II uniform buttoned at the neck, with the label CAPTAIN HUTCHINSON sewn onto the left breast. My concern about not fitting in had obviously been wasted energy: I'd have had to wear a tutu if I wanted to stand out. The doctor waited for the roar of a 727 overhead to die down before he turned to me.

"I can offer you only a Sazerac, I'm afraid," he said dryly. "We drink only Sazeracs on Turnaway."

"Sazerac it is," I said.

"Glorious, isn't it?" Elias said from his chair, with a proprietary sweep of his arm that included the Sound, the entire north shore of Long Island, Manhattan, the Bronx, and the great vault of aquamarine overhead, now striated with pinkening fronds of cirrus and dissolving vapor trails.

"Sure," I said blandly, accepting a highball glass from the doctor. When Elias received his, he stood up and raised his glass to a passing swallow.

"To Ben Givens. May his stay bring joy and friendship."

"To beautiful Turnaway," I added.

"Manapinock."

"Manapinock," I repeated, unsure if my toast had been corrected or amplified. The doctor didn't join us but retired to an uncomfortable-looking ladder-back chair by the sideboard, where he sat silently sipping his Sazerac for the rest of the cocktail hour. Elias and I sampled our drinks, nicely chilled, and savored the sudden quiet that had descended on the evening. I watched as a single puff of black smoke rose and dissipated from a tall chimney poking above the treetops on Hart Island.

"How old were you when your mother died?" Elias asked abruptly, startling me from a reverie.

"How's that?"

"I asked, how old were you when your mother died?"

"My mother died in childbirth."

"I knew it, I knew it," he said, clapping his hands in a kind of joy. "And your father?"

I took a deep breath and looked Elias straight in the eye. "I was four," I said without blushing.

"Any brothers? Sisters?"

"No."

"I knew it," he exulted again. "I told you we were like brothers, you and I. I'm an only child too, if you don't count Ross, and my mother died when I was a baby. I hardly remember her at all."

"I'm sorry."

"Oh pooh pooh." Elias flapped his left hand as if shooing a noisome fly. "My father taught me everything I need to know anyway."

"What about Dr. Ross?"

"Ross is not here to teach me—he is here to protect me."

"Protect you against what?"

"Against the people who destroyed my ancestors. Until I can propagate my seed, my blood is all that stands between the Siwanoy and extinction. I am a warrior, it's true, but I am only one warrior, and they are many. But Ross has protected me well all these years. He saw me to manhood and he will see me to fatherhood, I have no doubt. Do you see?"

"Uh-huh."

The sun set and we went into dinner, Ross serving us like a butler. We ate schnitzel and potato dumplings with gravy, washed down with iced water. The doctor sat stiff and prim as always, cutting his meat with tiny mechanical strokes and eating it with his eyes on his plate. He didn't participate in the conversation unless he was directly questioned; in fact, he acted just like somebody eating alone in a noisy restaurant. I had a funny feeling that he wasn't always this

reserved—that he was somehow reacting to my presence—but since
Elias seemed blissfully unaware of it and actually spoke about the
doctor as if he weren't there, I decided to ignore it, too. I concentrated instead on getting the heavy food down in the humid summer
heat.

"Do you ever do any of the cooking?" I asked Elias. He laughed.

"I sometimes cook for myself"—he sneaked a quick smirk in the
doctor's direction—"but Ross won't eat my kind of food. He cooks
when we eat together."

"What's 'your kind' of food?"

"Oh, you know, good old American food—dried fish gruel, hominy
mush, beaver tail, steam-fried bread, that sort of thing. Not exactly
Ross's national cuisine."

I turned to Dr. Ross. "Where are you from, originally, Doctor?" I
asked.

"Austria." He did not look up from his plate.

"How long have you been here?"

"Since a boy." Still he did not look up, but his hands stopped in
midair, his implements poised above his food like a pianist's fingers
above a keyboard.

"Did you change your name?"

Still he did not look up, but gently lowered his knife and fork to
his plate, folded his hands in his lap, and sighed. All this while,
Elias chewed on his meat noisily—it was not the best cut—and
stared eagerly at Dr. Ross as if he were a contestant on a TV quiz
show. Finally, the doctor spoke.

"My name was Rosen."

"My father met Ross just after the war," Elias piped in.

"Elias, will you take some more cabbage?" the doctor asked quietly.

"No thank you. He found him in a refugee camp when he was—"

"Then I shall clear the table now," the doctor snapped, standing so
abruptly that his chair legs squealed against the floor. He proceeded
to clear the table efficiently, piling every dish onto a tray and disappearing into the kitchen. Elias and I sat in silence until we heard the

water running in the sink, then Elias raised his eyebrows, rolled his eyes, and made a goofy smile.

"You were saying?" I pressed him, but he gave me a blank look. "About?"

"Your father and Dr. Ross."

Elias just shrugged as if my question made no sense. "Oh, it was nothing."

"I'll go help him with the dishes."

"No, no, he likes to do it by himself." Strangely, a look of near panic crossed Elias's face and he grabbed at my forearm.

"Nonsense," I insisted, freeing myself. I strode around the table and through the swinging door into the kitchen. Dr. Ross, having removed his jacket and donned a gingham apron with lace frills on the collar, stood over the enormous old sink, rag in hand. The moment he saw me, however, he rolled down his sleeves, turned off the water and stood motionless, staring out the window into the dark woods.

"Can I help you?" I offered weakly.

"Thank you, no. You may return to the dining room."

But I couldn't leave it at that. "Dr. Ross," I said in a conciliatory tone, "I'm sorry if we've gotten off on the wrong foot."

"Mr. Givens, I assure you there is no wrong foot. But I hope you will remember that you are here for Elias's sake and at his request only. What Elias will choose to tell you about himself in the course of your . . . recreation, is his own business. But as to my personal life . . . you understand?"

I nodded, retreating backward into the dining room.

The rest of the evening was subdued. Elias and I retired to the porch, listening to the cicadas and watching the distant stream of glowing pearls that flowed endlessly across Throgs Neck Bridge. He told me about something called the Mahkohkwe—the h pronounced like the ch in loch: "Mach-koch-kway"—meaning "Red Woman." She was some sort of mythical creature that was supposed to arise and save his people from extinction. But my mind was somewhere else, brooding on the day's events, and I hardly heard him. It couldn't have been much past nine o'clock, but I made my excuses and headed up to my bedroom. There I lay naked in the dark with the French doors open. I'd come upstairs to think, to go over the day's events and try to make sense of all the contradictions and mysteries through the nonsense. But the night air, the silence, the heavy supper, and the pills all acted on me, and I fell straight to sleep to the hooting of barn owls, as coolly and evenly spaced as an SOS telegraphed from a sinking ship.

The owls' call was still reverberating through my dreams when I was pulled from a very deep sleep by an insistent, prodding hand. It was Elias, his eyes gleaming maniacally in the dark, his body silhouetted against the glow of the muslin curtains. "Hunt's on," he whispered breathily. "Just wear shorts. No shoes."

"What about Lyme disease?"

"What's that?"

"From deer ticks?"

"My deer have no ticks," he said, genuinely offended by the suggestion. He stood over me as I fumbled for my sweatpants in the dresser.

Dawn was just a stain on the eastern horizon when we crept into the thick of the forest, Elias leading the way. Except for his hair, he looked like your stereotypical Hollywood redskin: leather flap over his buttocks, a quiver full of wooden arrows on his back, bent double, raising each knee almost to his chest when he walked and pointing his toes like a ballerina when he lowered it again. When his arms swept aside obstructing branches in slow, exaggerated arcs, the overall effect was of a diminutive Nijinsky, but the best I could do was to stumble and stomp through the undergrowth like a clumsy giant. Any bird or bunny not alerted to our approach would have had to have been deaf. I spat and swore as the brambles caught at my arms and shoulders. We gave up after about an hour. The sun had just crept over the hedge of trees as we tramped back across the lawn to the house. Overhead, the first plane of the morning dipped its wing above Pelham Park. He didn't say anything, but I could tell Elias was put out by having to return empty-handed from my first hunt. Dr. Ross, in suit and tie, was waiting for us on the front porch. Elias and I filed past him like a pair of chastised schoolboys. I found it strangely disturbing for the doctor to see me barechested and vulnerable. Elias ran upstairs; I followed, limping.

On the landing, as I turned to enter my room, Elias rapped me on the back with his knuckles and gave me a bright, conspiratorial grin. This seemed to be some kind of invitation to adolescent roughhousing. I went into my room and shut the door. A full minute passed before I heard his door close, by which time I was already dressed. I slipped down the stairs without waiting—it gave me a little thrill of vengeful pleasure to imagine Elias standing stoically by the door for a good long stretch, like a faithful but stupid dog, before he figured out that I wasn't on the other side.

The doctor was already seated at the breakfast table, *Times* in hand, eyes downcast. He greeted me with a cough. The coffee was hot and strong, but the porridge offended my nostrils and I pushed it aside. The doctor was completely hidden behind the wings of the Metropolitan section; I reached for one of the others stacked by his right elbow but withdrew my hand at a sharp rustle of the paper, as threatening as any rattlesnake. I sighed and drank my coffee, contenting myself with what I could read on the front and back pages of the Metropolitan section. It didn't take me long to figure out that this was yesterday's newspaper. Obviously, since the mail boat didn't arrive until late morning, it was impossible to get the day's news in time for the breakfast table, but the doctor seemed to prefer reading outdated news to upsetting the tradition of the breakfast newspaper. Then again, what could it possibly matter, out here where the passage of time appeared to have little impact or urgency, whether the news was two days old or twenty? What could the news matter at all?

I heard Elias bouncing down the stairs three steps at a time before he burst into the room, dressed in his ridiculous golfing suit and saddle shoes, his arms outstretched like a talk-show host making his entrance. He didn't seem at all bothered by the little trick I'd played on him. "Old Ross keeping you entertained, then?" he asked without the least hint of irony. Ross and I harrumphed at the same time and with about the same intensity.

As he wolfed down his porridge, Elias mapped out our morning's activity. "I thought we might go fishing," he said. I choked on my coffee. "You'd be surprised what you come up with. Shad, carp, snook, an occasional striped bass. Of course, it's nothing like when my people fished these waters. Then they were teaming. Just for the asking you had sturgeon, pike, trout, flounder, thickheads, sheeps- heads, you name it. And shellfish? Lobsters, conches, periwinkles, terrapins, oysters as big as my hand." He held up his hand, fingers splayed; it was a small hand for a man, but it certainly would have made a large oyster. "Why, good god, when the fish left the bottom ground in early spring, it was like—"

"Elias," Dr. Ross said in a low monotone, eyes on his paper as usual. "Perhaps our guest would prefer to fish than to talk about fish."

"As a matter of fact, I was thinking of taking the launch out for a spin," I suggested.

Elias jumped to his feet, setting his empty bowl to rattling, and clapped his hands. I'd noticed that he had this gift of completely ignoring a put-down as if every word said to him was coated in an unction of goodwill. To me, the doctor's constant interruptions and snide asides would have been intolerable, but Elias seemed oblivi- ous. I found this trait so exasperating that I couldn't help adding my own insults, like the subjects in that famous experiment who were encouraged to administer ever-increasing electric shocks to their vic- tims just to see how they'd respond. But with Elias, no matter how high the voltage, his response was always the same. It was his good luck, I guessed, that he couldn't feel it.

"Come along." He laughed, and I was about to follow him from the room when the doctor called me back. He spoke almost in a whisper.

"Mr. Givens. Elias has a very developed imagination. I urge you to take the things he tells you with a grain of salt."

"You mean the fish?"

"*Ach* no, not the fish," a note of real impatience in his gargly voice. "But he will tell you many stories. He is not a liar because he truly believes them, but please remember there is always a reverse to the story he tells you. Listen. Agree—always agree. And doubt."

Elias stuck his head through the door. "Come on, lazy bones, unless you want schnitzel for supper again," he laughed. Dr. Ross threw me one meaningful glance over the top of his wire-framed reading glasses—the first time he'd looked up from his paper, so far as I could tell, since I'd entered the room—and nodded curtly. I ducked out and followed Elias upstairs.

Alone in my room as I changed into my "hunting" garb, I took a minute to think about the doctor's warning. My little vacation on Turnaway was certainly turning into a fascinating study. On the one hand, you had the doctor, who manipulated Elias—or appeared to manipulate him—like a marionette. And Elias let him do it, as if he had no will of his own. But is anyone really that naïve? I doubted it. It was almost impossible to imagine that, on some deep subconscious level, all this condescension was not absorbed and festering. I know only too well what living with someone cold and distant can do to a young and impressionable boy. If I were Elias, I'd be brimming over with self-loathing and bitterness. But on the other hand, Elias must also have some power over the doctor. Why else would Ross go to the trouble of warning me against his stories? It was too much to hope that these two shared some dark secret, but it was fun to speculate, especially since I had two whole weeks ahead of me with not much else to do. I'd need to keep my eyes open. I smiled to myself: suddenly, I realized what had made me come to Turnaway.

"What's the story with Dr. Ross?" I asked Elias, struggling to keep pace with him through the undergrowth.

"What do you mean, 'story'?"

"Where's he from? How'd he get here? What's he to you?"

"He's my brother," Elias said matter-of-factly.

"Your brother?"

"Not my real brother, silly. Does he look like an Indian? During the war, my father was an army cryptologist, like many Indians,

because of their language skills. He met Ross in Germany—he was
just a boy then, an orphan. My father adopted him and brought him
back to America."

"So you've known him all your life? You trust him?"

"Of course. I was only fourteen when my father died. Ross was
nearly a doctor by then, but he gave it all up to take care of me. My
life is in his hands. I could not survive without him."

"But he's such a cold fish."

"You're wrong, Ben," Elias said hastily. "He is not cold. He's
watchful, that's all. He trusts few people."

"If he's your brother, how come his name's different from yours?"

Elias seemed to ponder this, as if for the first time. Finally he said:
"I don't know. I suppose he wanted to keep something from his old
life. I have two names, too, you know. Many people do."

I was ready to press him further, but just then we emerged from
the woods onto a tiny cove facing west toward the Bronx mainland.
Elias put his finger to his lips and leapt silently from the pebbled
shore onto a small boulder jutting from the water. He squatted on the
boulder and peered intently into the dark water, in which I could see
nothing but the reflection of the overhanging chestnut boughs. After a
minute or two, he jumped back onto the beach and reached up into
the crotch of a small birch tree, from which he pulled a bow, apparently handmade, no bigger than a lyre, and a spool of thread that had
been hidden there. Returning to the boulder, he continued staring
into the water while all the time, his hands acting independently of
his eyes like those of a blind man, he withdrew a foot-long dart from
his quiver, snagged a loop of thread onto a notch in its shaft, then
raised the bow and projectile to his cheek. He mumbled something
under his breath that did not sound like English, and then it seemed
to me that before he'd even had time to aim, he let fly with the dart at
a spot in the water about five feet away. He immediately began
hauling in the thread. When the dart emerged from the water, there
was a plump, wriggling fish impaled on it, blackish in color, some
sixteen or eighteen inches long.

"Bass for supper," Elias whispered.

In one fluid motion, he slipped the dart from the fish's midsection, grabbed his catch by the tail and gave it a brutal and startling whack on the boulder. The fish stopped wriggling, but Elias was already setting himself up for the next shot. Within five minutes he'd speared three smallmouth bass. He turned to me with a satisfied smile signaling the end of our labors.

"Ah, country living," he said, beating his fist on his skinny bare chest. I could see the New England Thruway snaking away through Co-op City just over his right shoulder.

"Uh-huh," I sneered. Elias immediately detected the scorn in my remark.

"What's that?" he asked defensively.

"This isn't the country, Elias," I said with some condescension. "This is New York City."

"This is the country." He sounded like a cranky child denying the obvious. "Look around you," he said, sweeping his arms in toward the woods but keeping his back firmly turned against the cityscape behind him.

"Why don't you turn around?"

Elias was silent, staring into the woods with eyes wide.

"Turn around, Elias. Go on."

He cocked his head at the sound of a bird crying in the woods. He concentrated his whole attention on that cry, as if nothing else existed in the world but that birdsong. Now I understood what Dr. Ross had meant about agreeing with Elias: the moment you contradicted him, he slipped into denial. If he had to, he could deny evidence shoved right under his nose, in all good faith. It was quite a talent— as awesome and frightening in its own way as levitation, you might even say, if you saw him do it. Clearly he'd developed it as a strategy for dealing with Ross, for living in isolation with such a man. And suddenly, all the glee I'd felt only a few minutes earlier at the prospect of toying with this boy evaporated. He'd worked all his life to build himself this armor against loneliness. Maybe it was useless and pathetic, but it was all he had. If he didn't want to turn around and face the city, who was I to force it on him?

"Forget it," I sighed wearily, and that seemed to snap him out of his trance.

"Let's go for a swim," he said, then leaped onto the boulder and plunged into the water in a sloppy shallow dive. By the time he emerged, my little bubble of compassion had burst. "Come on in," he laughed.

"I don't think so," I said coldly. "I think I'll take the launch for a spin." I dusted off my pants and turned to go.

"Oh," said Elias, and he looked so crestfallen, crouching there alone in the water with his wet hair molded to his scalp, that even his ears seemed to droop.

"Want to come?" I said impatiently.

"No, I don't ride in the launch. Is it your legs?"

"How's that?"

"I've seen your scars, you know. Is that why you won't wear shorts or go swimming? Are you embarrassed by your legs?"

"Don't be stupid. I just don't feel like swimming."

"Sorry."

I sighed again. "Tell you what. I'll wait here while you swim if you come for a ride with me in the launch, later."

Elias didn't answer.

"Is the water clean?"

"I believe our average coliform level for August is about eight hundred."

"Is that safe?"

"It's safe enough for humans. For fish, I imagine it would be like living in a perpetual shitstorm." He blushed and giggled. He obviously wasn't used to swearing; he'd just done it to impress me. To cover his confusion, he disappeared beneath the surface in a blur of arms and legs. A moment or two later, he reappeared some twenty yards away, spluttering and beaming like a kid.

I sat on the boulder, dangling my feet in the water, and watched him for about half an hour while he played. A circle of buoys offshore kept the noisy pleasure boats at a distance, where the sound of their engines was no more intrusive than a persistent mosquito. At one point, I saw the launch go by. There were three men in it, all standing close to the helm. One had his arms stretched wide open toward the island. But by the time I'd noticed it, the boat was already speeding away and the pilot blocked from view, so I couldn't be sure. Meanwhile, for all he noticed these distractions, Elias might have been Huckleberry Finn playing in the Mississippi, joyously oblivious as he was to everything but the caress of the water, the heat of the sun, and the pleasures of companionship. The way he smiled at me, or looked for my approval of every trick and dive, you might have thought he hadn't been in the company of someone his own age in a very long time—if ever. I know now that that was true: he'd been swimming in this cove since he was a little boy, and it wasn't the sun and water making him so happy—it was not being alone.

When he was done, Elias stretched himself out on a flat rock and dried his naked body in the open air. Just beyond the perimeter buoys, a pair of speedboats roared by, two shrieking waterskiers in tow.

"This island must be worth millions," I said thoughtfully. "The last undeveloped private acreage in the whole city. Why don't you sell it?"

"I haven't left the island for fifteen years," Elias said. "What possible use could I have for your millions?"

"You could buy yourself a thousand acres upstate. Spread out, stalk deer, be private. You'd never have to hear another jet-ski again."

Elias propped himself on one elbow and turned to me with a quizzical gaze, water streaming down his face. "Now Ben, do you honestly expect me to believe that you would simply sell your house, leave your home, move away to some place you'd never been, where you know nobody, just for an easy, quiet life?"

"Well . . . sure I would. In a second."

"Oh I see." He lowered himself onto his back and lay in silence, staring up at the blue sky for a long time. Not having eaten anything since last night's schnitzel, I was grateful when he finally glanced at the sun and declared that it was time for lunch. But before we left, he returned the bow to the cleft in the birch tree and retrieved a small paring knife that had been hidden there. He began cleaning the fish.

First, he'd slit one lengthwise along the underbelly, then reach into the cavity, grab a fistful of guts, and yank. The guts he threw over his shoulder into the water, followed by the tails, the dorsal fins, and the heads, which he'd sawn off awkwardly with the smooth blade. The bloodiness of the operation shocked me, not because of the gore, but because I'd already grown used to thinking of Elias in a certain way, as a gentle, lonely boy who dressed in plus fours for dinner and was too sensitive to hurt a bunny. When you find someone like that wrist deep in fish guts, you can't help seeing him in a different light. The operation itself made me queasy, but I could hardly begrudge him his due of my admiration. For all his playacting, Elias had real and extensive survival skills. He was an authentic stalker, hunter, butcher. Still, a lengthy dissertation on proto-Algonquian pottery shards managed to dampen a lot of my enthusiasm on the walk back to the house.

Showered and changed, we came down to the dining room to find our places set with cold borscht and stuffed cabbage but the doctor nowhere in sight or hearing. We sat down and I waited demurely to begin my meal, but Elias, absorbed in the task of modeling a facsimile of Turnaway Island out of the sour cream in his soup, didn't seem to take the doctor's absence amiss.

"Where's the doctor?" I asked innocently.

"Oh, I guess he's in town," he answered without looking up from his bowl.

"Shopping?"

"Yes, probably," he answered in a vague, dreamy sort of way. "He goes off from time to time." Having completed his island, Elias began circumnavigating it with a grain of rice. Strangely, I couldn't get another word out of him until lunch was over and we'd changed out of our formal clothes.

And now here we were, in the third hour of the first of many lessons I would eventually endure on Lenape culture. One thing he'd made only too clear was that I was required to be a patient student. He wasn't going to tolerate interruptions or digressions, which was fine with me since I was happy to lie on my back, a blade of grass between my teeth, and let his singsong countertenor lull me into a daze. It wasn't so much that Elias wanted to lecture me as that he took my interest in the subject completely for granted. I don't know why, since I never encouraged him; but then again, I never specifically discouraged him either. He assumed, I guess, that if I wasn't openly rude, I was his friend and ally. I soon came to find this childlike, guileless quality of his deeply irritating, mostly because his knowledge seemed to be inexhaustible. Though my eyes were still open, my mind had long since hitched a ride on a passing cloud and was far, far away.

"Long before the Europeans came," he was saying as I yawned my way out of a daydream, "the Lenape had been overlords of the Iroquoian tribes of the northeast. But the Five Nations overcame us and we began to pay tribute to the Mohawks, the easternmost and fiercest tribe of the Five Nations and the closest to Lenapehoking. We called them Mengwe, which means 'pricks.' We, the Lenape, were known as 'grandfather' to all the Algonquian tribes of the north-east, but to the Mengwe we were 'nephew.' It wasn't until much later that they made us 'women.' They made us wear the petticoat: we weren't allowed to negotiate our own treaties or fight on our own behalf. It was humiliating, but there's—"

At that moment, the doctor emerged from the woods on the path leading from the jetty. He skipped along swiftly in his funny, birdlike gait, and his brow was furrowed with concentration or worry. We silently followed his progress along the path. Just before he reached the back porch, he stopped cold in his tracks and looked up, as if he'd suddenly become aware of being stared at. He shaded his eyes and peered around in all directions, seeking the source of his distraction, until they lit on us all the way across the lawn. His stare was like that of a man gazing in perplexity at a heavy sofa that he's expected to get up a narrow flight of stairs. He looked at us this way for a good fifteen seconds and then disappeared into the house without so much as a nod or a greeting. We watched after him for a little while, until Elias, whatever thoughts he'd been thinking at that moment lost forever, recalled our attention to the lesson.

"As I was saying, so long as we paid our annual tribute of wampum to the Mengwe they tended to leave us alone. . . ."

I never did get my outing on the launch.

At supper, Ross was silent as usual. Since he rarely spoke, it was never easy to gauge his mood, and since the mildest way to describe his attitude to me was that it was generally civil, it would have been unreasonable to expect anything more friendly. Even so, I'm pretty certain that I wasn't imagining the particular brooding quality of his behavior that evening. It wasn't anything he said or did—as always, he ate methodically, primly, staring at his plate—nor did he glower or refuse to answer the trivial questions put to him. It was just a mood, a radiant grimness coming off him like an odor, suffusing the room. Elias felt it, too—he was more than usually talkative and flighty, making up ridiculous stories and excruciating puns, as if he was trying to counterbalance the weight of the doctor's gloom. But it was hopeless: as much as I turned my back on the doctor—I always sat between them, in the center of the table, while they occupied either end—and nodded my head in time to Elias's babble, I could no more ignore the sullen presence at my back than I could have ignored a hot coal on my neck. I couldn't help wondering what had happened on his trip to the mainland to make him so upset. I spun idle conspiracy theories in my mind as I pretended to listen to Elias, but it also occurred to me that I myself might be the cause of his irritation. He'd already made it clear that he was against my visit. Now, here we were at the end of my first full day on Turnaway: I seemed to be getting along just fine with Elias, and it looked as though I might stick it out for the whole two weeks. For a man like the doctor, fiercely protective and deeply set in his ways, I could see how a disruption like me would be annoying, if not downright maddening. I shrugged it off. It wasn't the first time I'd been made to feel unwelcome in somebody's home; now it just made my adventure all the more realistic, like knowing that one of the make-believe desperados at Wild West Kingdom was out gunning for you and you alone.

Even so, I found myself unnerved by the prospect of two weeks of this cold-shoulder treatment—and the doctor was very good at it. I remember, as a boy, having dinner at the house of a friend, an only child, whose parents were in the process of a cruel divorce, and that's exactly how it felt that night. We hadn't made it halfway through our "rat tails" and rice when the conversation petered out altogether and we had to eat on in oppressive silence. So no one was sorry when Elias threw his cutlery onto his plate, gave vent to a drawn-out and obviously false "ah!" of satisfaction, and headed for the door. I stood to follow, lingering in a backward glance with the thought of offering Ross a hand with the dishes; but one look at him, bent over his unfinished dinner—he hadn't even looked up when Elias left the room—made me think better of it.

Upstairs, Elias turned into the dark, narrow hallway that branched off the main landing. It led to a steep stairwell, which rose and twisted to the left beneath a bull's-eye window. At the top was a heavy, paneled door; Elias had to butt it with his shoulder before it opened with a grating protest. We stepped up and into a lozenge-shaped room with a 360-degree view above the tree line. We were in the tower. It was furnished with a desk and chair looking southeast and lined with low bookshelves below the windows, overflowing with books. A stainless-steel wind chime swung lazily from the ceiling, but the breeze through the open windows wasn't strong enough to set it going.

"My study," Elias said.

In the center of the room was an iron ladder reaching from floor to ceiling. Without turning on the light or saying a word, Elias started climbing. At the top he raised his arm to push aside a trapdoor, then hoisted himself up and out. The outline of his head, black against the deepening purple of the evening sky, appeared in silhouette in the opening.

"Come on," he said quietly. I climbed the ladder uncertainly, hugging it tightly with both arms, wishing I'd remembered to take my painkillers. I finally emerged onto a widow's walk from which the entire city of New York, from Pelham to Wall Street, spread away like an impossibly frivolous stage set. It was about eight o'clock. A warning beacon flashed at regular intervals from the chimney on Hart Island. The sun had only just sunk behind Newark. The tops of the highest skyscrapers still glowed in its last beams, while far below, lights were beginning to flicker on among the already twilit apartment houses of Bayside and the woods of Little Neck. It's a strange thing about New York summers: all day long, the skies are tentative, always seeming to strive for an effect—any sort of effect—but never achieving it, like an indecisive chef endlessly tampering with his sauce as he prepares it. One minute it's one thing, the next another, the light shifts, the clouds realign themselves in quick succession. And then, at the end of the day, you realize that all this time it's only been rehearsing for the sunset. I'm not lyrical by nature; if you've never seen a New York sunset I'm not about to try and describe one for you. It's like a battlefield, that's what, all smoke and blood—that's as far as I'm prepared to go. But on Turnaway the show didn't end there. As the darkness invaded, the lightning bugs came out against the black backdrop of the woods. Above the tree line, the glittering city and a few hardy stars; below the tree line, the dancing fireflies. The tops of the trees were like the shore of a lake, with the lights of the city reflected in the waters below. With a balmy breeze and an easy conscience, it's the sort of pretty scene that somehow makes people feel duty-bound to grow pensive. I know I had—all of a sudden, out of nowhere, I found myself thinking about the transience of joy and the tenacity of loneliness. And I know Elias had been, too, because, after a seemly pause and deferential nod to the view, he cleared his throat and began saying what he'd brought me up here to say.

"You know, you shouldn't imagine me an idiot," he said quietly. "I'm very well aware what you think of me, what you must think of me. No, it's alright. I couldn't expect you to feel otherwise."

As a matter of fact I hadn't even considered contradicting him, but I felt there was more coming, so I kept my silence. After another long, dramatic pause, Elias spoke, staring out toward the city.

"I'm not entirely without experience, you know. I used to visit New

York quite regularly with my father. Museums, libraries, lectures, that sort of thing. I even attended elementary school on City Island, believe it or not. So I'm not a complete bumpkin. I see the city. I know it's there. I can hear it. If I choose to."

Another long pause.

"I'd like to tell you a story, if I might. It's about my ancestor, Wampage, the great Siwanoy brave. He lived in a village called Lapechwahacking—meaning 'plowed field,' more or less—which was right here, across the bay in Pelham Park. He was straight and handsome and true, my ancestor Wampage. He could shoot an arrow further, tell a story better, dance longer than any other warrior in the region. He shaved his head with a hot rock and wore his hair in a long roach that reached right down to his waist. He painted his body with the juice of the bloodroot. He was always in demand to speak at the council fire, and many women had known his kiss. His best friend was Cokoe, a Poningo warrior from a village near Rye, and they often were together on all sorts of adventures.

"Well, one day, Wampage was sent up to Alipconk, an important Wekweskik village, to deliver a string of wampum. The string was a gift and an invitation to Sauwenarack, the sachem, to the annual Big House ceremony at Lapechwahacking. The string was quite valuable—lots of purple sewan—and Sauwenarack was an important chief and the dance was one of the holiest ceremonies of the year. That's why Wampage was entrusted with the mission. Cokoe came along to keep him company. They accomplished the mission, a three-day walk up the river valley along the Wekweskik trail. But on their return they encountered a party of Mengwe carrying tribute to Onondaga. There was an exchange of words—perhaps Wampage had failed to show enough respect to the Mengwe, or one of the Mengwe had called him a woman. Now, Wampage was a warrior and a leader—he would have stood up to any man. But against four ferocious Mohawk, with the might of the entire Five Nations behind them, he knew better. He and Cokoe fled, because he knew that if they were caught and identified, the Mengwe would destroy Lapechwahacking and murder or enslave its inhabitants. So they ran.

They ran all the way down the Wekweskik trail, through Wekweskik village and Nappecamack they ran, with the Mengwe hard on their trail. Day and night they ran, as silent as deer, as swift as hawks, through Menantanch and Achqueehgenom they ran. But the Mengwe stayed with them, their fearsome barbed arrowheads ever ready to fly. Finally, after running for thirty-six hours without a stop, Wampage reached Ranachqua, home of his friends the Wekweskik. But he could not run for help, because it would be easy to kill these four Mengwe—he didn't need anyone's help for that—but not the hundreds who would come after to avenge them. So he led them through the woods, avoiding all signs of human settlement, around Quinnahung and Snakapins, bustling villages full of children, until he reached Asumsowis. This was a summer fishing station on the Aqueanonk shared by the Wekweskik and the Siwanoy, and Wampage knew just where the dugouts were hidden in the undergrowth. He and Cokoe dragged one from the bushes and launched it and themselves into the water. The Mengwe were so close behind, however, that they didn't have time to cover their tracks; the enemy found the remaining hidden canoes and set out across the bay in pursuit. But now Wampage was at home; he knew the waters and currents and islets of Aqueanonk better than anyone and he guided the canoe in and out among the rocky islands until the Mengwe's heads were spinning. Finally, he pulled in at a small wooded island that his people had sometimes used in the past as a fishing station; the Mengwe rowed right past, into the open waters of Maminketesuck, too proud to admit they were lost, and nobody ever saw them again.

"That night, Wampage held a big feast in Lapechwahacking to celebrate his escape. They ate venison and beans and oysters out of season. And there he announced that, to thank the little island for saving him and Cokoe, he was giving it a name—Manateyung-pachgen-auke—'the island place where I turned aside.' As was usual among the Algonquians, the unwieldy name was condensed to Manapinock, which the English settlers later translated as 'Turnaway.' And Wampage announced that Manapinock would always be among the Siwanoy a sacred place where kinfolk and friends could find refuge from enemies who would destroy them. And so it has been, throughout the centuries, down to the last Siwanoy—a refuge, a sanctuary from the destroyers."

Elias turned to face west, toward the Bronx. From up here you could see clear across the borough to New Jersey. You could see the hills and valleys that Wampage must have run while evading the Mohawk; you could see the rivers and creeks he must have forded; you could see Pelham Park, where Lapechwahacking had stood, and Pelham Neck, where the Siwanoy had cast their nets at Asumsowis. With his eyes half closed, gazing out upon this fantasy landscape, Elias seemed to be trying to conjure up its ghost. In the way you can see all sorts of mirages by narrowing your eyelids to slits, he was willing the trees and wigwams and planting fields to rise again from among the tract houses, the projects, the golf courses and crumbling ghettos. I understood then, by the way he'd hunched his back and drawn his head between his shoulders, that Ranachqua was more real to him than the Bronx would ever be. A kind of horror overtook me, almost a nausea, at this picture of self-delusion and false nostalgia, and I shivered.

"Shouldn't they have called it Turnaside Island?" I asked to break the tension.

"I guess so."

"The Mengwe have been gone a long time," I said, in a tone more compassionate than I was feeling.

"Have they?" Elias said, surprising me with the bitterness in his voice.

"Look out there, Elias," I said with a sweep of my arm over the city, and I'm sure he read the contempt behind my gesture. "Nobody out there is trying to destroy you."

Elias followed the sweep of my arm. "I don't think so," he said. "The Mengwe are still out there." His eyes scanned the horizon, then dipped toward the black shore of Turnaway Island, invisible now but present in the rhythmic clopping of waves against its stones. He peered down into the darkness like a nervous sentry, then scanned the horizon again. This time, as his gaze swept first to the right then back to the left, it came to rest squarely on my face. Though his eyes were hidden in pools of black shadow, I felt his gaze upon me like a sheet of moist clay, molding itself in the dark and clinging to my skin and sinking into my every porous cavity, and filling them with sadness.

The very next morning, right after breakfast, Elias drew me aside in the dining room. "I want to show you my project," he whispered like a conspirator. He led me to a door beneath the staircase in the foyer.

"This way," he said, and raised a hollow racket as he ran down a flight of old wooden stairs into the basement. I followed cautiously.

Elias stopped halfway down the stairs and motioned for me to do the same. Below us was an enormous rectangular table or platform, probably fifteen feet by twenty. It filled almost the entire room, leaving only a narrow passageway along the periphery of the walls. The stairs, situated against the center of the longer wall, provided the best vantage point from which to take in the whole scene. The entire surface of the platform was covered by a landscape, the kind of precise, ultrarealistic miniature made by architects or model train enthusiasts. But this landscape held no trains.

At first, I didn't quite understand what I was seeing. Clearly, it was a model landscape, but in my experience such a thing usually serves as a setting or showcase for something else that its maker wants to highlight: a condo development, for instance, a train circuit, a historic district, a bridge. This model had none of those: no little electric-powered drawbridges or switching lights, no tennis courts or marinas, no highways or ramps with tiny, motionless cars, no playgrounds bustling with minute children. It was just one great unbroken stretch of primordial jungle, a segment of the Amazon basin maybe. Mostly, the surface was covered in trees. Their fluffy crowns, made of some kind of dyed cotton wool, followed the varying contours underneath, revealing hills, valleys, escarpments, islands, that sort of thing. Besides the forest, there were swamps, rocky outcroppings, beaches, and of course water. There were many islands and many bodies of water separating and girdling them—rivers, streams, ponds, inlets—their surfaces made of blue-stained glass except for an occasional pristine waterfall modeled of plaster and painted a greenish azure. Toward the nearer end of the table, the larger waterways converged into a wide bay. But apart from the specific characteristics of the topography, there was nothing that I could see to distinguish the tract of land represented by the model from any other forest: it was just woods and water. It had no apparent purpose. Surely this wasn't "the project"?

And then it all came into focus. This wasn't just any tract of primeval forest—this was a very, *very* particular tract. I felt like an idiot for not having seen it sooner, but it wasn't as obvious as you might imagine. Once I recognized the contours of Manhattan, its long, spindly neck to the north and broad hips to the south, the other boroughs fell into place. This was a model of the land and waterways of New York City (except for Staten Island, which was still in progress, just a blank of blond tabletop), perversely denuded of buildings, bridges, roads, and every other landmark of civilization. Even Coney Island was just a white beach. It all felt a little obscene to me. I shuddered violently and tried to look away, though I didn't want to offend Elias. But he was already down there, strolling up and down the length of the model, blithely pointing out its salient features and curiosities like a wing commander preparing his squadron for a raid. I tried hard to concentrate on what he was saying; it was a little like being forced to attend the autopsy of a loved one: the only way to get through it was to avoid looking at the face. I soon found that by focusing on the particular, on details, I could blot out any sense of the overall picture, and that helped a lot. Once the roaring subsided and the swarming spots had vanished, I was able to pick up the thread of Elias's exposition.

He was giving an overview of Manhattan, pointing out the irregularities of the shoreline, how virtually every inch of the waterfront has been smoothed out, straightened, shored up, filled in, or filled out in modern times. And it was true: the minuteness of his detailing—you could see where the shore was rocky, where it was sandy, where bare, where overhung with towering oaks—revealed hundreds of tiny inlets, baylets, and streams, none of which now exist. Four or five large streams flowed down the hills of the East Side into the East River. Downtown, a large pond covered most of what is now Chinatown and poured its waters into the Bay. Elias showed me how the Harlem River formed a sharp double-S curve where today its two loops have been straightened, stranding the northernmost outcropping of the island in the Bronx.

The strange and unsettling part of it all was that it made Manhattan look like any other island, really. It could have passed for the setting of some *National Geographic* documentary on rare Micronesian primates. From its central spine, the island sloped down to the surrounding waters. It was remarkably hilly—you don't notice it on the streets, but even today it has surprising heights and abysses, almost daunting, some of them, at least in scale. Manhattan Valley was a real, deep valley. Central Park was a plateau of dunes and sandy wastes—the only part of Manhattan not densely covered in hardwood forest. The other boroughs were the same—vast stretches of woodland interrupted in many places by creeks, marshes, and some small rivers, which today have all but disappeared. Rockaway Peninsula and Riker's Island didn't exist at all, and Hell Gate had four islands where today there's only one. There were many little anomalies like that, but to me they were insignificant compared to the overwhelming prospect of forests covering all the familiar landmarks. Lincoln Center—gone; the Empire State Building—gone;

Yankee Stadium—gone; Grand Central Station, the Staten Island ferry terminal, the Brooklyn Heights promenade, the General Post Office Building, the World's Fair globe in Flushing Meadows, the Public Library—all gone. To me, it was sickening, apocalyptic— uncivilized.

Not that there were no signs of life among the trees. Elias was eager to point out all the paths and villages secluded throughout the woods and re-created in painstaking miniature: rounded huts and Quonset-shaped lodges, eensy-weensy canoes, and even racks for curing meat and fish. He showed me how all of midtown, the business center of the modern world, had been shunned by the ab- original inhabitants for lack of fresh water. All the settlements downtown—Sapokanikan, in the present-day meat-packing district, and Nechtanc, near South Street—were Matouack villages, while all the settlements north were Lenape. Each had its own streams and its own fields cleared for planting. There were plenty of "roads," too— the Wekweskik road ran the entire length of Manhattan to the landing beach at Saperewack, then continued north into Mahican country. You could see the embryonic beginnings of Kings Highway, Flatbush Avenue, Northern Boulevard in Queens and Brooklyn—they were all there, eerily: narrow dirt paths connecting villages, fishing stations, and cornfields. Familiar names kept cropping up, too, as Elias danced around the edges of his creation, pointing to tribal lands and landmarks—Maspeth, Rockaway, Jamaica, Gowanus, Canarsee, and so on—now nothing but stream and forest. That was it—woods and water, water and woods, as far as the eye could see. I put on a show of fortitude, but finally I had to turn away, overwhelmed. Elias went on talking, oblivious of my condition; I wanted to make him stop, to scream or hit him, but he just kept on talking.

"I come down here often," he was saying, "especially in winter, when the snow is thick on the ground and it is very quiet. I come down here sometimes at night. I come down here if I'm not feeling well.

"Sometimes, I look at this place and I dream that I go back in time, before the coming of the *shuwonnock*—the salty people, the whites. I travel up and down the eastern shore and I warn all the

Wapanaki, Algonquians and Iroquois and Muskogee, about those who will soon arrive, the evil ones made by the foam of waves crashing against the lands of the night. I warn them of what they will do. I say, in the words of my people: 'You will want them to live with you, to build homes and to plant corn, as your friends and allies. Because they will be hungry, and thought children of Kishelemukong, and not songbirds who lie.' They will know me as a prophet, as Wulamewet— 'He speaks truth.' And because the *shuwonnock* come insidiously, a few at a time at the beginning, they will be easy to kill, and they will not get fat off our lands and their industry will not prosper, and they will stop coming after awhile. And then we will finish our work that was begun. We will fish in peace, and plant our corn in peace, and our children will play at the water's edge and sing the songs their parents teach them. And I will see it all, it will be me there with them."

My head was in my hands at this point, and it took me a few moments to realize that his voice had trailed off into silence. As usual when he told stories about his forebears, he'd drifted off into the twilight zone again. There was no telling how long the trance would be on him. This time, it had come on so strong that he was still distracted and ill at ease by bedtime that evening.

When I think about it, it was probably this episode more than anything that set the tone for the rest of my stay on Turnaway, and maybe even for my entire relationship with Elias. I knew then that, even if I were ever to become his friend, there would always be this tension between us. If it was true that we were somehow "complementary," it could only be in the way that insulin and blood sugar are complementary. I mean, it had been clear to me almost from the beginning that Elias was a nice guy—"nice" in the sense that he was friendly, generous, open, cheerful, that kind of thing—in other words, everything I wasn't. Plus, he was healthy and good-looking. He was surely the sort of person that most people say you can't help liking. But for me, "nice" has never been much of a criterion in my choice of friends. "Nice" somehow doesn't quite register with me as a desir-

able or even a positive attribute. Frankly, it hardly even sounds like
a compliment to me. I don't think that's callous—it's just that "nice"
is almost never enough, unless you're talking about a dog. On the
other hand, even an idiot could see that there was more to Elias than
that.

So the next two weeks were difficult, sometimes tense, often irritating. The two of us circled warily around each other, testing vulnera-
bilities, exploring each other's defenses without leaving ourselves
exposed. He wanted something out of me—my allegiance—and I
wanted something out of him—his motives. Some people just want to
be liked; others need to know why they're liked. But there are some
of us who are not liked, and I think we know why, so we're pretty
confused by people who claim to like us. Every transaction has to
balance out, doesn't it? It was my job to resist, Elias's to push and
needle me. At least, that's how I saw it at the time—my childhood
taught me to see most relationships, even the most successful ones,
in terms of antagonism, vying for control, getting the upper hand. It's
very possible—and I say this with the advantage of hindsight—that
all Elias really wanted from me was my companionship and that all
he wanted to offer me was something he loved and thought I would
love, too. Anything's possible, even face value, however implausible.
I fought as hard to maintain my cynicism as I've ever fought for
anything in my life, but Elias was no slouch, either.

Over the next few days, we fell into a casual routine. The weather
was his accomplice. One day seemed to blend into the next, each as
perfect as the next in that late New York summer, when the air is
fragranced with apple and sweetgrass and the sky is swept clean by
salt-laden breezes off the New England banks. Even I found the so-
called pleasures of nature hard to resist.

Our early mornings were always devoted to hunting, but we never
seemed to catch anything. We both knew without saying so that our
failure was due to my clumsiness. Try as I might, I couldn't master
the "Indian creep," as Elias called his high-stepped, silent stalking
technique. Somehow, as his daintily pointed feet descended into the
underbrush, they seemed to twist and sidle around every little plant

like garter snakes, settling on the lichen without disturbing the least shrub or twig. To me, with my bad legs and dislike of green things, it all looked like a solid, impenetrable trap; all I had to do was look at a bush to make it start crackling. I imagined a host of forest creatures above my head, guffawing, hugging their bellies, and rolling around in mirth at my attempts to catch them unawares. It was humiliating, and I seemed to be making no progress. Still, Elias insisted on taking me out every morning. "You'll never learn without practice," he'd say kindly. "Watch me."

I did. The talent meant nothing to me—it was about as useful and relevant to my life in the city as ice carving to a pygmy—but the challenge was irresistible. In the darkness before dawn, I even strapped on a loincloth to make the task easier. Believe it or not, I eventually figured out the trick—not very well, of course, but I did. It wasn't so much a question of where you placed your feet, as I'd thought—though that was important, too—as of consistency of motion. If your movements were the least bit jerky or variable in their speed, you'd make noise; but if, in lowering your foot, you moved it in one slow vector, never pausing, never accelerating, like a ship sliding beneath the surface of the ocean, you could persuade the plants to part silently before you instead of bending under protest. As a matter of fact, once figured out in principle, it isn't as difficult as it sounds.

These efforts of mine weren't a total write-off, either, since I finally got to see Elias catch a bunny. The mystery to me had always been how he hunted without arrows, a snare, a slipknot, a net, or even a deadfall. On my fifth morning, I found out. At the time, I wasn't even aware that he'd sighted his quarry. One moment I was staring, half bored, half asleep, at the spiky knobs of his spinal ridge, the next I saw an indistinct flurry near his right foot, as if he'd stepped on a nesting bird. A moment later a bunny was swinging by its ears from his fist. He held his prey up to me with a triumphant grin, then grasped it firmly in both hands and held it aloft, like Abraham did Isaac. A pallor of sublime devotion suffused his boyish face. You'd have thought he was about to slit the bunny's throat and drink its blood, but the rapture soon subsided. He perused the rabbit thought-fully, bounced it once or twice in his left palm, then flung it headlong into a clump of creeping ivy, muttering in Indian.

"Too small," he said matter-of-factly.

"Too small for what?"

"For the pen."

Over the next few days, Elias caught several rabbits. Like some hard-core angler, he always threw the smaller ones back with a curse; the larger ones—those weighing over eight pounds—he would release into one of the teeming pens, after having displayed it vain-gloriously to the supremely indifferent Ross. On a few occasions, Elias made me bellwether, but of course I never caught a thing.

Every morning after the hunt, the three of us ate breakfast together in silence. I was allowed to read the sections of the paper that the doctor discarded. That first week, the *Times* happened to be running a three-part article on nearby Hart Island, the city's potter's field, serviced by inmates on work-release from Riker's Island. You could see Hart quite clearly from any number of spots on Turnaway—it was always bustling with activity, and the smokestack was rarely cold. According to this article, Hart Island already held nearly a million bodies and was running out of space. I thought my hosts might be interested in the issue, given its proximity, and I tried to engage them on it. But Elias never took any interest in the outside world and the doctor just snorted contemptuously when I brought it up. "Non-sense," he said. "Those poor people are cremated, not buried." Our morning meals continued in silence.

After breakfast we often waited down by the dock for the mail boat, dangling our legs over the water and making faces at our reflec-tions. Since we were up so early, we usually had well over an hour to kill, and I soon came to see that Elias had structured our schedule on purpose to give us this time to talk at leisure. He tried his best to draw me out, picking his topics as carefully as a rabbi, with an eye to the instructional shared experience. But in the end, he did most of the talking. It was during our mornings on the dock that I learned most about his childhood.

As I'd suspected, it had been a lonely one. When not teaching anthropology at Columbia, his beloved father Andrew was often away on field trips in Central America and elsewhere. When he was at home, his idea of having a good time with his son seems to have been exhuming skull fragments and tibias from the collections in the Heye Foundation. They never went to ballgames or amusement parks or even the movies, the sort of thing I'd have wanted to do with a father. To me he sounded like a well-meaning but self-absorbed kind of guy, with no idea of what a young boy might need; Elias adored his memory nonetheless. True, his father did send him to a regular school for a while, the parochial school on City Island, but he'd been so far ahead of his classmates and so quirky in his habits and interests that Andrew had pulled him out and hired tutors for home study. Dr. Ross was away at college and medical school through most of Elias's boyhood. A series of ineffectual nannies threw up their hands at the boy's ungovernability.

When Elias was fourteen, Andrew Hutchinson died of unknown causes—a spider bite, Elias suspected—in the jungles of Guatemala. He left only the tiniest of annuities to keep Turnaway running—nothing for his sons, nothing for their education and future. The impression I got was that he'd been more absentminded than brutish. He didn't sound like the kind of person who would deliberately shut his only son away from the world. But without insurance or an estate, it had come to the same thing. Elias was effectively marooned on the island, the only place he could live for free. The tutors had to be sent away. Ross managed to finish his studies on hardship scholarships, but as soon as they were done, he came home to take care of his strange little brother. The island closed in on itself. After that, Elias was mostly self-taught, hence his incredible expertise in a narrow range of subjects and his total ignorance of science and the arts. Gradually, I formed a picture of Elias as an adolescent—lonely, maybe, but immersed in sophisticated studies of his own design and not very interested in the company of his peers. As far as I could make out, after his father's death, his one brush with normal human relations had been his "initiation into manhood" by Felicia when he was sixteen—an affair the older woman had soon put an end to but which they both seemed to look back on with fondness. Other than that, nothing: no friends, no outside interests, no relations with any-one but his adoptive brother, who was old enough to be his father.

But it was Andrew Hutchinson who loomed largest. I tried more than once to get him to recognize the man's obvious shortcomings as a parent—his long absences, his reliance on surrogates, his glaring selfishness—but Elias couldn't hear it. He idolized his memory of his father, and he couldn't accept my indifference to my own.

"You don't remember your father, do you, Ben?" he asked me during one of those rambling conversations on the dock.

"Not much."

"That's very sad. My father, he made me everything I am today. My life with him was one unending universe of the imagination. He filled it with his stories. Stories, stories all winter long, Indians and magic and heroic deeds. He always said: 'They belong to you. These are your stories, Elias.' "

"Did you ever stop to think that stories are for children?" I had to say it, but I tried to say it as kindly as I could.

"No. Never. Stories are blood. Sometimes, all that keeps me going is the memory of my father and his legacy of stories. That and the Mahkohkwe. You missed that, without a father. Still, I suppose he loved you very much."

"I doubt it."

"That's silly. What makes you say such a thing?"

"Just a hunch."

We heard the distinctive sound of the approaching mail boat. Elias, as usual, jumped to his feet and paced the dock until the boat was close enough for Felicia to cast him a mooring line. She could easily have handed him the meager delivery from the deck of the boat, but she always landed and took a few minutes to chat. They spoke in Spanish, and from what I could make out it was just small talk, but of the nicest kind. It was clear that she cared for him like an old friend—in fact, Elias told me she'd had the same route, her first and only since joining the service, for fifteen years. She was only a few years older than him, and of course they'd had their famous "liaison," but she talked to him like a mother, always asking after his health, his recent discoveries and adventures, and admonishing him to take care. She was never anything but friendly and generous with me, but even so I could tell she harbored a little seed of mistrust, like the doctor only much less obvious. I could understand it, too. After all, I was brand new to a way of life that had been getting along just fine without me for a long time. She was protective, and I liked that about her.

Once she'd left, the late morning was usually given over to swimming. The hot and humid season was pretty much played out by Labor Day, and after that the water sports around our island dropped off significantly—even the air traffic into La Guardia seemed to have been rerouted to suit my holiday schedule. The first few days I refused to swim. Even as a boy I'd never amounted to much at sports, but Elias was right, too: I was embarrassed by my puny legs, which were crisscrossed with livid scars up both thighs, and exposure to sunlight would only make them more hideous. The rest of me was no great shakes, either, especially compared to his body, lithe and sleek as an otter. So I'd been happy at first to perch on a rock and watch him play, or to catch up on my sleep in the woodland shade. But Elias was relentless.

"What better therapy for your injuries than swimming?" he'd goad me day after day.

"I'm not interested in therapy."

"But how do you expect your legs to grow stronger if you don't exercise them?"

"I don't."

"It's not your legs you should be ashamed of, Ben," he'd say to me, shaking his head sadly. "It's your attitude."

Finally I relented, just to get him off my case. I remember that first swim. It was the first time in years I'd voluntarily undressed in front of another person. Elias politely turned away as I peeled off my T-shirt and jeans, but even so I was ashen with shame and fear. I didn't know what scared me most: nakedness or the water. I couldn't help recalling the trauma of my shipwreck, but at the same time, exposing myself to the Bronx shoreline a bare two miles away seemed like the most vulnerable position I'd ever been in. I trembled like an idiot on the verge, ankle-deep in the waves, then closed my eyes and plunged. The water closed over my head, cold and cleansing. I opened my eyes into the green twilight and saw clams and oysters sleeping at my feet. The only sound was the distant thrum of speed-boats, rising and fading through the depths like a heartbeat. When I emerged, Elias was right by me, smiling warmly.

"Isn't that better?" he said, beckoning me toward the deeper water. I followed.

Sometimes, instead of swimming, we'd play in the fire pump out back, behind the kitchen. It was just an old bore-hole pump sunk into an artesian well, but the doctor liked to keep it gassed up and primed, so we tested it every so often and made a game out of it. It turned out that, in all the years of his life before I came along, it had never occurred to Elias to turn the hose on himself, just for the fun of it. Other times he gave me shooting lessons with his beautiful ashwood longbow. It was handmade and deadly—Elias claimed you could kill a deer at a hundred yards with one well-aimed shot, and with the precision of his target practice, I believed him. Once, too, he took down the massive oak war club that hung over his bed and gave me a chilling demonstration on the proper way to handle it against an enemy.

So, all in all, these morning games of ours were innocent and lighthearted. I won't pretend that I didn't enjoy them or that I couldn't feel their effect on me. It was a little like having a second childhood, only for me it was all new, since I'd never done anything like this the first time around. Neither had Elias, for that matter, and his enthusiasm was infectious—not the kind of reaction I was used to inspiring in people. I was amazed to find myself relaxing. I was eating and sleeping better, without painkillers for the first time since my accident. My instinctive contempt for Elias was gradually losing its hard edge; like a caterpillar dissolving itself inside its cocoon, it would soon emerge, completely transformed, as affection. I'm not saying that my acquaintance with Elias made me a new man, any more than a shot of morphine will alter your personality forever. These were all queer and uneasy changes for me, and I fought them. But still and all, the way I figured it, as long as I was getting my free ride I might as well enjoy it. So I gave in to the spirit of Elias's games. They were also among the few times of the day when it was easy to forget the ever grimmer presence of the doctor up the hill, hovering over us like a carrion vulture.

He was elusive, to say the least. I'd catch the odd glimpse of him through the greenery, returning from the dock with groceries or the mail; once I saw him down there talking to some guy in a dark suit, an encounter that I'm pretty sure he never mentioned to me or Elias. He was always shuffling through mysterious papers at his desk in the library. Every so often, the telephone would ring. It was never—not once—for Elias. Dr. Ross would snatch up the receiver, turn his back on whoever had answered the call, and speak in hushed tones that definitely qualified as a whisper. Who was calling, or what they talked about, I never did learn.

Occasionally, we'd meet him at the noonday meal that followed our morning activities; more often, a cold platter of meats and salads would be waiting for us at the house, the doctor nowhere in sight. I was aware of all the time he spent tending to the lettuce and the bunnies, of course; it was obvious to me, no matter what Elias chose to believe, that the rabbit compound represented more than some halfway house for wayward bunnies, the way Elias had described it. This was no pastime—it was a business of some sort, that was certain, and the doctor seemed to be running it professionally. He also spent at least part of every afternoon on maintenance—a losing battle, but he kept at it. No matter where you were on the island, the sounds of his hammer, saw, and squeaky wheelbarrow could always reach you. Late at night, too, long after Elias and I had gone to bed, I could still see rectangles of light projected from the library windows onto the lawn, and hear the scratch of the doctor's fountain pen or the leafing of dessicated pages directly below my bedroom.

So without actually spending much time with him, I could account for a large part of his day. But there were also hours on end when he seemed to disappear from Turnaway as effectively as if he'd vanished like a shadow in a dark corner. I often tried to coax Elias into telling me what he knew about the doctor's free time, but he was always evasive in that naïve, disarming way of his, surprisingly discreet and respectful of the doctor's privacy. I never did figure out how much of this could be set down to ignorance, how much to reticence, and how much to a blind eye. He tried to tell me that the doctor spent long hours with his entomology, but I knew better than that. I never once heard or saw him enter the lab at the end of the hallway. With all that dust and neglect up there, I'd have been willing to bet he hadn't kept that hobby up in a long, long time. And I was happy to suspect something far more interesting—something that demanded cunning and secrecy and intrigue—but what that was I could only guess at, since the doctor never let me get close enough to ask questions of a personal nature.

Of his past, all I knew or was ever able to find out by questioning him directly was that he was born in Austria and that he'd been brought over to America as a boy by Andrew Hutchinson some time after the war. It was my guess that he was Jewish and that his parents died in the Holocaust. If my estimate of his age was about right, he couldn't have been more than ten years younger than Andrew, more a brother than a son, which might help explain why he was more a father than a brother to Elias. Andrew hadn't even been married when he'd adopted him, and the doctor had been older than his own adoptive mother. He was already a grown man when Elias was born. Did he somehow blame Elias for their mother's death in the delivery room? Had he resented their father's diverted attention and affection? There was no way of knowing.

Elias would tell me little anecdotes about growing up with him after they were orphaned; about the long, long hours Ross put in as a medical student and intern at Montefiore Hospital; how sometimes it seemed to Elias—a teenage boy—that he was alone on Turnaway for days on end, and how, when Ross did come home, he was so exhausted he slept for sixteen hours straight and spoke little while he was awake. The overall impression was of a cold, withdrawn guardian fulfilling an unwanted duty. And yet, according to Elias, it was Ross's own decision to return to Turnaway to look after his young brother instead of starting his own practice. It was hard to credit, that kind of altruism, but here he was—shoveling shit, fixing clapboard, mixing cocktails, doing the dishes in a frilly apron. Not only that, but Elias's anecdotes were always punctuated with selfless deeds and kindnesses that the doctor had performed for him. I couldn't deny that I'd seen these kindnesses with my own eyes—the tender removal of a splinter, the meek sewing and laundering of clothes, distant errands for minor items, that sort of thing. One evening early in my stay, after some cutting remark I made, Elias had turned to the doctor for comfort. They didn't say a word, but the doctor took Elias's hand in his own and held it for a few minutes while I, impenitent, glared into the sunset.

Whatever he may have been to his brother, he was a complete cipher to me and obviously wanted to keep it that way. In the evenings, when Elias and I took our Sazeracs on the porch, looked at the stars, or told stories from our experience, sometimes the doctor would sit with us and sometimes he'd unaccountably disappear; but he never joined in our conversations or contributed stories of his own. Elias seemed perfectly content with this order of things, rarely speaking to the doctor except when he needed a service. When he did, he often called him *nohwesh,* Munsee for "my little father." The doctor always performed the service with the silent efficiency of a servant, expressionless and graceful. But, unlike a servant, once he'd completed his task—say, filling our water glasses or setting out fresh ice for our Sazeracs—he'd resume his seat at the side of the porch, never out of earshot, yet never, or rarely, speaking. Even in the worst heat he wore long-sleeve shirts and usually a jacket, and he never allowed me to help him prepare dinner or clean up in the kitchen, as if he had something at stake in it. I remember one evening when I bugged him long enough—it seems very symbolic to me now, somehow—he relented and allowed me to prepare the drinks. He was a good cocktail mixer himself and I was eager to impress: just so much bourbon, so much pastis, bitters, syrup. I gave mine a sip and beamed proudly—every bit as good as the doctor's. I served him first in his old ladderback chair in the corner. He just barely wetted his lips, then looked up with a subtle smile that was only part approval. What the other part was—mockery? triumph?—I didn't figure out until a few moments later. I stepped over to Elias, handed him his frosty highball glass, then hovered over him as he closed his eyes, tilted his head back and took a long draught. The next thing I knew, he was gagging and choking, his eyes watering, the color drained from his face as if I'd served him paint thinner.

"What in god's name was that?" he finally managed to cough out when he caught his breath.

"It's a Sazerac," I stammered abjectly, pounding him on the back and dabbing a napkin across his soaked gray-flannel vest. "Just like we have every night. It's the same recipe, even."

"For god's sake Ben, how could you be so stupid?" Elias shouted in a tone of real anger I'd never heard him use. "You don't serve alcohol to a Native American!"

"I'm sorry, I didn't know." I turned to Dr. Ross for some sort of moral support, but all he did was radiate that same mocking smile.

"I'm sorry, Mr. Givens," he said smugly. "I thought you were aware. Elias always drinks sassafras tea. The color is quite similar to our cocktail." This was the kind of weird, unanswerable hostility I had to put up with on a daily basis as Elias and I got to know each other and settled into our routine.

During my first few days, I tried to establish the after-lunch hours as my time to paint. I had a pad and some watercolors that I'd brought with me from the city and I'd set up a jury-rigged easel on one of the beaches or at a window in the house. Turnaway didn't offer much besides nature to paint; that was hardly my strength, but I felt like I should stick it out. Also, I thought I could make my own contribution to our joint entertainment by giving Elias impromptu lessons. He knew almost nothing about the fine arts, but it turned out he knew just enough.

"You're not very good at this, are you?" he said, shaking his head at a rendering of Orchard Beach.

After that, I decided to give painting a rest. Elias had his own plans for that time slot, anyway. Our daily anthropology lessons were mostly held on the lawn, but sometimes, if the weather threatened or he needed to use illustrations, we'd go up to his study in the tower. That's where I came to realize the incredible extent of his learning—the hundreds of books on Native American subjects, each one filled with margin notes in Elias's elegant, old-world script; the dedications and acknowledgments of his help that appeared in many of these

scholarly works; the numerous typed monographs he'd written himself; plus the textbooks, histories, and case studies in half a dozen
European languages, all annotated by Elias—it was more than impressive, I can tell you. It added an aura of authenticity to our
lessons, impromptu as they were.

At first, they were dry afternoons of ethnography, archeology, some
local geology, pre-Columbian history, and a little linguistics. Elias's
knowledge was daunting—he could have taught Native American
studies at any university in the country—but it just wasn't for me,
and besides, there was something about his wistful tone that put me
off. All that mumbo jumbo about animal spirits and vision quests
leaves me cold. Maybe you can't love a subject without wanting to
live it. I can understand that some people need a place to escape to,
but Elias—I sometimes had the feeling that he'd have given up
refrigeration, electricity, antibiotics, nylon, citrus fruit, or toothpaste
before he'd relinquish one arrowhead from his quiver or one deerskin
thong of his breechcloth. That's what I wanted to tell him—I didn't
believe in anything he was teaching me, even as I absorbed the
lessons.

But as the week wore on, these lessons took on a craftsy tone, as
Elias illustrated native ways with native industry. The things he
knew how to do—it was revolting. He taught me to recognize herbs
with ridiculous names: burdock, pennyroyal, sweet flag, cicely. He
made red dye—"the color of peace"—from bloodroot and sumac. He
wove hemp from dogbane and basket nets from wild grass and bass-
wood fiber. He made shoes from braided corn husks. He could strip
bark from a chestnut tree without damaging it, and use that bark to
thatch a steam lodge framed with bent saplings. He cooked meat and
hominy porridge by dropping heated rocks into a deerskin bag filled
with water. He made ax handles, arrowheads, hoes from antler, and
incense out of sweetgrass. He grew corn and beans and squash in a
plot he'd slashed-and-burned—all for succotash. He fashioned a rattle from a gourd and dried jack-in-the-pulpit seeds. He made wampum beads from quahog shells.

As if this wasn't all dismal enough, most of these handicrafts were
practiced in the time-consuming, labor-intensive traditional fashion.

It can take hours just to prepare a bowl of gruel if you have to start from scratch. To pass the time he'd continue his ethnohistories or tell stories about his ancestors, among whom, he claimed, was the famous puritan heretic Anne Hutchinson. Now I happened to remember from school that Anne Hutchinson was murdered in the wilderness by the Indians, but I didn't think it would be smart to point out the apparent irony—Elias didn't seem to cotton on to irony very well. In any case, he wasn't interested in his European heritage. Instead, he mostly talked about the great Wampage, whose actual Indian name, non-Europeanized and unpronounceable, means "chestnut burr." I heard a lot of Wampage stories then and in the weeks to follow, and it soon became clear to me that Wampage was more than an ancestor—he was an Ancestor. All the Siwanoy and their Lenape and Mahican kin were well made, strong of back, fair of limb, clear-eyed; but Wampage—to hear Elias tell it, it was like being descended from Odysseus, Beowulf, and Gilgamesh rolled into one: two thirds divine, one third human. He lived in a pre-Columbian wonderland of vague date: when someone tells you that his ancestor helped create the seasons by tying up one wing of the Snow Eagle, you don't think to ask what year he did it in. There were other stories like that—which I don't imagine even Elias expected me to believe—stories about how Wampage fought with Moose and gave him his crooked snout, or how Skunk's stripe was a reminder of how Wampage saved him from the White Corn Devil, or how Wampage's hunting prowess was a personal gift of the Deer Queen. That sort of stuff.

Mostly, though, Wampage was just a man among men—a hero, of course, but a human hero, and the stories concerned his adventures and misadventures in the natural world, usually accompanied by his sidekick Cokoe (whose Indian name, *Kokhos*, means "owl"). Whenever Elias told a Wampage story, he went into a kind of trance and recited it dramatically, as if it had been rehearsed or learned by heart. Here are Wampage and Cokoe caught in a sudden squall on the Sound and blown clear up to Montauk country. Here is Wampage piercing three pigeons with one arrow. Here is Wampage seducing the beautiful daughter of a Raritan chieftain by coming to her at night dressed in a wolf skin. Here are Wampage and Cokoe stealing a valuable tobacco pipe from a self-important local sachem and leaving a dried dog turd in its place. Here they are engaged in an eating contest that ends when Cokoe vomits up a live guinea hen with its feathers still on. Here they rescue a young Tappan woman from slavery among the Mengwe. Here Wampage lulls a bear to sleep by imitating the snores of its mate, then kills it with a stick through the heart; and here he and Cokoe devise a convoluted plan to foil a Mengwe attack, essentially by inserting quail eggs up their own rectums.

You never knew what might draw a story out of him. Any chance occurrence, like a vireo passing low overhead or the sound of a branch falling in the woods, might trigger some association with an event from Wampage's life. Likewise any subject we might touch on in our lessons. Usually, the tenor of the story reflected Elias's mood—when he was in his melancholy, his story was all suffused with nostalgia for lost things; when he was feeling cheerful, the story was equally upbeat and humorous. But if it was impossible to guess what would bring it on, you always knew when it was coming. Elias would suddenly grow still and solemn, his eyes focus on some remote, invisible kingdom, and his body begin to sway back and forth, rhythmically. It was as if he were putting himself into a mild trance. Then he'd fall silent before beginning. I can remember my shock and concern the first time it happened, one afternoon on the lawn. We'd been discussing Lenape cuisine when Elias cut himself off in midsentence and started to sway. I thought he was going to throw up, but then he began to speak.

"Here camps my story. Many years ago, the village of Lapechwahacking celebrated the harvest with a great feast. Kin arrived from throughout Manhattan and Sewanhacky and Ranachqua to join in the festivities. There was an abundance of fish and chowder and cornpone and bean stew and meats: venison, bear, turkey, and dog. There was a great revelry of dancing, singing, storytelling, and oration, for it had been a very good harvest that year and there would be an ample sufficiency of provisions for the coming winter. Much tobacco was smoked, of which Wampage and Cokoe, being renowned speakers, enjoyed their share.

"The feast was to last four days, and sometimes the oratory continued through the night. Now, Wampage was known throughout all Lenapehoking and beyond for his powers of speech and his beautiful deep voice, and all year long those who were to attend the feast in Lapechwahacking looked forward to hearing him tell of myths and visions. So when the guests were gathered around the great fire under the full harvest moon, and the *hopokan* was passed to Wampage, they all fell silent. Wampage stood to speak, he stretched his arms to fill his lungs with air, he opened his mouth—and out came the voice of Raccoon. Try as he might, he could not find his own voice, but only the high-pitched shriek with which Raccoon calls in warning to his kin. The gathering of warriors and sachems burst into laughter. Unable to speak, Wampage was forced to hand on the pipe to the next speaker, a Matinecock called Mahenas, who enthralled the audience with his story.

"The next day, Wampage pampered his throat with sassafras tea and poultices. By the fall of night he felt his voice to be in full form, and at the gathering he accepted the *hopokan* with great confidence. He stood up and planted his feet firmly. But this time, when he opened his mouth, out came the voice of Loon—*kee-a-ree, kee-a-ree*—and again Wampage was forced to pass the *hopokan* without speaking, while the others all laughed until they held their sides in pain. Finally, they stopped only to hear Mahenas camp his story by the fire, which brought him great honor.

"The next day, Wampage and Cokoe discussed these events and decided that Wampage had been the victim of witchcraft. No doubt, an evil shaman, a *mĕteinu*, had invaded his body. Therefore, Cokoe stood guard over Wampage all day long, determined to protect him from any shaman who might put Wampage under a spell by inserting objects into his body. Cokoe allowed no one to touch Wampage that day while he ate, bathed, sweated in the lodge, and went about his other duties. Not even Wampage's own mother was allowed near him, and in this way he was protected right up to the very moment when he was called upon to speak.

"Again, he stood. Again, the guests fell silent. Again, he planted his feet and stretched out his arms. Again, he opened his mouth—

and barked like Dog. The guests roared with laughter, and old Winhampas singed his toes in the fire. Only Mahenas did not laugh at his rival, but merely smiled into his chest like a man who has concealed wealth. Wampage sat down again in shame, but resolved to get to the bottom of his humiliation. He had a plan.

"That night, when the guests had gone to their beds, Wampage and Cokoe crept silently through the village. They stopped outside the lodge of Paurigos, where Mahenas and his people were staying. They tiptoed around the lodge until they heard Mahenas's voice—he was lying down with his wife on the other side of the elm-bark wall. They listened with their ears to the wall, and this is what they heard him say to his wife:

" 'The spells of Mahkatape the *mëteinu* have worked very well. On the first day, I placed the shinbone of a raccoon in Wampage's fry bread, and he spoke like Raccoon. On the second day, I placed the beak of a loon in his fish gruel and he spoke like Loon. Today, I placed the whisker of a dog in his venison stew and he spoke like Dog. Tomorrow, I will place a turkey claw in his grape dumplings and he will talk like Turkey. Then I will be known as the best storyteller among all the tribes on the water!'

"When Wampage heard this, he knew just what he must do. The next day, at the communal feast, Wampage made certain to sit next to Mahenas. Mahenas's wife, Amimi, brought each of them a bowl of *shëwahsapan*. Just as Wampage was about to eat his first dumpling, Cokoe came along and distracted Mahenas with a question. Wampage switched the bowls, and watched as Mahenas ate all the *shëwahsapan* that had been destined for him. Mahenas, in turn, smiled as he watched Wampage enjoy his dumplings.

"That night was the last night of the feast. The stars danced in the heavens and a gentle autumn breeze tickled the waters. The *hopokan* was passed around the fire, and each man spoke what was in his heart—happiness at the good harvest, sadness at leaving friends and family. When the pipe reached Wampage, many half-suppressed giggles could be heard. Wampage stood and prepared himself to speak, as he had done on the previous nights. Mahenas sat and smiled politely. But when Wampage began to speak Mahenas's smile faded, for his rival spoke in his most powerful, beautiful voice. At times it sounded like a thundering waterfall, at times it sounded like the wind through the salt-marsh, at times it sounded like a bear crashing through the undergrowth, at times it sounded like a gentle tide. But at all times it sounded like Wampage, the great warrior. And this is what he said:

"'There are many stories among us of animals taking on their human form and walking among people. Also, there are many stories of humans taking on their animal forms, and of *manitowak* impersonating people and animals. When the *mësingholikan* puts on his mask for the Big House ceremony, he becomes the *mësingwe,* as we know. We have *petakhuweyok, tangtititawenik,* and *wemcheknishak* wandering about our forests, and do we ever know what they look like or who they are pretending to be? The wife who leaves your wigwam in the morning to sow beans in the field may be the terrible *tehataongelemhes* in disguise when she returns at night. The son who is lost in the woods on a hunting expedition could be Snow Boy or Munhake the Badger when he returns. The fact is that nothing in this world is certain and nothing and no one can be said for sure to be the thing or person we believe them to be.

"'No, it is not easy to discover the truth. Sorcerers are very clever at hiding their magic, and spirits are usually reluctant to reveal their disguises. That is understandable. In fact, many among us believe that the only way to unmask sorcery is by using sorcery or trickery. But I do not believe that is true. Sometimes, all that is needed is to ask a direct question. Only the great Mahtantu himself can look you in the face and lie without blushing. If my words are not as straight as the ashwood arrow shaft, let the Mengwe come and flay the skin from my body. Not only that—I will be happy to prove the truth of my words by unmasking a changeling in our very midst.'

"A general gasp arose from the gathered guests, followed by a murmured tone of disapproval. Idle boasting was frowned upon in Lenape society. But Mahenas and Amimi looked distinctly uncomfortable. Wampage continued.

"'Now, all of you here know me. You know I love a competition and you know I love a wager. So I will bet anything you like that there is an animal spirit here with us, and that he will reveal himself under my questioning.'

"The murmur grew, but Wampage was unabashed. He strode through the crowd and stopped before his own sachem.

" 'Well, Maminepoe,' he said loudly and boldly, for all to hear. 'Tell us: Are you a *manito*?'

"The crowd roared in merriment, while Maminepoe looked about in confusion. Eventually, goaded by the taunts of the guests, Maminepoe shouted, a little louder than necessary: 'No! I am no *manito*!' which only made him more ridiculous and caused the laughter to redouble. Wampage moved on.

" 'What about you, Owenoke? Are you a *manito*?'

"Owenoke, in the spirit of the game, mimicked Maminepoe's confusion. 'No, I am no *manito*!' he stuttered, and all roared even harder. Wampage moved on.

" 'And you, Cokoe?'

" 'I am no *manito*!'

" 'And you, Pemgaton? And you, Ipawahun? And you, Megtegichkama?'

" 'I am no *manito*!'

" 'I am no *manito*!'

" 'I am no *manito*!'

" 'And you, Mahenas? What are you?'

"By now, the laughter had grown so loud, and the guests' eyes so filled with tears of mirth, that no one might have noticed that Mahenas had failed to answer if Amimi had not wrapped her arms about her husband and cried out loud, in a desperate shriek, 'No, my Mahenas is no *manito*!' The crowd immediately fell silent, while Wampage glared down upon the cowering Mahenas.

" 'Well, Mahenas? What about it? Are you a *manito*?' he demanded triumphantly. Mahenas shook his head dejectedly.

" 'What's that, Mahenas? Speak up. *Are* you a *manito*?'

"Mahenas only shook his head, while all looked on in horror and anticipation.

" 'What's that, Mahenas? We can't hear you?'

" '*Yuup! Yuup!*' Mahenas had spoken. The guests were stunned. None but Wampage dared speak in the presence of the spirit.

" 'Aha!' he said. 'So you are a *manito,* are you?'

" '*Yuup!*'

" 'You see, I told you all I had to do was ask him a direct question. And what sort of a *manito* are you, may I ask?'

" '*Yuup!*'

" 'You sound like Turkey to me. Are you Turkey? Can you fly?' Wampage picked up a heavy club. Mahenas jumped to his feet and began edging away. Wampage jabbed at his rival and Mahenas turned on his heels and fled toward the water, with Wampage and the rest of the guests close behind.

" 'No, you can't fly but you certainly can run,' Wampage yelled as he pursued him to the water's edge. 'Perhaps you're Rabbit? Let's see you jump, Rabbit.'

"And Mahenas jumped right into the dark waters of Maminketesuck and began swimming away into the night, while Wampage and the rest hooted in derision behind him.

" 'You're no Rabbit, since you swim so well! You must be Terrapin. Come back, Terrapin, come back!'

"But Mahenas kept swimming all the way to Madnank, and he was never seen in Lapechwahacking again. Later, when Wampage explained what had happened, all agreed that he had behaved wisely, and Maminepoe even gave him a gift of an eagle feather for entertaining them all so well."

Elias lapsed into a dreamy silence, staring off across the bay. At these moments you had the impression that the liquid surface of his eyes was not a mirror but a window onto that other time. If you looked closely enough they would not show you a reflection of Eastchester Bay and its bobbing white sails, or the gray sprawl of the Bronx beyond; instead, you'd see Aqueanonk and the precarious perch of Lapechwahacking at the edge of the wild, primordial forests of Ranachqua. At times like this, when he'd mesmerized himself by the sound of his own voice and was deep in the grip of one of his stories, it was obvious that his hold on this world was far weaker than his presence in the other. It was as if Elias were an old man living in the memory of his glorious youth, allowing his soul to wander free in that vanished place; but it was worse, far worse, since Elias was so young and the place he escaped to wasn't even one he'd ever known. This kind of behavior could make me angry, even a little sickened, but it was hard, like I said, not to feel sorry for him. It's pretty fair to say that Wampage loomed large in Elias's psyche, but I wouldn't know how to describe the love in his eyes and his voice when he spoke of his cherished ancestor. I would never want to be that far gone, I would never want to yearn that much for someone who was dead. I couldn't stand it, not if I had my whole life before me, like Elias. It made me want to yank him so hard out of that imaginary world of his that the door to it would snap shut behind him forever.

I don't know what made me feel so strongly about this—it's not as if there was anything personal at stake in it for me—except maybe that, after all the time I'd been spending with Elias, I was actually beginning to feel the powerful lure of that world myself. Despite my resistance and distance, I could feel it tugging at me, like a riptide. For a moment there, as I watched Elias, I stopped struggling and allowed myself, too, to be carried along by the current. Why resist? It was sort of like being dead—it was nice, the dead voices, the dead forests, all the dead so much happier than me.

I was hardly aware of the motorboat pulling up to our jetty, and it was only when he began to shout my name that I noticed Dr. Ross waving to me from the bottom of the lawn, trying to attract my attention. A glance at Elias told me he was still in the spell of that long-waned harvest moon, listening to the echo of Siwanoy laughter as their cousin splashed his way across the Sound, and I left him dreaming on the crest of his hill as I joined the doctor below.

Dr. Ross seemed uncharacteristically excited. He beckoned to me urgently as I strolled across the lawn to join him at the mouth of the path leading to the rabbit hutches. I refused to be hurried, ambling slowly in his direction, deliberately closing my eyes and holding my face up to the sunlight as if I hadn't a care in the world. He was pretty worked up by the time I reached him.

"Please," he said quietly, leaning in toward me as if he were sharing a secret. "I have a heavy load today. You will be good enough to help me." I followed him to the hutch compound.

By the gate in the compound fence was a stack of bottle-green plastic crates with latticework air vents on either side. As we approached, I could see twitching pink snouts poking through the vents. There were six crates teeming with bunnies. On the side of each crate, the words ATHOS FINE MEATS & GAME, OYSTER BAY, NEW YORK were emblazoned in yellow letters. Dr. Ross explained to me that, having already loaded the stock, he needed my help carrying the crates to the waiting delivery boat.

"Athos," I said dubiously as I hefted a surprisingly heavy load of bunnies onto my right shoulder. "That's your 'home for bunnies'?"

Dr. Ross grunted under the weight of his cargo but didn't even bother to answer. We walked side by side down to the dock.

"Don't you think Elias should be doing this?"

Still, Dr. Ross continued to ignore my questions.

"He really believes there's a home for bunnies, doesn't he?" I pressed on. "He doesn't even know about the butcher."

That got him. The doctor stopped in his tracks and lowered his burden delicately to the ground. His face, as usual, didn't give much away, but it was clear that he was struggling to restrain a rising anger. The pupils of his gray eyes as he turned to me were as tiny as lice.

"Mr. Givens," he said. "Really, none of this is your business."

"Why don't you ask Elias to help carry the rabbits?"

No answer.

"Is it because he believes your lies?"

Now the spittle was showing white at the corner of Ross's mouth, and he was trembling with rage. I think it was all he could do to keep himself from striking me.

"Elias is my brother," he said. "I do not lie to him. He knows where these rabbits go."

"Then why not ask him to help?"

"What kind of a person are you, Mr. Givens?" There was acid in the doctor's voice. "Can you really be so cruel as you seem?"

"I'm thinking of Elias."

"Well then, think this of him, use your eyes and your brain to see him as he is," the doctor said. "Elias knows many things, many truths, and yet he chooses to live as if he did not know them. It is easier for him, and for me. I help him to live as he wishes. You can see for yourself that he is equipped to live no other way."

We continued on in silence. It seemed very clear to me that if Elias was incapable of surviving outside this sheltered, hothouse life, it was the doctor himself who was in large part to blame. I seethed with resentment but said nothing—one, because the doctor was angry enough at me already and I was afraid he'd have an apoplectic fit; and two, because we'd reached the dock, where a longshoreman type was waiting beside a small, battered launch. He took our crates and dropped them unceremoniously onto the deck of his boat, then folded his arms across his chest and glared at us impatiently. The doctor and I turned back toward the compound for our next load.

"Let me ask you a thing," Dr. Ross said when we were out of earshot of the dock. His outburst seem to have exhausted most of his anger. "Why do you suppose Elias wears these funny clothings, these suits from other times? Why, eh?"

I thought a moment. "He enjoys the fantasy, I guess. Dressing up."

"Yes, well, as I thought you would say. But not so, not so. He wears his grandfather's suits, yes, and his father's suits, because he can afford nothing else. Nothing else. We are very, very poor people. These rabbits, you see, they are our main source of income. Not pets—organic, range-bred game. And the fish Elias kills—it is not a hobby. We need the fish. Clothes, fish, rabbits—sustenance, you see, sustenance. But to Elias—he knows the truth, he prefers to believe the fantasy. Why should he not? Who are you to tell him differently?"

"But the reservation, surely—there are government subsidies, a casino . . . ?"

"For once and all, Mr. Givens, for once and all—there is no reservation, please! No Manapinock, no Siwanoy, no subsidies, no nothing. It is fantasy, purely. Turnaway is private property, mine and Elias's, jointly." We retrieved the remaining crates and headed back to the dock.

"So Elias isn't an Indian?" I asked, surprised to find myself a little disappointed. "No Lenape blood?"

"Maybe just a little, who knows?" the doctor acknowledged. "But not what he claims. It was his father, Andrew, who taught him the language and ways. But Andrew was an anthropologist, not an Indian. He learned it all from books and real Indians."

We walked the rest of the way to the dock in silence, which gave me some time to wrestle with my confusion. It was hard to know which version to believe. On the one hand, it was a lot easier to accept Dr. Ross's account of Turnaway than Elias's—after all, whoever heard of a tribe with one member? But then again, it had always seemed clear to me that Ross had his own agenda when it came to Elias and that he'd been trying to discredit Elias's ways and beliefs in my eyes from the very beginning. One thing, in any case, had been made very obvious by this whole issue—Elias was never going to be coaxed out of his shell while the doctor was around to browbeat him. I couldn't know what the doctor's game was, maybe, but he was certainly capable of lying to further his ends. I was never going to discover the truth by asking direct questions.

Back at the dock, we handed over our last crates, the doctor signed some papers, and we watched the launch pull away, carrying our bunnies to their fate. It wasn't until we were halfway back to the house that I cleared my throat tentatively.

"Dr. Ross," I asked casually, like I was just making conversation. "How much do you suppose Turnaway is worth?"

The doctor's bushy eyebrows shot up. "Worth?" he asked suspiciously.

"It's an island of, what, ten acres?"

"Twenty."

"A private island of twenty acres in New York City must be worth millions, wouldn't you think?"

"I have no idea."

"Really? You mean it's never been assessed? Not even for tax purposes?"

"One assesses a property one intends to sell, and I have no intention of selling. As for taxes, Turnaway has never paid. The island was sold to the city during the war of independence and awarded by George Washington himself to Elias's ancestor, John Hutchinson, for heroism at the Battle of Glover's Rock. This was the edge of wilderness then, not worth much."

"But now? You must have been tempted to sell. You must have had offers?"

We'd reached the house, and the doctor paused on the porch steps before heading for the door. "Really, Mr. Givens," he said stonily. "I find your conversation vulgar and annoying."

"You don't like me very much, do you?" I shouted at his back. Again, he stopped, turned around and fixed me with the weary gaze a teacher reserves for an eager but hopeless pupil.

"I like you fine, Mr. Givens. What you represent I abhor."

"I don't represent anything."

"Oh you do. You represent everything that is not Turnaway. You are what Elias calls a Mengwe."

"No I'm not."

And now the doctor sighed, his features set in such infinite lassitude that his entire face became a spider's web of wrinkles and crow's feet.

"Please now, for once, please just listen to someone's voice other than your own," he began. "You believe you know Elias. You think he is a simple person to understand. You know him for ten days, you know nothing. Nothing. I have no idea what you intend, but I wish you will be wise enough to leave him alone."

I had grown used to being woken up at some ungodly hour, but even so I was a little disoriented when Elias shook me awake in the pitch dark that night and told me to get dressed. I didn't bother to ask why since, whatever his reason, it would have been pointless to try to refuse him. There was a large silver moon in the sky, not quite full, and I figured we were going after some bit of wildlife you can only hunt by moonlight. Elias led me half asleep through the kitchen, out of the house, and down the path to the western jetty. From the slope of the beach where it fell away beneath the walkway, Elias dragged a canoe—a real old-fashioned Indian canoe with sweeping rounded ends and smooth wooden struts. He dragged it to the water's edge and shoved a paddle into my hand. We launched the vessel and I jumped in front. In a few minutes we were out on the bay, where the surface of the water in the moonlight looked like aluminum foil that had been crumpled and smoothed flat again. Elias showed me the right way to paddle, and despite my awkwardness we were soon leaving a creditably straight, rippling wake. The air was warm and moist, the dew already falling, and we paddled on through the night, the darkness broken only by a bright halogen beacon on the north shore of Hart Island, sliding away to our left. Elias leaned forward and tapped me on the shoulder, then pointed toward the light.

"My people used to bury our dead over there, on Hart Island," he whispered. "Now it's a refuse depot for discarded *wapsichik*."

"You ought to see Fresh Kills," I joked, but he ignored me. "Where are we going?"

"You'll see."

We paddled on quietly for some twenty minutes or so, heading in the direction of Orchard Beach, each of us lost in private thought. I was thinking about the dream Elias had described to me in the basement, the one where he goes back in time to change history and save the Indians. A dream like that, it was about everything I despised—nostalgia, wasted sentiment, false hope—and yet I had to admit I knew it well. I used to have a dream of my own like that, and out here in the silent bay in the dead of night it suddenly returned, unbidden, from the lost kingdom of childhood. On the surface of it, there wouldn't have seemed to be much in common between my dream and Elias's, only there was. They were both dreams about something that can never be taken back, something you have to live with for the rest of your life. I got to thinking that maybe every dream that ever was shares a common ancestor: the dream of the family that should have been. The difference between us was that Elias indulged dreams like that and I reviled them.

The Bronx shoreline was nearly upon us, lines of tiny breakers folding silver onto the beach in the moonlight. We came to a jutting headland to the north, black and ominous against the blue-black sky.

The canoe bottom scraped and squeaked against the pebbled beach as we glided straight ashore. Elias leaped from the canoe behind, his splash the loudest sound I'd heard in half an hour. Without a word he led me through thick bracken onto a steep uphill path. I was just able to make out a reflection of moonlight on his taut Achilles tendon—otherwise I'd have been lost in the murk. I stuck out my hands blindly and touched a smooth surface of stone to my left, which continued unbroken as we climbed. Our path was following the curve of a massive boulder. We hadn't gone far when Elias stopped abruptly and I walked straight into him.

"Shh," he said. "Don't move."

Now that he'd stopped walking, I could no longer see him at all. In order not to lose all my bearings, I looked straight up, where the crowns of the trees were outlined against the starless sky. I heard sounds, what seemed like a frantic rustling of dried grass, and a moment later the clash of striking stones accompanied by a little shower of bright sparks. In that split second, I was able to see Elias, on his knees, striking flints into a little pile of dessicated straw or grass. Two or three more attempts were enough to set the grass smoldering, and when the first tiny flames leapt up Elias scrambled for more grass, then twigs, then branches. Within two minutes he had a viable campfire going and I was able to make out our immediate surroundings. It was nothing special: a little clearing, no more than twelve paces across, with a dusty dirt floor, completely enclosed by thick woods on three sides, and on the fourth by the smooth boulder, which rose to a rounded summit some eight feet above. The moon rose and glowed in a patch of sky. The clearing was like one of those hidden places passed on from generation to generation of high school students, a place to meet and smoke and trade secrets and have sex in, though in the dark and silence of night it did have a kind of eerie tension about it.

"This is Wampage's grave," Elias said in an awed whisper.

"I thought it must be," I said.

"We're on Hunter's Island," he continued. "Most of the old Siwanoy from Lapechwahacking are buried here."

"Uh-huh."

There was a silence and I had the distinct impression that Elias was expecting me to come up with something a little more dramatic to mark the occasion. Old bones and ancestors don't generally inspire me, but I did my best. I cleared my throat.

"Are you going to conjure up his spirit or something?"

I don't suppose I got it quite right, because there was another long pause before Elias answered. He was facing away from the fire, directly toward the boulder, so I couldn't see the expression on his face.

"No," he said coldly. "We don't do things like that. In fact, I'm not even supposed to pronounce the name of a dead man at night, in case his spirit grows lonely and answers the summons. The only reason I can say 'Wampage' is because it's so different from the original that he would never recognize it."

"I see."

We sat there for ten minutes before another word was spoken. I fed the fire with any piece of deadwood at hand and stretched myself out along the dirt, my hands behind my head, staring up at the moon and listening to the flames. Elias continued facing the rock wall, and though he was still and quiet, I had the feeling he was praying. Finally, as if there'd been no interruption in our conversation, he gazed skyward and spoke. His eyes were completely swallowed up in the shadows cast by his cheekbones.

"But I do talk to him sometimes," he said. "Not that he answers."

"What do you tell him?"

"Oh, this and that," he said sheepishly, rocking his head back and forth. "I tell him about my troubles, sometimes. It can be a difficult situation, mine, but so was his. I feel he can empathize. Not that I complain, mind you, that would never do in a *kihkai*. And of course I tell him about the Mahkohkwe."

"The mack . . . ?"

"Mahkohkwe. Mahkohkwe, Ben. Do you never listen to my stories? I told you about her. The Red Woman."

"Oh, yes, yes, that. The one who's going to be the mother of your tribe?"

"Precisely. I tell Wampage all I know of her. How I hope she'll get here soon. What she looks like."

"Maybe it's not my place," I began hesitantly. "But these old legends, you know, they don't always pan out."

Elias turned to me now for the first time, a look of incredulity on his face. "You really don't listen to me, do you, Ben?" he said. "I told you, the Mahkohkwe is not some 'old legend.' She's a real woman."

"I know that's what you want to believe, but—"

"Not believe. I know she's real. I've seen her. Did you think she was foretold, like something out of one of your medieval romances? Did you really think I'd believe in something like that? No—she's a real person. I saw her about two years ago on Manapinock, on the dock. The most beautiful woman I'd ever seen, I'll never forget her. And she was an Indian, without a doubt. I called her Mahkohkwe then, for red is the color of peace and love."

"She was on Turnaway? Did you talk to her?"

"I never had the opportunity. I was wearing my *sakutakan*. I ran upstairs to change and by the time I'd returned she was gone. No trace. I asked Ross but he hadn't seen her. You know, we get trespassers on Manapinock all the time—sightseers, real estate developers, that sort of thing. I have no idea who she was or what she was doing on Manapinock, but I do know this. She is the Mahkohkwe and someday I shall find her and make her mine."

"How do you expect to find her, cooped up on Turnaway?"

"I don't know, Ben. I don't know." I'd never heard him sound so desperate, so helpless.

"You're going to have to figure it out."

"Yes."

There had been a moment, early in my stay on Turnaway, when I'd imagined I understood what had brought me there. Now, suddenly, I was sure.

Two nights later, I stood on the balcony of my room. It was a lovely late summer's evening, balmy and breezy. A lurid sun was turning the sky to milky red. There was just enough moisture in the air to make the distant vision of Manhattan shimmy and waver, its glass and concrete as insubstantial as a projection on a cotton sheet. After just two weeks on Turnaway, it had never seemed so far away to me in all my life. It was difficult to imagine walking its streets again, breathing its air.

Dr. Ross had been right about one thing: I was wrong to imagine that I knew Elias and how he thought, and now I knew just how wrong I'd been. When a diver looks up through the depths at a world of undulating docks, pulsing shorelines, and billowing houses, he knows they're really solid, that it's only the medium he's seeing them through that makes them appear tenuous and insubstantial. Elias saw things differently—he was the fish, unaware of the water in which he moved. If the world overhead seemed unreal and incorporeal compared to his own, then that's the way it was. Manhattan wavered and shifted in the distance because it was just so much gossamer. The only solid ground, the only foundation on which he could walk and live without its giving way beneath his feet, was here on Turnaway. That was the lesson I'd spent the past two days learning—the one that I was playing back now, over and over, trying to understand how I could have been so stupidly, disastrously mistaken.

As far as I could make out, my problem was that, despite everything I found so unreasonable and pathetic about Elias's way of life, I'd really come to like him over the past weeks. I remember what I said about "nice" people, and it still holds true, but Elias was an exception. Unlikely as it seems, we'd become friends. On Hunter's Island, he'd reached out for me like a person in need. I don't have much experience in that area, but I'm sure I heard him do it. Still, the big mistake—and maybe I'm not the first person in history to have made it—was in thinking that just because I liked him, I knew him. Because I thought I knew him, I thought I could influence him. And because I thought I could influence him, I took matters into my own hands. And there it was, the moral of the story: never try to help someone who doesn't ask for help.

My friend. It's true I liked him, and who wouldn't? He didn't have a mean bone in his body; he could be funny, attentive, intelligent, big-hearted, even inspiring at times. He was loyal, patient, generous to a fault. But the fact is, a lot of people share those quirks to a certain degree; if you had to give your time and attention to every Pollyanna who came along, where would that get you? In any case, it's not a person's qualities that make you want to help him, it's his foibles—and that's where I try to draw the line. Other people's addictions, insecurity, and self-loathing don't generally inspire much philanthropy in me—in fact, to my mind, the do-gooder's attraction to other people's weaknesses is one of the most pathetic weaknesses of all. But in Elias I'd come across something new, something so grotesque and threatening that it was impossible to ignore: his helpless innocence. It was an insult to me and a defiance of all my values. It had irked and provoked me from the beginning; gradually it had come to frighten me; now, I'd become determined to strip him of it. It wasn't his fault; it had been forced on him and I couldn't blame him for it. Nevertheless, it had become a real and immediate danger to him, like a dormant virus suddenly awakening. So help me god, I never wanted to save anyone in my life until I met Elias.

It was that damned "project" of his that started it all. Despite everything I've said, I would probably have let it all slide if it wasn't for that project. I'd have been saddened, maybe, by Elias's plight; I'd have dreamed up wild, impractical schemes; I'd have felt frustrated and helpless; but in the end I'd probably have just thrown up my hands at a bad situation and kept my nose out of it, like I usually do. But there was something about that project that pushed me over the edge—it was a rebuke and a challenge. You don't wave a red flag in front of a bull unless you're looking for action, and you don't show me a model of Manhattan covered with trees and babbling brooks if you're not ready to face the consequences.

And so it was that the very morning after our excursion to Hunter's Island, I cornered Dr. Ross in the dining room while Elias was still upstairs changing out of his hunting garb.

"Dr. Ross," I said hesitantly, as if the idea had only that second crossed my mind. "I'd like to put something to you."

"Hmm?" He was already suspicious.

I hesitated once more, then took the plunge. "I'd like to invite Elias to stay with me awhile. In the city. Kind of like a reciprocal visit."

The doctor stopped with a segment of grapefruit halfway to his lips and stared up at me with a perfectly sincere facsimile of wide-eyed amazement. "You are joking surely" was all he said.

"Not at all."

"It is out of the question," he dismissed me and resumed his breakfast.

"Why?"

The doctor grudgingly folded his newspaper and glanced at the ceiling before replying. "You have scolded me once already for making Elias's decisions. Now I say the same to you, Mr. Givens—why not ask Elias himself?" He'd timed the question just right for Elias to hear as he scampered through the door, dressed in tennis whites.

"Ask me what?" he chirped as he set upon his oatmeal.

"Nothing," I muttered. "We'll discuss it later." Elias shrugged cheerfully.

After breakfast, I brought him up to the widow's walk to get him away from the lowering, oppressive presence of Dr. Ross. I wanted to be up-front and candid with him: I would invite him to my apartment for the weekend. That seemed innocuous enough, hard to refuse without being rude. But when I put it to him, like the doctor he dismissed the offer with an incredulous laugh. "No, really, think, what could I possibly do in the city?" And he flicked his wrist toward its shining towers as if to say they meant no more to him than the termite hills of Botswana.

"What are you so afraid of? You used to go when you were a kid, didn't you?"

"I'm not a child anymore. And it is beneath the dignity of a Lenape warrior to go out in search of gratuitous thrills."

After that, I brought in my heavy guns. I worked him over good, citing all the pleasures and services of the city that I thought would most appeal to him: theaters, museums (the Museum of the American Indian, for instance), galleries, parks (such as Inwood, with its Indian caves), libraries, zoos, and so on. All wasted wind. He had everything he needed on Turnaway.

"When I was eighteen," he told me in all sincerity, "and I was considering what to do with myself, I had a revelation of sorts that changed my life."

"What was that?" I asked.

"That I should go on living exactly as I had always done. And that is precisely what I intend to do."

"That's a big mistake, Elias. I think you should learn some independence, how to get along in the world. I could show you that."

"But why should I? What use is it to me?"

We waited patiently for a 727 to pass on over the bay. "You never know what might happen," I continued. "You should be prepared. You've got to learn to stand alone."

"What could possibly happen, Ben? You're not making any sense."

"What about your Macocky? How're you ever going to find her if you don't go out into the world?"

"Let the Mahkohkwe be my concern, why don't you," Elias said peevishly, pursing his lips as he turned away.

We went swimming. I stayed close to shore, quietly observing Elias. He made no further mention of our conversation, but I hadn't expected him to. Instead, predictably, he clammed up on the whole episode. This was typical of him: whenever you asked him an uncomfortable question, or pointed out some inconsistency, or in any way threatened to burst his bubble, he got all flustered. He had a way of pretending to be so absorbed in whatever he was doing (usually something physical such as swimming or precision craftsmanship) that he couldn't possibly talk to you, let alone find time to fret over unpleasant topics. As long as he looked happy and distracted, he figured you could never believe he was preoccupied; before long he'd convince himself that he'd forgotten whatever was bothering him. He was like a child who starts playing more frantically when he hears his mother calling—the kid thinks it's a great act, but Mom isn't fooled. That's what Elias was doing with me now: he was playing the fool in the water, diving below the surface and staying under until he thought I might be frightened, blowing waterspouts like a whale, slapping the waves in mock panic, swimming way out to the barrier buoys and hailing passing boaters. That's where he was when I heard the sound of heavy footfalls in the woods behind me. I turned, expecting to see Dr. Ross come to call us in for lunch.

But it wasn't Ross. At first I saw nothing, but then the bushes began to rustle and shake; a moment later they were roughly shoved aside and a man emerged from the undergrowth. He was dressed in brown from toe to head: brown leather work boots; brown utility slacks; a brown T-shirt; a sleeveless vest of padded nylon, like the inner lining of a parka; and a brown baseball cap. The vest and the cap carried official-looking seals—they looked like City of New York but I couldn't tell for sure at that distance. In his right hand he held a plumb bob and one end of a tape measure, the other end of which disappeared into the undergrowth. A theodolite and tripod hung from his right shoulder. He was looking at the ground and seemed to be pacing off a distance. He was completely oblivious of me, as all but my head was submerged beneath the water some twenty feet away; I paddled quietly behind a rock for extra security and watched him from there.

He stopped just short of the waterline and aimed the plumb bob over some invisible landmark, with the tape at eye level. When the bob had stopped swinging and was almost perfectly still, he shouted "clamp!" and, when answered a moment later by another "clamp!," dropped the bob. A few seconds later, he was joined by another man, identically dressed, who reeled in the tape as he approached. They were both in their mid-thirties and a little overweight. The first man was partially balding and wore heavy, black-frame glasses. I knew right away that I'd seen him before. It was the guy I'd seen a week earlier, talking furtively with Dr. Ross down by the dock. He'd been dressed in a suit that time, but the glasses were unmistakable.

"I make it one twenty-seven," the second man told him.

"Good."

They stood silently, hands on their hips, facing away from me into the heart of the woods. The balding one took a handkerchief from his back pocket, wiped his brow and dome, blew his nose, then returned the handkerchief to its pocket.

"True metes and bounds in six weeks?" he asked the other.

"Most of the bearing trees standing. Here's one now."

"Monumentation's good."

"I can do it. I can do it."

They moved off again into the woods. When I was no longer able to hear their crashing and stomping—these guys made me sound like Bambi—I crept up out of the water and approached what one of them had called a "bearing tree." It was a big old chestnut. I ran my fingers over its gnarled surface. At chest height, a rectangle about the size of my shoe had been hewn out of the bark and into the living wood. Within the rectangle, running top to bottom, were carved the letters E4BT. This, too, I recognized from my former life in the civil service. It was a surveyor's bearing, used to demarcate corners on a plot of land being surveyed or prepared for development, and it was relatively new. It seemed to me that maybe I'd just witnessed something important, but I had no time to think it through. Elias, having sneaked up behind me, snapped the elastic on my bathing suit then plunged laughing back into the water.

For the rest of the day, we went about our usual business, but I was only going through the motions. I swam, ate, chatted, attended to Elias's lessons, but my thoughts were completely taken up with the implications of what I'd seen that morning. As far as I could tell, Elias hadn't noticed the strangers; if he had, he was doing a good job of pretending otherwise. That afternoon, he instructed me in the preparation of clay for firing in a pit. He took me down into a clearing in the woods where he'd already prepared a hole in the ground, a fire pit, and lumps of raw clay. My mind was busy elsewhere: Who were those men, and what had they been doing on Turnaway?

"The best rocks for firing are to be found in a streambed. You should select stones of the same size, and they must be well rounded and smooth. Otherwise they could explode when heated, with potentially lethal effect. . . ."

They were surveyors, that much was certain—the theodolite and plumb bob gave them away. I'd barely understood a word they'd said, but it was also pretty clear that they were surveying Turnaway, or at least part of it—the bearing carved into the tree testified to that. It had seemed relatively fresh, but not brand-new, so they, or someone like them, had been snooping around here before, taking measurements. Who did they work for? Their insignia had seemed to peg them as city employees, but they'd really been too far away for me to say for sure, and anyway lots of company logos are designed to look governmental. Still, there was one other thing I knew with relative certainty: these guys were no trespassers. I'd seen one of them on Turnaway before, talking to Dr. Ross. He knew they were around, they probably had his consent to be there, and if so, he had to know what they were doing. But he'd never mentioned their visits to Elias or me.

"When the rocks are white hot, you arrange them along the sides of the pit, in an even layer one stone thick, so that the heat is distributed evenly and concentrated in the center of the pit. You then cover the stones with grass and leaves to cushion the air-hardened pottery, and pad the spaces in between with moss. Finally, add more grass, then fill in the pit with earth. . . ."

There was any number of innocent explanations for the presence of surveyors on Turnaway. Probably they were just there for the Geological Survey, plotting the island for topographical maps. Or maybe they worked for the municipal or state fiscal units, charting the island for tax evaluation. They could have been hydroengineers, measuring the water table for future well-drilling, or oilmen determining how far their pipeline would have to be rerouted around this private island to some terminal in the South Bronx. Any of these explanations might be the right one, but none of them explained why Ross had kept their visits a secret.

"A traditional Lenape cooking pot, *siskuwahus,* was designed like a Roman amphora, with pointed or rounded bottoms, so that it had to be propped up in the fire or in the storage pits. However, by the mid-sixteenth century, ongoing commerce and warfare with the Iroquois had had a strong influence on traditional design and technology, so that . . ."

It was true I didn't care much for the doctor myself, and he'd bared his antipathy to me at every opportunity. He was cold, unresponsive, secretive, and I had no reason to love him or even to regard him with vague indifference. Except that his sun obviously rose and set for Elias. It was hard to believe that Dr. Ross could be involved in anything that ran counter to Elias's interests. He may not have been the warmest guy in the world or much given to displays of tenderness, but there was no doubt in my mind that his inscrutability was like that of a lioness, always tense and coiled and ready to spring in defense of her young.

At the same time, one valuable lesson I'd picked up early in life was that when you're feeling suspicious or think you're being played for a fool, you can be pretty sure it's paranoia; it's always when you're blithely going about your business that someone is giving you the shaft. And how much truer would that be for poor Elias, as vulnerable as any nestling when the folks were out hunting for worms. Unlike Elias, I couldn't just pretend to be unaware of the strange and mysterious goings-on around me. And I don't just mean the surveyors. I mean, too, the way Dr. Ross, regardless of what he was doing, always made sure to get to the mail first; the way he always turned his back and spoke in whispers when he was on the telephone; how he sat at his desk late into the night and sent the scratching of his fountain pen echoing through the darkened house; his unexplained absences on the mainland. I mean how Elias never received any mail, correspondence, or paperwork of the kind that home ownership usually entails. For Elias's sake, I wanted desperately to give Dr. Ross the benefit of the doubt. But now more than ever I had doubts of my own. Brother, father, protector: Is anyone really that selfless?

"You haven't heard a word I've been saying, have you, Ben?" Elias said in the tone of a vexed but indulgent tutor.

"No, I'm sorry. I was somewhere else. Let's go for a walk."

We set off downhill through the woods and moss beds, then turned left onto a path that would take us along the shore of the island to the dock. As we strolled, my eye began picking out surveyor's bearings that I'd never noticed before. Suddenly they seemed to be everywhere, at least one marked tree in sight at any given step, like closed-circuit cameras in a department store. The bearings were at eye level, clearly etched. Even though I was seeing them for the first time, it was almost impossible to imagine that Elias, with his sharp vision and intimate knowledge of these woods, had failed to spot them up to now. Still, I didn't say a word.

"What's bothering you, Ben?" Elias finally asked.

"Oh, nothing. Well yes. I'm worried about you, Elias."

"Not that again," he snorted.

"I'm serious. What would you do if you had to make it on your own? How would you survive?"

Elias paused thoughtfully before answering. I thought I'd finally reached him on some level. "I don't mean this unkindly, Ben," he said, "but I don't believe you have much to teach me about being a man. And since you mention it, I might ask you the same question. You have no job. You have no responsibilities. You have a secure income. What makes you qualified to lecture me on independence?"

"That's different. I had to struggle my whole life to find out what I didn't want. That's how it works in the real world. It's a luxury you have to earn."

"But in the end, after all that noble struggle, you only achieved your independence by accident."

"And that's exactly what I want to help you avoid. I was ready for it when it came, but you're not. Your father didn't do you any favors, leaving you stranded on this rock."

"I'm at home, you know, not in exile."

"What's the difference?"

We'd made the circuit of the island and reached the house. We sat on the lawn, gazing out at nothing in particular. It was one of those late summer afternoons in New York that leave you dozy and slightly intoxicated. We said nothing more as we watched the traffic jam on the Throgs Neck Bridge through a haze of rippling smog banks and flashes of chrome, sounding like a distant cattle drive. A few wisps of reddening cirrus lingered torpidly overhead. The sun balanced for one brief moment on the tip of the Empire State's radio tower, like a beach ball on the nose of a seal. Only the birds were gathering their energies for the dying day, chattering and swooping above the lawn for their evening meal. Only the birds, and me: we had plans for tonight.

Dinner—pork chops, boiled potatoes, and sauerkraut—was eaten in unusual silence. There was a tension that connected us and kept us apart, like guy ropes holding up a tent, evenly distributed and mutually balanced. Elias, I could tell, was deeply upset by the atmosphere in the room, enough at any rate to dampen his usual chatter. His glum silence cast a pall over the entire meal, and we were all glad to escape from the gloom and mustiness of the dining room to the views of the front porch, where Manhattan appeared as a black silhouette tonight before the crimson afterglow of the sunset and a fragrant coolness was just beginning to rise off the lawn. But even here, as we sipped our drinks, Elias and I couldn't manage to shake our oppression. The way friends do, we were wordlessly communicating our respective moods, feeding off each other's state of mind and sinking fast into blue funks. And when the doctor joined us after finishing the dishes and established his trollish presence in the corner, we all just gave up the evening for lost. It couldn't have been much past nine, and the sky barely dark, when Elias and I went up to our rooms, while the doctor remained downstairs to "see to some papers."

I had a lot of time to kill. The doctor didn't usually switch off the living-room light or begin his slow ascent up the stairs until sometime past one A.M. Even then, if the heat or a bad dream found me awake an hour or two later, I might often hear the sound of his shuffling or the whine of the faucet in his room down the hall. Playing it safe would mean waiting at least until three, and better until four, but I wasn't sleepy. Reading was impossible. I sat on my balcony for a while, looking out across the Sound and the darkened promontories of Connecticut, watching the occasional silent passage of a glittering yacht or a throbbing freighter to our south. The night was cool and, in early September, the cicadas were silent. I soon developed a dull ache in my hips from propping my feet on the railing. So I went inside, turned down the light, lowered the speed of the ceiling fan, and lay on the bed watching the lazy sweep of its blades fence with the shadows of moths attacking and clinging to the window screen. The hours passed. At four I rose, put on my slippers, and used my elementary command of the "Indian creep" to get me downstairs without raising the dead—or, I hoped especially, the living.

Knowing the way old people sleep, I wouldn't take it for granted that I could accomplish my mission without rousing the doctor. I prepared for the possibility of being caught. At the bottom of the stairs, instead of continuing on to the library, I turned right and down the hall to the kitchen, where I opened the refrigerator door and was temporarily blinded by its light. Since the doctor's room was directly overhead, I knew that if he got up he would see the light reflected on the grass beneath his window; if he was disturbed by a creaking floorboard, he would hear the hum of the ancient compressor and assume that someone was in the kitchen. And if I detected any movement upstairs, I'd have time to dash across the library and through the WC that connected it to the kitchen; I could be leaning innocently into the depths of the icebox by the time anyone reached me. Now, I retraced my steps past the stairs and made straight for the captain's desk in the library where the doctor took care of his paperwork. I felt safe enough to switch on the old gunmetal desk lamp by which he usually worked. I opened the flap and peered into the bowels of the desk.

Its interior was divided into compartments, drawers, shelves, and pigeonholes. As I might have expected, the papers were highly, almost obsessively organized—not one loose chit or receipt, not one wayward pen, not one piece of junk mail the doctor had forgotten to discard. To the left was an old Fairfield Yacht Club mug, its handle long gone, filled with sharpened pencils; to the right, a crystal inkwell brimming with India ink, and next to it, a trough in which lay a classic Mont Blanc of tortoiseshell and silver. Behind these was a rack of pigeonholes containing envelopes and stationery of various sizes; to the left of these, another row of compartments filled with correspondence, neatly classified.

The first compartment, working from right to left, contained paid bills, the second unpaid. The paid bills were scrupulously marked with the date, amount, and check number of payment in Dr. Ross's elegant Germanic script. They were the usual sort of thing: Con Ed, telephone, heating oil, credit card. The doctor had a $600 limit but his charges that month amounted to just one $47 purchase at Sears, Eastchester. No invoices from real estate developers, engineers, drilling companies, or anything of the sort. The next slot held copies of invoices, paid and unpaid, billed to Athos Fine Meats. The invoices were handwritten by the doctor on heavy rag stationery with the letterhead "Turnaway Island, New York, New York." I was surprised to find that the household took in almost $500 a month from the bunny business, more than I'd thought but still little enough to keep them well below the poverty line if, as the doctor claimed, this was really their only source of income.

The third slot contained correspondence from the New York State Department of Agriculture and Markets, dealing with certification and health standards for the doctor's "livestock husbandry enterprise." The most recent letter referred to the results of an unannounced inspection that had apparently taken place in May. The inspectors had found only minor violations of the code and there was nothing here that had anything to do with surveying, but still the letter had a funny effect on me. It was dated May 13, the very week I'd bought the *Spirit of New York*. It had been written before I'd ever even heard of Turnaway, and I found myself oddly moved by the image of life on the island going on normally without me. So recent, and yet we'd been complete strangers to each other.

The next slot also had only one letter in it, bearing the letterhead of a Manhattan law firm. It was dated from the previous November and addressed to Dr. Joseph Ross.

Dear Dr. Ross,

As per our conversation of the 4th, I am confirming that Yarden, Balin & Browne will require a retainer of $5,000 to initiate action in the matter we discussed. Because of the value of the real property you claim, I am sorry to inform you that we cannot consider your request to provide you with our legal services on a pro bono basis.

Please feel free to write or call me if you have any further questions.

Sincerely,
E. Praeger

I returned the letter to its slot, no wiser than before but far more curious. This could be something and it could just as easily be meaningless, but a $5,000 retainer was nothing to sneeze at. It wasn't easy to imagine what kind of circumstance, here on bucolic Turnaway, could possibly call for such an expense. A real estate transaction, maybe? I moved on to the next and final compartment in the desk.

Two letters from the Corporation Counsel of the City of New York. The first went back to the previous September.

Dear Dr. Ross,

The first hearing concerning the striking of Turnaway Island from the Register of National Historic Monuments will be held in New

York County Courthouse at 1 Foley Square at 10 A.M. on December 12. As I told you, you are not required to be there but it would be very much in your interest to do so. If you do expect to attend the hearing and to make a statement, may I suggest that you be represented by legal counsel.

Sincerely,
Jay Habner

The second was dated August 15, only a week before I washed up on Turnaway's beach.

Dear Dr. Ross,

As we discussed last night, Henry Gonzalez and Peter Giardino will meet with you on September 20 to discuss preliminary topological and geological surveying of Turnaway Island. You can schedule the dates directly with them. When we have a true metes and bounds description of TI, I will be happy to share all the results of the survey with you.

I'll be in touch.

Sincerely,
Jay Habner

I flipped through the checkbook stubs. There was no record to indicate that the doctor had ever paid the $5,000 retainer, and no incriminating evidence of any other kind either. That was the full content of the desk. There were three drawers under the flap, but they were locked. I had little experience as a lock picker, but I decided to try my hand at it anyway. I looked around for an appropriate tool and my eye fell on a loose brad wedged in the crack between two floorboards. It was as I was crouching to pick it up that I saw Elias, leaning against a column at the entrance to the room. There was no telling how long he'd been there.

"I couldn't sleep," I said lamely. "I was looking for something to read."

I'd made my pathetic excuse, but it was obvious that Elias was a lot more flustered and embarrassed than I was. His face was bright red, and he fidgeted crazily with the belt of his flannel bathrobe. It was as if he was the one who owed an apology, and he couldn't come up with a convincing one.

"I was downstairs," he stammered. "With the project. I heard something. Thought you were Ross. Bed now. Good night." He disappeared up the stairs. I gave him enough time to reach his bedroom, then followed him up. I threw myself on my bed and stared sleeplessly at the ceiling fan.

I hadn't gone through the doctor's papers looking for anything specific, and it was easy enough to admit that I'd found nothing conclusive—no "smoking gun," as they say, no contracts, no receipts, no indication of any agreements of any sort. Ross seemed to trust Elias enough not to hide his business documents, but with me around anything dubious would probably be kept in a locked drawer. Even so, a skeptical mind accustomed to suspicion doesn't need much evidence to incriminate. And like I said, I hadn't found much, but I'd sure found something. I'd found a phrase.

The striking of Turnaway Island from the Register of National Historic Monuments. It may not have been smoking, or even a gun, but it was a weapon of some sort if you looked at it the right way. I'd had no idea that Turnaway was a national historic monument. Nothing about the place was particularly monumental, the decrepit old manor least of all. Still, I figured there must be hundreds of cases like this, forgotten corners all over the country that found their way onto the Register for obscure reasons decades ago, through graft or incompetence. One thing I did know, however, is that a national historic monument can't be developed just any old how, even if it stands on private property. There are all sorts of codes and standards governing the least alteration to the property, and I was pretty sure they would not allow for any kind of wholesale development of the island. If someone wanted to turn Turnaway into a luxury marina, say, or a bonded warehouse, or a theme park, he'd certainly have to start by getting it struck from the Register. No doubt a long and costly process, involving lawyers and courts. Say, then, that this hypothetical developer managed to have the property struck from the Register: What would be the first step toward development, once the property was redesignated? Surveyors? And after? Hadn't I heard Giardino or

Gonzalez say something about needing the survey done in six weeks? What was going to happen in six weeks? Bulldozers? Demolition crews? Condos?

Granted it was almost five in the morning, I hadn't slept, and my mind was overwrought. Even so, it seemed like a logical series of deductions. I may be a cynic but I'm not usually susceptible to conspiracy theories. As I lay in bed, then, the certainty grew within me, grew and hardened and burned like a kidney stone: Dr. Ross was up to no good, and Elias needed to be warned. Once I'd gotten that straight in my head, once every suspicion had been funneled into that one simple proposition, I fell asleep. I woke up only three hours later in dazzling sunlight, my left cheek bathed in a pool of accumulated saliva and sweat.

Elias and I had long since come to an agreement about the morning hunt, which usually began around five-thirty: if I wasn't able to rouse myself without his help, he should go ahead without me. By now, judging from the sun's height above Long Island, he'd finished the hunt, imprisoned his captives, showered and dressed, and was just about ready for his breakfast. I heard the muted clatter of crockery downstairs as the doctor set the table. I heard Elias's bedroom door open and close and his light-footed tread on the stairs. I had a cold shower, ran a comb through my hair, dressed hurriedly. I took a deep breath and went down to join my hosts for breakfast.

Elias was telling the doctor about his dream. ". . . it looked like the *Half Moon*, and it was burning in the bay, and sinking. But as we came closer I realized it wasn't the *Half Moon*. It was Turnaway House, sinking and burning. . . . Good morning, Ben."

I ate my grapefruit in silence as Elias continued his account of the dream, baroque and tedious. Typically, he was pretending that our encounter in the middle of the night had never happened—not the slimmest reference or ironic inflection to indicate that anything unpleasant had occurred. As usual, the doctor kept his eyes on his plate as he listened. I watched for any sign that he'd been tipped off, but since he always behaved as if he suspected me of every dirty trick, it was impossible to say. In any case, again, nothing out of the ordinary. When Elias was finished, it was my turn. I made up a story of a sound night's sleep and of being attacked by Peter Stuyvesant in a wet suit, which I knew would please him. We finished breakfast, changed, and strolled down to the beach. It wasn't until we'd drawn ourselves out of the water and lay sunning on a large, smooth boulder, and when I knew from experience that Elias would be feeling a little dopey, that I made my move.

"I saw a couple of guys walking around the island the other day," I said nonchalantly. "Any idea who they were?"

"Trespassers, I suppose. We get them from time to time." He was playing dumb, but I knew immediately from his tone of voice that he'd seen them, too. With his hunter's eye and instincts, he was incredibly perceptive; if he'd seen them, as I was now sure he had, he'd certainly have noticed their instruments. How, then, could he have helped wondering about their presence on his terrritory, just as I had? But he'd prefer to beat himself into the ground and twist logic into pretzels rather than admit to himself that he'd seen and understood what he'd seen.

"They were surveyors, Elias. *Surveyors.* What were they doing here?" Elias leapt to his feet and began pacing the surface of the boulder like a caged leopard.

"How should I know?"

"They weren't trespassing, Elias. They were doing whatever they'd been hired to do. Now you didn't invite them here, so who did? *Who* knows what they were doing?"

Elias dived into the water and swam to the farthest buoy. He hauled himself halfway onto it and bobbed there, staring out across the water toward New Rochelle. I'd never been so confrontational with him, and I'd done it on purpose. If I beat about the bush or tried to spare his feelings, he'd be certain to find a way of avoiding the issue. But this wasn't something he could drive from his mind with a five-minute rumpus, that was certain. I waited. Sure enough, he soon pushed himself from the buoy and swam toward shore in a paced, pensive backstroke. He stopped some ten feet from the rocky beach, where the water reached to his hips, but crouched so that only his head was above water when he turned and spoke.

"Wouldn't you like to tell me what you're thinking, Ben?"

"I'd just like to ask you a few questions."

"You can ask them," he said warily.

"Elias, who really owns Turnaway?"

"Well, the tribe does."

"Besides the tribe. What about Ross? What's his stake in it?"

"He has no stake because he's not a member of the tribe."

"Why not?"

"He never applied, and besides he'd never get in. You have to prove you're at least one-eighth Indian, and he's an Austrian Jew from way back."

"Did you ever sign a proxy? Was there maybe something in your father's will?"

"Ben, does this have anything to do with last night?"

I sighed. I'd been trying to avoid this. I'd wanted to guide the conversation, force Elias to come to his own conclusions so he wouldn't need to hear it from someone else's mouth, especially mine. But he'd anticipated me and now I had no choice. He wouldn't want to hear it—I knew that from the start—but he'd have to. He had no choice either.

So I told him everything I knew and suspected. I told him about the surveyors and the mysterious phone calls. I told him about the strangers I'd seen with Ross on the launch. I told him how Ross had tried to warn or scare me away from the day I first washed up on the beach. I told him about the letters and the lawyers and the city agencies. I told him about the National Historic Register. I told him everything. He never moved from his spot in the water.

"Now I'm not saying I understand what's going on," I concluded breathlessly, trying to end it as quickly as possible. "Maybe it's nothing. But *something* is going on, Elias, and you're being kept in the dark. All I'm saying is, you should ask Dr. Ross about it. Get some straight answers. Of course it's up to you, but you're going to have to take some responsibility. You've got to take charge of your life, before it's too late."

He remained motionless for a while, submerged now up to his nostrils, contemplating me like a crocodile. Then he kicked off from the bottom and spread himself into a full back float, arms and legs akimbo. He blew a gentle spout of water from his mouth, the way swimmers do, and his body turned gently on the momentum from his kickoff. From that moment until the end of our conversation, he remained in that position, on his back, eyes skyward, wrists twisting in lazy paddling circles, and rotating slowly like a pinwheel in a gentle breeze.

"You're planning to leave Turnaway tomorrow, aren't you, Ben?" The question was put serenely, musingly, and took me completely by surprise.

"I am?"

"Yes, I think you are. Well, I'd like to tell you something before you leave, and I wish you would listen carefully to it. Ross has been my brother and my father ever since I was orphaned. My real father loved him like his own son. He has seen me to manhood with no thought for his own comfort. He has maintained the house and property against all odds, with his hands and his ingenuity, where lesser men would have been content to let it fall into utter ruin long ago. He has devoted his entire life and soul to me. So now listen when I tell you that it is perfectly impossible—*impossible*—that he should have done or planned to do anything at all to harm me or Manapinock. It is simply not possible. I trust him more than I trust myself. With my life. And when you and your kind have long since disappeared, he'll be there, always. Do you understand me? He is worth a thousand of you. You can't even imagine what it might be like to love the way he loves. You Mengwe." He scissored his legs and was propelled out toward the buoys, beyond earshot of the shore.

My last evening on Turnaway should have been the best of all, sampling cocktails on the porch with my new and future friend as we watched the sun set, again, reviewing the pleasures of our vacation together, looking forward to those to come, and later, out of the doctor's earshot, cementing our friendship with a final story and a manly embrace on the widow's walk, with the great metropolis at our feet. Instead, Elias had avoided me for the rest of the day and I hadn't had the stomach to show up for dinner. I heard it going on downstairs, the scrape of cutlery and an occasional muffled voice rising through the floorboards. I'm sure there was a place set there for me, unwelcome as I now was in Turnaway House, but there was no room for a Mengwe at the table.

The next morning found me alone with the doctor at breakfast. It was standard procedure for him to hide behind the paper, as he was doing now, but it felt even more like a snub this morning—and a particularly triumphant one—than it had on others. Afterward, I went upstairs to pack. When that was done I sat on my bed and held my breath, trying to pinpoint Elias's whereabouts in the house or on the grounds by the noises he'd normally be making at this time of day. But I heard no creaking of floorboards, no splashing of water, no crackling of fire, no hoeing of soil, no tearing of fabric. The house seemed to have been deserted by all but the grandfather clock in the front hall, ticking off the increments of my betrayal. A breeze awakened a loose shutter outside the kitchen, and it coughed. A tile settled with a sigh into a more comfortable position on the roof. Two squirrels quarreled over an acorn in the forest canopy. And then a two-engined jetliner began its banking descent into La Guardia. I rose with my bags and trudged heavily down to the dock without encountering a soul. I waited an hour, dangling my legs above the water and kicking my heels against a rotten pylon, until Felicia came to carry me home.

The graveyard shift at a Wall Street law office pays a lot better than the civil service and even more than I'd banked on. I could work as many hours as I wanted, and often did twelve at a stretch. Nobody bothered me or wanted to be my friend—nobody is anybody's friend in a law office at four A.M. Report early, clean starched shirt every day, reports triple-proofread, perfect courtesy to my superiors, initiative, enthusiasm, last one home every morning—in a month, I'd already earned enough to buy a better second-hand dinghy than the *Spirit of New York* ever was, or to make a down payment on a new sailboat. Data processing, I discovered, is easy, impersonal, and sometimes exactly what a man needs to clear his head. It made me regret all those wasted years in the civil service even more poignantly.

It's very easy to fall back on old habits. Everything was so familiar and comforting: the sitcoms, the Chinese food, the big, empty double bed, the privacy, the late mornings. There had even been an anonymous message on my machine to welcome me home from

Turnaway: "You are a sick fuck." That was auspicious, to say the least. I was home.

As a kid, all I ever wanted was what everyone else had. I didn't want fancy cars or superhuman powers, like my friends did. Sometimes I'd walk down the street and see some bland, white-bread kind of guy in a business suit—that's the guy I wanted to be. I envied his normal life, uncomplicated thoughts, and simple worries. It didn't seem like a lot to ask for, but I had to work harder than most to get it. The civil service exam was the least of it. Maybe I was the last person on the planet to find out it wasn't all worth the effort, but blind slavishness can be a useful discipline to acquire and it was standing me in good stead now.

I worked and minded my own business. I minded my own business like I never should have stopped doing. It's amazing how much you can accomplish when you really knuckle down and stop thinking all the time. That's what makes the world go round, as a matter of fact. It separates the wolves from the sheep. Not that I saw myself as either: being a wolf is too much trouble and being a sheep, well, I knew only too well what happened to sheep. I was a hippo: wallowing, untouchable, no natural enemies. Yes, it *was* good to be home.

Still, I wouldn't want to give the impression that I'd simply washed my hands of Turnaway or given it up as a lost cause—far from it. From my very first day at home, almost from the minute I set my bag down in the living room, I'd tried to get in touch, to set things right. Dr. Ross answered my first call and immediately hung up. My second and every other attempt that day were thwarted by a constant busy signal. The next day, amazingly, my call was picked up by an answering machine, though where they got the money for one—or where they'd found one in the North Bronx on a Sunday morning without a car—were questions worth asking. I left a message to the effect that I was sorry, I took back everything I said, and I'd do anything to repair the trust and affection I'd so thoughtlessly betrayed, so please call me. Needless to say, neither of them did. I feel pretty certain that Elias would have been willing to forgive me, but that Dr. Ross held him back and convinced him that no one in the outside world could be trusted. In any case, it was the only message I left, since my name was in the phone book and they could look me up whenever they had a change of heart.

Also, I wrote a letter. I won't recall it here, since there were some maudlin passages in it that I knew would appeal to Elias's sense of melodrama but were otherwise kind of purple. I don't keep copies of the letters I write in any case, but the gist of it was the same as my message, only in greater detail—regret, sorrow, hope for the future, and all that. It, too, went unanswered. What more could I do? No matter what it is, no matter what you say, it always seems to be about what you leave unsaid.

I'd done what I could and I could do no more, so there was little point in agonizing over the situation. My friend may have been in trouble, but he'd explicitly told me to butt out. Whether or not my feelings were hurt isn't important—I know better than most when I'm not wanted. Mostly, when I thought about it, if I thought about it at all, I was more angry at Elias than anything else for being such a sap, but finally even that was his responsibility, not mine. Like it or not, the whole mess was out of my hands. In the past, when I'd found myself in similar situations, I took it as my cue to walk away and get on with my life. Some people have accused me of being cold or unsympathetic on that account. Some—not many, since few are masochistic enough to get involved with someone like me, and those that are tend to do it for the pain—have even called me hateful.

Well, I know how I come across but I can't help that. My feeling is just that sympathy without action is mere sentimentality. If I can help, fine; if not, I won't lose any sleep over it. What good does it do anybody to wring your hands over the plight of some orphan or homeless person or war-torn country without lifting a finger to help? You're only fooling yourself if you think your tears and indignation make you a better person, and I have enough troubles without lying to myself on top of it. The way I see it, you can't torture yourself day after day for the rest of your life over a situation that, no matter how painful it may have been at the time, you were powerless to change or alleviate.

And that's exactly what I did, and did well, that first month off Turnaway. I fell into a beautiful, lulling routine. Up at two, lunch at a

Greek diner on Eleventh Avenue, where I often ran into the street-girls from my corner. They were just getting up, too, and could make good company if I was in the mood. Afternoons I spent combing through the classifieds in the dailies and the boat magazines. I wasn't ready to buy just yet, but I wanted to get a feel for what was on the market, what sold quickly and what ads languished in the columns month after month. I wanted to get it right this time. In this season, the new offerings were pretty slim, so I usually had time for some painting on the waterfront or an art class at the ASL in the late afternoon. Dinner from Peking Garden West at home, followed by a few hours of TV or a rented movie. Then on to work, finishing just late enough to make sure the papers had hit the stands and my favorite William Street diner was open. Then home to bed. I won't say the routine was iron-clad, but it was close enough to perfection to restore my lost serenity.

And then in late October something happened to knock it off course. I was flicking through the paper one morning when an article caught my eye. It was about Davids Island, a former military base in the Sound, just off the coast of New Rochelle. The article was about the most recent of many failed attempts to develop the island commercially; it discussed the hurdles any developer has to overcome in environmentally sensitive projects, particularly on islands in metropolitan waters. An aerial photograph of the island caught the tip of a wooded headland of Turnaway a mile or so away to the southeast. The article never mentioned Turnaway, but that hardly mattered. The certainty just quietly took its place in my mind, as naturally as the lone standing passenger in a subway car taking the sole empty seat. I'd known it all along, so I wasn't even surprised or dismayed. It was a simple fact: Dr. Ross was in secret negotiation with developers over Turnaway. Elias was on his way out.

That afternoon I abandoned my usual program and took a stroll through the garment district to the Empire State Building. I got on line with the tourists and rode the express elevator to the observation deck. The building's shadow under the crisp northern sun stretched like a thermometer under the tongue of Central Park. Standing in a stiff but still warm and fragrant mid-autumn breeze, I waited my turn for the viewfinder that stands on the northeast corner of the terrace. When it came, I deposited my quarter and trained the telescope down and in a general northeasterly direction. When the quarter dropped and the view appeared, I found myself staring down on the skeletal globe from the 1965 World's Fair in Flushing Meadows. I swung the telescope up and to the left, and the blurring landscape within the lens swept in an arc through Flushing, across Riker's Island, into the East River, and up the Bronx River valley to Yonkers. A level sweep to the right sent me hurtling over Pelham, Eastchester, the Sound, until I came to a jarring halt and hovered over Kings Point. Now I floated gently backward as far as Pelham Park, then forward again, then back, then forward in ever-diminishing echoes until my eye came to rest over Eastchester Bay and its islands, and in particular one emerald button with a white microdot in the center. Not one detail emerged from that fuzzy little emerald at this distance, but I went on staring until my five minutes were up and the black shutter descended. I dropped in another quarter. I stared unblinkingly, as if that tiny green stain—which sometimes shimmered and disappeared behind the exhaust of jetliners on their final approach to La Guardia—were the protruding nose of some enormous, submerged sea creature just about to arise and burst forth after a thousand-year sleep. And when these five minutes elapsed, I reached into my pocket only to find that I was out of change. Back on the street, I wandered the sidewalks in an unusually pensive mood for the rest of the day, hardly noticing the deepening chill of the evening with its harbinger of a north Atlantic winter near at hand.

The following Saturday I rented a car and drove out to the south shore of Long Island. I had a number of appointments to look at boats. Again, I wasn't really ready to buy, but I wanted to see how the real articles held up against the ad copy. I thought the experience would help me avoid wasting time on duds when I began my search in earnest. After a disappointing but educational morning, I decided to cut my excursion short and head home. But I did a funny thing on the Expressway. Without planning or even giving it a second thought, I took the Port Washington exit and drove up through Manhasset all the way to the north shore. I parked at the foot of the lighthouse and walked to the water's edge.

From Sands Point beach to Turnaway is a little over a mile. Other than a few inaccessible rocks and islets, the beach is the closest piece of solid ground to Turnaway. I squinted through a pair of binoculars that I happened to have with me and brought the island into focus. From this angle I had an unobstructed view of the southern and eastern sides of the island—my shipwreck beach, the swimming cove, the widow's walk peeking above the treetops like a periscope. But there was no visible activity except for the black dots of songbirds playing above the forest canopy. I don't know what I expected to see—a golf course? A canning factory? I drove home.

I spent the next few weekends looking at boats from Freeport to the Moriches. Usually, at the end of a day, I ended up taking the same detour to Sands Point. I didn't have any particular goal in mind and I didn't examine my motives very carefully. I had a car and this was as nice a drive as any. That was all the reason I needed.

But I was soon bored with Long Island and its dismal tracts, and turned my attention to the wealthier coastal towns of Westchester. It was just a change of scenery, but I brought along my binoculars just in case. On my way to Larchmont on my very first day, I peeled off the Hutchinson River Parkway and drove to Orchard Beach. I walked to the far northern edge of the beach and climbed the great boulder on Hunter's Island—it's still called an island but it's attached to the mainland now—which Elias claimed to be Wampage's grave. From the top, I had a sighting through Middle Reef and East Nonations to the Turnaway dock some two miles away. Again, there was no activity of any sort, and the island was exactly as I'd left it, the launch tied up to the pier and bobbing prettily on the sparkling water. On a whim, I returned to my car and drove the five minutes to the Fordham Street landing on City Island.

Overnight a nor'easter had blown in, washing the sky and bringing Canadian winds; I beat my arms against my chest in an effort to keep warm. The mail boat was tied up and banging against the dock; Felicia was late. At the land end of the dock, a group of four craggy

men huddled around a kerosene heater. I'd heard Felicia once describe them as "wharf rats"—jacks-of-all-trades afloat, ready to pick
up any menial work that offered itself. They looked none too friendly.
I clopped the heels of my boots against the loosened old boards of the
dock to give myself courage and alert them to my presence. As I
neared, one of them looked up briefly, then ducked his head and
returned to the murmured conversation around the heater. When I
spoke up, not one of them would meet my eye.

"Can I get a ride to Turnaway Island from any of you?" I asked
hopefully. You'd have thought I was asking to go to Frankenstein's
castle.

"Sorry, weather's gettin' up."

"Got a prior commitment."

"Boat's outa commission."

"No can do, sonny. Too busy. Sorry."

It was obvious that begging wasn't going to do any good, so I
headed for the end of the dock, feeling their hard, priggish eyes on
my back. I stood there for a while, huddled in on myself, watching
the seagulls fight over a slick of garbage. Then I heard footsteps and
turned to see Felicia striding purposefully toward me down Fordham
Street. I hurried to meet her. When I caught her eye, some twenty
yards away, she gave me a big, welcoming smile. But a moment later
it vanished as if she'd just remembered I was suffering from rabies.

"Hello, Felicia," I said, offering my hand. After hesitating, she
took it reluctantly.

"Hello, Ben," she said.

"Can you take me across?"

"No I can't," she said, her features hardening. "I'm sorry. I'd like
to help you, but I got orders from the doctor not to let you over to the
island." She pushed past me.

"Felicia, come on!"

"No, no, no. Sorry." By now she'd jumped onto the deck of her
boat and was already casting off. I could tell she bore me no personal
ill will, but it was just as obvious that she had no intention of giving
in. She offered one last sheepish smile, then headed out into open

water without a backward glance. The wharf rats stared silently as I retreated to my car.

🐞

I kept up my occasional trips to the Empire State Building but stopped going to see boats. There wasn't much point to it, since I'd got a pretty good idea of what was available and I wouldn't be ready to buy until the early spring in any case. Besides, renting a car every weekend was expensive. The smartest thing to do was to save my money, knuckle down to work, and forget all about Turnaway.

I feel pretty sure I'd have done it, too, if it wasn't for a phone call I received one morning a few days later. I monitored all my calls through the answering machine and I'd been in a deep sleep when it picked up. But the voice at the other end brought me bolt upright and had me scrambling for the receiver before the caller hung up.

"Elias!" I shouted down the phone.

"Ben? Is that you?" He sounded confused and disoriented.

"Of course it's me. Who else?"

"Ben, I've had a disagreement with Ross. I'd like to come stay with you for a while."

"What kind of disagreement?"

"A terrible disagreement. But that's not important. I've come to see that you were right. I must be independent. I must learn to be my own man. So I'd like to come to New York and live with you while I search for the Mahkohkwe."

"Hold on there, Elias. Isn't that being a little rash?"

"I don't understand, Ben. You were the one who suggested—"

"Yes, but not because you've had a fight with your brother. You should do it because it's the right thing to do."

"But I do, I do. I've thought about it a great deal and—"

"Listen Elias." I made my voice steely and merciless. "I know what I told you and I'm not going back on it. But I just don't think you're ready. I was wrong about that. You just want to trade one caretaker for another, not strike out on your own. I think you should make it up with Ross. Try to find a balance with him first before you go off on some wild goose chase. I can't be responsible for you that way."

There was a long pause, and when he finally broke the silence Elias sounded stunned, crushed.

"Are you saying I mustn't come, Ben?"

"Yes. I don't think it would be a good idea. Not just now."

"I see. Well, thank you just the same."

"That's okay. Take care, Elias."

"You too, Ben."

So that was the end of that. If, like I said, it doesn't matter what you do and the only thing that counts is what's left unsaid, then maybe it was impossible to know if I'd done the right thing. I'd faced a similar sort of decision after my accident, and it had been a defining moment in my life. When the police came to interview me in the hospital, I'd had a big choice to make: should I tell them what I'd told Elias (and everyone else), that I'd slipped in a puddle and fell? Or should I tell them the truth: that I'd been pushed by a man who thought I'd wronged his sister? Did I want justice or did I want my easy money? You can't base decisions like that on intuition, can you? You have to act on your own experience. I learned a lot about myself mulling that one over, maybe more than I cared to know, but one important lesson I did learn was that you can't reveal someone's personality for them. They have to discover it for themselves, like I had. Why lay the responsibility or the blame on me? I was nobody's father figure: whatever I had to teach Elias I'd taught him, and now he was on his own. And I was pretty sure that, whatever might happen to Turnaway in the future, the doctor would make some provision for him. Elias was *his* brother, after all, not mine. It's always easier to know who you're not than who you are, and I was neither mentor nor martyr; if nothing else, that was a given.

I'd once offered Elias my help when he hadn't asked for it, and he'd rejected me. Now he'd asked for it and I'd turned him down. It wasn't a question of justice, but I had my own needs to think about now. It was easy to predict what kind of a burden Elias would be as a protégé: needy, helpless, insecure. He'd certainly screw up the life I'd built for myself with hard work and luck, one I'd waited a long, long time to enjoy. If I let him do it, I'd only end up resenting him, and who would that help? I mean, we all end up on our own at some point, don't we? Better he figure that out for himself. You couldn't call what I'd done a betrayal. It was more a sort of harsh act of kindness. I *had* done the right thing, and I wasn't going to distract myself by fretting over it.

I went back to work with a vengeance. I increased my hours and logged spectacular overtime. I cut back on my socializing and entertainment, such as they were, and focused single-mindedly on my goal. I dropped my painting and art classes. When this was all over I was going to have the best little pleasure craft on the water, all paid for and insured, and then I'd never have another day of worry or doubt. And it would be seaworthy, too, and I could go anywhere I wanted. The bank could wire me my annuity wherever I happened to be—Nova Scotia, Cape Fear, Key West, the Tortolas. All those beautiful, empty miles. All I'd ever need again was a cash machine and a flat horizon.

One morning, after a long night's walk, I was sitting in the diner on William Street over a cup of coffee. I was daydreaming about my boat, just staring out the window, when a man walked past. I couldn't see his face, but he had long, stringy gray hair and wore beat-up blue overalls with a plaid patch over one buttock. I threw down a pocketful of change onto my table and hobbled out after him, my hips aching as they always did after a ten-hour shift.

By the time I reached the street, the man was at the corner. He turned right onto Fulton Street. I broke into a light sweat as I hurried to catch up, but I'd barely closed the gap between us when he came into view. Shooting pains up both thighs and into my lower back prevented me from going any faster. He crossed the street in the middle of the block and had to dash ahead of an oncoming truck, increasing the distance between us. A moment later he disappeared into the Fulton Street subway station. There was no way I could catch him now, but I pressed on anyway, just in case. I crossed the street, turned into the station entrance, and almost crashed headlong into the man, who'd stopped at a newsstand and was fishing in his pockets for change. He didn't look anything like my father. I turned on my heels and limped back to the diner.

It had been a long while since I'd made that mistake. Every time I did I'd sworn it would never happen again. At this point I couldn't even be sure he was still alive. If he was, and I saw him, I might not recognize him, and I certainly had no idea what I would say. What could there possibly be to say after all these years? In a way, I hadn't really lied to Elias when I told him my father was dead. He'd haunt me less dead than he did alive, that was for sure. Looking for fathers—was there ever such a pathetic delusion? You might laugh if it wasn't so sorry.

The muffled click of the front door latch woke me up in the pitch dark, my heart bouncing sickeningly off my ribcage. There was a stranger in the apartment. I rolled over, with the vague idea of hiding under the bed, and my eye caught the glowing digits of the alarm clock. Then it came back to me. It was 5:07 A.M.—hunting time.

I lay in the dark and my imagination expanded into the eerie void of that silent hour. I tried to picture Elias in his loincloth, stalking his prey through the empty streets and lots of Hell's Kitchen—hard to imagine our New York squirrels, rats, and feral cats submitting to his tender attentions with the docility of a domesticated bunny. Not to mention all the human predators that might be stalking him. I probably should have warned him of the dangers. In fact, I was reluctantly beginning to suspect that it might be my duty to drag myself out into the bleak, frigid morning and lead him home to safety. But then I thought of his amazing stealth and dexterity with a knife and I convinced myself that he could take care of himself, unused to the streets as he was. And in any case, by now he could be anywhere and how could I be sure of finding him even if I did go? I tried to relax and go back to sleep, but I was too high on adrenaline from my abrupt awakening. I had to laugh. Elias had been in New York less than twenty-four hours and already I was as jumpy and protective as a mother hen.

When I'd called him, the very day I'd spotted my father's look-alike, I'd tried to discourage him from leaving right away. "Take your time," I'd told him. "Prepare yourself. Talk it through with Ross." But no, he was bubbling over with excitement; waiting was out of the question. "I'll see you first thing in the morning," he had said, and hung up before I could respond.

Early the next morning, Elias had stolen away in his canoe, which he ditched under the wharf at Fordham Street. Unfortunately, I'd forgotten to warn him it was Thanksgiving. It was impossible to hail a cab on City Island, of course, and he'd wandered around the island for an hour in a biting wind, looking for an open store or business where he could call for a car (I didn't have the heart to ask why he hadn't used a pay phone, since I knew very well that such high-tech was beyond him). Finally, he'd stumbled on the storefront office of a radio-car service. The one available driver was on a run to Arthur Avenue, and Elias had had to wait another hour. When he was eventually settled in the back seat of an '82 Continental, the brawny, pockmarked driver turned to ask him if he had a preferred route into Manhattan. Elias said "overland." By the time they hit the on-ramp to the Major Deegan, Elias was farther from Turnaway than he'd been in fifteen years. He kept his eyes closed all the way to the Triborough Bridge.

When I heard the prearranged signal from the street—three short blasts on the limo's horn—I slipped on my bathrobe and hustled down the stairs to the front door. I opened it and prepared to welcome my old friend with open arms. But Elias just stood there in an old gray overcoat and porkpie hat, a look of horror on his face.

"What shall I do?" he whispered. "He wants money. He's threatened me."

"Wait there."

I hobbled up to my apartment, grabbed my wallet, and hobbled back down. The driver was leaning against the passenger side of the car, hulking and angry. I handed Elias a fifty-dollar bill and stood at the top of the stoop, hugging myself against the cold. A young mother and her three-year-old happened by at that moment, and the child stared unabashedly up at me as they strolled past. Meanwhile, there was some sort of commotion brewing between Elias and the driver, who was pounding the roof of his car with his fist. I called down to Elias to let the driver keep the change. He did so, reluctantly. As the car pulled away, he snatched up his old-fashioned cardboard suitcase and gazed up leerily at me hovering on the threshold. He glanced down the block and at the garbage-strewn gutter, then skipped up the stoop, his eyes on his shoes, alligator wingtips I'd never seen before. I ushered him in.

"What's 'tipping'?" he asked.

"I'll explain later," I said.

I offered him some tea—sassafras, which I'd taken to drinking at his example—and he mumbled his assent. When I returned from the kitchen, he was sitting stiffly on the edge of my couch, hands on his knees, trying to pretend that he hadn't been casting a curious eye over my little hovel. It's true I'm no decorator, but it wasn't the drab interior that interested him. I don't think he'd ever been inside someone else's home before. He'd never watched television and didn't read magazines, so he'd had no idea what to expect. Finding himself inside my very ordinary floor-through, with its warped pine floors and galley kitchen, was like being abducted into an alien spacecraft. At the same time, he had no idea how a guest was supposed to behave. I don't know where he got his model from, but he was as awkward and formal as a thirteen-year-old at his own bar mitzvah. He'd neatly folded his overcoat and draped it over the suitcase, but he'd forgotten to remove the ridiculous hat.

"You can relax, you know," I said, snatching it from his head and skimming it across the room onto the dining table. "This is your bedroom now. The couch folds out."

He smiled weakly but gratefully and sipped at his tea. Now that he was finally here, with me, in the city, the reality of what he'd done seemed to be sinking in. I knew the feeling: I'd felt the same every time I'd found myself in a new foster home. You were never too sure you understood why you'd had to leave the last one, and you couldn't fully trust the motives or goodwill of your new guardians, but there was no turning back. It could go either way. Maybe they were craven hypocrites like all the others had turned out to be, or maybe these were finally those fabled creatures you'd heard about in wild rumors, the ones who would end up adopting you and making you their son. It may sound far-fetched, but I had experience and I recognized that same fear and uncertainty in Elias now.

"Why don't you tell me what happened?" I said, trying to sound like a caseworker who'd once been very nice to me in a similar situation.

"I told you on the telephone," Elias croaked, his voice cracking. "Ross and I have had a disagreement.

"Tell me everything."

So Elias began to tell his whole story, his almond eyes liquid with emotion. It was an outpouring. I don't remember interrupting him even once, but still it seems like he spoke for hours, subdued, even ashamed at times, but determined to get it all out.

It seemed that, after my expulsion from Turnaway, Elias and Dr. Ross had made monumental efforts to settle back into their old routines. Elias began to get up even earlier than usual, an hour before dawn, and to hunt with such single-minded zeal that before long the pens were overflowing with inmates. As a result, the butcher from Port Washington, who couldn't get enough of the fluffy white beasts, began coming twice as often, and Dr. Ross was able to use the extra cash to make long-needed improvements to the house and property. Both of them felt that they were finally beginning to "put their house in order," literally and metaphorically, and they congratulated each other energetically every mealtime on work well done. The arrival of the cool autumn breezes put a healthy bloom on their cheeks, and their appetites for food and conversation increased. After years of trial and error, Elias finally perfected his pemmican recipe. He'd begun working on the Staten Island section of his project. His pottery designs evolved new and intriguing flourishes. The doctor even dusted off the long-neglected entomology laboratory. In short, not only did Elias begin to feel that he could get along fine without me, he even seemed to be better off, more capable of exploiting the new energies I'd helped to unleash. It goes without saying, the doctor never tired of demonstrating how much happier they were in their traditional arrangement, without me and my disruptive modern notions. And for a while it had been true—Elias had been able to put me and my accusations out of mind and to thank his guardian spirits that he'd escaped the devil and his temptations.

But even Elias couldn't live in denial that deep. "I hadn't even been aware that I'd been sitting on a Pandora's box. Not only had you found it—you pushed me off and opened it," he told me portentously. There were a number of unresolved issues that continued to haunt him, despite all his eagerness to ignore and forget them.

First of all, naturally enough, he missed my company. Who could blame him? I'd been the first real visitor to the island since he was a kid. I had a sense of humor, a ready wit, and at least a limited capacity for fun, unlike Dr. Ross. Now, I don't think of myself as being vain or boastful: it was only normal—you don't have to be a child to want to spend time with people your own age. When he was little and his father was still alive, Elias had received other kids on Turnaway—cousins, local schoolchildren, Boy Scout troops, that sort of thing—but they'd mostly found him strange and dreamy and excluded him from their games. That hadn't been any great hardship, since he was always the first to exclude them from his. Apparently, Andrew Hutchinson had been a little concerned by his teenage son's growing detachment from the world, but he died before he could do much about it. After that, the visitors gradually stopped coming. Since then, from what I could gather, only two other strangers besides me had ever spent more than one night on Turnaway. One had been Elias's aunt, Andrew's sister from Rhode Island, who arrived one month after her brother's death, spent four days rummaging through his belongings and, finding almost nothing worth inheriting, left again in a huff. Elias had never heard from her again. The other had been a septuagenarian Lenape, a tribal elder and one of the few remaining native speakers of her ancestral language. Elias had written to her in Oklahoma with an open invitation and a round-trip bus ticket. The woman had spent six weeks on Turnaway with Elias, instructing him free of charge in the language and lore of his people, and had left with the promise to return the next year for an even longer stay but had died of emphysema four months later. So was it any wonder that Elias had come to see my shipwreck on Turnaway as an "act of Providence" (his words), or that he continued to feel my presence like a missing limb when I was gone? Dr. Ross's company had come to seem increasingly inadequate.

Inadequate, and strange. This was another issue that had been raised by my expulsion. Now, Dr. Ross had been a member of the Hutchinson household for many years before Elias was even born. Elias had grown up with him, knew him as intimately as any blood relative. Certainly he was aware that Ross had his eccentricities, but it had never occurred to him that they might in any way be suspect. Ross was just Ross. But my accusations, like it or not—and Elias very definitely did not like it—had knocked that planet out of its orbit. He told me that it had been like a toothache—ignoring the problem just wouldn't make it go away. Behavior he'd accepted all his life as normal was suddenly seen in a new light. Like most fearful people, Elias was very conservative: he wanted things to stay as they'd always been, and he surely would have given a lot to make this new insight go away; but my words had stayed with him, vexing and irritating like a stubborn mosquito.

For the first time in his life, he allowed himself to be curious about Ross. He still dismissed my accusations—even now he refused to accept any suggestion that the doctor had betrayed him—but it was precisely because he wanted to exonerate his guardian that he was tempted to scratch this particular new itch. Knowing Elias and his ways, that seemed about right to me: if he'd really suspected Ross of wrongdoing, he'd have found a way to forget the whole thing. Most of us, I suppose, are lured from under our rocks by the scent of danger or the prospect of witnessing carnage. But Elias wasn't like most people: all he wanted was to be left alone in his illusions, and he'd been lucky enough to live in a situation where he'd been able to get away with this for a long time. But then I came along and undermined it all. Proud as I was of my disruptive influence, he saw it as a bad thing that had to be set right. The first step in that direction was to do away with all these petty, nagging doubts about the doctor once and for all.

It had taken a long time for Elias to reach that stage of decision, but things had moved pretty quickly after that. He told me—though he hardly needed to—that the last thing he'd wanted was a confrontation with the doctor. He planned on asking a few innocent, direct questions; the doctor would answer them willingly and honestly, and all qualms would be laid to rest. Easy and painless. But that's not what happened. The barometer had been dropping all day.

No sooner had the first question left Elias's lips than the doctor had puffed himself up with righteous indignation. A bitter argument had ensued, the first of Elias's adulthood.

"How can you ask me such questions?" the doctor had spluttered, the color rising to his cheeks as they sat by the fire in the library on a mid-November evening. "I who am your teacher, your brother, your guide and protector?"

"I was only curious, Joseph, I didn't mean to—"

"I think your mind has been poisoned, Elias. I think your Ben and his ill-considerate ways have made you lose all your faith in me. I think he has turned you against the only person in the world you can trust. Is not that so?"

"No, Joseph, I have not lost my faith in you. I was only curious to know, to understand, why we might have secrets from each other or why we should."

By now, the doctor was on his feet, pacing and gesticulating. The fire in the hearth cast stark, pulsating shadows throughout the room, which seemed to surround and threaten Elias, perched knees-up on the leather ottoman.

"Elias, I cannot tolerate this suspicion. I have not deserved it. It is not for me to be suspected, do you understand? If there are secrets here, it is you who are keeping them, not I. If there is loyalty in question, it is yours, not mine. If there is a stench of betrayal in the air, it is your doing, not mine. Do you understand? Do you understand?"

Elias was so cowed by this unanticipated rage that he didn't respond, just sat there pressing his palms together between his knees. The doctor continued to prowl around the room, as if in every darkened corner and recess there lurked a small, dangerous rodent that needed to be kept constantly in check. The flames crackled and the imperfectly seasoned firewood popped explosively. Outdoors, a gale was building against the brittle windowpanes. The softened leather of the doctor's slippers on the ancient Persian carpet sounded like the footfall of a cat or an assassin as his pace gradually slowed. Finally he stopped before an east-facing window and spent some time examining the crumbling grout on the upper sash. When he eventually spoke, his words were at odds with his tone, which was not that of a man mortally offended, but of one who was deeply ashamed of himself.

"I will not have you question me," he said in a whisper, then turned and stalked briskly from the room.

They ate breakfast together the next morning as if nothing had happened. But something had happened, something important and fundamental, and somehow Elias understood that it was useless to try to ignore it away as he'd done in the past. He knew from the very start that the doctor's rage was as unprovoked as it had been unanticipated. By almost any standard Elias had been a model of tact and deference, and no one with a clean conscience—let alone a dear and trusted friend—should have been able to find cause for offense or anger in his questions. He may have been no Mae West when it came to intuiting men's ulterior motives, but he could draw his conclusions as well as the next guy when he put his mind to it. And his conclusion was that Dr. Ross had been acting behind his back and had something to hide. It was not necessarily against Elias's best interests—he found that unlikely—but it was definitely something that, as nominal head of the household and Chairman of the res, he felt he had every right to know. The doctor had no business keeping secrets from him and even less flying into a blind rage when asked to give them up.

"And that, dear Ben, was when I decided to call you. I knew that nothing could ever again be the same between Ross and me. He knew it too—that's why he'd always mistrusted you. He'd given his entire life to me, but now the time had come. . . . Well, I suppose it comes to everyone.

"It was a terrible blow when you rejected me. I thought I'd understood your arguments perfectly. I imagined you'd be thrilled to have won me over. I didn't know what to do. I suppose one could say I fell into a depression, if that's possible. Manapinock had never felt like a trap before. It was awful."

In the silence that fell, I suddenly became aware of the smell of roasting turkey and yams seeping up through the floorboards from somewhere in the building. It seemed ironic and right for both of us that Elias had reached me on Thanksgiving day. I thought about this for a while like a religious man. Then Elias spoke as if he'd been reading my mind.

"What made you reconsider, Ben?"

"Well, I never did find out what happens to Wampage in the end."

Elias shrugged in a tentative sort of way. "We'll stay here for a while, if that's alright with you?" I nodded. Again we sat quietly for a few minutes. In that serene moment, a last practical thought occurred to me.

"Does Ross know where you are?"

"No," Elias said with false bravado.

"You'd better tell him."

"It's late. I'll call him in the morning."

"The phone's in the bedroom. You'd better do it now."

Elias shut the door behind him. A few moments later I heard the rise and fall of his reedy voice like wind through cracked masonry. Calm and measured at first, it grew agitated, then angry, then strident, and then was cut short; after a pause, it reassumed a conciliatory tone, and shortly afterward I heard Elias return the receiver to

its cradle. He waited a minute before opening the door. As he entered the room, we exchanged meaningful glances full of seriousness
and commitment. Then Elias gave in to a sheepish grin.

"He sends his love," he said.

That afternoon, I took him downtown by subway. He told me that, on
his very first day back in New York—he always scoffed when I
insisted that he'd been living in New York all this time—he wanted
to see the site of the first European settlement in the area. His father
had never allowed him to indulge in "tourism" on their few visits
together all those years ago, but Elias was eager. He thought it would
help him begin, as he said, to "colonize the city" in his mind.

"It was just about here," he murmured, almost as if to himself,
"that the *Tiger* burned in 1613." He hugged his elbows to his chest
and leaned over the steel balustrade. He stared straight down into
the gray water, its grime-smeared surface slopping against the marble parapet. I followed his gaze, then lifted my eyes up and outward
to the jagged industrial shores of Jersey City and the great mouth of
the Hudson opening into the Upper Bay, where the Statue of Liberty
guards the oil towers and container cranes in the Arthur Kill. I knew
these waters well; at one point early in my recovery, they'd been like
a second home to me. From the Verrazano to the George Washington,
every inch of shoreline is developed—factories, docks, high-rises,
ferry terminals, sewage treatment plants, warehouses, parking lots.
Planes and helicopters hum overhead; boats of every kind ply the
waters; industry and commerce own the river and its banks. It was a
soothing spectacle for me, a reminder of my place in the world of
damaged goods. But Elias wasn't seeing any of it; I could tell by the
way his hooded eyes had glazed over. I strained to do what he did
naturally, without effort: to see this vast harbor as it was in 1613,
nothing but trees, sea birds, the brackish, fish-teeming waters of the
Mahikanituk and, in one little corner, a miniature drama easy to
overlook in the eye's broad sweep across the landscape: a wooden
boat, no bigger than a modern tug, burning in twenty feet of water,
while a small knot of men, some clothed, some almost naked,

watched in silence from the shore. But it was no good. At best I could visualize its ghost, like heat ripples rising off asphalt, but Elias *saw* it. If I could do that, if I could make all the buildings and people disappear, I wouldn't have the faintest idea where I was, even if I was right here on Manhattan. I shivered against the cold and Elias interrupted my thoughts.

"Not there, silly," he said. "This way." He turned around and nodded toward the spires of the World Trade Center, towering above us and blotting out the entire eastern sky. "In 1613, the spot we're standing on was a hundred yards off shore. The *Tiger* burned in the middle of the plaza between the towers. Wampage was there. He saw the whole thing."

"How do you mean, Wampage was there?"

"Yes, you didn't know that, did you?" He smirked, pleased with himself for shocking me. "Wampage was born around the turn of the seventeenth century. He was a young boy when Block landed. For him, and for most with him, it was their first look at a European."

I have to admit I *was* a little shocked. With his stories of woodland spirits, deer hunts, and tomahawk-throwing contests, Elias had never placed Wampage in a specific historical setting. I'd never thought of him as having a place in "real" time. For me, he'd always lived in that never-never land of mythology along with Samson, Pegasus, David and Goliath, and other heroes from childhood cartoons. It was weird, almost creepy, to discover suddenly that he was a contemporary of Shakespeare and Elizabeth. I'd have to change the whole way I pictured him.

We sat on a bench, hunched against a nasty wind under an ash gray sky, and Elias grew somber. I knew what was coming next. Sure enough, a story began spilling out of him a few moments later.

"Early one fall morning when Wampage was in his eleventh or twelfth year, Cokoe came running into his family wigwam and shook him awake.

" 'They're here, they've returned!' he cried.

" 'Who? Who are here?' Wampage groaned, annoyed at having been torn from a dream in which he was outrunning a great wolf in a contest of speed.

" 'The salty ones!' Cokoe was almost beside himself with excitement and impatience. 'They have returned in their floating longhouse. Hurry or we'll miss them!'

"On the ebbing tide they made it to the tip of Manhattan in two hours and rounded its rocky shores, steering their little seining canoe into the choppy waters of the Mahikanituk. Directly before them, about a mile away, the mountainous bulk of the *shuwonnock*'s floating longhouse came into view. Great sheets, each as big as a cornfield, flapped from poles in the roof and gleamed blindingly in the morning sun. From a distance, Wampage took them for giant wings of goose down. He had certainly never seen anything like it, and as it loomed ever larger he kept thinking it could not grow any more, but it did. Finally, the little canoe was bobbing in its shadow, and Wampage had to shield his eyes against the glare as they roved up and ever up its slick wooden walls and intricate workings. At the top, a strange-looking red-faced man, covered head to toe in folds of cloth, his chin sprouting fur like a dog, shouted and waved a heavy gleaming stick at the boys. There was a large crowd gathered on shore, and they steered their dugout that way.

"Of course, Wampage had heard of the *shuwonnock* before. This was now their fourth visit in as many years. The first time, the rumor had gone up and down the valley that they—possibly spirits of some sort, emissaries of Kishelemukong—had killed a number of Wekweskik and Tappans by sorcery, and another time that they had stolen away two warriors to their home in the spirit world beyond the salt sea. Now it was known that they were mortal men. In the past, Wampage's mother had not allowed him to call on the camps of the *shuwonnock*. They were widely held to be unpredictable, very unmannerly and possibly dangerous, but they carried remarkable, magical objects with them in their longhouse vessel that made it difficult to resist paying their camps a visit when they appeared, as they had been doing at every harvest. As they neared the shore, Wampage and Cokoe could see small clusters of Canarsee men and women gathering curiously around the *shuwonnock*, who were holding up various articles for them to examine. The boys beached their canoe between two boulders and joined one of the groups.

"In this group, four awestruck men were passing back and forth an implement about the size and shape of a tomahawk. It had a polished wooden handle the length of a thigh bone, at one end of which was affixed a smooth flat stone the size of a hand, with one edge straight as a flint. Wampage squeezed between two of the gawkers and intercepted the implement as it passed between them. He was shocked by the weight; as he ran his hand over the surface of the blade he understood that it was not made of stone but of some material, cold and dense, that he had never come across before. The *shuwonnock* at the center of this group, a man who was a head shorter than the shortest of the Canarsee and smelled like an old bear even though he wore no grease in his hair, made a sweeping, chopping motion in the air with his left hand, evidently to illustrate the function of the tool, and said: *'Bale-tyeh.'* Then he spread both hands out, palms upward in the gesture for giving, and said: *'Wampum.'* The Canarsee laughed at his ugly mouth and bad manners but understood exactly what he wanted. The boys wandered to the next group.

"Here the people were passing handfuls of what appeared to be pebbles to each other, amid an ongoing chorus of *'shishtamwe!'* and *'nuwi!'* and *'keku haye?'* But again, when Wampage got his hands on one of the controversial pebbles, he found it to be made of an entirely new and marvelous material—transparent like ice but not cold, smooth like sewan but perfectly round and uniform, with a tiny hole through the middle of each pebble, like a wampum bead. Indeed, here was a necklace of these pebbles strung together, greatly admired by men and women alike. The *wapsit* distributing the pebbles, more red-faced and evil-smelling than the first, kept repeating over and over: *'Omaga! Omaga!'* They all knew he was trying to say *'Amohkwe'* but they ignored his rudeness until one old man, exasperated by the unpleasant noise, removed the beaver pelt from his own shoulders and held it out to the stranger. But the man became even ruder, refusing the exchange of gifts with an angry bark and holding up ten fingers. *'Omaga! Omaga!'* he shouted, while the Canarsee looked at each other in bewilderment. The boys moved on.

"Here was the leader of the visitors, easily recognized by his cloak of beautiful red cloth, his pale, refined features, and his quiet manner of dignity so contrasting with those of his underlings. He sat in counsel with the local Canarsee and Hackensack sachems, while a Lenape speaking the Unami dialect, a stranger from the south country, acted as interpreter. A large audience had gathered to listen to the halting conversation, which centered around the strangers' plans. As Wampage and Cokoe drew close enough to hear, the interpreter was explaining in his heavy accent that the white men would shortly be returning to their home to avoid the dangers of the northern spirits on the salt sea.

" 'Why does he call them "white"?' Cokoe whispered to Wampage. 'They are as red as cranberries.'

" 'Shh!' said Wampage.

" 'And now,' said a seated sachem, holding up his hand. 'Ask Borok how many moons he intends to stay here with his men?' A general hum of approval went up from the crowd at the sagacity of this question.

"The interpreter turned to the *shuwonnock* chief and spoke in his language, which to the boys' ears sounded as if the speaker were choking on quail bones. Borok asked a question and pointed at the sachem. The interpreter blushed and remonstrated, but Borok insisted.

"The interpreter said: 'Forgive me, Uncle. Borok wishes to know your name so he may address you with respect.'

"The sachems grumbled at this and the one spoken to looked distinctly uncomfortable, but finally, at the urging of the majority, he broke the taboo: 'Kakawashe.'

"Borok nodded. 'Crackewasco!' he said, and launched into a garbled monologue. Eventually, after much confusion, it came out through the interpreter that they were waiting for Kitchawank and Wappinger hunters to come downriver with beaver pelts for which they had traded, and then they would leave. In the meantime, Borok asked that he be granted a patch of land on which to build a council fire for him and his men.

" 'How much land does he want?' one sachem asked. When the question was relayed to him, Borok sent one of his men away, who returned with the hide of a large animal that had been soaking in a barrel of saltwater. The man held up the hide and Borok coughed. 'This much!' said the interpreter, and all the sachems and people laughed at the pleasure of granting such a modest request. Someone in the crowd pointed out that this was not a suitable place for a camp, and the entire group rose as one and trooped some ten minutes down the ragged shore, to a clearing in the woods at the edge of a small planting field. Kakawashe held out his arms and said: 'Here they may build their fire.' All looked at Borok for the appropriate displays of gratitude. The red-clad stranger bent his body at the waist, apparently in some sign of respect, then held out the hide, which he had folded and carried with him. One of his men took it and advanced into the center of the group. Kakawashe stepped forward to receive his tribute. But then a strange thing happened.

"Instead of presenting Kakawashe with his gift, the bearer dropped to his knees and spread the skin flat on the ground. He reached to his belt, retrieved a long-bladed knife and began to cut at the hide. He cut away a strip at its edge, no wider than a man's finger, and continued to saw at the skin without breaking the strip, while the Indians stood around bemused. The *shuwonnock* cut and cut, gradually spiraling inward toward the center of the hide, until the entire thing had been reduced to one long thong piled high before him. When he had done, he stood up and carried the pile to his chief, who took it in his arms and motioned for Kakawashe to accompany him. With Kakawashe following uncertainly behind, he set off into the planted field, which was bursting with ripe corn, beans, and squash, while the man who had done the cutting held on to one end of the thong. A few minutes later, Borok and Kakawashe reemerged on the beach at the far end of the field. With one end of the thong still in his hand, Borok strode down the beach and rejoined his confederate, closing the leather circle that now fully encompassed the planting field. The *shuwonnock* all burst into laughter while Borok, grinning from ear to ear, spoke to the interpreter, who frowned and scratched his head and seemed to need several repetitions to understand what was being said. Finally, he turned perplexedly back to the group of sachems waiting patiently for an explanation of this odd ritual.

" 'Borok says you made an agreement, Kakawashe, and you must now honor it,' the interpreter said timidly. 'You agreed to give him as much land as could be contained within that skin. The skin now contains this entire cornfield, and the field and everything in it is now, by rights, for Borok's own use.'

"The sachems all looked at one another, wide-eyed in wonder and confusion, shaking their heads at the meaning of all this. Could the *shuwonnock* actually have meant to trick them, or was this a misunderstanding? The land was everyone's, and there was corn aplenty to feed the *shuwonnock* all winter if need be. Why would they want or need to trick their way to anything the people would gladly have given them? Why hadn't they just asked? Kakawashe made the interpreter repeat everything and return to Borok to explain again, when the stranger very rudely began to raise his voice and exhibit impatience. Finally the gathered sachems could only conclude that, for whatever reason, he had meant what he said—he wanted the whole field. Of course, in spite of the weak objections of the family men who had planted and tended the field, Kakawashe had no choice but to grant the request, which he did with a raised forearm and a feeble shake of his forelock. Borok grabbed one of Kakawashe's hands and pumped it up and down, while smiling broadly in a display of emotion almost as unseemly as his anger. He then led his men away to gather their belongings, while the Indians stayed behind to rehash what had happened and vow not to be duped that way again. Wampage and Cokoe giggled softly at the way Kakawashe had been fooled. They didn't really understand the purpose of the ruse, and it was certainly lacking in dignity, but as boys they couldn't help admiring any clever display of tricksterism. This Borok and his men, these *wapsichik*, 'white men'—they were going to be great friends."

The wind had driven us off the waterfront, and as Elias's story unfolded at a leisurely, thoughtful pace we'd wandered through the plaza, across Church Street, and down the gray canyon of Broadway. A cold, wet fog was reaching across the bay from Secaucus, driving a mewing flock of gulls before it. I thought we'd been strolling at random, but as if he'd choreographed it to the inch, Elias came to an abrupt halt on the crowded sidewalk above Bowling Green, north of the old customhouse, just as his story was ending. Pedestrians glared and grumbled as they circled around us.

"It was just about here," Elias said, almost as if to himself, "that Adriaen Block inaugurated the disinheritance of my people that October morning. Wampage was a witness to it all." He added the last thought as if Wampage were standing next to us to corroborate the whole thing. Like a patient coming out of anesthesia, Elias emerged slowly from the grip of a story; there was always the danger that he'd slip back into a kind of afterglow, a reverie between the two worlds. When that happened, snapping him out of it could be difficult. I could see this was about to happen now, but it was too cold, standing there exposed to the winter whipping in off the bay, for me to allow it. I snapped my fingers a couple of times like a hypnotist, six inches from his nose.

"There's something I don't understand," I said. "You've never mentioned any white people in your stories about Wampage. But now you tell me that he'd been in contact with them since his childhood. Where have all these white people been?"

Elias warmed to my question, as I'd hoped he would. "You have to understand, when Block left Manhattan, his camp fell into disuse. The *Tiger* burned and its replacement, the *Onrust*, disappeared in the Delaware. The whites didn't establish their first permanent settlement in the area until seven years later, and even then it took a few more years for their presence to be felt. After all, New Amsterdam was hardly more than a squalid little village to start with. Wampage lived nearly twenty miles from that settlement, and he went about his business well into adulthood quite unaware that his people were on the verge of disaster. How could he know, all the while he was doing what young warriors had been doing in Lenapehoking for countless generations, that some committee of fat old men three thousand miles away had already decided to rename his home and destroy his people? He couldn't know."

We'd reached the lip of the stairway that descended into the Bowling Green station. I placed the palm of my hand lightly on the small of Elias's back, just to make sure we were moving in sync, but even as his left foot was poised above the first step he checked himself and turned around, so that now my palm was resting on his belly. I could feel it rise and fall, with underlying flutters like a panicked rabbit, and then he placed one of his own hot hands over mine, holding it there, squeezing. He stared in confusion up the long vista of Broadway toward the scene of that ancient fraud.

"I still don't understand it," he murmured, shaking his head. "Why did they do it? Why didn't they just ask us?"

The next morning I lay in bed, all jumpy and unable to get back to sleep, waiting for Elias to get home from his first "hunt" in Manhattan. A pool of dirty light was gathering beneath the blinds, and I decided it was pointless to lie there fretting. I threw on some clothes and went out for breakfast. The girls were already there, just coming off their night shift. They seemed genuinely glad to see me, even though I hadn't been a customer in a long time, and I told them a little about the friend who'd come to stay. After breakfast I picked up a few groceries at the supermarket and headed home.

"Hey gimp!" my landlord bawled cheerily from the stoop as I approached. "See you got yourself a roommate!" He winked at his cronies gathered round him, and they all laughed evilly. Elias must have gotten home while I was out. I winced at the thought of him trying to push through this group of neanderthals in his loincloth and moccasins, but I wasn't going to be put on the defensive. I sidled right up close and looked him in the eye.

"You planning to squeeze more rent out of me for a guest?"

His mirthful leer became mean-spirited. "I just like to know who's living in my house," he muttered.

"It's not your house, it's my apartment. And he's a friend from college. Is that a problem for you?"

"A college roommate? No, thweetie, no problem." More guffaws. I pushed past him up the stairs.

Elias was already preparing our morning tea when I shuffled into the living room. To my relief, he was dressed in baggy sweatpants and a gray sweatshirt, which he must have taken from my drawer. He was wearing my white leather Reeboks on his feet, though they must

have been at least two sizes too big. I had to stand and admire him—
I'd never seen him dressed in modern, casual clothing, and it was
like seeing a whole new man. In his own clothes—his Indian getup,
which included leather breeches and a full-fledged bearskin robe for
winter, or his hand-me-down suits, the newest of which dated to the
first Eisenhower administration—he'd always looked to me like a
method actor preparing for a role. It's hard to explain, exactly, but
even at his most relaxed he always looked like somebody else. Now,
however, with his long hair tousled by the wind, his cheeks flushed
from exertion and the cold, draped in rumpled sportswear, he suddenly looked modern, natural—real. It was almost like seeing him
for the very first time: boyish, slight, almost gaunt, with high cheekbones; slate gray eyes; blue-black hair; jawline curved like a cradle;
full, nut-brown lips; tiny ears. His hip was cocked as he stood at the
stove, pulling the fabric of the sweats against his frame and empha-
sizing the slim muscularity of his long legs. He blushed when he
caught me staring at him, then went back to his preparations.

"Where's the catch of the day, Wulamewet?" I teased him. He
laughed with pleasure to hear me use his adopted name, which I
almost never did.

"You can laugh if you like, but you'd be surprised," he said,
pouring boiling water into the teapot to warm it, then emptying the
water into the sink. "I only went for a walk, but I saw plenty of game
for the having. Canadian geese and ducks on their way south, striped
bass heading out to the deep water for the winter, squirrels all fat and
plump, ready to hibernate, wood pigeon, very tasty when young. A
good hunter could feed himself all winter in your city if need be. And
don't forget, we Lenape eat dog."

"Disgusting savages," I said. He handed me a mug of sassafras
tea.

"What time do you suppose the Empire State Building opens?" he
asked disingenuously.

Of course, we were the only two idiots up there that morning. The
eighty-sixth floor has a glassed-in walkway, but Elias insisted we
remain outdoors. We leaned into a steady gale that forced us to shout
at each other and made the open promenade feel like an Arctic

wasteland. Still, though the sky was dark with low, roiling clouds scudding for the Jersey shore, visibility was very good—twenty-five miles, according to the sign—and the landscape was laid out below us in sharp, late-autumn focus. I tried pointing out the city's famous landmarks; Elias nodded and commented politely, but his eye kept straying to the horizon, beyond the city proper. And when we came to the west side of the promenade, with its view overlooking the Hudson and New Jersey toward the Delaware Water Gap, he gave up any pretense of interest in Madison Square Garden or the great commercial docks. Finally I just shut up and let him dream.

"It's the first time I've seen it, you know," he eventually said.

"Seen what?" I shouted back over the roar of the wind.

"Lenapehoking."

"That's New Jersey."

"It's Lenapehoking."

"It's New Jersey. *New Jersey.* Look at it—where are the tepees?"

"Wigwams."

"Where are the wigwams? Where are the longhouses? The trackless wastes? All I see is tract housing. Does Lenapehoking have freeways and gasworks? Do the Indians live in factory outlets and oil tanks? Come on, Elias—it's New Jersey. Can't you see it?"

Elias was silent and sullen for a few minutes, his shoulders hunched against the cold, staring stonily through a blowing cowlick at the putrid marshlands across the river. "I know what I see," he muttered, and we moved on to the northern façade, where he was soon clicking his tongue and delighting over the telescopic view of Turnaway that I'd been enjoying regularly since the early fall. He was disturbed by the way foreshortening in the viewfinder made the projects of Co-op City seem to loom like a cresting wave over the tiny island.

"Four hundred years ago you wouldn't have seen more than a few dozen longhouses from up here," he said.

"Smart," I sniffed impatiently. "Four hundred years ago there was no 'up here' to see from." He cast a glance of withering pity in my direction but didn't answer. Soon afterward, we retreated indoors, down to a coffeeshop off the street-level lobby. We were the only customers, and the neon lights barely cut through the gloom of the day.

"I don't understand why you refuse to see the city as it really is," I said, pursuing my chain of thought.

"I might ask you the same question," Elias dodged.

"Come on, Elias, I'm serious."

"So am I."

"Look, do you want my help or not? It's a big world out there, you're only going to hurt yourself resisting it. Don't fight me—let me guide you."

Elias glared belligerently at me through the rising steam of his tea. For a moment it looked like he was planning some kind of petulant comeback, but finally he lowered his eyes submissively and heaved a big, resigned sigh. "It's an entire lifetime of habit. I can't change overnight."

"Take your time, Elias. It's human nature not to be able to break out of your mold. It's not about character—people are the same, it's their circumstances that change them. If Al Sharpton were rich, white, and female, he'd be Brooke Astor. You'll come round, you'll see."

"I have no idea what you're talking about."

"I'm saying, take it slow. Don't worry. We've got plenty of time."

I had no illusions about the work ahead of me. I don't mind admitting that I'd been a pretty hopeless student of aboriginal Lenape customs and history, but Elias turned out to be truly awesome in his ignorance of urban civilization. All it took, that first day, was a one-minute tour of the neighborhood to show me what I was up against. A pygmy straight out of the jungle could not have been more helpless. Elias had to be taught from scratch every little skill most of us take for granted: crossing the street on the light, reading a bus or subway map, riding an escalator, ordering a meal in a restaurant, calculating sales tax and counting change, talking to strangers, negotiating crowded sidewalks. You name it, he couldn't do it. He was most dangerous to himself, because he had the naïve fearlessness and curiosity of a toddler. I was terrified to let him out of my sight for a second, though I had my limits. Nothing could persuade me to leave my bed before sunrise to go "hunting."

But first things first. Every tourist to New York is warned not to attract attention to himself by looking out of place, and that seemed like a priority for Elias. He'd packed only what he considered to be his very best clothes, including his father's Navy uniform and khaki safari outfit, complete with pith helmet, and his grandfather's plus fours and tartan kneesocks. I explained as gently as I could that he was welcome to continue dressing for dinner at home if he wanted, but that under no circumstances would I allow him to walk the streets in that clothing. He seemed to understand, and invited me to choose a more suitable wardrobe. My own clothes were too big on him and he had no money of his own, so I dipped into my savings and we went shopping downtown.

Since he was a blank slate with no opinions, I had to come up with a look for him. We settled on a kind of commercial version of the "grunge" look: baggy jeans, work boots, floppy sweaters, and plaid flannel work shirts, topped off with a gray woolen mujahed cap. Posing for the mirror in a crowded outlet on Canal Street, surrounded by milling trendsetters ten years his junior, Elias didn't quite know what to make of himself.

"I think it's perfectly . . . *grovey,*" he said dubiously.

He was a little self-conscious in his new duds at first, walking jerkily like a marionette, shaking his ankles with each step. But in the end I think he was pleased with how it turned out. With his long, glossy hair and slim build, the look was a natural for him, and he turned a few heads on our walk home through the Village.

But clothes are one thing and behavior is something else. When we were together I could keep close tabs on him, but it was impossible to monitor him twenty-four hours a day. Like I said, there was no way I was going to drag myself out into the frigid morning to join him on his hunt. I had no idea where he went or what he did—he talked vaguely about "the waterfront" and "parkland"—but I had to assume he could take care of himself out there if he had to. Sure I worried, but he wasn't a child, after all. It wasn't until he'd been with me nearly a week that I had any reason to suspect that he was in over his head.

I was on my way home with the paper one morning when I ran into Annie, one of the prostitutes who worked the corner of Eleventh

Avenue, just as she was coming out of the Galaxie Diner. She was dressed in a rubberized miniskirt and white cowboy boots, and looked like she'd had a rough night. Still, I'd been a good customer and casual Samaritan to her in the past, and she always had something nice to say to me. Now she slipped her arm through mine as we walked together, hugging against me for warmth. Her voice was raw and gravelly from the cold.

"You know that friend of yours you introduced me to? He's some cutie, but boy is he weird."

"Yeah, he's kind of peculiar."

"The other morning, Desirée sees him walking down Forty-fourth, figures he's out for a date. It's a quarter to five, freezing cold, what else would he be there for? So she makes a beeline for him, right? But he gets to the train tracks, over the fence, down the embankment, and disappears into the tunnel. She's standing there another hour, no business, up he comes again, practically dancing down the street. What's he, a junkie or something?"

"I don't think so."

"Maybe he's got a boyfriend down there. Rich guy, likes to go slumming."

"I doubt it."

"How 'bout you, Ben? Party tonight?"

"Dream on."

"I sure could use a night in a warm bed." She hugged herself and shivered melodramatically, not that it did her any good.

"When did you ever get inside my bed, Annie?"

"Yeah, well, a nice harmless thing like you, a girl can always hope. Come see me." She gave my arm a squeeze and headed up Ninth, her white thighs quivering like tapioca.

Elias was drinking tea and staring out the living-room window when I got home.

"What've you been doing down on the tracks?" I demanded. He didn't seem surprised or disturbed by my tone.

"I am building a sweat lodge," he said calmly.

"A sweat lodge? Are you crazy?"

"There are no trains running anymore, you know."

"I'm not worried about trains. Those tunnels are filled with all kinds of people."

"I know. I've met a very nice gentleman named Sonny, a Negro gentleman. He's been helping me locate the materials I need."

"Listen, Elias. You don't know what you're doing. It's too dangerous for you down there. What do you need a sweat lodge for, anyway?"

"It will bring on the visions I need to find the Mahkohkwe. After all, that's my principal reason for visiting your city."

"What about a sauna? There's a health club just up the street. Wouldn't that do just as well?"

"No, it wouldn't."

"Wait here."

My landlord was at home, alone, thankfully. He was always much easier to deal with when he didn't have anyone to impress at my expense.

"A sweat lodge? What the fuck is a sweat lodge?" His bulk filled the frame of his front door, exuding suspicion and pepperoni.

"It's a kind of steam room," I whispered meekly. "It would only be temporary."

"You want to build a *steam room* in my garden? What the fuck for?"

"It's a health thing." I explained the benefits of steam to the skin, the lungs, the circulation. "And especially the heart," I added, eyeing his paunch meaningfully. "You could use it any time you wanted."

He gave this a little thought while he reached under the overhang of his belly for a scratch. "And it's not for any faggoty stuff, right? 'Cause I wouldn't want any of that going on in my garden."

"I promise."

He scratched again. "Well, sure. What the fuck, the yard's a mess anyhow."

Elias and I spent the rest of the day shuttling back and forth to the gardening center in Chelsea. We cleared away a patch of sickly forsythia at the bottom of the trash-strewn yard, near the back wall of a photographic-chemicals plant. We dug a shallow pit, over which we constructed a dome of bamboo poles and waterproof tarp, for want of saplings and birch bark. We wrapped it tight with nylon cord, leaving one waist-high flap as an entrance. Elias dug another, deeper pit nearby, in which to build a wood fire for heating rocks, which would then be lowered with metal tongs into the hole at the center of the lodge and sprinkled with water to create steam. My landlord watched the whole operation from his kitchen window on the first floor, shaking his head skeptically, but he showed a kind of sincere interest when it was all done and Elias beckoned him down and demonstrated its use.

"Nutty," he cackled in praise.

From then on, Elias spent the first hours of every day in his lodge, seeking the mystical revelations that were supposed to help him pick out his destined mate in a city of four million women. I tried it once or twice, but all I got were palpitations.

I took some time off work to help introduce Elias to city life and get him used to its dangers and complexities. It was well worth it for me to lose the income—even though Elias was completely dependent on me financially—in exchange for the real satisfaction of being his guide around town and seeing it through fresh eyes. Except for a few vacations here and there, I'd spent my whole life in New York; now, with Elias by my side, I was surprised by how much pleasure it gave me to be sharing my home with someone else. It was only now that I came to understand what my appearance on Turnaway must have meant to him. For me, it was even what you might call moving to realize how right he'd been all along about us having something to teach each other.

So I showed him the whole town, up and down, with the pride of ownership. I took him to all our great monuments and a lot of our lesser-known glories. We ate ethnic, the whole globe in five boroughs. We explored every museum from Washington Heights to Soho. We saw opera at the Met, performance art in the East Village, and the Knicks at the Garden. We attended uptown openings and downtown poetry bashes, piano recitals at the Y and underground after-hours clubs. Not to mention the Statue of Liberty. Basically, we went everywhere and did most everything you can do in New York. I kept Elias busy, and he was mostly game for all of it, even though so much went over his head, confusing and even frightening him at times. A lot of it struck him as a waste of time, typical *shuwonnock* distraction, without real usefulness or spiritual vitality. He was completely baffled by Christmas, for instance, and the Stock Exchange.

Still, at first he made an obvious effort to appreciate it all. If nothing else, I think it made him happy to see me so enthusiastic about anything. And it was true, whenever I showed him something he could respond to, like the Public Library or the Botanical Gardens, I felt as proud as if I'd built it with my own hands. But it didn't take me long to notice a certain kind of detachment, the same dreaminess that had come over him on the observation deck of the Empire State Building. Sometimes he actually seemed to float down the street like a ghost, untouched and unseen by the material world. When I first noticed this, I took it as a sign that I was pushing him too hard, boring him or asking him to assimilate too much new information at once. But gradually I began to understand what was going on.

I'd somehow imagined that, since we were standing side by side and looking in the same direction, he was seeing what I was seeing. But it wasn't so. He had this incredible map in his head—a miniature of his project at home—that corresponded to aboriginal New York, circa 1500. Wherever he went, whatever we saw, no matter how interesting or historical, Elias knew exactly what had been there or in the vicinity when it was nothing but trees and corn, and he'd trot out an anecdote about some event that had once taken place there, before the dawn of time practically. I was his guide on a tour of one New York, but he became mine on a tour of another. When I brought him to the Brooklyn Bridge and told him the story of its construction and invited him to admire the miracle of its form and structure, he told me of the village of Rechtauk that once clung to the banks of the river near Coenties Slip, where they weaved nets of such strength and suppleness that two children could catch enough shad in one day to last the entire village through the winter. When we went to City Hall, and I described the scene of Washington's inauguration, he took me to a spot not half a mile away, once a grassy meadow, where Chief Sawenarack and his warriors set out in great ceremony bearing a treaty belt to Onondaga. When we visited the echoing halls of the Public Library, a wonder as great as any of the ancient world, he told me of Chief Rechawanis, a man of such prodigious learning that he could recite the list of his ancestors all the way back to Turtle. When I took him deep into the subterranean vaults of Grand Central to dine at the Oyster Bar on lobsters that had been swimming off Georges Bank that very morning, he told me of a spot, ten minutes' walk from midtown, where the oysters once grew a foot wide and, if you knew how to approach them, could help you ward off evil spells into the bargain.

One day we went for a walk through East River Park. As we talked, we strolled past the housing projects and under the massive rusting tower of the Williamsburg Bridge. Elias told me that there, right there where we were standing, was the site of a terrible massacre of Wekweskik refugees—right there, across from the naval ship-yard and Wallabout Creek. But he also told me about a little freshwater brook that had once flowed and a deep, clear swimming hole about ten minutes' walk upstream where the Indian children had frolicked on hot summer afternoons, shaded by a canopy of ancient elms. He sighed wistfully.

"Ah yes, life was beautiful in those days."

"It's not as if your life is so bad now, you know," I said peevishly. "Your own island, a beautiful house, devoted servant. It's more than most people have."

Elias waved his hand dismissively. "That's like asking a house slave to be grateful for not having to pick cotton," he said. "This just isn't a natural situation. I can't be the only man on Earth who believes that he was born in the wrong time. Surely there are many who imagine they would have been happier in another era. It's all a matter of affinities, don't you see? Ancient Greece, Rome, the Dark Ages, precolonial Africa, shogun Japan, Renaissance Italy—for every time and place there ever was, there is someone alive today whose soul lives elsewhere. They don't belong here. A mistake has been made, a terrible mistake. I know where I belong, but even if I didn't, I'd know where I *don't* belong. What kind of affinity could ever induce anyone to want to live in the late twentieth century?"

"An affinity for nostalgia," I suggested.

"You have to see New York the way I see it," he went on, ignoring my joke. "For you, New York is the world, substantial and permanent. I try to see it your way—I really do—but I just cannot manage it. This place, this surface—it's an illusion, a mirage. For me, one good lungful of air could blow it all away. And what's left—the land, the rivers, the soil—for me, that is the only reality. And the people who live there, they'll be my descendants, not yours, no matter what their race."

"That kind of talk makes me sick," I said. "It's pathetic."

And on it went, tit for tat. It may seem now like it was a silly game, but at the time it felt like there was a lot at stake. No doubt, our visions were at odds. I felt defensive about mine, competitive even. His New York was a clean, wholesome place, full of nature's wonders and dangers, where honest labor and simple pleasures were the rewards of family and community, friendly cooperation, life in harmony with natural cycles, and other lies and myths. To him, it was a place that allowed human potential to come into its own fullness like a ripening berry, and that's what excited him so much. Oh, I'll admit it was concrete enough to him, but I saw the way his eyes glazed over whenever the passion came on him. My New York, on the other hand, was the real thing: stone, steel, and glass, where every building and every gutter was a tribute to the violent but real passions that move men. I don't mean to wax lyrical or anything, but to me New York is the truth about humanity made flesh—an ugly truth maybe, but since it's the truth, it has to be accepted, like it or not. My New York is the one that happened, not his.

I kept trying to remind Elias that he was here in the city for a purpose—to learn to live and think in the present, more or less—and that he wasn't helping himself by fighting my lessons and resisting my guidance. Did he or did he not want to be independent and capable of taking care of himself? He did, he insisted, but I was less than convinced; in fact, I sometimes suspected him of inventing superlatives just to keep up with me. But no, that wasn't it, he said. I just hadn't come up with any argument to persuade him that my way was better than his. For my part, it was hard to see that there could be any argument better than concrete reality.

From our bench in the rose garden of the United Nations, we had a sweeping view of the East River, from the Bronx in the north all the way to the Williamsburg Bridge and beyond. As always, the river carried a flotilla of garbage—tires, wooden crates, plastic bottles, boots, Styrofoam cartons—and its restless waters seemed to be forever moving in two directions at once.

"Look around you," I cried, exasperated. "Look at what you can see from here. Just look at it all! The great steel bridges, the billboards—Silvercup, Coca-Cola, Long Island City—the boats, hospitals, heliports, dockyards, schools, parks, churches, skyscrapers. And yes, even some trees! You've got all civilization right here from this bench. Now tell me something: in your day, what would you have seen from this spot, presuming it wasn't a salt marsh or a snake pit? Trees, trees, water and trees. Nothing but trees, and all flat along the river for miles and miles. A tepee or two—sorry, *wigwam*—a couple of canoes. Maybe, on a good day, a rack of venison set out in the sun to dry. Now you tell me: Where's the variety? What makes one place any different from the next? And why would you want to live in any of them?"

Elias stared at me in wide-eyed amazement, as if I'd just made the most ridiculous assertion of all time. "Now forgive me," he said tentatively, "because I do feel you're not a total idiot, but if you're not careful you're going to force me to speak to you in clichés, like a little child. My dear boy, it is the eyes that look but the heart that sees—don't you know that yet, at your age?"

"Don't give me that crap."

"Look, it's not terribly complicated. Where you see an undifferentiated mass of forest and water, the Lenape sees the places of his life. What do you know about those signs and dockyards and skyscrapers you love so much? Have you ever been there? Have they touched your life? Do you know the people who built those buildings or live in them? No you don't. But to my Indian, he can look at the shoreline and tell you, that's where you catch the fattest sturgeon, that's where the water runs deep and dangerous, that's where He-Who-Weeps-At-Night stepped on an urchin, that's where Touching-Bark Woman lost her virginity, that's where the soil is good for planting beans. This is his home, and nothing is more unique. You may not know that, Ben, because of the way you were raised. You can only have one home. That's what makes a place unique. And by the way, any Lenape could tell you that no two trees, even the most undistinguished pines, are so alike as any two skyscrapers you care to mention."

"My young Werther Running Deer, your imagination is in overdrive. The forests are gone forever but the concrete is here to stay. You'd better get used to it."

"It's not my imagination, it's my memory. I remember with my blood."

"Sees with his heart, remembers with his blood. . . . "

"Laugh all you like, but it's true. The problem with you people is that your blood has amnesia."

"I think you mean anemia."

I suppose it was inevitable that we'd have the occasional blowup. This wasn't our first, either—I was open-minded but no pushover. We always made up later, but this time I also learned an important lesson. Elias's interest in the Lenape wasn't historical or anthropological—it was deeply personal, anchored somewhere deep within his heart. I'd always known that about him, but now I realized that if I was ever going to win him over, help him find a place for himself in my city, I'd never do it by dragging him through monuments and anonymous public arenas. What he needed to see were the places of my life, where I'd been molded and educated, the sites of my triumphs and humiliations. New York could never be real to him unless it was as the filter of experience, the way scientists need to dye certain microorganisms to make them visible to the microscope. He made Lenapehoking real by tinting it with Wampage's life. Now I'd have to make New York real by coloring it with my blood.

So we stopped going to shows and readings and sports events and famous buildings. Instead, I took him to see the junior high school in Bensonhurst where I'd been beaten up every Friday afternoon for eighteen months for being a Jew. We walked through the courthouse

in downtown Brooklyn where my successive guardians had been chosen for me throughout my childhood. I took him to a quiet suburban
block in Flushing where I'd been abused by both foster parents until
I had planted a pair of poultry shears into my foster father's right
buttock. We sat on the Prospect Park bench to which I used to retreat
to read and nurse my wounds—for many years those books and that
bench were the only constants in my life. We went to the decaying
Ozone Park high school where, called like a truant into the principal's office in the middle of class, I'd first been introduced to Mrs.
Jampolski, the philanthropist widow who promised to pay my full
tuition at any university of my choice if I graduated and stayed out of
trouble. We stood outside the Park Avenue building where she'd
lived and died. We paid a call on the elderly Jewish couple in the
Seward Park Houses who kept me for four years—a record—but just
couldn't get by without the state subsidy they'd lose by adopting me.
One day we took the 1 train up to 116th Street, and I gave Elias a
tour of the Columbia campus.

We sat on the library steps in the quad, our faces upturned to the
pallid winter sun. Around us, students hurried by, their shoulders
hunched against the chill, or stood in tight little groups, conferring
with bowed heads. I closed my eyes; I couldn't feel the cold.

"I imagine you did quite well here, in your studies," Elias said
quietly.

"Pretty well, under the circumstances."

"Why join the civil service, then? Surely there were more challenging careers available to an Ivy League graduate?"

"There were. That's exactly why I joined the civil service."

"I often wish I had gone to university. I should have liked to make
some friends," Elias sighed.

"I studied very hard. I had a lot of catching up to do."

"I've read that the friends you make in college, you keep for life.
Is it true?"

"Not really."

"Still, you must have some friends from that time."

"Not really."

Elias sighed again. "How very lonely you came to be, Ben."

"Americans don't come to be lonely, Elias. They're born lonely. That's the beauty of this country—you can live in exile without ever leaving home."

Elias mulled this over for a while. I thought he was trying to come up with some sort of diplomatic response, but I was wrong.

"I don't quite see the pleasure or purpose of living in a big city if you have no friends."

"I didn't say I have no friends. I just said I didn't make any in college."

"Perhaps you could introduce me to your friends."

A sharp gust of wind from the river disturbed a carpet of brittle gray leaves on the lawn. I watched them wheel and glide across the quad until they were caught in the wrought-iron grille of the east gate.

"You already met my friend Annie, didn't you?" I said.

"Yes."

"We could have breakfast with her tomorrow, if you wanted."

"Well, we could do that."

The next morning, at six-fifteen, we slipped into a booth at the back of the Galaxie, where Annie and Desirée were already sipping coffee and touching up their makeup in the wall mirror. I took the place next to Annie and Elias sat by Desirée, who was dressed in a black leather bustier and sequined cling pants. They were surprised and a little annoyed by our intrusion at first, but when I explained that Elias had asked to meet some of my neighborhood acquaintances they seemed flattered to be included.

"Well, tunnel boy," Desirée said with an evil grin, running a long red fingernail down the back of his hand. "Ever find what you were looking for?"

Elias withdrew his hand and grabbed for his coffee cup like it was a life preserver. "I . . . that is . . . why yes, thank you," he stammered.

The women laughed at his confusion. Desirée turned to me. "We've been watching your friend," she said.

"We think he's sweet," Annie said.

Elias blushed wildly and buried his nose in his cup. The women roared, rocking back and forth.

"I say he's a cherry, Des. What do you say?"

"I believe you're right, girlfriend."

"Girls, you're embarrassing Elias," I interrupted before it got out of hand. This wasn't going the way I'd hoped—neither of them had ever spoken to *me* that way. "Why don't we talk like friends?"

"Friends can tease, can't they?" Desirée pouted, but they left him alone after that.

Breakfast came and I steered the conversation onto a more sociable track. I knew Elias would be interested in their lives—not so much their work but their fears, their stratagems for survival, how they kept their dreams alive, that sort of thing—and they were happy to talk about themselves. Both of them, but Desirée especially, were good talkers, peppering their monologues with vivid metaphors and philosophical asides, and Elias seemed to be engrossed. He hardly said a word the whole time, and it wasn't until I was mopping away the last of the egg yolk with my toast that I noticed he'd barely touched his oatmeal. The color was rising in his cheeks again, and it was obvious that the talk was striking an emotional chord with him. Desirée had been gabbing a mile a minute, her eyes locked on mine, so it wasn't until that very moment that I realized what was going on. Her left hand had disappeared under the table; I leaned slightly forward and saw that it was clamped onto Elias's upper thigh, gently clenching and unclenching. When she caught me looking, she smirked subtly. Just then, a napkin happened to flutter to the floor, and she stretched all the way across Elias to reach it, her breasts practically in his lap. Elias jumped out of his seat like he'd been bitten.

"Excuse me. I have to . . . the lavatory?"

When he was gone I gave Desirée a furious glare, but she just shrugged her shoulders innocently and mouthed a silent "what?" She leaned across the table and whispered something to Annie, and they both giggled. By the time Elias returned, they were ready to leave. I told them the check was on me and we all stood up. The women gave me a quick peck on the cheek then turned on Elias, who hung his head like a schoolboy.

"Come see us," Annie said, pressing her mouth against his cheekbone and leaving a patch of moist pink lipstick near his ear.

"First time on the house," Desirée purred, squeezing his biceps, and then they were mincing their way down the aisle, followed by a chorus of clucking and tsking from the bow-tied waiters. Elias and I sat down to our unfinished coffee.

Elias was quiet and solemn for the next few minutes. It was hard to tell if he was ashamed or angry at what had happened, but in any case he certainly wasn't charmed. I let him muse rather than risk making it worse with some awkward apology or explanation. But when he finally looked up and folded his hands primly before him like a politician about to make a public statement, I was surprised by the serene and melancholy determination in his voice.

"I think it's time I began looking for the Mahkohkwe," he said.

"Listen, Elias, I'm really sorry."

"No, please, Ben. Don't apologize. I'm very glad you introduced me to your friends. You've helped recall me to my true purpose in leaving Turnaway."

"Glad to be of service. But about this Mahkohkwe business, Elias."

"Yes?"

"It's just that—isn't it a bit risky to place all your hopes in one woman? What if you never find her? There are so many women in the world."

"Like your friends?"

"That's not what I meant. But you don't have to set your sights so high. Why set yourself up to be disappointed? You're a great guy, any woman in the world would be glad to get you."

"I might say the same about you. And yet you set your sights so low."

"Have another look, Elias. I'm glad to take what I can get."

"Well, I'm very sorry you feel that way, Ben. Nevertheless, I have told you before," he said haughtily, raising his nose. "I am saving myself for the Mahkohkwe."

"But what about urges? You're a man—you have needs. I know you do."

"Well, I do. But you know, a Lenape warrior must be very disciplined."

"Come off it! Your ancestors were a fun-loving bunch. Don't tell me they were above a little nooky now and then."

"Perhaps they did and perhaps they didn't," he sniffed. "But they could afford to. They were surrounded by women of the blood. But my seed is precious—I must preserve it to propagate the race."

There was obviously no getting through to him, so I let it drop.

But it soon became very clear that his intention to go out and search for the Mahkohkwe was no idle threat. If I'd somehow imagined her to be an obsession—born of loneliness and nurtured in self-delusion—that would soon dissolve in the face of the busy world, Elias proved me very wrong. In fact, from the very moment we left the diner that morning, he went about preparing himself radically for the impending changes in his life, the way a bride-to-be starts dieting the day of the proposal so she'll look her best in her wedding gown.

He disappeared into his sweat lodge that morning and did not emerge until suppertime, not even to eat or relieve himself. I know, because I sat in the living-room window all day long, worrying that he was doing himself real harm in his zeal. But when he did reappear he was visionary, his skin translucent and pink, his shining eyes fixed on some invisible prize like a saint before martyrdom. I hardly knew what to say to him—was this the same man who had allowed himself to be fondled by a whore in the back of a diner that very morning? But it seems he wasn't waiting for my comments. He floated over to the dining table and began to speak the moment he sat down, all but naked in his loincloth.

"I shall need some time to myself to complete my search," he said in a detached monotone. "The Mahkohkwe will reveal herself through milestones and markers that she has unwittingly left throughout the city."

"Kind of like a bear in the woods," I offered. Elias winced briefly but went on.

"These are very subtle markers. I will need all my concentration and spiritual equipoise to detect them. Yes, in a sense, I will be tracking her down like a hunter. But this is a hunt I must undertake alone, Ben, without distraction or hindrance. I would suggest you return to work, since there is nothing you can do to help me. Don't be hurt—finding her will be the greatest possible celebration of our friendship. You must know that without you I should never have found the courage to venture out in pursuit of her."

"That's just what worries me," I said plaintively. "I don't want to see you out on some wild-goose chase on my account, Elias. Even if she does exist, which I doubt, what are the odds of finding her? And say you do, by some miracle—what makes you think she's just going to throw herself at you and say 'Take me. I'm the mother of your race'? This is New York, Elias, not Bayreuth. Women just don't behave that way, believe me."

But Elias folded his hands in his lap, closed his eyes, and gave a Buddha-like smile. "You let me worry about that, Ben. I will find her."

"Well, I don't like it."

Like it or not, I went back to work—day shifts now, so that I could spend my evenings with Elias—and he went out into the city. The truth is, I was conflicted about this turn of events. I guess I was like any parent. On the one hand, I was worried sick about him every minute he was out of my sight. He was so inexperienced, and anything could happen. On the other hand, my stated aim had been to make him strong and independent, and nothing I taught him could ever do that as well as freedom and exploration. I had to button my lip and say a prayer every time he left me at the front door. I could try to influence or scare him into behaving sensibly, but he was used to getting his own way and finally ended up doing whatever took his fancy, even if it meant venturing into neighborhoods I'd specifically warned him against. I sometimes got home from work while he was still out, and then I'd spend the hours waiting for his return and fretting over visions of his body, bloody and stripped of its meager possessions, lying in a rubble-strewn lot in some forgotten corner of Brooklyn. He'd wander out in all weather and in every direction, bold and foolhardy like a child, and nothing could keep him out of any hellhole he considered his by right of first possession. There were times I thought he did it just to get a rise out of me, but the truth is, his head was in the clouds most of the time. I won't say that every tale he had to tell was calculated to fill me with horror and dread; but it's also true that I'm not so easily shaken as most parents.

He had a basic plan that seemed to give him great confidence, but sounded pretty half-baked to me. His idea was to visit all the neighborhoods of the city that had once been Indian settlements. He figured that if the Mahkohkwe had ever been in one of these neighborhoods, too—say, on the burial site of one of her ancestors, or a place where they had lived and loved—her Indian soul would have vibrated in sympathy and left its own signature there. If Elias's own inner antenna was sufficiently attuned and uncluttered, he hoped to pick up a trace of this vibration, like a scent, and use it to track her down, via triangulation or something. I don't claim to understand what he was really up to, but I wasn't shy about letting him know how crazy and pathetic I found the whole quest to be. Still, after his three-hour predawn steam, he was out there every day, walking the streets, sniffing around, letting his mind wander, following his inner map at whim. After supper, when the dishes were done and we relaxed in the living room, I'd grit my teeth and hear out the latest installment of his self-guided excursion through New York.

The funny thing is, more often than not Elias's particular interests took him into the uglier parts of town. I don't know why the Indians always seemed to live in areas that later became slums or gasworks, but they did. You might think, like I did, that these excursions were nothing but an extended graveyard tour, that Elias would grow tired and depressed after visiting the sites of ancient Indian occupation day after day—sites he'd dreamed about all his life and incorporated with loving care, each and every one, into his "project"—only to find them overlaid with asphalt, housing projects, body shops, garbage dumps, ganglands, whatever.

But no—he came back fortified and reinvigorated from each day's outing. How he did it I'll never know—it was like he wore these X-ray glasses from some science-fiction movie that allowed him to see through the present into the distant past. When he went to Bensonhurst, it was the settlement of Techkonis he saw. When he strolled along Kings Highway, it was the woodland path of Mechawanienk that guided his course. To him, the meat-packing district, with its bedraggled hookers and abandoned railroad trestle, was Sapokanikan, a landing beach for trade between the Canarsee and the western tribes. Most English and Dutch place-names really did sound as foreign to him as they would have to Wampage, and he avoided using them wherever he could. Now I know all this makes him sound crazy, and maybe he was, but in a good way. If you keep a dog on a short leash all the time then suddenly let him off it, he doesn't care where he is—he's just glad to be able to go at his own pace, anywhere he wants. Elias was kind of like that. After spending an entire lifetime cooped up on his tiny island, he was liberated, finally free to visit his ancient homeland, and it was joyous. It didn't take long for the effects of his new freedom to show. Every day, I watched Elias grow into his skin, into the identity he'd spent his life forging for himself. Before, it had been a fragile, empty shell. Now it was full, vital, vigorous. It was a beautiful process to watch, and I watched it with pride and, yes, maybe a little envy.

Not that every day was a picnic. Sometimes reality did manage to creep in around the edges. Like I said, crossing the street was always a harrowing experience for him, and he had a number of close calls. And then, when he finally got the hang of it, he was always forgetting about bicycle messengers speeding in the wrong direction and was knocked down a few times. He was always taking naps on somebody's lawn or pulling up their prize rosebushes looking for artifacts and vibrations. He got himself mugged in Inwood Park, propositioned by an aggressive transvestite in Tribeca, sworn at all over Forest Hills, had a knife held to his throat in Spanish Harlem, and spent six hours in the Tombs for trespassing on city property. Except for a few nicks and scratches, he generally came away unscathed from these adventures. More often than not, he wasn't even aware that he'd been in any danger.

Let me describe one of Elias's typical adventures on the town. On this particular day, he decided to visit the site of a Canarsee village in Brooklyn. In his mind's eye he could see precisely where that village had once stood; he lined up those coordinates with a street map, found the nearest subway stop, and was off. Riding the D train to Brighton Beach, he got off in one of the toughest sections of Flatbush and asked for directions to the intersection that marked the spot he was looking for. Now I may have mentioned that, whether or not Lenape blood actually flowed through Elias's veins, it was hard to peg him as anything but white. Black Irish, maybe, was the most exotic ethnicity his complexion suggested, not that being black or Hispanic in a neighborhood like that is any guarantee of safety. And anyway, if you really want to minimize your risk, you don't ask directions from teenage drug dealers carrying ill-concealed 9-mm pistols in their belts.

"They didn't seem terribly busy," he explained. "All they were doing was loitering on the corner, chatting on the phone or with passersby."

They told him to get lost. He told them he was already lost; they were suddenly eager to see him to his destination. He was touched by their solicitude. Surrounded by a gang of teenagers in quilted trenchcoats and mirror shades, he set off into the wild, unknown quarters of Flatbush.

And this is where the story gets a little hazy for me. According to Elias, in answer to some question he told them the nature of his mission and began describing the area and its inhabitants as they'd been in the sixteenth century. It seems he went into some detail. By the time they reached the vacant lot that marked the village site, his guides were thoroughly engrossed. It was hard to picture: soft little Elias in his oblivious-to-all-else storytelling mode, surrounded by vicious thugs in a faceless slum in Brooklyn, happily discussing the subtleties of Indian crop rotation.

"And they never made a move on you?" I asked, incredulous.

"No, they were very friendly after the ice was broken. I don't know why you should call them thugs, not having met them."

"They were carrying guns?"

"So? The Lenape always carried their weapons with them, and we were hardly thugs."

"I don't think these boys were hunting elk, Elias."

"Well, perhaps not. Nonetheless, they were perfectly well behaved."

I could only shake my head in disbelief. Every evening it was some nightmare or other, and every morning I begged him in vain to be more careful. He was going to go where he was going to go. If I objected, he'd tell me that I was just jealous because he was getting to know the city better than I did. That was ridiculous and I denied it, of course.

And then, too, cheerful and optimistic as he mostly was—and convinced that he was making progress in his search for the Mahkohkwe—his morale in the face of New York's horrors didn't always escape a bruising. I remember, for instance, one evening after he returned from a Hackensack site on western Staten Island, or Monocknong, as he insisted I call it. From the moment I stepped through the door and found him staring out the window with a mug of sassafras in his hand, I could tell that something had deeply disturbed him.

"You people are disgusting," he finally said.

"What'd I do?"

"Everything's disposable with you, isn't it? First Potter's Field, now this."

"This what?"

"Fresh Kills," he muttered, slowly shaking his head in disbelief. "Fresh Kills! You might think, mightn't you, even in this dreadful city of yours, that a name like that would mean something. That's one reason I went—it sounds like the translation of an Indian name. Limpid brooks. Shaded waterways. Ample, healthy game. Fat fish. Fresh kills."

I knew what was coming.

"A mountain," he went on after a pause to collect himself. "It was a mountain of garbage. Literally. Hundreds of feet high. Miles broad at the bottom. And the stench—I could smell it across the island. A stinking, putrid mountain of garbage. As if someone had thrown away the whole world. It was the most horrible thing I've ever seen in my life." Believe it or not, a tear trickled down his cheek, just like the Indian in the commercial.

"It's the city dump. Fresh Kills landfill," I said gently. "Anyone could have told you."

But he had no snappy answer to that; he was genuinely distraught, and shut himself in the bathroom for a long, hot bath that made the steam curl up from under the door. He remained quiet through dinner, but afterward he had a story ready.

"In those days, the first *shuwonnock* used to set their hogs out to forage in the woods. The hogs fattened on acorns and roots, at no expense to their owners, while the underbrush was cleared away in preparation for leveling the forest. Often, then, the first sign of white people in the vicinity was the sudden appearance of hogs in the woods. Many Indians thought they were demons sent by Mahtantu to harass the good people, and since the hogs were most often found uprooting the Lenapes' vegetable gardens and cornfields, not to mention the wild medicinal herbs on which their health depended, this view soon became widely held. No one dared approach or scare off the creatures, and as a result many gardens were destroyed before the truth was eventually discovered.

"Well, one day Wampage and Cokoe were hunting for pigeons in the woods of Manhattan, which belonged to their friend and ally Reckgawak, when they heard a strange and forceful rustling and crashing in the brush. Creeping stealthily toward the source of the noise, they crouched behind a mulberry bush and peered through its branches. There, in the clearing of an abandoned plot, were four of the oddest-looking beasts ever seen in Lenapehoking—pinkish gray like the flesh of a corpse, each had a bladder-shaped body on four stubby legs, the hooves of a deer, a tail like the tendril of the wild grape, a snout formed like a war club, and tiny round eyes that spun in their sockets like meadowlarks feeding at twilight. With every step they took, their noses deep in the grass, they grunted like whelping bitches, with the frequency and varied inflections of heated discussion. Wampage and Cokoe crouched at the edge of the clearing, awestruck and terrified, not daring to utter a sound lest these hideous apparitions sense their presence. Finally, Wampage leaned into Cokoe's ear.

" 'What are they?' he whispered.

" '*Manitowak,*' Cokoe replied. 'They have come from the spirit country to plague our people. So says Wapakhsin, who has spoken to one of them.'

" 'Why have they come?'

" 'It is said they are preparing the way for one more powerful and evil than they, sowing fear and destruction to ease his path, Mahtantu. They kill the crops with their gaze and breathe poisonous fumes from their nostrils. We must hurry or they will see us.'

" 'No, wait.' Wampage grabbed Cokoe's forearm as he turned to leave. 'We must wait.' Cokoe obeyed, as always putting his faith in his trusted friend. They waited in silence for several minutes, aware only of the horrible grunting of the demons and the rasp of their own labored breathing. Cokoe had seen Wampage in this stance before: brave as he was, he was too canny to be impetuous and always carefully sized up his enemy before deciding on a course of action. This is the measure of a great warrior. But even Cokoe's trust in Wampage was tested to the limit when, with no warning, his friend stood up and strode several paces into the clearing. Cokoe stood too, but remained in the shadows as Wampage beat his breast with his right fist.

" 'I am Wampage, the son of Tiyas,' he shouted, the shock of his voice echoing through the empty woods. The demons ceased their noises and leveled their tiny, malevolent eyes upon him.

" 'I am the fearless nephew of a fearless chief,' Wampage went on boldly, though Cokoe, who had often heard him harangue his foes, detected a slight quaver of trepidation in his voice, 'and I am a fearless war captain of the Siwanoy. Yuho!'

"The demons stood stock still, and all the forest trembled. The very breezes held their breath.

" 'I have flayed the skins of doughtier warriors than you,' Wampage threatened. 'I have many belts from those who have sued me for peace and many scalps from those who didn't get the chance. Yuho! I will open your bellies and tie you to a stake with your own guts and cut the flesh from your face in strips before I burn you. Yuho!'

"One of the demons snorted, and the four of them, their eyes never leaving the proud figure of the warrior, sidled toward each other as if banding together out of fear. Wampage gave Cokoe a sidelong smirk of triumph.

" 'Now listen to me!' he went on. 'You leave this place or I will do all these things. I will eat your testicles. Yuho! Tell your grandfather we are numerous as locusts. Tell your grandfather we are the sons of bears and the nephews of wolves. Tell your—'

"Wampage was cut off in mid-sentence by a shrill cry and the sound of snapping branches. Something was approaching the clearing from the opposite side. At the sound of the call, the demons perked up their floppy ears and began grunting in chorus, moving toward the source of the noises at the far edge of the woods. His chin raised in defiance, his fists clenched with tension, Wampage waited for the enemy to declare himself. Cokoe took another step deeper into the shadows. A moment later, the bushes at the end of the clearing parted, and from the gloomy breach emerged . . . two young *shuwonnock* boys, red-haired, dressed in leather breeches and deerskin vests, each carrying a loop of rope in either hand.

" '*Varkentje, varkentje,*' called one of them, and Cokoe recognized the high-pitched voice that had cut Wampage cold. '*Kom's hier, biggetje!*'

"The demons ran squealing toward the boys, and Wampage, some fifty yards away, instinctively stepped forward and reached for his weapons to defend the little Dutch boys. It was then that they noticed the Indian for the first time, a bone dagger in one hand, bow and quiver on his back, braided roach of bear-greased hair dangling down his neck. The boys grew pale and clung to one another but seemed rooted to the ground. Wampage, too, froze and did not move. Though the boys were clearly terrified of the warriors, they seemed to have no fear of the demons. Did the boys have command over the devil beasts? As if in answer to Wampage's unspoken question, the larger of the two boys pointed a finger to the creatures.

" '*Zwijnen,*' he said tentatively. '*Papa's varkens.*'

"Wampage nodded solemnly but said nothing. Encouraged, the boys moved into the demons' midst and began looping their ropes over the creatures' necks. They both kept repeating '*varkens, varkens,*' like an incantation to keep the demons quiescent, and their fearful eyes never left the two Indian men who watched in stony silence. When all the beasts were roped, the boys urged them, with some resistance, toward the woods from which they had emerged, and when all four animals and one of the boys had been swallowed up by the shade, the other turned back one last time toward Wampage and Cokoe.

" '*Jullie zwijnen,*' he said simply, then skittered into the shadows. The sound of giggling followed the *shuwonnocks'* passage as they fled.

"Wampage and Cokoe listened to the heavy, clumsy sounds of the boys moving away, and when they no longer heard anything but the hum of insects and the business of the birds, they returned to Lapechwahacking and related the afternoon's puzzling events to their people."

I sat and waited for Elias to get on with his story, but he continued to stare out into the blackness of Forty-fourth Street.

"Is that it?" I asked, disappointed.

Very slowly, he turned his head toward me, and as his eyes came into view I saw how cold with sadness and contempt they were. He just stared as if expecting and half wishing that I would melt away.

"I would have thought that was more than enough," he finally said, but I didn't understand.

On the whole, Elias's enthusiasm and growing sense of confidence survived these little setbacks. He'd mastered aspects of modern life that had completely stumped him at first, like pay phones and automatic tellers and the subway system, even obscure lines like the J or G. He was comfortable in his new clothes and had learned how to buy practical shoes and groceries. He even let me take him to the movies, and though they mostly bored or confused him, I still remember his excitement when he pointed out that the so-called Mohicans in one film we saw were actually speaking Munsee. It's not like he'd become a child of the city or anything, but he was definitely changing. His Wampage stories were becoming less and less frequent, as were his references to the Mahkohkwe.

You could hear the change, too, in his conversations with Dr. Ross, who had begun sending him a small monthly stipend, barely enough to cover his subway fares but still and all a welcome symbol. Now that Elias was out of his clutches, all bitterness and chest pounding had been set aside. They missed each other and spoke on the phone every week. Sometimes, just to gauge Elias's resistance to Ross's subtle ploys and insinuations, I'd listen in on the other extension. Like a child away at camp, Elias would run down his list of activities, and Ross would urge him to exercise caution and mind his health. I can't pretend that I didn't feel sorry for the old guy, all alone on his island, but I had to exert my authority over Elias and forbid him to accept Ross's repeated invitations to a weekend, or even a day, on Turnaway. I felt that he wasn't strong enough yet, that Ross would make quick work of his defenses and lure him back in no time. When you meet with Dr. Ross, I told him, it has to be as equals. Of course, it had always been my idea that Elias should return to Turnaway. I hadn't stolen him away for good, like Jack stealing the goose. As far as I was concerned, he was on a sort of sabbatical—to pause, to rest, to reflect, and maybe to learn. I had no doubt that the time would come, maybe even quite soon, when I could give my blessing to a reunion, but not yet. Elias was saddened by my intransigence, but he accepted my superior wisdom on this point.

But what could I do when the old man showed up on my doorstep one Saturday morning in late February? Slam the door in his face? Some people might, but not me. I showed him upstairs, where he and Elias engaged in a touching scene of silent reunion, which I observed from the doorway. The doctor then shuffled over to the couch—shuffled like a codger, which I'd never seen him do before—and sat down, very businesslike, his hands on his knees. He looked tired and sad.

"Elias," he said, never one to mince words, "when will you come home?"

Unprepared, Elias looked at me with panic in his eyes, but I raised my hands to my chest, palms forward in a gesture of neutrality. This was a good test for him—he was alone with the doctor, but I was there as a kind of symbolic prop, inert but present. Elias stared at him as if at a large, unwholesome mess he'd been asked to pick up. Finally, before he spoke, I saw him brace and stiffen his lower back.

"I don't know," he said with admirable resolve. Ross was visibly shaken.

"Please, Elias," he pleaded. "You should come home now. There is much you do not understand."

"Ross—Joseph," Elias said gently, almost whispering. "That's why I must stay here for now."

The conversation sort of petered out after that. It was obvious that Elias had no intention of giving in, though he behaved with all the love and deference that Ross could have wished for. It wasn't long after that the doctor shuffled back out the door into a waiting gypsy cab, looking even more defeated than when he'd arrived. After his car had pulled away, I gave Elias a big hug, but he wasn't in the mood to be congratulated.

So, all in all, it's fairly easy to see why, as the winter wore on, I was beginning to feel more and more optimistic about Elias and his prospects. He hadn't been a promising student, and I was inexperienced as a mentor, to say the least, and yet we'd made—let's face it—pretty remarkable progress. Progress—what else could you call it? Here was this man—this boy—who only three months earlier had been withdrawn, fearful, prone to fantasy if not delirium, dangerously naïve, full of denial and suppressed emotion, and so on and so forth—a cripple, let's say, to stretch a point. And now? Well, you couldn't exactly claim he was cured—he still preferred his fantasy world to this, his layers of defensive shell to the real, vulnerable identity beneath. But what strides! What a difference! Now, at least, he'd been forced to acknowledge the real world and its substance; now he knew it was a brick wall and not a mirage to walk through. Maybe he found it ugly, alienating, devoid of values—but at least he'd found it. You couldn't say it was *only* a first step—it was precisely *because* it was the first step that nothing, afterward, could ever be the same for Elias. Whether he chose it or not, New York in his mind was now a real alternative to Lenapehoking, manhood a real alternative to Peter Panhood.

I began to allow myself to cherish great ambitions for his future. Elias would return to Turnaway a new man, ready to assert his place as its master. He'd put a quick stop to whatever nasty little plan the doctor had cooked up for Turnaway. He'd put his foot down. What couldn't he do, if he had a mind to do it? Imagine, for instance, what a man like that—confident, articulate, charismatic—might do as a leader of Native Americans. The Mashantucket Pequots, the Golden Hill Paugussets, and the Uncasville Mohegans were all small tribes, but look what they'd done for themselves—Elias could do the same! Instead of living in some pathetic utopia, he could lead his people into a new era of prosperity, equality, cultural revival. Or, if he chose, he could turn Turnaway into an educational center, a museum, an arts colony. Or he could have a glorious career in academia. Or he could become an artist—all he needed to do was find a niche and market his talents. Or he could simply get married, have kids, lead a normal life on a beautiful island, filling Dr. Ross's old age with the sound of laughing children and a promise of continuity. Yes, and if he did any of these things, or explored any number of other possibilities I hadn't even considered, I would have been responsible for making it happen, I would have been the catalyst. He'd have become everything I'd hoped to make him, everything I knew I could never make myself. I don't mind admitting that, on some of those evenings when I allowed my mind to drift into fantasies of Elias's glorious future, I enjoyed a certain glow of self-satisfaction.

But then one evening in early March, I came home from work to find Elias on the sofa, staring into space as if in a trance. He looked terrible. His face, usually a lovely rose flush beneath an olive complexion, was pale as flour and kind of chalky. His clothes were ragged, his shirt pulled out of his belt and torn in strips in several places. His hair was a nest. The sole of one of his new Doc Martens hung loose, exposing a wet and soiled tube sock. He smelled funny, though I couldn't quite place the scent. I knew it, I thought to myself as I kneeled down to remove his boots for him; he'd finally gotten himself hurt. He didn't look too badly injured; maybe this would teach him a lesson. As he sat, catatonic, I checked his upper body for blood or wounds but found none.

I tried to press him for details of what had happened, but he just sat there, ignoring or unaware of me. I was beginning to worry—what if he'd been banged on the head and was suffering from concussion or shock? I was just about ready to call for an ambulance when he turned to me and smiled. It was no ordinary smile. If you've ever tried to coax a smile from an infant, and you waggle your fingers and coo and say "ye-e-ess, ye-e-ess," and the baby just looks at you confused, or bored, or maybe even a little frightened, then suddenly breaks into this shattering smile, then you'll understand the smile Elias gave me.

"What happened to your clothes?" I asked.

"I saw her," he said.

"Saw who?"

"The Mahkohkwe. I found her."

Elias never did manage to tell me how he'd gotten so disheveled that afternoon. It seems he'd been wandering the streets in a daze for some hours, but that was as much as he was able to recall. Now that he'd broken the news so dramatically, however, he could hardly contain himself.

"I tried to gain access to Pagganck," he said, leaning forward on the sofa. "Did you know they call it Governor's Island now? It serves as headquarters for your Coastal Guard. The guardsmen just laughed in my face when I explained my mission. They must have taken me for an unstable type. Then they threatened to eject me bodily. I managed to leave with my dignity intact and headed uptown along William Street, searching for the site of the possibly fictive settlement of Ashibic. It was, appropriately, at the corner of Maiden Lane that I happened to glance through a tall glass wall into the lobby of an office building. And there she was. I didn't need to look twice to recognize her—she stood out like a bead of purple wampum in a bowl of white. Her skin of moistened umber, her black hair, her white teeth—I have seen them all a thousand times in my dreams. She wore a suit of navy wool, and on her head a gleaming ring of nacre—"

"A headband," I interrupted.

"She sat on a bench at the side of the lobby, apparently waiting for someone to join her for lunch. I stood outside, staring in. I must have been pressing against the glass, because when I moved my nostrils left two little hearts of frozen vapor on the pane. I didn't know what to do. There she was, I tell you, just as I had always been expecting her, almost within grasping distance, and I didn't know what to do. It was impossible that I let her go without making contact, but it was impossible to imagine approaching her—my dream! my dream!—and addressing her. At any moment she might leave and the opportunity would be lost. I didn't know what to do!

"And then it came to me, with simple, straightforward logic. I understood it the way one understands things in a dream, as if there were no possibility of mistake—she was waiting for *me*! She was sitting there, tapping her left foot on the marble, glancing at her watch, smoothing down the pleats of her skirt, because *I* was late for our appointment! And when I understood that, it was easy. I didn't think about my clothing, my hair, my fingernails. I had no plan. I just pushed through the revolving doors, crossed the lobby, sat down next to her, and introduced myself."

"You spoke to her?"

"What else was I to do?" he pleaded, jumping to his feet. Nervous again, reliving every moment of the encounter, he began to pace the floor like a caged animal. "This was the Mahkohkwe! What should I have done—sent her a telegram?"

"Why not, for a start? At least you wouldn't come across like some nut off the street."

"But that's just it, Ben," he turned to me, his eyes round with the memory. "That's just it, you see. She wasn't afraid of me at all. She told me her name and shook my hand. She *had* been waiting for me after all."

"I don't get it," I croaked, wiping the sweat off my upper lip. "Start from the beginning. What exactly did you say to her?"

"I said: 'Hello, I am Elias Hutchinson. I am very pleased to know you.'"

"And she?"

"She smiled and shook my hand. She said: 'Emily Wolfe. How are you?' I said: 'Fine, thank you. How are you?' She said: 'Hungry. Shall we go?' And she stood up and we left the building."

"No!"

"It's all true. We walked about a block; our shoulders were almost touching. She walked fast, though her heels were high. She told me the name of a restaurant; she asked if I'd ever been. I said no, I was new in town. She said she thought I'd like it and she began describing some of her favorite dishes. And I was thinking, not quite believing this was happening: 'She likes linguine—how charming! She drinks Vernacchia—how delightful! Her name is Emily Wolfe—I love her!' And then we arrived at the restaurant. She had made a reservation. We sat in a booth."

"She thought you were someone else!"

"Well yes. It's true, she did, as it happens. It turned out she had been waiting for a client, a new client she had never met who was twenty minutes late. When I showed up she was so relieved she hadn't even heard me say my name. She had just assumed I was he."

"Jesus! So what'd she do?"

"Well, she was quite upset when I explained I wasn't her client. She wanted to leave. She said: 'But why did you approach me?' I said: 'I thought you were beautiful and I imagined we might like one another if we had a chance to meet.' Since I was a perfect stranger, I thought she'd accepted for the same reason."

"Did you tell her she was the Mahkohkwe?"

"Are you mad? Well, she thought about what I'd said and saw it was true, and then, you know, she laughed about it. She said she thought it was a wonderful story. I said, as you taught me, 'You can't be too careful about strangers in this town.' She said quite right and that she could not continue our lunch because she had to return to the office to see if her client had shown up."

"Ah, too bad."

"But before she left, she told me that I had intrigued her. I gave her the telephone number here and she is going to call me this evening."

"You don't seriously think she'll call, do you?"

But she did call, that very evening. Elias answered the phone in the next room. The conversation was brief—I could hear its cadence through the door—then Elias emerged, blushing and smiling shyly.

"We are to meet for supper next week," he said, all bashful. "Perhaps I am more attractive to the opposite sex than you credit me with being."

"Don't you believe it," I said, clapping him on the back. "She's the Mahkohkwe. She had to say yes—it's destiny."

"Oh yes. I'd quite forgotten."

That night I lay in bed and tried to figure it all out. The Mahkohkwe! If he'd told me he'd found the fountain of youth, or had bagged Bigfoot, or had encountered Wampage himself in the lingerie department of Saks, I couldn't have been more surprised. Or skeptical. The Mahkohkwe, as I'd always figured, didn't exactly exist. Sure, he'd made a big thing out of having seen her once on Turnaway, but I knew better—she was a legendary figure, a sort of bogeyman, a taboo. She was a placebo for experience—so long as she was out there, unattainable and otherworldly, Elias had a reason and an excuse to avoid any emotional entanglements. I figured that even he would have admitted that much, if pressed hard enough. So of course the last thing I'd have expected was that he'd put himself on the spot by actually *finding* her. He had a lot to lose. It was like those cults that predict the Second Coming—once you proclaim the arrival of the messiah, you'd damn well better be right, because one mistake and you end up in Waco.

So the way I had it figured, he'd finally come across a woman who fit the bill, someone who could pass for an Indian princess, and had taken his best shot. Of course he'd never seen her before, of course she'd never been on Turnaway, but if that was the fiction he needed to muster his courage, good for him. It was a big gamble, the biggest, and he'd been lucky. It had paid off. The only thing that made me uneasy about all this was what she would do once he sprung the Mahkohkwe stuff on her. I tried not to think about it—there'd be time enough for that after she'd broken his heart.

We put all that behind us as we went about preparing for the grand event. I made a conscious decision to stop fretting and concentrate on my friend's happiness instead. Poor Elias was a wreck all that week. I took a few days off to help him. Cinderella herself never went through such lavish grooming before the ball—but then again, the Mahkohkwe was no ordinary princess.

We scoured the city's boutiques for just the right suit. We had our pick—with his slim build and long legs, Elias was a natural clothes-horse. "You need something to express your individuality," I told him, and I knew just what I had in mind—loose-fitting, padded shoulders; pleats; single-breasted; two buttons. We finally found it in navy wool—since he knew for a fact that she liked navy—and it was on sale. Italian silk tie, white English linen shirt, blue suede shoes, and we were ready to go.

Elias was as jumpy as a kitten as the countdown began. Every day he wanted to call Emily to confirm and reconfirm their date, and I had a hard time talking him out of it. Once was enough, I promised him. I don't want to go into the sleepless nights, loss of appetite, restlessness, heartache, and mood swings, or the preoccupation with his personal appearance—any guy who's ever prepared for his first date with the predestined love of his life and mother of his race will know how Elias felt. He was a modest person to begin with, and I thought that the burden of anticipation and responsibility would crush him before the fateful meeting. But no, somehow we both made it, and when the great day dawned I sent him to the Plaza for his haircut, shave, and manicure. When he got home we went through a rehearsal dressing, which was supposed to be followed by a nap, but that proved too demanding. So we went to the movies, and by the time we were back on Forty-fourth Street there were only three hours left to kill. More pacing, more fretting. Finally, I packed poor forlorn Elias, armed with plenty of cash and my credit cards, into a cab

bound for the intimate bistro in Tribeca I'd chosen for the rendezvous. I stayed home and chafed, like any good mother hen, and every
car door that slammed in the street took a few minutes off my life.
But when the latch turned shortly after twelve-thirty, I was studiously
reading *Anna Karenina*. I yawned as I looked up.

"Well?" I said.

But there was no need to ask. He closed the door behind him and
fell back against it like a giddy schoolgirl. His eyes were closed, and
his face was so deeply flushed that even his lips seemed swollen and
a darker tone of rose. His hands, pressed flat against the front door,
were trembling noticeably. I couldn't be sure because of his color
and the odd shadows of the room, but there looked to be a smear of
red lipstick on his left cheek. He stood leaning against the door for
several moments before speaking, his voice almost squeaking with
overstimulation.

"The portents are good," he said.

Well, of course, he laid it all out for me in detail, from beginning to
end. The first very auspicious sign was that she'd worn red, since she
was the Mahkohkwe—the Red Woman—and red is the color of
peace and love. Elias said this showed she had an "instinctive"
appreciation of Lenape culture, a sure indication of her ancestry.
Had he actually asked her about her ethnic origins?

"Well, no. There's always time for that."

Anyway, to get on with his story, she'd had about her a light scent
of lilac, a favorite of Elias's from the bushes bordering the woods of
Manapinock. They'd been given a quiet table in a restaurant that is
dark and subdued to begin with, and they never ran out of things to
say to each other, from the moment they sat down to the moment he
dropped her off at her apartment in a Chelsea townhouse. I'd sent
them to a three-star restaurant, but he had no idea what they'd eaten,
except that it had been vaguely "tasty."

Well, and what had they talked about?

Elias blushed and said they'd talked about themselves. Her name,
Emily Wolfe, he knew already. (That name, he explained, was another good omen, since the three matrilinear phratries, or subclans,
of the Lenape are Turkey, Turtle, and Wolf. A Lenape can only marry

outside his phratry, so to Elias, a Turtle, the name Wolfe seemed to cry out eligibility.) She was thirty-one years old—three years older than him—and had grown up just outside town in Port Washington. ("Making her of Matinecock stock," he pointed out. "Close relatives.") In fact, her childhood home was on the waterfront in the village of Sands Point; Turnaway Island would have been in clear view of her bedroom window. "Did she know it?" I asked. "I'll get to that in good time" was all he would say. In case I hadn't guessed, her family was pretty wealthy, her father being the third-generation owner of a company that manufactured protective equipment for the police—riot shields, helmets, bulletproof vests, that sort of thing. Growing up, she'd spent her Christmases on the slopes of the French Alps and her Easters on the beaches of St. Bart's.

She attended her local public schools, graduated top of her high school class, and enrolled at Columbia. (It turns out she and I were there at the same time; we'd both been in the English department, but her name didn't ring a bell, not that someone like her would have been my friend even if I'd know her.) She'd gone on to Columbia Law and then landed a plum spot in the real estate division of a corporate practice on Wall Street. It was a typical eighties story: made a mint, married a partner, burned out, the market crashed, got a divorce. Sick of the corporate structure, she quit and became an advocate for the homeless. She'd taken a 75 percent pay cut, but she was still doing fine and only working a ten-hour day. Her work was less high risk but more varied and less stressful. She'd broken up with her husband almost three years earlier, but the divorce had only come through six months ago, and Elias was her first "date" since then. She wasn't ready for a "heavy commitment" yet, but she was "open to the possibilities" that life might throw her way. ("She smiled when she said that.") Her favorite color was ("of course") red. Her favorite food was ("of course") pumpkin pie. The best movie she had seen all year was ("of course") *Black Robe*. Her hobbies included playing squash and making pottery ("of course, of course"). She also liked gardening and had rented a garden apartment on West Twenty-first Street specifically for that purpose. Of course.

"I'm surprised she didn't wear her bearskin and moccasins to dinner," I said.

"She's the Mahkohkwe," Elias said earnestly. "I'm quite certain of it. She comes from Sint Sink—I mean Port Washington—she's a Wolf, she loves red and pumpkin pie and squash and . . ."

"Squash is a European game."

"But the *word* is Algonquian. She makes pottery and keeps a garden. It all fits. She's the Mahkohkwe. She must be."

I felt I had to speak up. "But anyone could fit those characteristics, Elias. You don't have to be an Indian to like red, and the Matinecock were forced to desegregate Port Washington quite a while ago."

"Yes, but I have very strong intuitions about these things."

"Sure, but you did *ask* her? Didn't you?"

It so happens that I was refilling my snifter at that moment; I had my back to Elias and didn't see his immediate reaction to my question. But the embarrassed silence that followed was answer enough—when I turned back to him, Elias was blushing and squirming.

"You see," he struggled for the right words. "It didn't seem quite fitting, somehow. You know, the intimacy, the warmth, the bond that was forming between us—well, raising questions of race, it just never seemed quite . . . seemly." He hung his head, knowing his excuse had fallen flat.

I was sorely tempted to give him a stern lecture about the importance of the truth and of starting a relationship off on the right foot. He deserved it and he knew it. I probably should have, but I couldn't quite bring myself to ruin the evening for him by letting reality intrude. And anyway, what the hell did I know about those things? This Emily probably wasn't half the sharp customer she sounded like to me.

"Did you at least get a kiss?" I asked, and had the pleasure of watching his face light up.

"A big one!" he said like a kid. "And another date for this weekend."

Their next date the following Saturday was just as successful as the first, maybe even more so, according to Elias. As luck would have it, the Joyce Theater was featuring a mixed company of Zuni and Pueblo Indians performing sacred dances and music from the Southwest. It was Elias's own idea to take Emily to the show, and he claimed that she'd been enraptured. "She sat through the entire performance in a kind of trance," he told me later. "Her eyes glazed over and her body swayed rhythmically to the beat of the drums. That's genes for you." Afterward, Emily had taken him to her favorite Thai restaurant in midtown, a first for Elias, which he thoroughly enjoyed. He finally seemed to be picking up some of the sophistication I'd run myself ragged trying to teach him.

They discussed the dance performance, Elias commenting in some detail on the more esoteric symbolisms of movement, rhythm, and costume. Of course, he said, the Southwestern cultures had never advanced to the levels of the woodland cultures of the East. Didn't she agree? "Yes, yes," she'd hastened to say, yet another sign of her Indian blood, Elias thought. I had my doubts, but I kept them to myself. At the end of the date, standing very close in the shadow of her doorway, they'd kissed again, this time at length.

"I'll be meeting her in the park on Saturday," Elias cooed. "Won't you join us?"

"I don't think that's such a good idea. You've only just met."

"No, I told her all about you, Ben. She's quite keen to meet you."

I had my doubts about that, too, but I agreed to tag along.

Because Elias felt he ought to have a new sweater for the occasion, we decided to meet in the park at noon. It was a clear, cool early spring day, and it seemed like all of New York had gathered at the Bethesda Fountain with rollerblades, puppet shows, kettledrums, Walkmans, and lovers. The fountain was on; its jets caught the sunlight and returned it to the plaza in a shower of sparkles, its splashes and gurgles interlaced with the laughter and music. Toddlers ran their fingers through its waters, dogs perched precariously on its lip and lapped, skaters dipped their cupped hands and cooled their red faces. A light breeze caught a frond of water and misted it across some sunbathers, who opened their eyes wide with shock and pleasure. I took a seat on the parapet at the edge of the fountain and tried to enjoy the weather.

A group of models in miniskirts and tank tops was being herded around by a professional photographer and his assistants. Some posed coolly under the lights and reflective umbrellas; some draped themselves across the stone benches waiting their turn; they were all tall, bored, and unapproachable. I watched them openly, like someone with no ugly impulses to hide. Except for the photographer and each other, they did not speak to or look at anyone in the plaza. They were stone. What did they want, these women? They wanted someone strong and attractive, I knew that much, maybe someone likable and uncomplicated. And what else? I didn't have the faintest idea. Even as a child I'd never understood how to please people, or what it was about me that put them off. Now, after all this time wandering among them, I was no closer to an answer. If people were all so mean and ugly and angry inside, why did they keep desiring each other? It seemed like the answer should have been easy, something any passing child could tell you off the top of his head, but I'd long since given up trying to figure it out. But then Elias came along, fresh from the wilderness, and in less than six months he'd found somebody to love him—at least, so he claimed. I'd studied him long and hard. It's true, he was good-looking and generous where I was scarred and suspicious, but there had to be more. And there was more: he'd found something in me to like, something I still couldn't see in myself. But if he'd found it, was it possible someone else could find it, too? The hope seemed so forlorn and ridiculous, like a clown trying to entertain the prisoners at Auschwitz.

"Here you are!" It was Elias, beaming, a black Barney's bag in the crook of his elbow. "Sorry I'm late. Did you see Emily?"

"No, she's not here yet."

"Why certainly she is. Emily!" Elias yodeled across the plaza and waved his free arm. One of the models, sitting at the far edge of the group, looked up from her book and waved back, laughing. She slipped the book into a canvas shoulder bag, stood up, and came skipping across the plaza toward us.

"I thought you said she's a lawyer."

"She is."

And now, as she came forward, I realized that, in fact, she was not dressed like the rest of the models and had never really been attached to the group at all. Anyone might have made the mistake. Straight, blue-black hair tied back in a simple ponytail; high cheekbones and thick, dark eyebrows; blue-green eyes and an olive complexion; a slim, athletic posture accentuated by a loose-knit sweater, a short, pleated skirt, and black tights. I registered it all in her brief stroll across the plaza. She planted a light peck on Elias's cheek, then turned the full force of her smile on me. I was stunned like a rabbit in the headlights of her beauty. I felt my heart sink.

"Elias talks about you so much, I feel like I already know you," she said, shaking my hand. Her voice was mild and mellow, a rich person's voice; her palm was cool and dry, a lawyer's palm.

"Let's walk."

We followed a path that wound along the banks of the lake, across a bridge, and into the Ramble. We walked abreast, with Emily in the middle, as she told me about her job. I clasped my hands behind my back like a military man.

"I do a lot of work with the local bureaucracies, liaison work between community boards and agencies establishing outreach programs, shelters, that sort of thing. But we're very short-staffed, so I also end up litigating on behalf of the homeless, class action suits against the state, mostly. I don't much care for the courtroom, though. That's not where you meet the interesting people."

"I see," I said. A pergola perched on a boulder high above us had just been vacated. Elias and Emily bounded up the stairway cut into the hillside and claimed it. By the time I caught up to them, my thigh bones grinding in their sockets, they were already draped arm-in-arm across the rustic benches, mooning at the view across the lake to midtown.

"Elias tells me you're a painter?" Emily asked earnestly, smoothing her skirt over her thighs. I looked away.

"Not really. I paint to pass the time, that's all. I have a lot of free time."

"I was sorry to hear about your accident."

"Never mind. I don't think about it much."

"How did it happen, exactly?"

"It was just an accident. Accidents happen."

There was an uncomfortable silence, then Emily did a funny thing. She crossed the pergola and sat right by me, so close I could feel the heat of her leg through her tights and my corduroys. She placed a well-manicured hand on my forearm. "I didn't mean to offend you. I'm sorry if you think I'm prying."

"No, that's alright. I just don't like talking about it, that's all."

"Okay, sorry," she said, but she left her hand on my arm until I pulled it away to look at my watch.

"Listen," I said, trying to sound sincere. "I've got to be heading home."

Elias jumped to his feet and grabbed me by the shoulders. Everybody seemed to be touching me today. "Home? What can you possibly have to do at home?" He sounded practically heartbroken. I wriggled free of his grasp.

"I have things to do. And besides, you two should be alone. You don't need me hanging around."

They protested, but I'm sure they were glad to see me go. Stepping out of the pergola felt like coming up for air after some scary minutes underwater. I took a deep breath of the scented breeze then lit out for Hell's Kitchen. My legs were aching. I spent the rest of the day reviewing the quarterly statements from my mutual funds.

That night, Elias waited diplomatically until after dinner to bring up the afternoon's fiasco.

"Emily thinks you don't like her very much," he said without a trace of blame or anger.

"Sure I like her. How could I not like her? She's the Mahkohkwe, isn't she?"

"Ben, what is it that's bothering you?"

"Nothing's bothering me, Elias. It's just that there's no place for me in your affair." I took a hefty swig of cognac. "I meant what I said today—you don't need me hanging around. You should get to know this woman by yourself. I don't need to be involved."

"But you're my friend. What touches me touches you."

"Not this. You're on your own."

Introspection is not my strong point, but that night I lay awake with the white noise blasting and tried to figure out what had made me behave so badly. I know I may be dense at times, but I don't think I'm a complete idiot. Of course it occurred to me that my problem might be jealousy. You don't wait your whole life for friendship, then watch it being snatched from under your nose, without feeling just a little jealous. It was only natural. Even so, after sniffing around in my heart for a while, I had to say that jealousy didn't really cover it.

The thing was, Elias wasn't just my friend—he was my responsibility. I'd taken it upon myself to be his mentor and protector; I'd done the mentoring part—in fact, I'd mentored myself silly on his account—and now, I felt, I was called upon to protect. But how? From a distance, Elias had once seen a trespasser on his property. Based on that one, shadowy glimpse, he claimed to have fallen in love and had invested that trespasser with all the power and mystery of a mythological heroine. Now he'd met someone who might or might not be that woman; who might or might not be of the appropriate genetic makeup; who might or might not have the least bit of interest in him. This was the person he was determined to woo, forsaking all others. How could I protect him from such a powerful delusion?

Elias had virtually no experience in dealing with the opposite sex, and now he was up against a pro: a divorcée *and* a lawyer. A little rich girl from a happy family, playing Mother Teresa with the homeless. But who was she? What did we know about her, except that she was spectacularly beautiful and obviously had Elias under her thumb? He was clearly at an unfair disadvantage, and my support could help even the field. Did protection involve saving him from heartbreak? On the other hand, I'd sworn to teach him to stand on his own two feet, to learn to protect himself like a man, like I had. Should I butt out and let him make his own mistakes so he'd know better the next time? That, too, seemed like a reasonable definition of protection, though I didn't like to think of him going through pain I knew I could spare him.

I don't usually care for the way people expose the ugliest and most hidden recesses of their thoughts as if the world was only waiting for their confession so it could continue orbiting the sun. We all go through it privately, one way or another, but this was a first for me. I'd never been so responsible for someone else in my life. People who have lots of friends, and who really look after those friends and take their responsibilities seriously, they go through this soul-searching regularly, I guess. But for me it was all new. I didn't know how to be a friend, what my responsibilities might entail, and I was groping my way through it. I wasn't convinced I had it in me to figure out what a real friend would do in a case like this.

I fell asleep just as confused and irritated with myself as when I'd gone to bed. To cap it all off, I had a nightmare that night, my first since I don't know when. It really wasn't much of a nightmare. I found myself at the top of a ridge in the middle of the woods. At my feet, the ridge fell sharply away in a rocky cliff to a sort of gulch or gully some fifty or sixty feet below. It was late autumn or early winter; the trees were mostly bare, and the forest floor was ankle-deep in maple, oak, and chestnut leaves, their brilliant reds and golds already fading. A cold, dry breeze made the treetops hiss, and I noticed that I was naked except for a leather breechcloth. I was suddenly afraid, even though the woods were perfectly silent except for the wind and the leaves beneath my feet. I began to move along the ridge as it sloped gently downward to the gully. And then I noticed that there was a path down there, running roughly parallel to the ridge. Not even a road, it was a mere footpath of beaten earth, and I knew that if I continued following the ridge it would lead me to the path. I became more and more afraid as I approached. Despite the silence and the beauty, there was a good reason, a reason I knew but had forgotten, why I did not want to be in these woods. I wasn't lost; on the contrary, if I joined the path and followed it, it would take me somewhere that would remind me of everything I'd forgotten. But I was scared enough to hesitate, and then I was scared enough to wake myself up.

After my performance that weekend, Elias was understandably leery about inviting me along on his dates with Emily. I could hardly blame him, but it didn't take me long to figure out what a big mistake I'd made in my petulance. How was I going to protect him if he shut me out? How could I know what, if anything, there was to protect him against if she remained an unknown quantity? Most important of all, there was always the slim chance that I'd been wrong about her—if she really did represent Elias's good fortune, and not some malignant threat to his happiness, shouldn't I at least make the pretense of being happy for him? I suggested he invite her to the apartment for dinner.

"Should I?" he squinted at me suspiciously.

"Yes, really," I said, taking his hands in mine. "I want to make up for everything I said. I want to start over. You could serve up a whole Lenape feast."

His eyes sparkled at the prospect. He immediately began making preparations, designing his courses and setting a date two weeks hence. That very night he presented me with a tentative menu for my approval: oyster and seaweed stew to start, followed by roast venison with cranberries, baked squash, fiddleheads sautéed with wild garlic and corn, and fry bread; for dessert, a sour-apple and maple tart. I suggested Muscadet to go with the oysters and a Côtes de Nuit for the main course. He agreed, since he knew nothing about wine and never drank it anyhow.

In the meantime, of course, he continued to see Emily two or three times a week, in the evenings mostly, since she worked longish hours. I was back at work myself, still on the day shift, so I wasn't seeing much of him and wasn't too clear on how he was spending his empty days. In theory, since he'd found the Mahkohkwe he was free to give up his dangerous sorties into the city's ghettos, but he didn't,

even though it seemed to me he'd scoured every last vacant lot. It
was a mystery to me how such a tiny handful of Indians could have
left such a wealth of evidence, but it was mostly the kind of invisible
archeology that only Elias could see, and he rarely came home after a
day's exploring without some new unexpected discovery to describe.
He was also taking the commuter trains up to Westchester now,
tracing the path of Chief Katonah's retreat through Mount Kisco,
Bedford, and Pound Ridge. On top of that, he spent at least two hours
a day in the sweat lodge, though now he was having to share it with
my landlord, who had taken to it like a pig to mud and whose waist-
line and temperament were already showing its effects. Elias told me
he was planning to introduce it to his cronies.

For the first time in months, I found myself alone after work. I
didn't always know what Elias and Emily were up to. Sometimes it
was dinner on the town—which she must have been paying for, since
he'd stopped asking me for money—sometimes a quiet evening at
her place. On Sunday mornings they volunteered at a soup kitchen in
Chelsea. It was shaping up to be a magnificent spring, and I suppose
they spent a lot of their time just walking around. I don't think they
were sleeping together—at least, he was always home by midnight or
one. In any case, it wasn't the sort of question you could put to Elias,
and he wasn't saying. In general, he was pretty circumspect about the
time he spent with Emily—I imagine he thought he was sparing my
feelings.

I fell back on my old habits, but kind of uncomfortably. Chinese
food and sitcoms just didn't seem to cut it anymore. Likewise, though
I'd started paying quick visits to Annie, Desirée, and the others
again, the cheap thrill was gone—it all felt a little sordid and pathetic now, somehow dirty and unhealthy; if I'd been thinking about
Elias and Emily, I was barely able to see it through to the end at all.
More and more, I found myself pacing the apartment absentmindedly, or just drifting off into blank, colorless abstraction. Worse, I
turned off my answering machine and eagerly picked up the phone
whenever Elias was out. It was usually Dr. Ross, who grew anxious if
Elias failed to call, as he always did when he was out with Emily.
The doctor and I would talk, often at some length, usually about

Elias. He seemed grateful to unburden himself, and I was glad for the distraction. Every so often, though, I'd pick up the receiver and get an abusive harangue from some anonymous caller. They were strange and sad, these messages from my old life. Was it really me, the one who had wronged them all so cruelly and now couldn't even recognize their voices? It was all so distant, now, that I wanted to urge them, gently and paternally, whoever they were, to free themselves and let it go at last. But they always hung up before I got the chance.

Finally, the big day arrived. After a particularly long steam, Elias spent an anxious afternoon in the kitchen and I steered clear until it was time to set the table. A wonderful fusion of aromas wafted through the apartment from the kitchen, where I'd never done anything more ambitious than boil an egg. As evening drew on and the patch of sky above our backyard ebbed into turquoise, I sat in the living-room window and watched my landlord shepherd his troupe of beer-bellied, cigar-smoking longshoremen, wearing nothing but their white boxers, one by one into the sweat lodge. At seven-thirty sharp, the doorbell rang. Elias bounded down the stairs while I stayed to light the candles, lower the lights, and find the appropriately mellow music for the occasion. A minute later, Emily and Elias slipped back into the room.

She wore a simple sleeveless dress of navy cotton that ended just above the knees. Her legs were bare, and her feet clad in red platform espadrilles. A black bra strap peeked out from behind the hem of her neckline, which had fallen slightly off one shoulder, but otherwise she was the image of cool perfection. I shuddered involuntarily as I leaned forward to peck her cheek and caught the subtle attar of lilac that rose off her collarbone. I quickly ushered the two to the sofa and went into the kitchen for the wine. I splashed a little cold water on my face before joining them.

Elias was talking about the meal he'd prepared, explaining where the recipes were authentic and where adulterated to suit modern tastes and markets. He described the difficulties, in a city that caters to every ethnic palate on the globe, of finding the ingredients of a native Lenape meal, including most of the herbs and a rare fragrant mushroom. He told us how he'd eventually located the mushroom growing in a stand of white birch just off the fairway of a golf course in Scarsdale, and how he'd almost been killed by a wayward tee shot in his effort to harvest it.

I sat in the armchair opposite the couch and watched Emily from the corner of my eye. I was determined to keep the promise I'd made to Elias and myself—to give Emily a second chance, to judge her with an open mind—so I made believe that she was just a mutual friend of ours and nothing more. From that angle I had to admit, as the evening wore on, that she appeared to be a fairly decent person. She and Elias hardly acted like lovers at all. They sat side by side on the couch, but they weren't all over each other; in fact, he never touched her, and she only tapped his arm or shoulder lightly to make a point. The two of them were genuinely affectionate with each other, exchanging shy smiles and glances all through dinner, without ever descending to pet names or sentiment. They complimented each other without flattery and disagreed without pettiness. She gave his conversation rapt attention, but she listened to me the same way, looking into my eyes as I spoke and sometimes making it difficult for me to keep to my train of thought. Every so often I even had to look away just to remember what I'd been saying. I had no way of knowing if she sincerely liked me or was just trying to disarm me, but either way I was charmed and a little bedazzled. I even found myself think-ing that she seemed like a real friend and companion to Elias.

We sat down to supper, and Elias served the first course in white gratin bowls we'd bought for the occasion. It was a little pungent for my taste, but I couldn't deny that the chef had a subtle touch. Emily complimented the wine and poured herself another glass. The talk turned to Elias and the amazing gaps in his education.

"I couldn't believe it," Emily said, a tiny string of kelp dangling from the corner of her mouth. She swept it in with the tip of her tongue before she continued. "Alright, I can accept, maybe, that someone might never have gone to the opera or the ballet. But when Elias told me he'd never even seen a movie before he came to live with you—I literally could not believe it. Whoever heard of such a thing?"

"You'd think it'd be a little limiting, wouldn't you?" I suggested.

"That's right!" Emily agreed enthusiastically, her eyes gleaming. "If I was going on a blind date—and don't think I haven't—and they told me: 'He doesn't know anything about art, music, theater, sports, economics, or literature, but he *is* a genius,' I'd say: 'Forget it! Are you crazy?' But Elias somehow brings this incredibly unique perspective to everything, it touches everything he knows and sees, like a sharp, sharp focusing lens—"

"Look, he's blushing."

"I'm sorry, Elias, I don't mean to embarrass you." She reached across the table and briefly squeezed his hand. "But you know what I mean, don't you, Ben?"

"Sure I do. For someone so book-learned, he's got real insight into people's hearts. He's been isolated for so long, like a hermit, so concentrated on one thing, and yet—"

"Excuse me," Elias said demurely, his eyes lowered. "I should clear the table." He gathered up our bowls and spoons and disappeared into the kitchen.

As soon as he was out of the room, Emily leaned across the table and touched the back of my hand with her fingernails. Her hair shone in the candlelight, and her lips were moist and red, like she'd been sucking on a pomegranate. I leaned forward, too.

"Has Elias said anything to you about moving here permanently?" she whispered urgently.

"No, not really," I whispered back, though I had no idea what secret we were supposed to be sharing.

"What do you think his chances are?"

"Well, he knows he can stay here as long as he wants, but—"

"I mean about tenure. He doesn't like to talk about it."

"Tenure?" She was talking so softly I could barely understand what she was saying.

"I mean, of course I'd be willing to consider Chicago but obviously New Brunswick is an easier commute."

"Emily, I have no idea what you're—"

At that moment, Elias backed through the kitchen door with a loaded plate in either hand. Emily instantly sat up straight and shook her head meaningfully at me, cutting our conversation short. I dropped back to my usual slouch and scratched my head in bafflement.

The rest of the evening was played out in boozy good cheer as Emily and I plowed our way through two bottles of wine and some calvados. After all the early praises we'd sung, everybody tried to outdo each other in self-deprecation. Elias made us laugh with the story of his first excursion on a city bus, when he'd accidentally kissed the wrist of a man who had stretched out his hand to press the buzzer. Emily was very funny on the subject of her boorish ex, Jeff, and their botched wedding ceremony at a liberal temple on the Upper West Side. I tried to describe my painting career in art-history jargon. It was probably one of the pleasantest evenings I'd spent in years, and the food and the drink made me feel suave and attractive, but I was distracted by this loop in my head that kept replaying the clandestine snippet of conversation I'd had with Emily. Had I misunderstood or simply misheard her? I didn't want to bring it up in front of Elias, since she'd obviously meant it to remain between the two of us, but I was burning for the opportunity to ask her what she'd meant. It never came up.

The party broke up around midnight. Maybe I'd had a little too much to drink, but I couldn't help admiring the smooth, curved muscles of Emily's underarms and shoulders as she slipped into her cardigan. We kissed good night like old friends and promised to see each other again soon. Elias escorted her downstairs to find a taxi while I started to clear the table. The window was open. I could see and hear my landlord and his buddies, still in their underwear, boisterously drunk on Bushmills around an open fire by the sweat lodge. They were being affectionately berated by an old Irish widow from her fourth-story apartment in the tenement next door. They responded with declarations of love and "Danny Boy." Elias returned to the apartment and joined me at my perch on the windowsill. A light, perfumed breeze was blowing into our faces, and a nearly full moon outshone the golden pyramid on the roof of a nearby high-rise. We listened in sated silence to the rowdy exchange until the old lady gave up her flirtatious harangue and slammed her window shut.

"Did you know she's Jewish?" I asked softly without turning my head.

"Irish, I rather think."

"I meant Emily." I felt Elias flinch at my side.

"And so?" he said defensively.

"I thought the Mahkohkwe was supposed to be an Indian princess."

"She's only half Jewish. It's not realistic to expect her to be full blood."

"What about the other half?"

Elias stared up at the moon.

"You haven't asked her yet, have you?"

He hung his head.

"Elias, I've got to tell you, I don't like this one bit," I said. "You're making a big mistake. Here you are on the brink of the one relationship you've waited for all your life, and you're starting it off with lies and half-truths. You've already allowed yourself to fall in love on the basis of a *hunch*. You've got to find out now, and she's got to know what you want from her. It's only fair to Emily, don't you think?"

He nodded.

"Anyway, what did you tell her about yourself?"

He muttered something unintelligible under his breath.

"What?"

"She thinks I'm an associate professor of anthropology at the University of Chicago, specializing in Native American studies. I am in New York on a leave of absence, having been awarded a fellowship to lead archeological digs at several Mahican sites in the Hudson Valley. I told her I was considering an offer from Rutgers in order to be closer to the sources of my study."

"That explains it. What about your family?"

"I'm an orphan. An only child. What am I going to do, Ben?"

"Your friends are your family."

"This is no joke. What am I going to do about these lies?"

"Tell the truth?"

"No, no, no." Elias held his head in his hands. "Be practical, Ben. What would I tell her, 'I am a Siwanoy chief and I have chosen you as my bride'? To you and me that may sound perfectly reasonable, but you must admit it might come over rather queer to her."

"Well—"

"No, I am determined to woo her on my own merits as a man. If she is to love me, she will love me for who I am and not for my exalted blood."

"Thank you, Lord Fauntleroy. In the meantime, how is she going to love you for who you are if you keep lying about yourself?"

Elias turned to me, wringing his hands operatically. "Don't be upset with me, Ben. I promise I shall set things right. I don't want this to come between us."

"What did you think? That it was going to bring us all together in some eternal bond of brotherhood?"

"Yes, actually, I did."

"Well you were wrong. There's only room for two in there. You've got to start getting a grip on the way things are in this world. You're screwing things up for all of us by clinging to your ridiculous fantasies. As far as I'm concerned, there is no Mahkohkwe. There's just you and a beautiful girl you happened to meet and you'd better make it work on its own terms. Tell her the truth and get on with it before you end up like me. That's my advice to you."

They met when the crocuses first appeared and their love bloomed at cherry-blossom time. A real fairy-tale romance—and wasn't it lovely? As the spring dragged on and threatened to lapse into summer, I saw less and less of my once bosom buddy. It seems he'd taken my advice to heart.

I guess this was the payoff for thinking of myself as a father figure to Elias for so long—I got what all fathers have coming to them. You try to teach someone to be independent and suddenly they *are*. Since that had supposedly been my aim all along, his victory should have been *our* victory. And on the face of it, it was a victory. I hadn't seen much of him since that dinner, but he was kind enough to spend his occasional free evening with me, and the change was pretty startling. I had to admit I'd never seen him so animated and witty. His entire body seemed stronger when he talked about Emily; his gestures were more flamboyant, his metaphors more daring, his clothing more natural on him. He was like a teenage boy who suddenly figures out that he's good at doing something he enjoys—the world begins to look different, problems become manageable, confidence is a matter of attitude. Suddenly, the admiration of others arouses the pride of accomplishment instead of the fear of being unmasked. All of this was evident just in the way he spoke her name: when he said "Emily," it was no longer as if he were asking you a favor; it was as if he were doing you one.

He'd keep me up to date on his progress with her. They did all the things he and I had done together and went to all the places I'd shown him first. By now, from what I could gather, Dr. Ross had expanded the bunny business enough to allow him to send Elias a monthly allowance of several hundred dollars. It wasn't much, but since Elias paid no rent and did not contribute to his own upkeep, it at least subsidized his affair. In any case, as I understood it, Emily usually treated, in recognition of Elias's meager "academic" salary. She had the sophisticated tastes of a rich girl and the purse to satisfy them, make no mistake—as an Indian, she'd have been fairly a-rattle in wampum. No little corner coffee shop for them—when they dined out, it was at Lutèce and Bouley. When they drove up to Storm King for the day, it was in a rented Mercedes convertible. When they went to the Met, they sat in a private box.

There's not much point in going on and on about it. Let's just say they behaved pretty much the way young lovers anywhere are expected to behave. There's nothing wrong with any of that, even if Elias was playing it under false pretenses—it's just that it all happened so fast and I had no chance to get used to the idea. It seemed as if Elias had gone overnight from being a timid boy who looked up to me for everything to being a carefree playboy around town who pitied me for missing out on the finer things in life. Maybe I'm exaggerating—maybe he'd never been quite as dependent as it pleased me to imagine, or maybe he wasn't quite as condescending now as it humiliated me to fear. All I knew was that suddenly my nights were empty. In the old days, I hadn't thought twice about my solitude. I could go happily for weeks with no more personal contact than a fifteen-minute, twenty-dollar fumble behind the Park Rite Dumpster. It was plenty—I'd taught myself to expect no better and I'd taught myself well. I'd felt no self-pity, no sense of anything missing. But the problem now was that I missed Elias's companionship and my life seemed even emptier than before he'd come into it. It brought back memories of my childhood, that emptiness, and I'd come so far and worked so hard to quash it. Even a good Wampage story would have been welcome, but I hadn't heard a single one since Emily had intruded on the scene. The truth is, like it or not, Elias's influence on me had been like one of those balloons they inflate inside clogged arteries to prevent heart attacks—it's life-saving for a while, but then the artery collapses even further into itself. I think that's how it works.

As much as I like to pretend that I can take anything life dishes out, the whole situation was beginning to take its toll. I could get through my workload, no problem; I had my painkillers, TV, and Chinese food to help me through the evenings; but my nights were being plagued by recurring nightmares.

I shouldn't really say "nightmares," since it was basically one dream, sometimes longer, sometimes very brief, but all more or less the same: I'm walking through the woods, I'm nearly naked, the wind is blowing, I'm afraid. Sometimes I turn and glimpse a large body of water through the woods, maybe a lake or a river, and granite, tree-topped cliffs beyond. Sometimes my way crosses a dirt path, and sometimes I take that path and sometimes I don't. Occasionally I'll hear voices in the distance, but I can't make out what they're saying and I don't really care. It's not the voices I'm afraid of. I'm vaguely headed somewhere, but it's not urgent. It's not my destination, either, that frightens me. Often in dreams you know something that you take for granted, a truth that can be perfectly natural in the context of the dream though it may have nothing to do with its action. For instance, I sometimes have a dream in which, years before the events of the dream take place, I've murdered my mother, buried her in a shallow grave or under the floorboards of my apartment, and forgotten her. Though the dream has nothing to do with my mother, that knowledge colors every event in the dream, just like it would affect everything you ever did or thought if you'd killed your mother in real life. Well, in my nightmare I know something like that, some secret, but I've forgotten what it is. I'm trying to remember it—and

what I'm afraid of, what makes this dream a nightmare, is that cru-
cial bit of information. I know in my dream that, whatever it is, my
whole life is going to change when I remember it. I also know that at
any moment in my wanderings, I might come across something, not
necessarily scary in itself—a bush, a view, an animal—that will
bring the occluded memory flooding back into my consciousness.
And that's what scares me so much that I wake up in a slick film of
perspiration, all my senses groping, like fingers, for something in the
real world to grasp on to. For a few seconds, after I know I'm awake
but before the atmosphere and images of the dream have dissipated,
I try to prolong the dream's struggle to remember, and sometimes at
that moment I sense myself closer to the answer than I was in the
dream itself. But that state of half-consciousness or dreaming wake-
fulness disappears much too quickly to be helpful, because there's a
long and complex string of associations that has to be made first.
And then I'm just left gasping, and instead of trying to remember I
try to forget, equally in vain.

Anyway, it's not that I attached much importance to my nightmare
or my efforts to understand it, but even I couldn't pretend that it
wasn't somehow connected to my present emotional confusion. It's
true that in the past, some people have accused me of living "in
denial," as if emotions were gemstones, pointless to own unless you
put them on display. Well maybe I do, but I'm not so insensitive as to
be unable to recognize my own unhappiness when it's kicking me in
the face. I like things to move along, to progress, to unfold like a
story. I was perfectly aware that my friendship with Elias had been
like that—a real story with a real plot, moving along with a purpose—until he met Emily; since then, it had felt more like an
extended session on an analyst's couch: self-indulgent, self-referen-
tial, hovering tirelessly like a stalker around the same petty griev-
ance. More than other people, I dislike being unhappy, because I'm
so sure that there should be an easy way to fix it. But my nightmare
kept reminding me, sometimes every night for weeks on end, that this
time I seemed helpless to help myself.

One night, Elias showed up unexpectedly at my apartment. He burst in without knocking—he still had the keys but he rarely spent the night there anymore—and his face was all flushed, his eyes watery. If I hadn't known better, I'd have sworn he'd been drinking. I was lounging on the couch in my underwear, watching reruns and massaging my scars with vitamin E oil. I had to scramble to cover myself, but Elias was too excited to notice my embarrassment, or even to bother with a simple greeting. He plopped himself down next to me and launched out breathlessly.

"There's something I want to tell you, Ben. I wanted to tell you personally because I think it will please you and perhaps help you lay your qualms to rest once and for all."

"Go on, then."

He paused for effect, then whispered with an ecstatic smile on his face, like he was announcing the second coming. "I have discovered beyond any doubt that Emily *is* the Mahkohkwe."

"Oh yes? How'd you do that?"

"That's the beauty of it! She did it for me. We'd been discussing the possibility of going away together, you see, and she was telling me of some of the beautiful places she had been in her life. Suddenly, she was describing a spot she'd visited in the Long Island Sound. It was a tiny, wooded island with an old Victorian house and rabbit pens. She was unable to recall its name, but there's no doubt she was describing Manapinock. To be certain, I asked her when she'd been. She said almost three years ago, which precisely coincides with my sighting. So you see, all your worries were for nought. She *is* the woman I've been looking for!"

I patted him on the shoulder. "Well, that's great news, Elias," I said. "And what was she doing there?"

"Sorry?"

"What did she say her reason was for being on Turnaway?"

Elias frowned in perplexity and bit his lower lip. "You know, I quite forgot to ask," he said quietly.

"How could you forget to ask? Wasn't that the first thing that crossed your mind?"

His frown became a scowl. "No, because I do not share your suspicious nature."

"Forget about suspicion. What about curiosity?"

Elias stood up. "I suppose it was foolish of me to hope you would take simple pleasure in my joy."

"Elias, if I don't look after your interests, who will?" I tried to place my hand on his neck, like a reassuring father, but he jerked away.

"You want me to be like that French poet," he snapped, "who was so poor he died of indigestion after eating two meals in forty-eight hours."

"What's that supposed to mean?" I asked.

"It means you think too much happiness is bad for me," he said. "It means you can't bear the idea of my being happy outside your company."

And then he left. I took a deep breath and then a stiff shot of scotch to calm myself. Why couldn't I have a conversation with Elias these days without getting angry or hurting his feelings? It's true he was maddening, but was it also possible that he was right? I called myself protective; he called me jealous. I'd always insisted that the only thing that mattered to me was his happiness, but I just can't help preparing for the worst to avoid disappointment. It's in my nature. I tend to think of this as hard-bitten realism, but the truth was I had no real reason to assume automatically that Elias's romance would end badly. So what if he started off with a little white lie? So what if he was a babe in the woods, in love with a driven, case-hardened professional used to getting everything she wanted? So what if they were planets orbiting the same sun but in opposite directions? They say opposites attract—well, why not? Look at Elias and me—fast friends, and who could be more different? Why shouldn't a disillusioned, love-starved woman be thrilled to meet a kind, good-looking, selfless, sincere, and intellectual man who honestly wanted her, even if he was barely able to cross the street by himself? Maybe he was exactly what she was looking for. If not, they'd go their separate ways. If so, she'd just laugh when he told her the truth. Suddenly, I couldn't figure out why I'd gotten so worked up about it all—far-fetched or not, there was every chance that things would work out fine.

But it wasn't that easy for me. I didn't enjoy Elias's luxury of being able to ignore things that were inconvenient or potentially unpleasant. It was obvious, for instance, that he hadn't "forgotten" to ask Emily about her visit to Turnaway—he just hadn't dared to. And if that was true, he'd almost certainly not looked into her supposed Lenape ancestry or told her about his own situation. I couldn't really claim to be surprised or disappointed. It was vintage Elias: he always retreated into fantasy when he felt threatened, and since he'd lived his entire life feeling threatened by the world at large, it would have been unreasonable to expect him to face one of the great challenges of his personal life with bold honesty. Who does?

The phone rang. It was Elias. He sounded like a broken man, his voice so dry and cracked that I hardly recognized it.

"Ben. Ben," he stammered. "I want you to know . . . to know . . . how deeply sorry I am."

"I'm sorry too, Elias. I hate it when we fight."

"Will you meet me tomorrow? I have something more I need to tell you." I could barely hear him.

There was a delay on the uptown subway, and by the time I reached the Ukrainian diner on Avenue A, Elias was already seated in a booth near the back, facing the door. Even at that distance he stood out from the crowd—whatever else I might think about her, Emily had done miracles for his wardrobe. He was looking better than ever, fully at ease these days in up-to-date fashion. His silky black hair was tied back in a slim, bobbing ponytail. He wore black, pleated chinos, a gray T, and a baggy black vest; on his feet, black patent leather oxfords and white socks. A pair of green-tinted granny glasses perched halfway down his nose. With his prominent cheekbones and gaunt good looks, he looked a little Eurotrashy, I thought—almost too good, like a model. He wasn't dressing himself on his allowance from Turnaway, that was for sure.

But as I approached I could tell that something was wrong. He was staring into space with that forlorn, distant look he usually had before launching into a story. His face, lean at the best of times, looked downright haggard, his complexion sallow. As I slid into the booth, I thought I smelled a faint cloud of alcohol on his breath. And throughout the meal, he was anxious and listless, fidgeting with a salt shaker and drawing abstract designs in the congealed grease on the tabletop.

"What's the matter, Elias?" I asked gently, erasing his artwork with a sweep of my napkin.

Without raising his eyes, he said: "I was thinking about something Flaubert once said. He said: 'Is it splendid or ridiculous to take life seriously?'" He paused. "I suppose he was right, really."

"Charming," I said. "Now what's really wrong?" He looked up sharply.

"Is it that obvious?" I nodded. He sighed. "I was thinking about the Dutch West India Company."

"The what?"

"In 1640, a Siwanoy chieftain signed away the tribe's rights to all the lands on the Long Island Sound, from Hell Gate to Norwalk, including the village of Lapechwahacking."

"No you weren't thinking about that."

"It was a terrible time, a time of desperation. Half the tribe was gone by then, killed in one season by smallpox. Mostly the children. A few men had been murdered in Fort Amsterdam by unscrupulous tradesmen and cutthroats. The Mengwe were pressing down from the north—"

"Elias," I interrupted peevishly. "I'm really not up for a Wampage story right now. Can't you just tell me what's bothering you?"

Elias gave me a flat, neutral stare that was hard to interpret. "I am telling you, Ben, if you'll just listen. As I was saying, the Mengwe were pressing down from the north, armed with muskets, driving unarmed Munsee refugees into the lands of their cousins, who were ill-equipped to receive them. The plantations lay untended, since the women were sick and the men had to travel ever further afield for pelts to trade with the *shuwonnock*. A European named Bronck had already laid claim to the Reckgawawank lands of Ranachqua, and now there were rumors of English arriving from the East, overrunning the lands of the Tankiteke as they had done to the Narragansett. All of this had happened in the twenty years of Wampage's adulthood. Now, in the prime of his manhood, with his glorious youth behind him, poised to take the leadership of his tribe from the ailing, broken-spirited Maminepoe, Wampage found there was little help his guidance had to provide. Few warriors, meagre resources, dejected hearts; there were now almost as many *shuwonnock* as Lenape in Lenapehoking, and the former were increasing like mosquitoes after the rain. All the Siwanoy had left was their land, and the Dutch wanted that.

"The morning after the deed was signed, Wampage and Cokoe sat down to talk by the shores of Aqueanonk, in Asumsowis.

" 'I think we have laughed in the faces of those *wapsichik* with this exchange we made last night,' Wampage said.

" 'I'm not so certain,' Cokoe answered with a rueful shake of the head. 'They often best us when we least expect it, because they think like snakes.'

" 'This time it is we who have bested the Long Knives,' Wampage boasted. 'Why, just look at the goods we received last night. Shirts, how many I cannot count, of the finest of their cotton. Coats, *red* coats. All the metal: kettles, adzes, axes, two plows. Plus a shower of guilders, and what cannot guilders buy in their town? Bread, cider, blankets, yes, to keep your women warm! And for all these riches, objects undreamt of in our own childhood, what have we given? Nothing. We have made our drawings on their parchment. Nothing! I tell you, it is good to take their possessions with one hand and give them drawings with the other.'

"Cokoe was dubious. 'I am not so certain it is all to the good. When have we ever benefited from our dealings with these *wapsichik?* Who has profited from their trinkets? They give us iron plows and steal our land. They give us kettles and destroy our game. They give us beads and kill our women with disease. Now they are moving our people off their lands throughout Lenapehoking and Sewanhacky, from Ackinkashacky to Roaton.'

"Wampage leapt to his feet, his face flushed with anger, and began to pace along the strand. 'Now that is not true, *dzho*. This Kieft may pursue us with his "tax," whatever that is, but who yet has lost their land? Have Reckgawak and his people left Ranachqua? Has Tackero abandoned Keskeskick? Is Sey Seys no longer hunting in Mareykawick, or Kakapeteyno in Canarsee? They are there today, all of them, and so they will be tomorrow and always. I predict it so. The *shuwonnock* cannot war with all of us!'

"Wampage had worked himself into a terrible lather. Like a young *ila* on his first war party, he was spoiling for a fight without considering the consequences. He got it into his head to visit the *shuwonnock* village and drink their liquor, just to flaunt his defiance. Though such boastfulness was not fitting and there was much work to be done—weirs to be set out, fields to be tended, meat to be dressed—Cokoe agreed to go along so that he might keep an eye on his friend. Wampage donned his new red jacket over his loincloth, popped his new gray felt cap over his greased roach, and slipped his copper stuivers into his left moccasin. Then the two men climbed into their separate *amocholak* and paddled down the familiar waterways, keeping a healthy distance from the Dutch scows anchored close to shore, with their aggressive, well-armed fishermen. They landed at Rechtauk, pulled their *amocholak* into the underbrush, and headed for Fort Amsterdam, passing by *shuwonnock* orchards and Indian cornfields along the road. Accustomed to using their noses in the hunt, they smelled the village long before they came to it, a peculiar and unpleasant scent of green-wood smoke and animal droppings.

"Soon the road widened, the forest dropped away, and they were in the outlying fields of the village, planted like Lenape fields with corn, squash, and beans, only segregated into straight rows. They passed farmhouses where wiry, red-faced *shuwonnock* women shucked peas or plucked the stunted, evil-tasting fowl they called *kip* and eyed the savages warily until they had passed. Men in the fields called out harsh insults in their ugly, turkeyish language. Just outside the village proper, the two braves came upon a tavern—a *hay bay,* one of the few Dutch words Wampage was able to pronounce—outside of which half a dozen burly, sweaty men roistered loudly at a table, sitting on a rough-hewn bench or on log stumps. When they saw Wampage and Cokoe, however, they stopped laughing and stared moodily, a rude *shuwonnock* custom Cokoe had never gotten used to. The Indians were each armed with a *temahikan,* a *hattape,* and flint blades; one of the Dutchmen slowly stretched out his arm toward a musket propped against the doorjamb. The others whispered to each other from the corners of their mouths.

"Suddenly, one of the *shuwonnock* stood up and bellowed. Wampage was about to reach for his *temahikan* when he realized that the man was laughing, beckoning with one hand and holding out a wooden tankard with the other. 'Don't go, it's a trick,' Cokoe cautioned, but Wampage strode purposefully forward, snatched the tankard, and downed its contents in one draft. By the time he had wiped the foam off his lips his eyes were already shining. He turned and called *'W'ndakha!'* to Cokoe, who was still standing in the middle of the road, then joined the *shuwonnock* at their table.

"Through a series of gestures and barks the *shuwonnock* challenged Wampage to an arm-wrestling competition, a game that was new to him but which he soon got the hang of. His first adversary was a fat, balding fellow with a filthy, stinking beard and pendulous lips. Wampage defeated him easily, to the mirth of the man's companions, then emptied the full tankard that was his prize. He turned triumphantly to Cokoe. 'You see,' he laughed. 'They may be *shuwonnock* but they recognize valor. It is an honor for them to lose to me.' Cokoe reserved judgment and refused to join in the game or drink cider.

"Challenger after challenger fell to Wampage's superior strength, and tankard after tankard of strong drink passed down his throat. After the third he was swaying, and the fourth caused his eyes to glaze over. Still he was determined to play on until every one of the ugly, smelly Europeans was defeated. Cokoe stood aside from the group, unspeaking, his arms folded over his chest and one hand on the hilt of his knife. Suddenly, one of the bearded men looked him straight in the eyes and smirked; Cokoe sensed a flurry of movement at his shoulder, but before he was able to react, he was knocked cold by a blow to the back of his head.

"When he came to he found himself lying in a ditch, his hair glued to a sticky wound that he palpated gingerly. Next to him lay Wampage, unconscious, his face smeared with dried blood from his broken nose, his ribs badly bruised, a stream of vomit caked on his chin and chest. His jacket, hat, and moccasins were gone, along with his stuivers. A *shuwonnock* boy of maybe twelve or thirteen was urinating on his feet. Cokoe made a feeble swipe, so weakly that the boy just spat and trotted off. Flies grazed at the corner of Wampage's lips.

"They were not far from the tavern. Cokoe draped his friend's arms around his neck and hoisted him onto his back. He retraced their steps along the path to Rechtauk, passing the same farms and the same hollow-cheeked women who had glared at them earlier. Now they grinned shamelessly. Once they had reached the woods, Cokoe followed the sound of running water to a stream, where he laid Wampage tenderly on a bank and tended to his wounds with a sponge of dampened moss. Wampage opened his eyes at the cool touch on his forehead, but said nothing for a long time.

" 'You see, *dzho*,' he finally spoke in a hoarse, cracked whisper. 'This is why we will never lose our lands. They can only best us by subterfuge.' "

By the time he'd finished his story, Elias was staring morosely into his water glass as if he were seriously considering jumping in and drowning himself. "That happened less than a mile from here, by the way," he added in glum afterthought.

"Elias, why don't you tell me what's bothering you?" I urged, tapping his knuckles. He gave me a surprised, querulous look.

"But I've already told you," he said. "It's that story. I always feel sad when I think about it."

I sighed. "Well alright, but what did you ask me here for?"

Elias smacked his forehead. "My god, I almost forgot. I asked Emily to marry me last night."

"She turned you down?"

"I'm not quite certain. She's a little shy, given past experience. She just needs more time."

"But you asked her about being a Lenape, right? You told her about Turnaway and all that?"

"What? Oh yes, yes," he said distractedly, dismissing the question with a backhand swat. "That's all come out as I said it would." But he looked as miserable as I'd ever seen him.

There was a long pause while I tried to think of something to comfort him. I couldn't come up with a single thing to say. More as filler, really, I asked: "I don't suppose Wampage was right?"

Elias snorted evilly. "Look around you. Does this look as if the Indians kept their lands?"

If there had been any hope for the conversation, that killed it. We paid the bill and headed for the street. Elias apologized for his mood but offered no explanation. I didn't attach too much importance to it. I just assumed he was upset because Emily hadn't given him a straight answer. That was understandable when you looked at all he had at stake. If Emily, the only possible Mahkohkwe, should turn him down, his whole world would crumble, and not only because he had real feelings for her. But I wasn't too worried on that score, either. I'd seen her with him: no matter what I might think of her or her hidden agendas, she really did seem to care for him. I was willing to bet she'd end up saying yes. Now that she knew he owned the last twenty-acre parcel of privately held, undeveloped real estate in New York City, I was certain of it. She was a lawyer, after all.

There was a message from Dr. Ross on my machine when I got home that night. I showered and took a painkiller before returning his call.

"Mr. Givens, I have just now spoken with Elias, who has told me of his plans to marry. Did you know of this thing?"

"Not until this morning."

"I see. And this girl, what do you know of her? Of what family?"

"Not much. She's a lawyer, divorced, rich parents, early thirties. Elias seems to think she's got Matinecock blood."

"This is all very serious, wouldn't you agree?"

"Serious enough for marriage, anyhow."

"I mean it is a grave situation, Mr. Givens, very grave. Precipitant. Ill-considerate. It should be stopped, should it?"

"Now hold on, doctor. I'm sure she's a very nice person, in her own way. I'm sure there's probably no cause for alarm."

"Mr. Givens, I must speak with you. Will you come to Turnaway, please?"

"Well, I—"

"It is very important."

We arranged to meet the next day; I wasn't too happy to lose a day's pay over his whim, but he was strangely insistent. I couldn't begin to guess what the doctor might have to say to me that was so urgent. I suspected that he was just lonely, and I was happy to keep him company for a morning, but I also figured that he'd try to enlist me in a campaign to sabotage the wedding. It was easy enough to see the situation through his eyes: if Elias got married, it was always possible that he and his wife would settle on Turnaway and raise a family there; that might not be so bad, but it would effectively reduce the doctor's status to that of a mere servant. But the other and more likely outcome was that Elias's wife would refuse to live in that drafty, musty old museum of a house, so inconveniently situated, and would insist on living in town, or worse yet in the suburbs, out of reach of public transport. Either way, the prospects for a happy, restful retirement for the doctor were looking pretty bleak, and nothing I could tell him was going to make it any easier.

My dream went a little further than usual that night. All of the regular elements were there: the bracing autumn wind; denuded trees and fallen leaves underfoot; the glimpse of water through the trees; the path on the valley floor, leading me on. Generally, in the course of the dream, I would walk for a while, looking around, encountering nothing in particular, until my free-floating anxiety woke me up before I knew what I was afraid of. But tonight I kept walking—the fear was there, but I passed through the first surge of panic without waking. It was like getting through a rite of passage, changing my perception of the world around me. Now, for the first time, I noticed that the woods were busy with animal life: a brown rabbit darted across my feet; squirrels, their cheeks bulging with acorns, scampered along the boughs overhead; a small herd of white-tailed deer browsed in a thicket to my left; songbirds called from the forest canopy. Suddenly there was a mighty beating of wings about my ears, and I turned to find an owl perched on my right shoulder. "Who?" it said, and I woke up to the sound of my own voice repeating the question.

I made my way to Turnaway on a fine, breezy early summer's morning. By this time I'd completely forgotten about Elias's prenuptial jitters. My main concern was how I was going to reach the island. The mail drop, I knew, was scheduled to coincide with the first high tide of the workday, since the natural channel between City Island and Manapinock isn't safely navigable at other times. But somehow I miscalculated, and by the time I reached Fordham Street the mail boat was already gone. This wasn't the first time this had happened to me, and I knew enough to go straight to the wharf rats—they'd never remember my face after all this time. I was right. It didn't take me long to find one idler who was glad enough to make ten dollars on the round-trip ride in his motorized skiff. I had to guide him: stay to the right of Rat Island, then straight up between the Chimney Sweeps and the Blauzes, forty-five degrees to starboard, skirting between Middle Reef and East Nonations, then due east to Turnaway. Any other route could be catastrophic, even to a small vessel, as I had once discovered—could it have been only ten months earlier? Just west of South Nonations, we passed Felicia in the mail boat, on her way back to Fordham Street. She waved and gesticulated, pointing back toward Turnaway, but we were too far apart for me to understand what she was saying. I cupped my ears but it was no good. She was probably just trying to tell me that Dr. Ross was expecting me.

But he wasn't on the dock when we landed, nor did I find him tending the rabbits. I was amazed to see that half a dozen hutches had been added to the compound; obviously, the reports of the doctor's success hadn't been exaggerated. The rabbits themselves were as plump and content as ever, and as I approached the house I noted that another large patch of lawn had been sacrificed to the lettuce patch. I called out from the porch, but there was no answer.

The door to the house wasn't locked, of course, and I pushed it inward. I shouted again; the only reply was the echo of my own voice.

I stepped inside, pausing in the front hall to allow my eyes to adjust to the gloom and the rush of emotion to subside within me. Nothing had changed, except maybe that the intensity of each perception was heightened by my long absence and conflicted nostalgia. The murk of the house was even thicker than I'd remembered, damper and more fungal; the warp of the floorboards was more pronounced, and the faded carpets more threadbare. Even the dust seemed more sprightly in the light that leaked through the front transom of milky stained glass. I took one step forward into the interior of the house and the gloom closed in around me. I called; if there was anyone in the house, they were either asleep, hiding, or dead. I turned into the living room.

Here, too, a few wayward shafts of light somehow dared to plunge through the grimy windows and frayed, yellowing paper blinds. They struggled into the plumes of dancing dust particles, clung to the backs of fat, playful fruit flies, and collapsed exhausted on the waxy floorboards. Everything was exhausted or dying. The headdresses, bows, loincloths, wampum belts, and moccasins on display looked on the verge of giving up the struggle against entropy; I had the impression that if I knocked one off its perch, it would disintegrate before it hit the floor. I tried it on a bone trowel; its echo off the floorboards flew away into the empty rooms like a frightened bat.

I turned, crossed the hallway into the library, and went straight to the captain's desk I'd once ransacked in the dead of night. I began shuffling through its papers; this time I knew what I was looking for. I found the personal correspondence. Yarden, Balin, Browne, Praeger, Habner, Gonzalez, Giardino. I sighed and returned the papers to their pigeonhole. No Wolfe. It had been a long shot anyway.

At loose ends, I sauntered into the dining room. The table was strewn with the remains of a meal—breakfast, judging by the coffeepot, now cold to the touch, and the two empty bowls encrusted with dried oatmeal. The dishes looked as if they'd been sitting there for hours, which was unusual, since Dr. Ross was normally pretty fastidious about cleaning up after meals. It suddenly occurred to me that the doctor had been alone out here for quite a while; if anything had happened to him, who would know—or care? If no one met her at the dock, Felicia left the mail in an old zinc dairy box, so it wouldn't strike her as strange for a day or two. You're always reading in the papers about bodies that go mouldering for weeks before they're found; this was exactly the way that happened. I was just steeling myself for a thorough search of house and property when I heard the back door open and the doctor's unmistakable shuffle across the kitchen floor. By the time I was through the swinging doors, the doctor was standing at the sink, his sleeves rolled up and the faucet running.

I didn't mean to sneak up on him, but the water was blasting thunderously into a galvanized watering can and I guess the doctor might have been a little hard of hearing, too. In any case, I was halfway across the room before I realized that he didn't know I was there behind him. I was about to cough to announce myself when my eye was caught by something. There, very sharp in the light from the window, on the inside of his left forearm, which he always kept covered in a crisp starched sleeve, were tattoed a letter and five numbers in faded blue. I stared at them until the doctor turned off the water and my shifting weight on a creaky floorboard caused him to turn and see me. His first shock gave way to a look of mild irritation when he caught me staring at his tattoo. He reached for a dish towel, dried both hands methodically, then slowly rolled down his sleeves, first the right, then the left, and buttoned them at the cuffs. Then he tugged at the sides of his shirt and dusted off his thighs. Only then did I notice that he was wearing dungarees, pretty casual workclothes for a man who usually gardened in a black vest and shirt buttoned to the collar. Life alone had obviously taken its toll on his sense of decorum.

"Mr. Givens," he said, stepping up to shake me by the hand. "Forgive me for keeping you waiting, there is so much work in tending the rabbits."

"I'm sorry to intrude," I apologized. "I should have waited on the porch."

"Nonsense, you can be at home here, you know." I smiled inwardly; this friendliness was a side of the doctor I'd never seen before. Solitude had softened him up. "Will you have some tea?" he inquired solicitously.

"Thanks, just some water."

"Well, let's take ourselves to the porch, shall we?" He actually chuckled when he said that. We went onto the side porch, just now fallen into shade as the sun swung round to the south of the house. We made ourselves as comfortable as possible in the old cane furniture. The doctor clapped his hands between his knees, then burnished his bald spot with his palms.

"Well, well, and here you are on Turnaway again after all these months?" he said. His jauntiness seemed forced. I had no idea why he was behaving so weirdly, so I just ignored it.

"Here I am," I said.

"A beautiful day for it, you see."

"So it is."

"Lilacs are in bloom."

"I can smell them from here."

The doctor didn't seem too anxious to broach the subject that had brought me here. We sat there in awkward silence, and again I couldn't help feeling that something was wrong. The doctor had a lot of quirks, but shyness was not one of them. On the other hand, I could understand and even sympathize: he wasn't used to having to appeal for help, especially to someone like me. He was actually squirming in embarrassment at that very moment, poor old guy. I gave him an out, rubbing my hands together in a "let's get down to business" gesture.

"So, what did you want to talk to me about, Dr. Ross?"

He startled like a rabbit caught in headlights; his eyes went round and wide, and I could even see his pupils contract.

"I? Talk to you?"

"You asked me here for a talk."

"Did I though?"

"Dr. Ross, you told me you had something important to discuss. So important it couldn't be done on the phone. Don't you remember?"

"I did?"

Now this was too strange. Within the space of five minutes I'd seen Dr. Ross—one of the least expressive people I've ever met, and I've known my share of cold fish—display shame, resentment, and sociability one after the other; and now, forgetfulness. Had loneliness made him senile?

"Doctor, are you alright?" I asked.

"Why yes, thank you, just fine, only—"

"You do remember calling me, don't you?"

Now he grew indignant. He puffed out his cheeks like a squirrel, and the little folds of skin under his eyes turned red. "But of course I remember. And naturally I remember inviting you for a visit. But as for something important . . . no, no, I think not . . . just a friendly visit . . ."

"Was it something to do with Elias?"

"Elias? Elias? What has Elias to do with it? No, no, no, no. . . . Why must it do with Elias? Elias is just fine . . . fine . . . Did you know he was to be married? Yes? Just fine, thank you . . ."

I made a mental note to call Elias the minute I returned to New York. I was deeply concerned about the doctor's state of mind and the effect of so much solitude on a lonely old man. Maybe it was a little premature to diagnose senility, but clearly his thinking was not at its sharpest. Elias would want to get him to a specialist right away, before his condition deteriorated any further. I tried changing the subject to calm him down, but my innocent question only seemed to rattle him even worse.

"Who was here for breakfast? Anyone I know?"

"Breakfast? No one was here for breakfast! No one . . . that is . . . oh, do you mean breakfast? Why yes, well, Felicia stopped in . . . for coffee. . . . She's an old friend of Elias, you know . . . asking after him . . ."

That made sense. Felicia was almost a part of the family; she'd have been checking up on the doctor, too, if she thought he was sick or in trouble. Maybe all her sign language on the boat had been a warning to me about his condition. Come to think of it, I seemed to remember that she'd tapped her right forefinger against her temple a few times—hardly subtle but eloquent enough, now that I'd seen the doctor. And now that I had seen him—he was squirming in his chair like a little boy, rolling his eyes and constantly glancing over his own shoulder—my only thought was to get away as soon as possible and warn Elias about what I could only imagine was some sort of breakdown, emotional, nervous, whatever. But at the same time, with the doctor acting so strangely, I didn't want to antagonize him by rushing off only moments after I'd arrived. So I made a little conversation, directing his attention to the beauty of the woods, stirring the naturalist in him, questioning him about the various bird and insect communities I knew he liked to monitor, asking after the rabbits, and generally trying to draw him out, make him forget himself and his troubles. I'm no therapist, but he did seem to calm down a good deal, to relax, and even treated me to a brief lecture on the latest phase of his studies into the ephemeroptera of Turnaway. Once I felt that his good humor was restored and that it might be safe to leave him to his own devices, I stood up slowly, anxious not to do anything that might upset or offend him, or make it seem that I was eager to be on my way. I looked at my watch.

"So soon?" he barked, leaping to his feet. He clapped a hand on my shoulder and left it there as he guided me around to the front of the house and down the porch steps, all the while keeping up a hearty patter. "I myself did not realize how late it has grown, and all the labor yet to be performed! You will forgive my not walking you to the dock? What a pleasure it has been to see you, Mr. Givens, a true pleasure. Again some time, can you? And to Elias you will say— hello? Well, I shall be off now. Goodbye, goodbye!"

He walked me as far as the edge of the lawn. His hand still on my shoulder, he gave me a light shove in the direction of the dock, where my hired skiff and pilot were waiting. I'd gone no more than ten yards down the path when I turned to wave a last goodbye, but the doctor was already scurrying away uphill—not toward the house but out past the lettuce field. A moment later, he disappeared into a dense cover of brush and brambles at the forest edge. I shrugged my shoulders sadly, still feeling the ghost of his warm palm there and a superstitious need to shake it off.

It wasn't until I'd reached home, deep in troubled thought over the doctor's condition, that it occurred to me that I didn't know how to get in touch with Elias. He'd never given me his new number, and the phone book listed no Emily Wolfe or E. Wolfe on West Twenty-first Street. Obviously, she was unlisted or still under her married name. Then I thought of looking in the business section, and there she was: "E. Wolfe, atty." I called right away.

"YBB. Can you hold please?"

I held. Vivaldi was piped down the receiver while I waited. Thirty seconds later, the receptionist picked up.

"How can I help you?"

"Emily Wolfe, please."

There was a short pause before the receptionist answered. "I'm sorry, she no longer works here."

"But I got her name out of the phone book."

"That must be an old phone book, sir. She hasn't been with the firm in over two years."

"I see. Do you know how I can get in touch with her?"

"I'm sorry, I don't have that information. But if it's an emergency I can let you speak with Mr. Praeger."

"Who?"

"Jeffrey Praeger. Ms. Wolfe's ex-husband. He's one of our senior partners."

"Oh, no. That won't be necessary. Thanks for your help."

I went down to West Twenty-first Street myself, only twenty minutes' walk from my place, and strolled its length from Fifth Avenue to Tenth in the forlorn hope of running into Elias, to no avail. I even considered calling all the Wolfes in Sands Point until I reached her parents, but I thought that might be pushing my luck.

Anxious as I was to let Elias know about Dr. Ross, I had no choice but to wait until he called me. I felt that he would surely be in touch in the next day or two with news of Emily's decision. In the meantime, I kept in touch with my "patient," bombarding him with daily calls and subtle inquiries after his health and stamina. But the funny thing is, he sounded perfectly fine over the phone, neither senile nor particularly cordial. In fact, the more I called, the more like his old self he seemed to become. Surly at first, he gradually grew irascible and then finally lost his patience with me.

"Is there a particular purpose to these calls you have been placing to me?" he asked pointedly. "You are concerned for my welfare, are you?"

"No, not really, I just—"

"I assure you I am quite well, Mr. Givens, and that any fears of yours are misplaced. It is kind of you to think so much of me."

So I stopped worrying about him. It had probably just been something he ate, anyway.

And still I waited to hear from Elias. Two, three, four days passed without a word. The doctor hadn't heard from him either. It's true we'd been a little on the outs lately, but I still figured that he'd bring his troubles home to me. I wanted him to, and I guess I was a little hurt that he was too wrapped up in Emily to give my feelings even a second's thought. If this was the way love led you to treat your friends, I was glad I'd never been smitten. Maybe if I hadn't felt so slighted and rejected I'd have been more alarmed by his silence— he'd never gone this long without at least a hasty call or visit—and I'd have made more of an effort to reach him. But as the days passed and I grew more and more resentful at my mistreatment, my wounded pride hardened like a tumor inside my chest and I resolved to stick it out until he came to me.

So when the phone rang one Wednesday morning, six days after our disastrous lunch, I let the machine pick it up. See how he likes being shut out for a change! But it wasn't Elias.

"Ben, it's Emily Wolfe," she said in a choked-up voice. I crossed the room and turned up the volume on the monitor. "I wonder if . . . I wanted to ask . . . Is Elias staying with you? I haven't heard from him in five days. I think he's missing."

I was at Emily's apartment ten minutes later. She let me in at the front door of the brownstone and led me to the far end of the landing, where her front door stood open. She was wearing a white, sleeveless vest and sweatpants, and her black hair was tied back in a simple ponytail. It bounced from side to side across her shoulders as she walked, barefoot, her heels never quite touching the ground.

Her place was small and cozy, hardwood floors, expensive-looking oriental rugs, and oversized pillows everywhere. I could see Elias's touch here and there—a handwoven basket on the wall, moccasins peeking out from under the skirt of the couch, that sort of thing— as if they were already a married couple. Potted trees and hanging plants gave the place a greenish, underwater tinge, but as we moved through the living room toward the back, where French doors looked out on to a garden of ferns and hostas, it grew brighter and fresher. Without speaking, Emily sat me down at a small table under a window and brought me a cup of coffee. But it wasn't until she took a chair opposite that I noticed the look of cold suspicion that had settled on her face.

"I have no intention of humiliating myself by cross-examining you," she said. "Why don't you just tell me what's going on?"

"Why are you talking to me like that?" I said, a nervous whine creeping into my voice though I'd done nothing wrong. "I've been waiting to hear from him for days."

"So you knew he was gone?"

"No."

Emily sighed heavily, disappointed but hardly convinced. She shifted in her chair and leaned forward, and once again I caught a hint of lilac.

"Look," she said, sounding every inch the lawyer. "When I hadn't heard from him in three days I called the University of Chicago. They never heard of him. Then I called Rutgers. They never heard of him either. What the hell is going on, Ben? You used to be his best friend—I have a right to know if he's keeping secrets from me."

"I swear I don't know. Did you call the police?"

"I was waiting to talk to you. Doesn't he have any other relatives he might be staying with? Other friends?"

"Not that I know of." I was breaking into a sweat. "Can I use your bathroom?"

The door she pointed to led into the bedroom. The blinds were drawn and it was dark, but a light shone from the bathroom at the far side. As I crossed the room—for some reason on tiptoe—my eye was caught by a couple of framed photographs propped on a bookshelf. The first was of Elias, sitting at a table outside a Village café. I knew the place, though I'd never have thought to take him there—it was ultratrendy, mobbed with club girls and fashion plates. But, in this picture at least, Elias fit right in with his black turtleneck and blue-tinted granny glasses. I'd hardly have recognized him—he was studiously looking away from the lens, like a self-conscious beatnik. The other picture showed him and Emily at a poolside, smiling for the photographer like the very models of youth and health. I had no idea where it had been taken, obviously some sort of resort. Elias was bare-chested and tan. Emily, in a black bikini, was glistening with oil or water; she had her hands behind her head, and her armpits were shaved smooth as glass. Feeling sick, I hurried on into the bathroom and splashed my face. By mistake, I turned the light off when I was done and barked my shin against a corner of the bed as I made my way back across the room.

I returned to my seat and took a deep breath before I spoke. "Let me tell you everything I know," I said in conciliatory tone, even though her accusations had left me testy and a little rattled. "The last time I saw Elias, we had lunch in the East Village about a week ago. He seemed—"

"Yes, he told me. He was upset because you two seemed to have so little to say to one another."

"He was very depressed when he got there. He wouldn't tell me what was wrong. I figured you two must have had a fight or something. Anyway, I had to wring it out of him, but finally it turns out he'd asked you to marry him and that you'd turned him down flat."

I had the satisfaction of watching all the color drain from her cheeks. She covered her mouth with her hand. "He said that?" she finally managed to whisper.

"He said that."

"But I didn't turn him down! I accepted—I accepted with all my heart. There's no way he could've mistaken me. Why would he lie to you?"

"I have no idea," I said coldly.

We sat in silence for a few minutes. I stared out the window at some irises swaying in the breeze. She didn't make a sound, but from the corner of my eye I could see the tears trickling down her face. Her lips looked swollen. I couldn't quite bring myself to reach out to her. I was torn between an impulse to take her cheeks in my hands and brush the tears from the corners of her mouth and my instinct to blame her for everything that had gone wrong. I don't know why it came over me so strong, but her vulnerability made me confused and irritated.

"Did you two ever discuss race or religion?"

She shook her head forlornly, unable to speak just yet.

"He never asked you about your ancestry?"

She swallowed her tears and managed a hoarse answer. "No, but he knows I'm half Jewish."

"What about the other half? Any Indian?"

"What?"

"Any American Indian? Native American? Lenape? Siwanoy? *Mengwe?*"

"What are you talking about?"

"Elias thinks you're part Indian. Are you?"

"Of course not. Do I look like an Indian to you?"

"You do to Elias."

"So what are you saying? That Elias is a closet racist and ran away because he thinks I'm an Indian? That's ridiculous."

"Then he never asked you?"

"Of course he never asked me."

I looked away, hating myself and hating her. My head felt like a fish tank, all the different and antagonistic species of emotions and ideas swimming around, nipping at each other, forming themselves into groups to attack one, then disbanding and regrouping to go after another. I had no idea which of them was responsible for making me behave so badly. I felt, somewhere, that it was wrong and mean to hurt Emily, but I couldn't help myself; from the moment I'd met her, there'd been something about her that constricted and pinched me, and I couldn't tell if she was doing it on purpose. It felt like she must be, like the time she kept asking about my accident as she wrapped herself all over Elias. But maybe, like me, she couldn't help it. I hated myself whenever I was with her.

"Ben, this isn't getting anywhere," Emily said wearily. She was standing behind the butcher-block counter that separated the kitchen from the dining area, washing dishes in the sink. "Maybe we should call the police now. Maybe it's not so complicated—maybe he was just in an accident."

"Maybe," I agreed. "No, wait. I just want to ask you one more thing."

"What is it now?"

"Do you remember you once told Elias about an island you'd been to? A little wooded island in the Sound?"

She squinted and pursed her lips as she struggled to recall. "Yes?" she said hesitantly.

"Did he ever ask you why you went there?"

"He asked me that exact question when he got home from his lunch with you," she said in a whisper. "The day before he disappeared."

"What did you tell him?

"Well, it was so . . . nothing, so trivial. There was this old man who wanted to hire my firm to represent him. This was when I was still at Yarden, Balin and Browne. My boss sent me to meet him because it was hard for him to get around. There wasn't anything that special about his case—we didn't handle it in the end—but what I was telling Elias about that was so incredible, was his house. Here was this old guy living all by himself in this amazing Victorian house on a private island—right here in the city, near City Island. It was a place called Turnabout. It was amazing, a little creepy."

"Elias wanted to know why the old man tried to hire you."

"Yes, I told him. Suddenly he went pale, I thought he was going to throw up. He ran into the bathroom. I heard the water running. He came out ten minutes later, I thought he'd seen a ghost. He said it was the shrimp he'd had for lunch."

"And?"

"And nothing. He spent the rest of the day in bed and left early next morning."

"No, I mean what did the old man want?"

"The city wanted to condemn the property and he asked us to handle the case for free because he was broke. It was pretty sad."

"Condemn? What does that mean?"

"They wanted to take the property by eminent domain. Turn it into a prison or something, I don't remember the details."

"They can't do that really?"

"Sure they can. It happens all the time. How do you think highways get built? Reservoirs, airports?"

"I see," I said. I stood up, but the room had begun to spin; I knocked my chair over and had to lean with both fists on the table. When I felt a little more secure, I straightened up and made to leave.

"I'll let you know if I hear anything," I muttered, but Emily hooked her nails into the sleeve of my shirt.

"Look," she said desperately. "I know something's going on here. Elias had exactly the same reaction as you. What is all this, Ben? What's going on?"

"No, I—" But her tone was so pitiable and, despite my confusion, her eyes were so blue and steady as I turned toward her, meaning just to loosen her grip on my clothing, that I had to say something. "Look, Emily, I think I may know where Elias is. I don't want to say anything until I find him, it's not my business. If I do, I promise you he'll tell you the whole story. If I don't . . . Anyway, call me tonight, okay?"

I didn't care that Turnaway was about to become the next Riker's Island. I wasn't thinking about Emily or my confused feelings for her. I was no longer interested in snooping and delving and prying into other people's lives, deciding what was in their best interests and what were the best recipes for their success. As I jumped into a cab on Eighth Avenue and headed for the Fordham Street dock on City Island, my only concern was to find Elias and keep him from hurting himself.

On the ride uptown I somehow became fixated on the tide chart in the *Times*. It was a very simple calculation, and I had plenty of time to make the mail boat, but I kept going over it again and again, coordinating my watch, adding and subtracting minutes, sweating over the consequences of missing the tide. The mind has its own ways of shutting out whatever it can't bear to face—the long, uncomfortable trip up the FDR and across the Bronx passed quickly. Like a lonely child who's lain awake all night long and finally sees the first smudge of daybreak against the black sky, I was unduly ecstatic to catch a glimpse of the navy blue roof of the mail boat's cabin bobbing against the pier as the cab pulled up to the gate. I paid my fare, ran along the dockway, and practically slid down the ladder onto the boat's deck.

"Hey, what the fuck do you think you're doing?" I turned to see a blond man advancing angrily on me from the cabin, waving his arms. He was wearing a uniform of tight shorts and white socks, and in my confusion I momentarily took him for some kind of crazed Nazi. But then I recognized the postal service emblem on his left breast.

"Where's Felicia?" I asked, backing away.

"This is government property. You can't be on this boat. Get off, now."

"Where's the regular carrier for this route? She always gives me a ride."

"That's strictly against regulations. She probably got fired. I'm the regular carrier now. Off, I mean it, buddy!" He shoved me roughly with his palm, and I complied. I soon found Lonnie, the wharf rat who'd piloted me last time, lounging with his peers among the bollards. This time he asked for fifteen dollars round-trip; I'd have agreed to any fare, the way I was feeling.

I found Dr. Ross among the rabbits, on his hands and knees in his dungarees before a hutch. This time I saw my chance to surprise him and took it cruelly. I waited until I was less than a dozen paces behind him then shouted his name. He skittered round on all fours to face me, blind terror pulling his lips over his gums like a cornered fox. But he recovered well when he saw it was just me: his eyes narrowed to puffy slits as he picked himself up nonchalantly, his hands trembling almost imperceptibly. I stood over him with my fists on my hips while he brushed the dust from his knees.

"I'd like to talk to you, Doctor," I said.

"What would you care to talk about, Mr. Givens?" he asked, though it was pointless to pretend he didn't know.

"Is Elias here?"

"No, he is not here. That was your question, is it?"

"Do me a favor."

"I will join you at the house in five minutes. Please help yourself to tea while you are waiting."

This time, instead of lingering like an idiot in the front hall to savor my nostalgia and wax lyrical over romantic decay, I bounded up the porch stairs, threw open the double front doors, and raced up to the second floor. I didn't waste a second on the portraits or the view from the great window at the head of the hall—I made straight for Elias's room and burst in without knocking. I'm not sure what I expected to find—hastily packed or unpacked bags, telltale wardrobes of up-to-date clothing, Elias himself lounging on the bed—but I was remembering the unexplained breakfast dishes and the doctor's strange behavior during my last visit. I'd figured out in the cab that Elias had vanished the very morning of that visit. I was certain now that he'd been here, somewhere in the house or on the island, hiding or being hidden, at the very moment I'd been innocently taking tea and making conversation. That would explain the doctor's quirkiness that day and his eagerness to get rid of me.

But though I'd been hoping to catch Elias unawares, if he was or had been on the island, I certainly found no proof of it in his bedroom—it was just as I'd last seen it, except for ten months' accumulation of dust and spider webs. His ridiculous clothes—his plus fours, Oxford bags, spats, clownishly wide ties, and double-breasted suits with winglike lapels—were undisturbed in their drawers and on their cedar hangers in the closet. The bed was made with the doctor's characteristic crisp edges; an authentic cobweb stretched from spread to pillow, like a sanitation wrapper on a motel toilet bowl. I ran a finger along the edge of the war club hanging over the bed, and it came away gray with dust. If Elias had come through Turnaway House, he hadn't stopped or slept in his room. I climbed up to the study in the tower, as empty and haunted as a ghost ship. From its windows I scanned the surrounding woods, but they were too dense with summer foliage to reveal anything. A quick foray through the rest of the rooms was equally fruitless, though the doctor's newly spruced-up entomology lab, an airless tomb a year ago, was now bright with Windex and lemon oil. Oddly disappointed, I returned to the porch, where the doctor was patiently waiting for me. He threw me a glance of long-suffering martyrdom as I collapsed into an old rattan sofa at his side.

"I hope you looked under the bed, did you?" he said wryly.

"Where is he really?"

"Really? Where he is really, I don't know."

"But he *was* here, wasn't he? When I was here."

"But now he is gone."

"Come on, Doctor. Where would he go? This is Elias. He doesn't know anywhere else. He's never been anywhere else. He wouldn't go anywhere else if he was feeling bad or frightened. Where would he go?"

"You tell me," Dr. Ross began innocuously, with a delicate needle of malice and bitterness in his voice that he honed to a sharp point as he spoke. "You have taught him the ways of your beautiful world. You have shown him by your shining example how to live. You have sneered at his gentle ways and schooled his ambition. He belongs to you now. So you tell me, do."

"You really don't know where he is, do you?"

The doctor slowly turned his head and leveled at me a ray of purest scorn. "Really," he said fatally.

I looked away. A flurry of birds exploded from the crown of a tree ahead, and I watched them rise and circle and dissipate. A blush-stained cloud floated into view between the porch roof and the tower gable, then floated out again. A dragonfly hovered about a nearby dandelion, and for one crystalline moment the surrounding bay asserted its ancient voice in one perfect, musical crash of tide against the stony beach where I'd first landed on Turnaway. After that there was silence, broken a moment later by a domestic flight banking lazily over Pelham in its approach to La Guardia.

"What's going to happen to Turnaway, Doctor?" I said as calmly as I could.

"It will be leveled. The house will be torn down. The woods will be razed. The hill will be made flat. The beaches will be made concrete." He spoke without looking at me, but his voice was so tired now, so unresisting, I don't think he had the energy left to turn his head again.

"For a prison?"

"No, not a prison. A cemetery. You have seen Hart Island—it is just across the water there. That was like Turnaway once. Only they have thrown away a million people there since then, and that can change the character of a place, doesn't it? It wasn't the first potter's field, either. It was the ninth. Now potter's field is full, just like a landfill it is full, and your city needs a new place to discard its dead. Turnaway will be the tenth potter's field—big enough to last fifty years, I'm told."

"How long has this been going on?"

"Three, four years now, the first letter."

"And when will it end?"

"Soon."

"How soon?"

"Soon enough."

I paused, panting as if I'd been running windsprints, but the impetus of my curiosity and horror kept me moving despite myself.

"Can't anything be done?"

"Nothing. The city is activated now and nothing will stop it."

"What have you done to try to stop it?"

"With what shall I try?" For the first time the doctor allowed a note of impatience to creep into his voice. "There is no money here for lawyers. There is no cause here for sympathy."

"What about legal aid, minority rights groups?"

"Oh you are a child, Mr. Givens. What minority rights? I have told you, there is no minority here. Legal aid? I think you have seen my tattoo, yes? I know a little about governments. The only thing you need to know about governments is that they are made of men. You do not fight governments, I have learned, you flee them. You run as fast as you can, if you can. Well I have flown my last flight. This nest was safe, now no longer. There are no allies to liberate me this time. Only a boy and a bulldozer."

"So you've done nothing to save the island? Nothing at all?"

"That is right. I have done nothing at all."

"And Elias? What's going to happen to him?"

"He will die. Without Turnaway he will die. With me, he was to live in perfect innocence and happiness until the day they came. It would all be over quick for him, and me. No pain, lingering. Now instead, thanks to you, he will die in misery. Even the Nazis allowed you the illusion of taking a shower, did they not? But your world is crueller still. Crueller . . ."

"You shouldn't have given up on Elias, Doctor. He was worth saving. You should have been the one to save him, not me."

The doctor shook his head sadly. "You think you have saved Elias, is that it? That he is changed now? Oh you are wrong, how you don't know him. Even now, it is your world he regards as fantasy, and your life is to him as a game. His Manapinock, to him, that is the only important thing. This here, now, while it remains, is all he regards as real. And I agree with him. There is nothing else but here. There is one home only and when you have lost it, it is gone. He cannot be saved. You cannot save him, I cannot save him."

I stood up. "Is that so? Then where is he now? If this is still his home, where is he? I'll tell you where—he's out looking for a place to start over, like I taught him. Somewhere he can put all this behind him, the lying, the illusions."

The doctor shook his head again. "I think not. I think he is looking for a place to die."

"And you just sit here."

"Where shall I look? You tell me."

All the way home, my teeth chattered and I shivered myself into a cold sweat of grief and rage. I could only imagine—and even that not too well—the holes and wounds torn through the child Joseph Rosen by his experiences in the war, and the empty spaces they'd left in the adult Ross to make him such a hopeless, helpless, heedless misanthrope. I've read the testimony of Holocaust survivors and I know what they say about its repercussions through the generations. But I didn't need to imagine the damage he'd done to Elias in its name. That damage was all too obvious.

All this time—it was incredible!—all this time Ross had known about Turnaway's impending destruction and, in the name of making Elias's last days happy ones, had kept him in the dark. His plan seems to have been based on the theory that, when threatened, it's better to live in ignorance and perish quickly than to have foreknowledge of your doom. It was a funny sort of attitude for a Holocaust survivor, I thought, but it must have been based on some sort of experience. Did he really equate Turnaway with the shtetl, City Hall with the Third Reich? Of course his plan had backfired. Had he really imagined that Elias was such a puppy dog? A younger, more energetic, less fatalistic man could have fought the condemnation, I'm sure of that—through the courts, the government, the media, grassroots activism. Elias himself—the new Elias—could lead the charge with energy, charisma, conviction. When the initial shock and anger wore off, he'd come to his senses, wherever he was, and enter the fray with flying fists. How could he not? This was his whole life being threatened. After everything I'd taught him, I just knew he'd never lie down with the wolves again, not willingly. He couldn't be a patsy, a victim like Dr. Ross—no matter what the excuse. I felt sure of it. By the time I'd reached Hell's Kitchen, new confidence was surging like adrenaline through my veins. All we had to do was find Elias.

I paced the little rooms of my apartment all afternoon, but Emily didn't call until early evening. I told her that we had to meet that very evening, that Elias could be in danger. We met an hour later at a local diner. I arrived first, she came in a few minutes later in miniskirt and sleeveless sweater. As her fiancé's best friend, I felt a sort of proprietary pleasure watching her turn heads as she passed, even as I resented every swish of her ponytail and every click of her heels.

I wasted no time laying out the whole truth for her, as far as I knew it anyway. I gave her the good with the bad, since I felt it was her right to know, even if Elias had chosen, for whatever reason, to put off the hour of reckoning. I told her the various versions of Turnaway's origins; I told her of Elias's beliefs about his ancestry and the central role they played in his life—even in his life with her, though she hadn't known it. I told her about Dr. Ross, his own background, his relationship to the Hutchinsons, his dissenting opinion on Elias's heritage. I told her about my introduction to their strange household, how my initial confusion and distaste had grown into affection and respect and finally concern for Elias's welfare; how

I began to suspect that a dark secret was being concealed on the island and how I was banished for daring to challenge the status quo; how Elias had come round to my way of thinking and had submitted himself to my instruction in the ways of the world. Finally, I told her about recent events, how all my suspicions about her had proven correct. I explained how it had only been today that I'd been able to connect her, through her ex-husband Jeff Praeger, to the "E. Praeger" in Dr. Ross's correspondence, and how much grief might have been prevented if I'd done it sooner. And then, in flawless detail, I demonstrated how her innocent remarks had broken Elias's heart and shattered his complacency about his ancestral home, where he'd intended to spend the rest of his days with his Lenape princess, resurrecting the fortunes of his people.

By the time it was all over, she was pale and trembling and all the mascara had run off her eyelashes. I wasn't feeling too well myself. I'd lashed into her with such relish in the beginning, but I'd had to watch her self-respect slowly wilt and all her composure crumble as I went along, and it had finally forced me to recognize the real person I was taunting. She wasn't any symbol of corruption; nobody had put her there just to make me feel inadequate. In any case, hurting her feelings had been no fun at all, the way I'd imagined it might be. It only made me feel uglier, and the uglier I felt, the more I wanted to punish her for it. I don't usually go in for this kind of kitchen-table psychoanalysis, but this time I had to admit that it wasn't her fault— it really wasn't.

She seemed to have accepted the truth as far as she could understand it, though I can't say whether she grasped the full extent of the deception that Elias had practiced against her. All she knew for certain was that the man she loved had lied to her comprehensively about his background, aspirations, and motives—that, and the fact that she'd been at least partly to blame for his disaster. I tried to make her see that he'd misled her not out of malice but from misguided insecurity. I think I succeeded. By the end of the evening, in any case, her feelings toward Elias didn't seem to be dominated by anger or resentment, but more by awe of his vast imaginary empire and by sadness at what he'd been driven to do in the name of love.

I really did share her sadness, since Elias had lied to me, too, and I was angry but I didn't let it show. There'd be plenty of time for explanations and tears when we'd found him. For now, though, I took charge. I talked to her in a firm, determined voice: I forced her to say that she still loved Elias and that she'd help me find him and put things right, if that was possible. I felt a lot better after that—it felt good to say the right thing for once—and she broke down and sobbed, which seemed to do her some good, too. When she'd finished dabbing at her nose, she squeezed my hand and smiled timidly as she thanked me for seeing her through this. She said Elias was lucky to have a friend like me. I smiled weakly.

No matter what I might have felt about her, I have to admit that she turned out to be practical and energetic. By the time I spoke to her the next morning to go over our plan of action, she'd already contacted her father and laid out the entire situation, no holds barred. Considering that he hadn't even known about Elias until then, he was a pretty good sport about it. He insisted we alert the police. He also put her onto a detective agency that he'd used in the past, and she was ready to go for it, at his expense, pending an interview scheduled for that afternoon.

It so happened that Emily was acquainted with Jay Habner, the Corporation Council lawyer who was handling the Turnaway condemnation. I remembered his name from Dr. Ross's letters. They'd worked together before, and she was certain that he'd be susceptible to friendly pressure, especially since she was pretty sure that he had a longstanding crush on her. She called him and he immediately agreed to meet with us the following day. And we were encouraged, too, by our meeting with the head of the detective agency that afternoon. He was young and handsome and brimming with confidence. Even with the meagre tips we were able to supply him—Delaware and Mahican reservations from Niagara to Oklahoma, Pound Ridge, Pelham Park: Elias could be anywhere—he was able to convince us that this was run-of-the-mill, a simple case even, and that if his best "operatives" weren't able to track down our missing man, no one

could. We left buoyed by naïve optimism, and hugged each other
with fraternal solidarity as we made our way back into the world, a
world where Elias was waiting somewhere for us to save him.

That night, though, as I lay in bed trying to wind down from the
day's excitement, I was again plagued by misgivings and confusion. I
was feeling suddenly alone and lonely. I hadn't felt that way in a long
time, and I couldn't help wondering why it'd come on me, though at
the same time I didn't really want to know. I told myself that I missed
Elias and that I was feeling his absence even more acutely now that
there was a chance I would never see him again. But there was
another voice, quieter but insidious, telling me that I wasn't lonely
like a friend but lonely like a man, and that it was getting to know
Emily that had done it to me. I had to deny it, of course, even to
myself, but I also knew that I was making it impossible to uncover
the living heart of my sadness, and that was the way it was going to
have to be. Not only could I never have Emily; I could never even
admit I wanted her. People like her don't want people like you, I kept
telling myself, over and over, like a mantra or an after-school punishment. But the image of her, the sound of her voice in my ears, and
the scent of her clinging to my nostrils continued to come back at me
there in the dark, like the number eight on a magic cue ball. Maybe
it didn't have to be Emily; maybe it could just be the possibility of
someone as beautiful and as loving for me. I could have that, too?
But it was no use, and I knew it. It *was* Emily, and that raised a
disturbing question: How *much* did I want her?

I tried to empty my head. I turned the white noise up to full
rainstorm, but it was no use. I tossed and turned and got up and
showered and lay down and listened to the Jeep Cherokees from New
Jersey cruising the whores on Tenth Avenue. When you're wrestling
with your conscience late on a summer's night in a noisy city, every
laugh drifting in off the street sounds like a harsh judgment. The
ugliness of my dilemma made me morose, and it was in that frame of
mind that, some time after two, to the sound of car windows shattering down the block and along the avenues, I eventually fell asleep
and had my dream.

There were all the usual elements—trees, leaves, water, wind—

leading up to the moment where, again, the woods are suddenly full of animals and I'm terrified, though the animals are benign. I turn and see Emily, naked, riding a full-horned stag through the woods, grinding her pelvis lasciviously into its backbone, but this is somehow perfectly irrelevant and I turn away, instantly forgetting her. The path I'm on has always followed a gentle downward slope, but now the gradient becomes steeper and at the same time the woods begin to thin up ahead. My fear builds to the point where, as I gaze into the ever-brightening forest, the sight of a glade or clearing in the distance, the flash of a bright color from the brush, and the distant laughter of a child are enough to bring me back into the milky predawn light of Hell's Kitchen, sweating and panting.

After another half hour of sticky tossing and turning, and with the first commuters arriving through the tunnel, I gave up the struggle and went out for an early breakfast. Annie and Desirée were there. They glared at me when I stopped at their table, but when I told them that Elias had disappeared, they seemed genuinely upset. Unfortunately, they hadn't seen him, but they reminded me that he had a friend, Sonny, who lived in the railway tunnel over by Eleventh Avenue. I'd forgotten all about Sonny, but I made a mental note to check it out. By the time I got home, there was already a message from Emily on my machine, reminding me of our lunchtime rendezvous and the need to phone Dr. Ross.

My nightmare—the first in over two weeks—set the tone for the rest of the day. First I called Dr. Ross for news—there was none—and reminded him to let us know the moment he heard anything. To say that he treated me gruffly would be an understatement. I knew he blamed me for Elias's disappearance, but that was all right, since I blamed him. I'd just hoped that we might be able to put our differences aside long enough to see our common goal through, but obviously he had a different agenda. I tried to shrug it off, but still it dogged me all day, like when you let a stranger's passing insult go unanswered.

My next call was to Lieutenant Dilombardi at Midtown North, who was in charge of Elias's case. He, too, seemed to think of me as his antagonist; he didn't quite grasp the concept of my calling for a

progress report. There was no progress as yet, but he implied that I
shouldn't be bothering him with check-up calls—he'd be sure to let
me know if something came up. Again, I shouldn't have let it bother
me—especially since most of my hopes were pinned on the private
detectives anyway—but I was feeling a little sensitive after my difficult night, and I allowed myself a few choice ironical comments
before hanging up.

My lunch with Emily did nothing to bolster my spirits. She seemed
haggard and dejected, and it showed in the bags beneath her
almond-shaped eyes and the frizzy nimbus of loose ends around her
hair, which was usually brushed to perfection. It turned out that
she'd had a rough, sleepless night, too. For one crazy instant, the
ridiculous notion crossed my mind that she'd been restless on my
account, but I dismissed it with only the tiniest pang of my old
bitterness. Anyway, her confidence of the day before had somehow
evaporated like mine, and the fears and efforts of the days or weeks
or months ahead were weighing on her. She felt she had to warn me,
too, that from what little she knew of eminent domain in state law,
she doubted that Habner would have much good news for us. We
lapsed into sullen silence over our salads, and it occurred to me that
a good hug might help dispel our blues. Instead, the hug we shared
on the sidewalk after lunch just made me feel sick to my stomach.

As far as Jay Habner was concerned, Emily's prediction was right
on the button. Without going into too much detail, and without using
the words *fiancé* or *boyfriend,* she explained our personal interest in
the matter and wondered about the status of the case. Was it too late
to reverse the process? Could anything at all be done? There seemed
to be some question of confidentiality, but Habner waived it without
much scruple at a coy bat of the eyelid from Emily. He clucked
sympathetically as he reviewed the file, glancing up every so often to
see if Emily was registering his humane emotions. He was a slovenly,
greasy kind of guy in a cheap suit, and his role in the imminent
destruction of Turnaway did nothing to endear him to me. I didn't
much care for the way he ogled my best friend's fiancée either.

"Oh, no, no, no," he said, shaking his head as he closed the file, as
if destroying peoples' homes was the most painful thing in the world

to him and not a part of his basic daily duties. "You should have come to me two years ago, at least, if you wanted to challenge this condemnation. Everything's already in place, the final public hearings were held months ago. Nobody representing the property ever showed. Dr. . . . whatsis . . . Ross seems to have stopped answering our correspondence about a year ago. The final environmental impact statements have been handed in, the surveyor's work is done, the engineer's plans are drawn up, the contracts have been assigned. In other words, this is as done a deal as you could want. As far as I can tell, the only delay is some snafu with the DOT and the Coast Guard over permits to dredge a channel for heavy equipment to be barged in."

"How long might that take?" Emily inquired desperately, as if some grounds for hope could be placed in the delay. But Habner dashed that idea with a callous snap of his fat fingers.

"Could be any day, there's no knowing. All I can say for sure is that the property is scheduled to be cleared before winter so that construction of facilities can begin first thing come spring." He smiled smugly, as if he'd just been a big help to us.

"What does 'clearing' mean?" I asked.

"Clearing. Clearing. As in 'everything must go.' House, trees, fields, beaches—clearing."

"And there's nothing that can be done to stop it? What about some sort of injunction."

"Cato Institute already asked for one. Denied."

I had a sudden inspiration. "What if," I said, leaning toward him conspiratorially, "what if an ancient burial ground were discovered on the property? Like an Indian burial ground? They'd have to halt construction then, wouldn't they?"

"Sure they would," he grinned evilly. "But we're no idiots, we've been burned on these goddamn burial grounds before. We went over that island with a fine-tooth comb, didn't find so much as a wishbone."

That was that. We thanked him glumly and turned to go. Emily put her arm around my waist, quite low around my waist actually, as we left the room. My heart raced, just a little bit, to feel the heat of her palm on the scar above my hipbone, but when she removed it the second we were out the door I realized that she'd only done it to tweak Habner.

It would be nice to say that there was more we could have done, but there wasn't, either for Turnaway or for Elias. What else could we do? All the legal avenues, it seemed, had been exhausted—Mr. Wolfe's high-powered attorney had looked into it and assured us that Habner had been telling the truth. We considered hiring a publicist, getting public opinion on our side, but we agreed that it was really much too late for that, too; at best it would only prolong the agony and subject Dr. Ross to unnecessary harassment. As for Elias, Mr. Wolfe was paying top dollar for the detective work. I'd call in every so often with my intuitions, which were received politely but without much encouragement, and I supplemented their work with a lot of walking in neighborhoods I thought might attract Elias: Wampage's "grave" on Hunter's Island, Inwood Park, the meat-packing district, Spanish Harlem, and other sites of Lenape settlements and stations. I even drove out to Fresh Kills on the off-chance that he'd found some sort of home out there in the salt marshes, but it was too disgusting, and Elias was even more sensitive than I was. It was hardly likely in any case that he'd be padding around town like some homeless man. What we were really afraid of, Emily and I, and what we finally admitted to each other in whispers over a quiet meal in the Village, was that Elias had crawled off to some secluded spot, sacred or special in Indian lore, and done away with himself in despair. What we didn't dare to admit, however, was that of all the likely causes of Elias's disappearance, this was the most likely. And as the days mounted and became weeks, any optimism we'd felt at the outset was drained of all blood, a hollow shell with no life in it at all.

One day, more out of boredom, almost, than despair, I remembered my vow to look for Sonny. I crossed Tenth Avenue and found a hole in the chain-link fence along the railway embankment. I squeezed through and clambered down the steep slope along a well-worn path that cut through the weeds and young ailanthus. At the bottom, everything was quiet and hot, like in an arroyo, and there was a pervasive smell of goldenrod and creosote. I peered into the tunnel and was surprised to see a diesel engine in it. The diesel engine was moving very fast in my direction. I jumped off the track and fell into an old tire as the train thundered past. When it was gone I picked myself up and began the painful climb back to the street. I didn't think any homeless people would be living in that tunnel anymore.

At the top of the slope, an old black man with white hair and frayed dungarees was sitting on a chair, drinking water from an Evian bottle. He was shielded from the street by a makeshift screen of plywood and plastic bags. I must have gone straight past him on my way down; I hadn't seen him, but he'd watched my entire descent and near accident without saying a word. Now he was laughing at me.

"There been trains running through there four months or more now," he chuckled in a friendly way, offering me the bottle. "They give us some warning but I guess nobody thought to alert *you.*"

"Are you Sonny?" I asked.

He pulled the bottle to his chest and frowned mightily, his bushy eyebrows coming together. "No I ain't Sonny. Sonny long gone," he said suspiciously, but I knew it was him.

I explained why I'd come. His frown melted away and he smiled ruefully to himself.

"No, I ain't seen him in a long time, long time," he shook his head. "He come to give me one last lesson and say goodbye. Crazy boy, that. Nice though."

"Well, thanks anyway," I said, turning away.

"You Ben?" he called out after me. I spun around. "I knew it was you!" Sonny burst out laughing, slapping his knees and rolling his head. "Ha ha! That Injun boy was always good with words, described things just as they are! Got you just right, Ben, yes he did!"

"What'd he say about me?"

"Think I remember? No sir, old man like me." He dabbed the sweat off his forehead with a handkerchief and took a swig of water. I thought he was going to continue, but he just sat there, hanging his head and laughing softly to himself.

"Well, thanks again." I waded through the weeds and bent down to the hole in the fence.

And still and always, I had that awful question hanging over me, casting an even darker shadow on the whole enterprise. I knew that I could never, ever look in the mirror and put it to myself directly, but it lingered around me like body odor. I felt like I was living a double life: traitor to Elias on the inside, liar to Emily on the outside. I couldn't let it interfere with our search, that much was certain; if anything, it made me redouble my efforts, as if I were trying to outrun it. But it was always a step ahead, opening the door for me when I went to meet Emily, pulling back the sheets when I climbed into bed at night, alone. What would happen when we found Elias? Would my joy be tempered with resentment? Was it possible I might even regret our success? What if we failed to find him, or worse yet, what if he turned up dead? How authentic would my mourning be? With Elias as far above me as a buffalo to a frog, could I even pretend to imagine I could take his place and carry off his princess? Nothing I could ever do again would be guiltless, and nothing I could ever feel again would be sincere. The paradoxes of my situation were piling up and haunting me by night; by day, I found myself walking around in a fog of dread and exhaustion. It was becoming all too obvious that something had to be done, and soon, to avert a major breakdown. Either I was going to have to talk to Emily, to unburden myself, or— or what? Kill her?

We spent a lot of time together in those weeks, comforting and supporting each other, sharing our thoughts and fears. We got together almost every day, usually over dinner, and when we couldn't we always spoke on the phone. A real intimacy developed between us. I came to see her the way I thought Elias saw her, with clean eyes. I got to know her moods, what made her laugh, what triggered her melancholy. I found myself repeating little phrases and verbal tics I'd picked up from her; I'd hear them over and over again all day long, in her voice. I came to miss the scent of lilac when she wasn't there.

It was obvious that she liked me for my own sake, too, the better she got to know me. And that made it worse—even if I felt like a dog being scratched between the ears every time she laughed at one of my jokes—because the more she came to like me, the more she got to know what she must have thought was the "real me," the more I felt like I was putting on an act, and I hated myself. For the first time in my life, a kind and beautiful woman wanted *me* for company—it wasn't love and it sure wasn't desire, but it still felt nice. And yet I couldn't allow myself the swagger and ease that any other man might expect to feel in the circumstances. It wasn't fair, I guess, but I couldn't very well revert to my old sour self. I couldn't very well make her dislike me, not without disillusioning her about the "real me," at least. So I moved forward. And since I hadn't had a straight thought in my head since I'd met her, I don't think I can be judged too harshly if, just once, I let down my guard and made a mistake.

Emily had chosen the venue, a quiet bistro down four steps from the sidewalk on a quiet Village street. She'd been gazing at me in an eerily soulful way throughout our meal. She'd silently taken my hand and held it in hers. The skin of her shoulders glowed in the candle-light. Emily sometimes got this look in her eyes that wavered halfway between anger and passion. I had no idea what it meant, but I'd seen it flashing on and off again all evening.

As usual, we'd been talking about Elias since cocktails, listing all his qualities and recalling incidents from his life, the way you do about a recently deceased friend. Suddenly I found this little gobbet of irritation rising in my throat. I was beginning to feel a little tired of all these damp-eyed eulogies. Elias wasn't the only person in the whole wide world, after all.

"You know, Emily," I said casually, as if the thought had just occurred to me. "I always thought it was funny, how you and Elias got together."

"How do you mean?"

"Well, you know, what with him being so new in town and you being so . . ."

"So . . . ?"

"Attractive."

She gave me a long, curious stare, as if she didn't quite get what I was driving at. I could feel my heart throbbing in the arteries of my neck. I swallowed hard and pressed on.

"I mean, you could have any man you want."

She still hadn't got it. "But I do, Ben. I have Elias," she said earnestly. "There isn't a girl in New York who wouldn't be glad for someone like him."

"Yes, that's not the first time I've heard that," I said a little too morosely, pulling my hand from hers. I saw the light of understanding suddenly switch on in her eyes. Now she saw my meaning and it was too late to take it back. There was a breathless silence between us while she tried to figure out how to respond, but she never took her gaze off my face. Finally, she reached slowly across the table for my hand, like she might for a wounded bird, and took it in her cool, dry palm.

"You know, Ben, Elias talked about you all the time," she said gently. "He described you perfectly."

"Ah?" was all I could manage, not being in the mood to be comforted.

"I remember one time very clearly," she went on in the same tone of voice. "He said that you're a much better person than you think you are."

"He said that?" I interrupted despite myself.

"He said that he'd once promised to teach you something. That was what he wanted to teach you. He was afraid he'd failed."

"Now there's a loss to the world."

Emily squeezed my hand. "But he was right, Ben. I used to doubt it, but you proved it tonight. He *was* right."

I know she meant it kindly, but for me, at least, my stupid confession only added to the deepening gloom of the days ahead. I couldn't help taking every act of friendship from Emily as an act of pity. It was selfish of me to feel sorry for myself with Elias missing, and I knew it, and that made me feel worse. Every time she called or smiled at me I felt grateful, and every time I felt grateful I felt pathetic and disloyal. There was no way out of it, and I was sinking fast.

Emily did everything possible to keep me up and functioning, focused on our task, not that we were getting anywhere. She sent me gifts of comic novels and Caribbean music. She treated me to expensive dinners and a boat ride up the Hudson. She bought me new shoes. It was almost as if she were wooing me, though I knew it was exactly the opposite—she was keeping me at bay. I was even invited out to dinner at the ostentatious colonial family mansion in Sands Point. For the first hour of the meal, Mrs. Wolfe, soused on dry martinis, questioned me about myself as if I were the boyfriend. Suddenly it seemed to dawn on her that she should be asking about Elias, whom she'd never met, and she switched from one topic to the other in mid-sentence. Mr. Wolfe, on the other hand, had already formed an opinion of Elias—based, I think, on an ill-informed comparison with the rejected golden boy, Jeff Praeger—and I got the impression that he was forking over a small fortune to find him just for the privilege of throttling him with his own meaty hands. After dinner he offered me an enormous Corona and asked pointed questions about my personal life; when it came up that I was Jewish, he threw an unconcealed smirk of triumph at Emily and slapped me chummily on the back. "You married?" he winked. Even though we laughed about it later, it wasn't so absurd that it didn't make me uncomfortable, in the circumstances.

But moments of jollity were rare enough during that terrible time, and they hardly put a dent in the general and growing bleakness of our outlook. We were like a family meeting daily at the hospital bedside of a comatose sibling: without progress or deterioration we had little to discuss except our sense of helplessness, and that wears thin after awhile. Day after day we met, pointlessly going over old ground again and again for that elusive clue. Day after day we heard the reports from the detective agency, ever less optimistic, ever more fanciful, ever less discriminating in the leads they were willing to follow up. They'd already disinterred a couple of anonymous stiffs from a mass grave in potter's field, and a month after Elias's disappearance an operative was dispatched to Flin Flon, Manitoba, to look into a possible sighting. Day after day I spoke to Dr. Ross, who in his hostility, wasted no words in telling me he knew nothing further. Day after day I called in to my answering machine for a message from Lieutenant Dilombardi, who was no longer accepting my calls. Day after day I pined after Emily, and night after night I punished myself for my guilty craving. I even thought of paying a visit to the corner, but in the end I knew it would just make me feel worse. And day after day I lost more and more hope. In a situation like that, or at some protracted deathbed, you get to the sickening position of look-ing forward more to a change—any change—than to good news. It was now mid-August, almost exactly a year since I'd met Elias and seven weeks since his disappearance. The weather was oppressive with humidity and the air rancid with ozone and rotting garbage.

When the change came, the break we'd been waiting for, it came with no warning. After a morning kicking around midtown with no particular purpose, poking my nose into the pocket parks and librar-ies, I was resting my aching legs on a shaded bench in Tudor City park when I heard someone call my name from across the street.

I turned toward the sound, but there was no one around except a letter carrier pushing a three-wheeled mail cart ahead of her. It wasn't until I realized she was coming my way and waving at me that I recognized Felicia. She was very glad to see me and gave me a big hug.

"How you doin', Ben-ja-*man*?"

"I'm fine. I looked for you on City Island. They told me you got fired."

She looked indignant. "No *way* I got fired. I put in for a transfer, *papí.*" Her face grew suddenly somber. "After what happened to Elias and all, you know? I couldn't take it, I had to move on."

"You know about that, do you?"

"Sure, sure. Any news about him?"

"Nothing. We're going crazy."

"I know what you mean. I couldn't bear to see him like that neither."

"See him like what?"

A flicker of confusion passed across her face. "You know, after what he did to himself and all."

"Did to himself? He disappeared himself, that's what he did."

Her confusion turned to horror. "Disappeared? My god, my god. Since when?"

"Almost two months now."

Now she looked really perplexed, and squinted one eye at me suspiciously, as if she thought I might be lying to her. "What two months? I seen him on Turnaway just a few weeks ago, before I transferred to Manhattan. He weren't no disappeared then, that's for sure."

"That's not possible. I was out there myself, I even saw you on your boat. The doctor was as worried as I was."

"Well, somebody's been lying to you, 'cause I saw that poor boy that very morning and it was the doctor took me to him. Camped out in the woods he was, and what a mess. Blood all over him, paint on his face, naked 'n covered in shit. You think I'd forget that? *That's* what made me get out, honey. I like that boy too much to see him like that."

I don't remember if I said goodbye to Felicia; I can't imagine what she must have thought of my demented getaway. I barely remember anything of the next few hours, in fact. All I recall is bounding down the stairway out of Tudor City onto First Avenue, hailing a cab, then sending it away at the last minute. I found a working pay phone and tried to reach Emily, but she was at lunch. I ran to Forty-second Street, sweating profusely in the miserable humidity, and hailed a cab that slid straight onto the ramp to the northbound FDR. Construction in Harlem slowed us down, and I remember tapping so impatiently on the window that the driver had to say something. After the Third Avenue Bridge it was smooth riding, and we made good time to City Island. I didn't even bother looking for the mail boat and Lonnie wasn't there either, but a crony of his who recognized me offered his ferrying services for twenty dollars. I jumped into his flat-bottomed aluminum tub and we lit out, with me standing at the prow like Washington crossing the Delaware.

I scrambled up onto the Turnaway dock and ran headlong up the hill toward the house, ignoring the shooting pains in my hips. On my way I shed my jacket, shirt, shoes, and socks, leaving them on the path where I had flung them, soaked in sweat. Reaching the crest of the slope, I stopped for a minute to catch my breath and consider my next move. Directly in front of me, a pail of feed in either hand, stood Dr. Ross, halfway between house and hutch. I ran straight for him, and he froze like a startled rabbit when he saw me coming. Without slowing my pace, I flew right by him and headed for the woods. No sooner had I passed under its canopy than the brambles caught at my pants, which I promptly tore off. Now I was bounding almost naked through the woods, peering into the shadows for any sign of Elias. I smashed through that undergrowth like a Sherman tank, crushing entire carpets of lilies of the valley underfoot and sending herds of panicked bunnies scrambling for safety.

I was on a downward slope and could just make out the water at the bottom. Somewhere along here was a path that led around the periphery of the island, connecting the two beaches with the dock. When I came to it, I turned right and sped toward the larger, half-moon beach where I'd first washed ashore on Turnaway. I came to the path that led from the beach to the house, the one Dr. Ross had used to bring me, dazed and injured, to my sickbed across from Elias's room. I crossed the path and pressed forward through the thickest section of the woods, the part most favored by the deer, but I saw neither beast nor man. Soon I'd gone halfway around the island and found myself back at the intersection. I continued along the peripheral path, heading for the small secluded beach where I'd first watched Elias harpoon and gut his bass, and from which I'd spied on the surveyors. Still, I saw nothing out of place in the forest. I was about to come full circle, having run the entire circumference of the island, when a strong scent of wood smoke wafted across my nostrils and I stopped dead.

It was coming from the right, uphill. Turnaway wasn't so big that anything could stay hidden in its woods for long, and I'd probably dashed right by it on my first pass without noticing. Now I saw the column rising from a clearing and heard the sharp crackle and pop of green twigs burning. Shifting to the silent creep, and squeezing my hands against my hips to still the pain, I sidled some thirty feet up the slope to the edge of the glade. The fire was burning in a circular hearth of rough stones. A tiny hut of bent saplings and reed mats, no bigger than a pup tent, stood to one side. To the other was a pyramidal frame of whittled branches hung with strips of drying meat and gutted fish. A longbow leaned against the hut. Several large bones, some with shreds of charred meat still clinging to them, lay scattered in the dust. In the center of the clearing, between the fire and the hut, sat a naked man hunched over a length of animal sinew stretched between two poles stuck in the ground. He was scraping patiently at the sinew with a sickle-shaped stone and humming a Lenape harvest song.

Obviously, I was expecting to see Elias. When a branch cracked under my heel and the man suddenly straightened and turned to look for an intruder, I was expecting to see Elias's face. I was hoping to see Elias's bright, open smile break out when he recognized his old friend. But when the man in the clearing did turn, and did smile, even then it took me a full five heartbeats to realize that it was, indeed, Elias.

I was transfixed: it was like confronting a hideous ghost mask from some savage primitive religion. I was so struck with horror that, even though I knew who I was facing, I still considered running away. Instead, I stood rooted like an animal in the beams of an oncoming car and for the first time understood how the earliest *shuwonnock* in America imagined that they'd stumbled on a land of devil worshippers.

I should point out that Elias was not naked, as I'd thought at first. He was wearing a *sakutakan*—a deerskin breechcloth, six inches wide at most, that did nothing to conceal his private parts. A long white feather was tied with a length of grass to his hair, or what remained of it. A deerskin pouch hung on a thong around his neck. He wore sandals made of braided corn husks.

His entire body from the waist up was painted. His torso was red on the right side, black on the left, cleanly divided straight up the middle; his face and neck were the same, only with the colors reversed. I'd once seen him make this paint, suspending ground bloodroot and powdered charcoal in a base of tallow. It was very greasy stuff, not easy to wash off, and his body gleamed and gave off a rancid odor. In addition to the paint, he had chevrons tattooed on his cheeks and horizontal lines on his chest and upper arms. The Lenape used to burn and pulverize poplar bark and apply it with sharpened fish bones. Elias had demonstrated their technique for me, and it was as indelible as any modern tattoo. Some of the wounds on his chest were already infected from the grease and dirt.

He'd mutilated his ears to conform to Lenape standards of beauty. Probably using a sharpened clam or mussel shell, he'd cut three or four strips from the helix of each rim so that they hung loose like palm leaves. The lowest strip on each ear was being stretched with weights of stone attached with threads of sinew. Elias must have begun the process when he'd first arrived, because the weighted strips now reached almost to his collarbones, like long, flesh-toned pendant earrings.

I recognized, too, the traditional fashion in which Lenape warriors wear their hair. It was all gone, with the exception of a roach, about two inches wide, that sprouted from the left side of his head, near the crown, and hung down about three inches below his shoulder. He'd used the ancient native technique of removing the hair from the head and cheeks by burning the stubble with flat, heated rocks—I could tell because he'd burned his scalp in several places, and the healing scars were visible even beneath the bloodroot paint. The roach was heavily greased, probably with lard or tallow, since the more traditional bear grease would have been hard to come by.

Elias batted away some flies that had congregated at his nostrils, then scratched at a nasty-looking rash on his inner thigh, high up near the crotch. He coughed wetly but continued smiling at me. An Algonquian *siskuwahus,* shaped something like an amphora, was propped up at the center of the fire. Elias stirred at the embers with a pointed stick, then used the same stick to stir the bubbling contents of the pot. From where I stood, it looked and smelled like *namesisapan,* a gruel of hominy and dried fish. Elias burbled something unintelligible at me in Munsee, and it wasn't until he repeated it that I realized he was actually talking in English.

"Did you see Cokoe?" he asked gently.

"Who?"

"Up there, behind you." He pointed over my shoulder and I turned. Perched on the bough of a chestnut tree about twelve feet up was a small barn owl, brown and gray, silent and intense as it gazed directly down on me, returning my stare as candidly and accusingly as any police interrogator. I shuddered involuntarily and turned back to Elias. "A pet?" I asked, and a brief look of alarm crossed his awful painted face.

"No. He's my *manito*. He revealed himself to me in a vision when I was a boy. Now he has come as a guardian to protect me. Cokoe and Wampage—the owl and the chestnut burr—together again after three hundred years."

"You're not Wampage, Elias."

"Perhaps not, but I am his direct descendant. I have inherited his spirit. *Na alahksit ila pe!*" He coughed again, wiping a splash of rust-colored spittle from his chin.

"Elias, you have to give this up now."

He looked at me impassively, almost as if I hadn't spoken at all. He looked at me that way for a good ten seconds, then turned to stir his *namesisapan*. But when he spoke, it was with icy, deliberate responsiveness.

"I'm not going anywhere, Ben. I've made that mistake already. Manapinock is my home."

That's when every fear, frustration, and resentment I'd suppressed for two months finally came spewing out. I jumped to my feet and began ranting and raving, striding up and down the clearing, waving my arms, stamping my feet, scaring away the owl, going red in the face, losing my breath, scolding, pleading, urging, threatening. I don't remember my exact words; they were probably obscene, repetitive, and racially insensitive. But I pulled no punches, venting my anger over the heartache and worry he'd put Emily and me through, the shameless abandonment of his friends—his only true friends—getting Dr. Ross to lie to us, making us search the entire continent, fearing the worst, spending a small fortune, while all the time he was right here on Turnaway, indulging his childish fantasies about some ludicrous and barbaric way of life, risking death by infection and exposure, dreaming pathetic dreams of dead heroes and dead civilizations, when there was a beautiful, intelligent woman waiting for him, a woman most men would kill for, and his best friend, too—that is, waiting for him—two people ready to help and support and nurture him. And all for what? Twenty acres of woods getting plowed under in the name of progress? Did he have any idea how much those twenty acres were worth, how much the city was going to compensate him for the loss of his property? Most people would be grateful for such a windfall. . . . Anyway, that was the gist of my rant. I couldn't say exactly how long it went on, but Elias sat imperturbably stirring his stew throughout. When I was done, he waited a few moments, then sighed.

"Ben, I think you've missed something important here," he said quietly. "I'm terribly sorry that I hurt you and Emily by disappearing as I did. And as for lying, I never asked Ross to do any such thing. But you're quite mistaken if you think I'm hiding here. I'm not hiding—I'm guarding, along with Cokoe. When you find a home, Ben, you'll see what's worth preserving. So long as I occupy these woods, as my ancestors did, Manapinock will remain untouched." As he spoke, the owl returned to its perch overhead and resumed its eavesdropping.

"Wake up, Running Deer. They're coming in whether you like it or not."

"No they are not."

"They are, Elias, you little jerk, they're—"

"You know, all this reminds me of the time Wampage and Cokoe were chasing after—"

"I don't want to hear about Wampage!" I was hysterical, almost screaming in his face. "If it wasn't for Wampage you wouldn't be in this mess. Forget Wampage, will you? You make me sick, Elias, you really do. Fuck Wampage."

I turned my back on Elias, and during the deep silence that followed I didn't dare look around or meet his eye. I was trembling all over. I heard the stick rattling in the pot and poking through the fire. I heard Elias hack and scratch his thigh. I heard the wind rustle the treetops and saw Cokoe hop onto a lower branch, eyeing me warily. Finally, I heard the sound of a stone methodically scraping at sinew. I had the rest of my say with my back still turned to my friend.

"You can think what you want about me, Elias. I know you're thinking that I've turned out to be a cruel, lousy friend. Maybe you even blame me for everything that's happened. But I'll tell you one thing. I'm not leaving this island until you come with me. I'll be up at the house waiting. You're going to have to leave some time, you know that. I'll wait as long as it takes. You know where to find me."

I left without looking back. When I reached the top of the slope, Dr. Ross was hovering anxiously at the edge of the woods, squinting into the shadows. He stepped away timidly as I emerged from the undergrowth. My jacket, shirt, pants, and socks were neatly folded and draped over his left arm; my shoes were hooked by the heel over his index and middle fingers.

"There'll be one more for dinner," I said as I brushed by him on my way to the house. I stormed upstairs and into "my" bedroom, where I took a long, cold shower then lay on the bed with my forearm over my eyes. Only the feeblest of breezes disturbed the gauze curtains. Within moments I was bathed in an oily sweat. My head and thighs throbbed. Outside, except for an occasional powerboat and the regular rising and falling thrum of air traffic, the afternoon was quiet. I fell into a dazed, uncomfortable sleep with visions of Elias, like some grotesque dormant talisman buried in the heart of the forest, spinning through my head. I awoke at twilight, my throat parched, to the smell of frying meat rising from the kitchen. My clothes were neatly piled by the doorjamb. I showered again, dressed, then headed downstairs.

Too wiped out to face the inevitable clash with Dr. Ross just yet, I went straight to the phone in the library. Emily wasn't home, and I didn't want to leave the news on her answering machine, so I hung up. I tried to check my machine, but Turnaway had a rotary phone and I was unable to punch in my access code. I tried to think of someone else to call, anyone, but I'd run out of excuses: the doctor could be avoided no longer. I strolled down the entrance foyer to the kitchen and found him draining breaded schnitzel on paper towels. He conspicuously did not turn around as I entered.

"Feeling better, yes?" he said in a monotone that revealed nothing.

"Thank you."

"Will you eat?"

"Maybe a drink first."

"Help yourself. Nothing for me."

I made myself a Sazerac and took it to the front porch to watch the sunset's afterglow fade from the underbellies of thunderheads massing over Jersey City. Even as I stood there, the last of the day's light was gone, and thunder rumbled in the far distance while heat lightning played on the fringes of the horizon. I thought about Elias down there, sitting by his smoky fire, sweating into his paint, fighting off the mosquitoes, muttering to himself in an almost extinct language, and listening to the approaching storm. Well, it wouldn't be his first drenching of the summer. A good soaking might even wash away some of the mud between his ears. The thunder rumbled closer and I felt the first cool breeze being pushed ahead of the rain. I downed my drink and went in for dinner.

Schnitzel, mashed potatoes, peas with ham on a hot August night—the doctor had started without me, and a crackly skin had already formed over the pond of melted butter on my potatoes. I sat down and began to eat in silence. Our cutlery scraped and chimed, as if the knives and forks were in conversation. As the wind picked up outside, the window began to bang and rattle in its frame. Lightning flashed, much closer now, followed by thunder still some miles off. A low hiss announced the first of the rain. The doctor speared the last pea fastidiously with the middle tine of his fork, and when he'd slid it thoughtfully into his mouth, he wiped his lips and pushed his chair away from the table. It wasn't until he stood and was about to clear his place that I spoke.

"Isn't there anything we can do?" I asked.

The doctor sighed wearily. "Perhaps we have done enough already," he said without malice.

"Anyway, I'm glad he's alive, at least."

"You should be." The doctor took his dishes into the kitchen, and I listened to him clattering around while I tried to finish my meal. Eventually I just pushed my half-eaten meat away in disgust. A moment later the doctor returned with a tray bearing a silver coffeepot and two china cups on saucers. The voice of the rain rose from a patter to a roar. As he poured and served, the doctor spoke in a low voice, full of sadness and regret, that was occasionally drowned out by the thunder. At particularly loud claps we would both look to the door and beyond it to the lone warrior sheltered in the dark, dripping woods downhill. The doctor spoke in a gentle but steady torrent, as if he'd waited just a little too late in his life to say this.

"Elias, even when he was a boy, I worried for him. I was an *interne* then, at Montefiore, the hours I worked I never saw sleep. But on weekends I came here, Andrew was still young—only ten years more than me, was it? Only ten, eleven years—all alone on this island with his son. And Elias—how did he love his father! A god, a more-than-god, and when Andrew told a story, that boy, his eyes were wide and shiny like Moses himself was talking. And Andrew didn't know—he thought he would live forever, plenty of time to explain that these Indian stories were just *stories*. The boy believed, the poor motherless boy, he believed, he believed everything because it was his father who laughed at the Indians in the movies, who spoke their language better than they did—his papa was cowboy *and* Indian, he did not need anything else. But no, Andrew died—he was my father, too, I cried more for him than for all my dead in Austria. And now Elias was mine, a strange boy, fourteen years old, my brother—but young enough to be my son, a strange son to me though I loved him. We found each other strange. I did my best. Was it not good enough? Was it not? Another boy, he'd have grown up, the stories of his boyhood he would leave behind or remember fondly or forget or regret or something. Only Elias—that is what he took of his father, only that. Sometimes I almost thought him crazy—no friends, no sports, always bad or distracted in his schoolwork, no college. He worried me. Yet he speaks how many languages I can't count. Yet like his father he is a great scholar, a historian, you can't even know what a mind. . . . And now he sits in the rain, he kills himself, I know him, he *will* kill himself."

The doctor paused as the thunder boomed almost directly overhead. He seemed so tired; I've never seen such weariness. But he went on.

"Anything we can do? What haven't I done, what wouldn't I do? More important is, what have I done? Give the boy his stories—it is all he has. What can it hurt the world, one boy dreaming forever on his island? One little boy . . . I have seen that place where no one dreams, I lived there. There is too much reality already in the world. Too much reality. One boy dreaming . . . one man dreams . . ."

The doctor lapsed into a sort of reverie. The storm was at its height, and every loose board in the house groaned and creaked and every pane of glass rattled like a machine gun and the wind moaned in the chimneys, which is why, I suppose, we didn't hear the front door bang open or the gale rush in, and it came as quite a shock when the dining room door swung back and Elias was standing there for all the world like an ambassador from hell. He was dressed and painted just as I'd seen him earlier, only now he was very, very wet. His breath came in shallow pants. He smiled vaguely, as if at strangers whom a good friend was about to introduce, and passed a hand across his bald, dripping scalp.

"I can't stay long," he said matter-of-factly. "I've just come to tell Ben a story." Then his eyes rolled back into his head and he collapsed in a heap in the doorway.

By ten that evening the storm had passed away to the northeast and a nearly full moon was pushing its way through ragged clouds on the woods above Kings Point. A shard of its light fell on the foot of Elias's bed, where he lay in a deep sleep for the first time in many weeks. In the moonlight, the umber chevrons on his cheeks were barely visible and the roach, tucked neatly beneath the collar of his cambric pyjamas, not at all. There was no smile on his face, but he did seem genuinely at peace. The fever had abated.

It had taken us close on two hours to get him this far. After carrying his limp, stinking body upstairs, we laid him on my bed, which doubled as the house infirmary, while the doctor ran a hot bath next door, dosing the water with salts and antibacterial soap. I read his temperature as 102.5 degrees. I snipped away his *sakutakan* with a pair of surgical shears and when the bath was ready we laid him in it. In the end, it took three fresh tubfulls of water, the last lukewarm, to remove the layers of greasepaint, tallow, and dirt from his wretched body. Between the first and second baths we had to remove him from the tub before scrubbing and disinfecting it. We had to be extremely careful with him, covered as he was with wounds fresh and not-so-fresh, infected and healing, scarred and scabbed, loose and encrusted. I think the doctor was surprised by my calm and gentle touch in tending to the ravaged body. When Elias was finally as clean as we could get him, we laid him on a white sheet on my bed. He tossed his head and mumbled in a delirious faint.

The doctor injected him with antibiotics and something to reduce his fever. He swabbed, disinfected, and dressed the wounds on Elias's chest, face, head, and ears. One of the head burns had turned pustular, and he had to lance, drain, and suture it before applying a bandage. Finally, he gave Elias a thorough examination, palpating his limbs, glands, and abdomen, putting the stethoscope to his chest and back, looking into his eyes, ears, and throat, before diagnosing a case of double pneumococcal pneumonia compounded by exposure and malnutrition. It was true—Elias had lost a good fifteen pounds, and he'd been wiry to begin with. The doctor said that, given adequate bed rest, medication, and a varied and plentiful diet, the patient was in no real danger and should be back on his feet after a brief and comfortable convalescence. Having said that, he lapsed into a meditative silence.

"What concerns me," he finally whispered as we stood at the bedside, "is that recovery requires the cooperation of the patient."

"What do you mean?" I asked once we'd tiptoed from the room.

"I mean that I have known for some time that his condition has been deteriorating. Elias is quite capable of feeding himself from the woods, and even his knowledge of herbal medicine is excellent. He could take care but in his depression he doesn't try. I saw this when I visited him—not enough cleaning, not enough eating, not enough shelter. But what could I do? I could not force him to take medicines, I could not force him to disinfect wounds. He did not care enough to do it. And now—what shall I do? Tie him to his bed?"

"But he came to the house of his own free will. Why do you think he did that?"

"To tell you a story, isn't it?" the doctor said wryly before taking his leave for the night. Exhausted by our labors, I popped some pills and went to bed a minute or two later. It wasn't until I was snugly under the sheets and half asleep that I realized I'd forgotten to call Emily. Well, at this point it could wait until morning. I fell asleep to the persistent hooting of a nearby owl.

I slept late, unused to the bucolic silence of the island, and by the time I got to the phone Emily had already left her apartment. I left Turnaway's number on her machine, without letting on why it was so important for her to call me there as soon as possible. Then I went upstairs and found Elias, pale but smiling, enjoying a breakfast of poached eggs, seven-grain toast, and coffee. The storm had freshened the atmosphere over the Sound, and a cool breeze was blowing through the open windows. I was startled to see an owl—presumably Cokoe—perched on the windowsill, his back to us, gazing out pensively over the forest toward Long Island. His mouth full, Elias beckoned me over and slapped the bedcovers by his side. The clean white muslin patch on his head flashed in the morning light, but his bald scalp was already dulled by the finest fuzz of new-sprung hair.

"I'm very sick, it seems," he said lightheartedly as I sat beside him.

"Nothing a good kick in the pants wouldn't cure." But he didn't find my joke very funny and his face went as solemn as a child's.

"Just because I'm lying here in white cotton pyjamas eating poached eggs, you mustn't think that anything has changed, Ben," he said soberly. "I wouldn't want you to get your hopes up. I've only come to tell you this story, you understand, before I send you on your way."

"You're not going back to your tepee and succotash, Elias."

"It's a wigwam, Ben, and I'm quite capable of taking care of myself. And you needn't smirk. I'm very serious." He coughed painfully into his fist and wiped the reddish stain on a towel by the bed.

"Okay, okay. So tell me your story already."

"You may have guessed it's about Wampage. It's the very last, because after this there are no more stories left to tell about him."

"This one begins in the Christian year 1642, in the twenty-first year of Maminepoe's chieftaincy over Lapechwahacking and its tributary bands.

"There had been a war on for three years between the *shuwonnock* and the Algonquian nations—the Lenape, the Mahicans, the Matouack. Kieft and his evil secretary Van Tienhoven had broken promises, levied taxes, and massacred native men, women, and children from Matawuck to Madnank. In the sale of Siwanoy lands by Chief Tokaneke, Van Tienhoven was now claiming Dutch ownership of vast tracks which Tokaneke had had no authority to sell. The Siwanoy, already weakened by plagues, liquor, and crime, were angry and restless. In accordance with their law, they had avenged crimes committed against their own—it was one such act of vengeance that had unleashed the war—but these crimes were mounting up too fast to be avenged. And now, suddenly, from nowhere, a band of *Kwenashikanak*—Englishmen—had arrived from Sint Sink and were building a house next to the *sackerah*, the path that led from the village of Lapechwahacking to the summer fishing station of Asumsowis. Why they had come, or who had asked or allowed them to live and build on Maminepoe's land, no one could say. All that was known was that the group of *shuwonnock* was led by a fiery woman they called Anne and that she had been cast out by her own people.

"One day, while heading to Asumsowis for the day's oyster harvest, Wampage heard the sound of metal tools working somewhere off near the plantation along the shores of Aqueanounk. He and Cokoe and a group of braves followed the sound to a site where a young *wapsit* was planing boards near the stone foundation of the house of Anne. Because it would be dishonorable to kill him, Wampage gathered the man's tools, put his axe on his shoulder, and gestured for him to leave. But on the return trip from Asumsowis that evening, Wampage found the man still at work. Again, he gathered up the man's tools and bade him be on his way. That night, Wampage and Cokoe determined that the *wapsit* had been given fair warning and that, if they found him there again, he must die.

"The next morning, Wampage walked the *sackerah* alone—if the *wapsit* was there, it would be more honorable to kill him man-to-man. But the interloper was not at the worksite—in his place was the woman Anne, sitting on a tree stump as if she'd been waiting for Wampage. Though not quite young, she was tall and straight like an Indian woman. Her hair was red as a fox's coat and, like all *shuwon-nock*, her direct gaze was a challenge and a provocation. She spoke a few words in Narragansett, which Wampage could understand from his travels among the Mohegan and Pequot, and they talked.

"She told him of her god and his love of people who act straight and true, regardless of their faith, and how she had been exiled from one *shuwonnock* settlement after the other for her beliefs, which offended the hypocrisy of her people. She had been friends of the Narragansett, she claimed, and now she desired the friendship of her hosts, the Siwanoy, whom she knew understood the cruelties of white people. Wampage, who had lost his wife Sasappis to the recent plague and needed a mother for their children, admired Anne's hair and white skin. He pictured to himself how he would make her buck and claw beneath him. She too was a widow, he knew, with children of all ages and thus in need of a husband. Who finer than Wampage? That she was no friend of Kieft or the Dutch in general made him like her all the more, and he agreed to allow her to build her house.

"Through the winter Wampage often stopped at the house to talk with Anne and offer her people food and protection. She always received him like a friend, even with a special sparkle in her eye, he thought, not like the other *shuwonnock*, and she tried to acquaint him with her god. She called herself 'a great wonder in heaven.' She claimed to be 'a woman clothed with the sun who had fled into Lenapehoking, where God had prepared her place.' He was not interested in that, but was quite certain that this proud, vital woman had noticed his fine hair, his strong muscles and black eyes, and that she wanted him as he wanted her. In the spring, he planned to marry her.

"But in February of that winter, the war took a terrible turn. Eighty

Wekweskik men, women and children, refugees from the Mahican, were slaughtered in the night at Rechtauk, on Manhattan, by Kieft's soldiers. It was the worst depredation yet, and at a great war council of all the tribes it was decided to attack and kill all the white people outside the fortified town and to destroy all their property. A false peace was concluded with the English and the attack was scheduled to begin after the harvest. Only Wampage had any reason to oppose this course of action, but he dared not say it to the gathered *sakimawak*. Instead, he stepped forward and claimed the right to kill Anne and her people, who had taken his land, and his bravery was applauded.

"The corn was harvested in August and soon news of attacks by the Hackensack, the Raritan, the Wekweskik, the Reckgawawanc, the Haverstraw, and other tribes began arriving at Lapechwahacking. But Wampage and his men made no move against the *Kwenashik-anak* on their land. Cokoe began to wonder, and to hint—the hunting season would soon be upon them, they must head inland. But Wampage would not move. Finally, Maminepoe lost patience—his brother *sakimawak* had all fulfilled their vows of revenge but not he. Wampage must wait no longer. It was late in the month of *Winaminge* that Wampage and his men finally struck the *shuwonnock* settlements. But before the attack, early in the morning, Wampage walked along the *sackerah* to Anne's house, where she received him warmly, as was her custom.

" 'Where are your men?' he asked her in Munsee, which she was learning.

" 'They are in the forests today, choosing trees for our new barn.' She spoke haltingly and with frequent mistakes, but Wampage understood because he knew her heart.

" 'And which of these men will be your husband?' he asked. 'Collins? Underhill the captain? Perhaps Cornell?'

"She gave him a strange, uneasy glance, but answered: 'I have no need of a husband but he who is most glorious.'

" 'And if one of these should ask you to be his wife, what will you answer?'

" 'I will answer: "Let Him who is *sakima* of all take me as His wife, for I will have none other in this world." ' "

"Wampage went away, determined that Anne should somehow be spared in the day's killings, for she had as much as promised that she would be his wife when Maminepoe made him *sakima* in his place. That day, terrible deeds were done, and the plantations of Cornell and Throckmorton at Snakapins were put to the torch and most of their occupants killed. Anne's farm, isolated from the others by the waters of the Aqueanonk, was closest to Lapechwahacking but the last slated for destruction. The warriors did not descend upon it until the late afternoon.

"Wampage approached the house alone, and the man named Collins met him. Wampage asked Collins to tie up the mastiffs, who were none too friendly to Indians and had been known to bite, and Collins was happy to comply. But the moment the dogs were immobilized the war party came whooping down out of the woods and began the slaughter. None who were found were spared. The cows and pigs were burned in the barns, Collins and Anne's children Francis, William, Mary, and little Anne were all hacked to death. Young Katherine tried to flee but was caught at the fence, dragged back into the barnyard by her hair, and had her head chopped off in one blow by Cokoe's *temahikan.*

"In the meantime, Wampage had entered the house and found Anne cowering in the larder with her youngest daughter Susannah. Wampage sent Susannah into the kitchen while he tried to calm his betrothed and reason with her.

" 'You will be my wife,' he told her in a soothing whisper as he kneeled at her side. 'You have nothing to fear. You will be spared because of my love for you.'

"Anne simply stared at him blankly, her eyes wide and wild with terror, her teeth chattering. Outside, screams and war cries mingled with the growing roar of the flames. After staring at Wampage for some time, Anne began to mumble under her breath in English.

" 'What are you saying?' Wampage asked her. 'You will agree to be my wife? Is that what you are saying?'

" 'Your wife?' Anne answered in Munsee.

" 'Yes. You told me this morning. You said you would be the wife of the *sakima.*'

" 'Sakima?'

" 'Yes. You must hurry if I am to save you. You will marry Wampage and save your life?'

" 'Marry Wampage? I? Marry you?' Suddenly, confusingly, she began to laugh. Wampage stood up.

" 'Why do you laugh?' he demanded.

" 'I? Marry *you*? You, a filthy heathen savage? I love my God. I will marry him, I said.' She closed her eyes and began to mumble again in English. Wampage hesitated only a moment before burying his hatchet deep in her forehead and then, in one swift arc, removing her scalp with his blade and tucking it neatly in the belt of his *sakutakan.* When he stepped into the kitchen he found Pemgaton holding young Susannah by the arm and about to plunge an iron dagger into her chest. Wampage called to him to stop and he obeyed immediately.

" 'This girl is reparation for my dead wife. I will take her.'

"Wampage did take her. When the last traces of Anne's settlement had burned to the ground, Wampage and his warriors vanished with their families deep into the hills of Cantito, beyond the frontier, where they remained for some ten years before returning to Lapechwhacking to sell their lands once and for all to Thomas Pell. But from the moment he killed Anne, Wampage renamed himself Annhook, in honor of his slain enemy, and that was how he was known until his death."

Elias lowered his chin to his chest and closed his eyes. He was panting heavily, clearly in pain, and clutched at his ribs. Though a mild breeze was dancing through the curtains and the morning sun had turned the Sound into a field of liquid diamonds, the atmosphere in the sickroom had grown as heavy and portentous as a funeral. I wanted to yell, maybe slap a little sense into Elias; I kept my silence as long as possible, but finally I had to say something.

"So that's the last of Wampage, is it?" I said jauntily. "What happened, he die after that?"

"No," Elias said resentfully. He sank back into his despondent musing. We sat like that for a few minutes. I watched the wind ruffle the owl's tail feathers.

"There's something I don't understand," I eventually said; in that silence my voice sounded loud and stupid, but I pressed on. "If Wampage killed Anne, how is it you're related to her?"

"Wampage took Susannah with him into the wilderness, and there, when she was old enough, she bore him a child. When she was ransomed by the Dutch, at the age of fifteen, she was already a mother, a secret that was kept from her so-called benefactors. Actually, she was very reluctant to leave the Siwanoy, whom she had grown to love, and Wampage the father of her son. But it was part of a peace treaty—she had to go. She took her son with her and renamed him William."

"How did he come by the name Hutchinson?"

"She married a man named Cole in 1651, but she could hardly bring a half-breed to the marriage. She gave William to her uncle Edward, Anne's brother, who raised him as his own in Boston, as a Hutchinson. When he was a man he somehow learned of his true birthright and returned to Eastchester Bay. His great-grandson John was the Hutchinson who received Turnaway from President Washington."

"What a soap opera. Do you really expect me to believe you're descended from Wampage and Susannah?"

"I don't care what you believe. But now you know, you can leave."

"What did happen to Wampage?"

"Please, Ben," Elias passed his hand over his eyes and coughed. "I'm really very tired. Will you go now?" His face was red and some of his scars had gone livid. A light sheen of sweat had formed above his lips, which were badly chapped and trembling. And yet, despite all this, I had the distinct impression that Elias was avoiding my question. I was ready to force the issue, but the owl, without moving its body, had swiveled its head and was staring at me with open hostility. I left the room, peering through the crack of the door as I closed it—Elias was staring intently out the window and licking his lips.

I met the doctor coming up the stairs to give Elias his morning examination. We didn't speak but exchanged significant glances, the way people do over a sickbed; then we went on our ways. I'd just reached the bottom of the stairs when the phone rang. It was Emily.

I told her the situation and she began to cry, first with relief and then in anguish. When she'd calmed down she told me that she'd been on a date the night before. She'd accepted an invitation from Jay Habner in an attempt to butter him up, maybe milk him for information and determine if the situation was really as desperate as he'd made out. His hands had been all over her from the moment they met in some revolting civil servants' bar on lower Broadway, and for all her pains she'd learned only that it was even worse than we'd known—the problem between DOT and the Coast Guard had been resolved and the heavy equipment was due in by early September. Jay himself was deputed to ensure that the "squatters" had vacated the property and to coordinate the eviction with the U.S. marshal's office if they hadn't. This gave Emily the opening for the one high point of the evening—the opportunity to harangue Jay loudly in front of his colleagues and empty a tankard of Dos Equis in his lap before storming out of the bar.

We made arrangements for her to call that evening when she got to City Island, where I would pick her up in the Turnaway launch. The doctor was coming down the stairway as I hung up, a look of concern shadowing his features. It seemed that Elias's fever, which had responded well to the previous night's dose of penicillin, was up to 104 degrees and that the congestion in his chest had gotten worse. The doctor had dosed him up some more, but if he failed to improve he might have to be moved to Montefiore for observation and tests that couldn't be administered from the primitive infirmary here. A little gloomy and oppressed by the day's increasing humidity, which promised another storm by evening, we ate our lunch in silence on the porch, plagued by mayflies. Beads of sweat kept rolling off our faces into our kasha varnishkes. After the meal, the doctor returned upstairs to check on Elias, uncharacteristically leaving me with the dishes. But I'd barely begun to clear the table when he was back, ashen-faced, to tell me that Elias had vanished.

I'll just replay the facts as I remember them instead of trying to piece together a coherent sequence of events out of a very sketchy sense of what really happened over the next eighteen hours. A lot of it is still foggy—Daphne and the doctors tell me the trauma will fade in time, leaving my memory clear—and some of it is a little too raw to be looked at head on just yet. It's easier for me to make it quick and a little glossy. Maybe the day will come when I'll be ready to flesh it all out, draw conclusions, "make sense" of it all, but right now I'm happy just to get it out any way I can, since the days spent on your back are so long and the nights are so haunted and sleepless, even cradled on the phantom tide of the white-noise machine. It's true, I could tell it into a tape recorder, but then I'd have to listen to it all over again, and sometimes I think that if I never hear my own voice again it'll be too soon. I'm sure Daphne feels that way too, but she's not saying.

It took us less than five minutes to find Elias—he'd returned to his bower, the first place we thought to look. He was squatting naked on the bare ground, and by the time we got to him he'd stripped the poultices from his suppurating chest wounds and had begun applying bloodroot paint to his pectoral muscles. He was mumbling in Munsee, though I couldn't catch the gist of his words, and he didn't respond to our voices. But he had very little strength in his limbs and allowed himself to be led back to the house, passive as a sleep-walker. Cokoe followed at a safe distance, hopping through the grass like a rabbit. We washed Elias, redressed his wounds, and put him back to bed. The doctor took his temperature—105 degrees—and gave him a mild intravenous sedative. He was asleep almost immediately. It was about two P.M.

That afternoon, Dr. Ross made arrangements for Elias to be admitted to Montefiore Hospital. Since he himself was not affiliated with any institution and was unwilling to bring his patient to the emergency room at Jacobi, he called in a favor from an old medical school acquaintance who found a bed that would be vacated the next day. In the meantime, he contacted the pharmacy on City Island and arranged for erythromycin to be delivered to the Fordham Street dockmaster, where I could pick it up when I went for Emily. Throughout the afternoon, the doctor monitored Elias's temperature, which gradually rose over several hours to 106. Without the appropriate blood tests it would have been dangerous to give him any more penicillin. By the time Emily called, at around six P.M., Elias was tossing fitfully.

The round trip to City Island didn't take long—fifteen minutes each way, allowing for my lack of skill in the shallows and a heavy chop in the water from all the unsettled weather out on the Sound. The air had cooled off a little and it was no longer clear if a storm would be breaking that evening. Still, I was glad to reach Turnaway safe and dry, and Emily and I hurried up the path to the house. We were halfway across the lawn when we saw Elias and the doctor struggling together near the rabbit compound. Elias was naked and his chest was again smeared with red and black greasepaint. Although he was obviously very weak, he held a tomahawk in his right hand, which the doctor had pinned to his side but couldn't shake loose from his grip. Like me, the doctor had seen what that tomahawk could do to a fish or a melon, and he didn't dare let Elias go. Emily and I raced over and quickly disarmed and subdued the patient, who collapsed like a ragdoll once the weapon had been pried from his fist. We again carried him upstairs, bathed and bandaged him, then put him to bed.

This time, for his own safety, we bound his wrists to the bed frame with twisted sheets. Emily and I hovered anxiously at the foot of the bed while Dr. Ross went through his examination in dismayed silence. Elias was conscious though delirious, his eyes rolling, his lips speaking, though not necessarily to any of us. The time was approximately seventy-twenty P.M. The doctor was about to put him under for the night with the strongest dosage yet of sedative when Elias seemed to catch sight of Emily for the first time. His gaze, previously wandering and unfocused, fixed on her and he smiled. *"W'ndakha ohkwe"* he said. I nudged Emily, urging her to approach so Elias could speak to her. When she stood over him, he gazed up at her with what might have been moist-eyed appreciation of her beauty.

"Ngahta wewihul ohkwetit," he said quite clearly.

"I think he's asking you to marry him," I whispered.

"Yes, I will marry you, Elias," Emily said.

"Witawemak ohkwelwe kittakima."

"Um . . . something about a chief's wife."

"Anishik ktahwal."

"I love you."

"I love you too."

Then the doctor sedated Elias for the night and we shuffled out. We looked to Dr. Ross, but he shook his head. "It is something else," he said thoughtfully. "But without tests. . . . Well, we will know tomorrow."

We spent an anxious evening together, first around the supper table, where our breaded chops stuck in our throats, and then on the dim porch, its gloom barely pierced by a shaded sixty-watt bulb. There was a healthy gale blowing that smelled of the rain we'd been waiting for all night. But though the lights of Kings Point and New Rochelle were obliterated in the fog, and though the roar of late-arriving planes into La Guardia was muffled by layers of densely packed cloud overhead, and though the gong of Execution Rock sounded fierce and urgent through the crashing tide, no storm came. After a final check on the sleeping Elias—his fever was steady at 105.5—we all went to bed around ten forty-five P.M.

Since all three bedrooms were occupied, Emily and I shared my bed. I knew it was a stupid thing to do, but I couldn't help myself. We fell straight to sleep, but the storm broke with terrific claps of thunder and woke us up in the middle of the night. Disoriented and half asleep, Emily moved closer and flung an arm over my bare chest for comfort. The scent of lilac invaded my nostrils, and I was suddenly overwhelmed by the melancholy certainty that Emily would never, ever be mine. I don't know why it came on me like that, but it was so sickeningly strong that it brought tears to my eyes, as if I'd been winded by a sucker punch. I wanted to get her off me, but I was also confused and aroused by the heat and smell of her body. I could feel her heart beating from a vein in her smooth, scented armpit. The rhythm of her breathing had been broken by a sharp gasp at the first explosion of thunder, but it was quiet now, as if she were holding it in anticipation. I didn't know what to do. Then she heaved a deep sigh and rolled completely away, so that she ended up with her back to me, one sharp shoulder blade jutting against my nose. Her breathing resumed, shallow and rhythmical. I got up and made a cot for myself in the wicker armchair by the window, but didn't get much sleep that night.

Shortly before dawn—there was a glow out toward Norwalk, but the birds were still silent, except for the owl—I heard light footsteps outside in the hall: the doctor, sleepless like me, checking on his patient. My bedroom door clicked and squeaked open a few inches, as it often did when someone walked by, the boards being so old and warped. I didn't move, waiting in the half-light for the doctor to come shake me by the shoulder with his update, but no one came. I fell into a restless doze—I was still too uncomfortable to sleep properly—and when I opened my eyes the sky was bright and the nuthatches were busy in the treetops. It was six thirty-four A.M. by my watch. I slipped into a pair of shorts and padded across the hall to do my own checkup on Elias. His door was slightly ajar. I peeked in and it took a second or two for my mind to register the empty bed, the flaccid sheet-ropes dangling from its frame, and the light stain on the wall above the headboard where the war club had hung.

I woke Emily, who leaped straight out of bed, wide awake from the second I squeezed her bare shoulder, and then the doctor, who'd been in a deep sleep from which he startled in confusion. Emily plunged down the stairs, out the front door, and down the gentle slope of lawn. I limped after her, leaving Dr. Ross to pull himself together before bringing up the rear. Surely, Emily and I would be able to handle Elias between us.

I caught up with her in the empty bower. There were footprints in the fresh mud of last night's storm, but no sign of Elias. We agreed to split up, Emily searching in the direction of the dock, I toward the crescent beach. But we hadn't gone three paces when a sharp cry rang out in the cool morning air from the direction of the house. We found Dr. Ross sitting on the front steps, cradling his head in his hands, rivulets of blood leaking between his fingers. He waved toward the door, indicating that Elias was somewhere inside. Emily stayed on the porch to tend to the doctor, while I rushed up the stairs and through the front door.

After that I don't remember much—little flash cards of memory, like those freeze-frame sequences you sometimes see in slapstick movies. I know that the sun had just risen because I remember catching a glimpse of its reflection, gold through red, in the puddle of blood on the doctor's head as I climbed past him up the stairs. Next I see myself in the front hall, my nose in the air, trying to determine the source of the smoke hanging in the dusty air. I stumble on the red-stained war club. Then I notice the thick plumes curling up from under the kitchen door.

The flames in the kitchen surprise me with their intensity, rising as they seem to be from the floor. The smoke is dense and I cover my mouth and nose with my right hand, which already begins to sting from the intense heat. I crouch down low to where the air is still a little transparent. And that's when I notice two naked feet sticking out of the doorway to the larder. From the vantage of my position just a few feet above the floor, it looks like one foot is in front of the other, as if I'm underneath watching someone on a tightrope high above.

At dawn, every building in New York looks like a monument. When the light comes slanting in broad sheets down those narrow canyons, and their endlessly repeated horizontal elements undergo some sort of epic foreshortening, it happens to tenements and their fire escapes, brownstones with their high stoops, skyscrapers glass and stone, cast-iron warehouses, apartment buildings towering over the canopy of Central Park, police stations and post offices and hospitals. In that brief still moment of sunrise, when the first light breaks over Brooklyn and rolls cascading across the river and spilling down the side streets, each and every edifice comes into its own, like a hopeful soul rising to its final judgment.

This morning, when I woke up to find Cokoe missing, the city was being transformed by just such an event. Maybe *transform* is the wrong word, since it never lasts long. Soon enough, the stone and glass and steel and concrete remember that this is not, after all, the first day of creation. Strange, disconnected snippets of memory begin to filter back, memories of jackhammers and traffic jams and spilled blood and parades and wrecker's balls, and as the day wears on we all assume the weary, pallid look of people and things that are doomed to remember their own true natures. But at night, if we're lucky, we sleep that sleep, and in the morning we are again blessed with transient forgetfulness.

That oblivion was what inspired me to launch into my story this morning. If I'd known how exhausting it was going to be I'd never have begun, but it dragged me along with it and here I am, every surface of my body ablaze, enough heat escaping through my damaged skin to warm a bath. I'm so worked up and uncomfortable I know I'll never sleep tonight, not *that* sleep certainly, not for a long time. I can count on Daphne for a sedative, but it's not the same thing. She's almost ready to leave for the evening, going back to her husband and kids in East New York. I can hear her in the kitchen, rattling through the dishes. She's had a long day.

Elias had hovered between life and death for two days after the fire. His injuries from the flames were minor, just some second-degree burns on the soles of his feet, but the double pneumonia and smoke inhalation were brutal. The police were called in to investigate because of the way he looked when he was rushed into the emergency room at Jacobi. Emily reenacted for me the doctors' horrified reaction to his mutilated ears and singed, scabby scalp. Dr. Ross was questioned over and over again by the police detectives in charge, even though he'd been badly hurt himself. It seems they were looking into the possibility of some sort of satanic ritual abuse or cult sacrifice. I'm sure they'd have done the same to me if I'd been in any condition to answer questions. In the end, though, because they found such massive pneumococcal infections in both lungs and some trace of pneumococcemia, the fire was ruled accidental rather than arson, since they figured he couldn't have been in his right mind when he doused the kitchen with kerosene and set it alight, trapping himself in the larder. But we know better—Elias set that fire not because of his delirium but in spite of it. It stands to reason.

Like I said, I don't remember any of this. Emily tells me I was some sort of hero, risking my life as I plunged through the flames and dragged Elias out the back door by his armpits. Somehow or other the owl had found its way into the kitchen, and it almost took my eyes out when it panicked, clawing and beating through the smoke-blackened air. Dr. Ross, bleeding profusely, had already managed to hook a hose up to the well pump behind the house and was training a feeble stream into the heart of the blaze, but by that time Emily had called the fire department, and the Coast Guard responded speedily with its fireboats. It's hardly imaginable, given the age and condition of that old trap, but they managed to preserve the better part of its structure. Their zeal, I'm told, was commendable—and their emergency medical assistance kept my injuries from being much less severe than they might have been—but hardly worth the trouble. The building is going to be razed to the ground in early spring, weather permitting.

Dr. Ross wasn't seriously injured either. It turns out that Elias had barely enough strength at the end to pick up the war club, let alone wield it to its lethal advantage. The doctor's head wound required twenty-five stitches and an overnight stay in the hospital. He waited faithfully at Elias's bedside for three days, as quiet and transparent as a ghost, but the minute Elias's suicide watch was lifted, the doctor vanished. Emily hasn't seen or heard from him since then, but she expects he'll be in touch eventually. He made it clear that he needed to go off by himself, so it's not as if we have to worry about him now. All she knows is that, before disappearing, he paid a visit to Jay Habner's office and accepted the city's offer for Turnaway. Even at below market value, that offer must have been enough to make him a wealthy man. I don't imagine I'll hear from him again, but who knows?

As for Elias, Emily tells me he's doing as well as can be expected, in the circumstances. The pneumonia's gone and he can walk, at least. Emily doesn't think he's any danger to himself at this point. In any case, he's got a long, court-ordered stay ahead of him at the psychiatric center she found for him up the Hudson Valley. It's a plush kind of place, I'm told, but he can afford it. He's a rich man, too, now, of course, since the money from the sale of the island was split straight down the middle. He hasn't said a lot since he regained his faculties, but he has asked after me, according to Emily. He hasn't made any plans for the future yet. I'll go visit him just as soon as I can, cheer him up, offer some real estate tips.

Emily comes to see me every day when her work schedule permits. She's very nice to me, and I always look forward to seeing her and inhaling her soothing perfume. Still, I know that once I'm back on my feet she'll do the same as Cokoe, because like him she's got a home to go to. I don't think she's going to make it here tonight, though; she'd have been here already if she were.

With all this time weighing so heavily on my hands I've been doing some research. Emily and Daphne have very kindly brought me the books I need from the library. What is known: Wampage did live in Lapechwahacking, he did murder Anne Hutchinson and take her name in 1643, he did kidnap Susannah into the wilderness of Westchester then return her to her uncle several years later, and he and Maminepoe did sign away their lands under the Pelham Oak in 1654. After that he seems to have fallen away into toothless impotence, retreating further and further inland with the Wekweskik as they signed away their territories piece by piece. His last treaty was signed alongside Chief Katonah in 1703, by which time he must have been close to a hundred years old. If he did father a son by Susannah, his white grandchildren were living in Boston by then, Brahmins to the teeth. But there's no way of knowing if William was his son or not, none at all. As for Turnaway, in his book *New York City in Indian Possession,* Reginald Bolton makes no mention of any island called Manapinock. As far as anyone can tell, it was always called Turnaway, though like most of the oddly named islets of the Bay, no one knows how it got its name. The Pells sold it to Oliver Delancey in 1774, along with Hart Island, and Delancey sold it to the city in 1784. The city later presented it to John Hutchinson in recognition of his role in saving Washington's retreat to White Plains. That's all I know.

I can hear my landlord and his buddies in the back yard, chanting Irish folk songs around the fire by the sweat lodge. The birdcage is swinging and creaking in the breeze. I hear Daphne rummaging in the coat closet now. I'll be all alone in a few minutes. I can't say I look forward to this part of the day anymore. Then again, it doesn't mean much for me to admit that I'm easily confused these days. A lot of that has to do with my discomfort, but I can't imagine things being so different when I'm better. All in all, it's hard to imagine what sort of wisdom I'm supposed to take from all this. Sometimes, as I lie here looking out the window just after the sun has set (as I'm doing now), when redbricked buildings that a moment ago were blazing gold have fallen under blue shadow, I'll admit that New York can seem to me to be wearing its doom and its decay like a faded bridal veil. Not exactly a cheery thought, but if I've learned anything from all this, it's that everything, even a great big city like New York, has an outer skin that can be peeled or burned away.

On a more positive note, my nightmares have stopped. The last time I had one, just a few nights ago, I finally got to the end and found out what all the fuss was about. I passed through the woods, through the animals, down the path, and into the clearing. The bright colors that had frightened me so badly turned out to be the harmless designs of handwoven blankets draped over bark-thatched huts, and the voices those of children playing at the edge of a river. As I emerged from the woods, a woman broke away from the communal hearth to welcome me, and several naked children gathered at my feet. I was in a Lenape village near the northern tip of Manhattan and I'd just come home after an afternoon's hunting. That's what I'd forgotten and what I suddenly remembered as I embraced my little daughter. It wasn't half as terrible as I'd imagined.

ACKNOWLEDGMENTS

The author wishes to offer his sincere thanks to Dr. David Oestreicher for his patient and invaluable help with all aspects of Lenape history, culture, and language.

ABOUT THE AUTHOR

JESSE BROWNER works at the United Nations in New York, where he lives with his wife and daughter. *Turnaway* is his second novel.

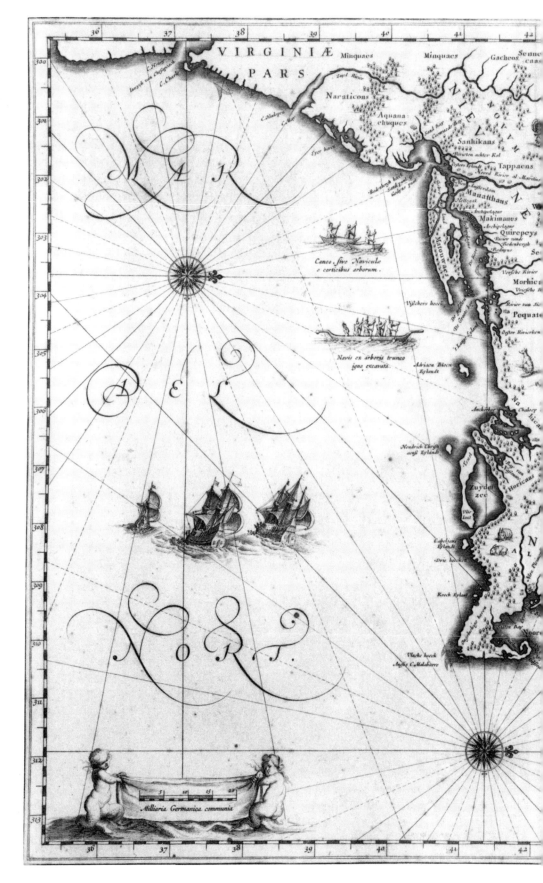